The Virgins Wreath

By Bob Looker

Books by the author:-

Auxiliary Forces series

Three Days

18th Century Smugglers

The Virgins Wreath

Virgins Wreath

First published in Great Britain in 2014
By R.J. Looker Publications

Copyright © Robert J.M. Looker 2014

The right of Bob Looker to be identified as the author of this work has been asserted by him in accordance with the Copyright, Design and Patents Act 1988

All characters and events in this publication, other than those clearly in the public domain, are fictitious and any resemblance to real persons, living or dead, is purely coincidental.

All rights reserved. No part of this publication may be reproduced, stored in a retrieval system, or transmitted, in any form or by any means, electronic, mechanical, photocopy, recording or otherwise, without the prior permission of the copyright owner.

ISBN-13: 978-1-4929-9083-3

A CIP catalogue record of this book is available
From the British Library

Printed by CreateSpace, an Amazon.com Company
Available from Amazon.com and other book stores

Dedication

Stella — My mother, a woman of great strength.

Angela — My step-sister, without her I doubt that I would ever have known about the smugglers of Jevington, the original inspiration for this book.

My wife — Who has supported me throughout the years I spent developing this story.

Rob — My son, who has helped me a lot with advice and in the preparation for publication.

CHAPTER 1
I'm in charge now

In 1786, fights between two men in Aldfriston, the village that dominated the Cuckmere Valley, didn't normally warrant much comment.

The River Cuckmere ran beside the village taking its navigational waters from well above the village down to the English Channel, some two miles away. It was in part because of its navigational properties that had an influence on the village and why these two men's activities were of equal importance to the economy of the village.

The older man was Brian Cockburn; he was in his late thirties and starting to put on some extra weight. He stood five feet four inches tall, had long black hair, tied in a ponytail, and was clean shaven. His rugged features had become weathered over time.

Brian had run the largest gang of Free Traders (smugglers) in the Cuckmere valley for seven years. He controlled his gang with good organization, rough justice against anyone who crossed him and his knowledge of how to get people to turn the other way.

Several smaller groups of Free Traders operated in the valley. They did so only at the behest of Brian. He let them continue to operate as long as they didn't challenge him or get in his way. Because of his success, Brian enjoyed a higher standard of living than most working men in the village.

During the last six months he had started to want to enjoy the trappings of the wealth he had accumulated and began to take things a bit easier. It was this lacklustre approach to his business that had caused this fight.

Brian had given over more of the day to day control of the Free Traders operation to others in his gang. He had retained full control of the money, ordering and distribution of the contraband; for that is where the real power and wealth lay.

In the recent weeks he had begun to realize that the control and discipline of the gang was slipping away from him. He was aided by his lieutenants; men he could trust with his very life and who would use their considerable strength to assert Brian's will. His problem now, was that his will was being asserted by one of his lieutenants.

The second man in the fight was his main lieutenant, George Styles. He was a big man, who stood five foot eleven inches tall, had broad shoulders and large hands. He was a very large man, physically fit and for Brian's purposes, he also had a ruthless streak.

George didn't have the face of an angel; his eyes didn't radiate heat, even when he smiled. His face was oval with a pointed chin, with a large nose that showed it had been broken several times. His lips were large and had the appearance of stretching right across his face.

At times he had tried to hide his chin with a beard, so that when people heard of his deeds, wouldn't recognize him. He relied on his reputation to ease the way, but on occasions would have to use his strength to ensure his will.

Brian was leaving more and more of the running of the gang to George and his lieutenants, Neal and Simon who were accepting George's lead.

George would arrange for all the men to receive, unload and hide up the contraband, when it arrived at the coast in a French Lugger. On good nights he had well over one hundred men under him, eager to earn extra money to feed their families.

A night's work, with the Free Traders, could earn them the same as a week's wages working for the Lords of the Manor or their Tenants.

Brian had now woken up to the fact that he was losing control of the gang and the valley.

His long time friend Neal Turner had told him that George was trying to close down the other gangs in the valley and in particular the one working out of the hamlet of West Dean.

Brian couldn't allow this. His brother-in-law, Henry Lake, runs the West Dean gang of Free Traders. If Henry was not making money his family would starve. Brian would then be responsible for providing for Henry's family. If not, Brian's wife would make his life unbearable.

Another reason for allowing these smaller gangs to operate in the valley, was that he could tip off the Riding Officer (men who worked for the Customs/Excise Authorities and patrolled the area) about the activities of the smaller gangs, leaving room for his gang to operate virtually undisturbed by the authorities.

It was now time for Brian to re-establish his authority as the gang's leader. The only way he could see how he could do this was if he confronted George in full view of members of the gang and the village.

It would be no use to just strut about and give orders, if the men then turned to George to check if he'd approve. Brian had to show that it was he, who the men should turn to. It was him who paid them and ensured that they were kept out of the range of the Riding Officer and Magistrates.

Neal told Brian that George was going to move some contraband from one of the many hiding places, south of the village, to a barn near to George's own house.

Brian realised that this would be the opportunity he was looking for. Time to establish his authority and show that George was being disloyal to both him and the gang.

No goods were moved without Brian's or George's say so. Anyone so much as approaching any of the hideouts was liable to get a good beating or kicked out of the gang. The latter being a greater punishment as it would mean that their families would go without. Without the support of the gang and in particular the money they earned from this work, they may have to resort to stealing. The punishment for this was deportation to one of the penal colonies.

Brian had never allowed goods to be moved in daylight; for fear that it would be reported to one of the constables or be spotted by one of the roaming patrols of Dragoons.

With the war with France over, the troops had returned to England. The Government was losing revenue, as a result of the smuggling along the south coast. They stationed Regiments of Dragoons, in various towns along the coast and with orders that they were to work with the local Riding Officers to prevent further smuggling.

An added benefit was that there was less likelihood of the French raiding the towns and villages, along the south coast, if they knew that English troops were on hand.

The nearest barracks to Aldfriston was in South Bourn; (now known as Eastbourne) some nine miles further East along the coast, where a Regiment of Dragoons was stationed. The Regiment covered an area from Newhaven, to the West, across to Fairlight in the East and up to ten miles inland.

Before Brian set out from his home that day, he had cleaned his flintlock pistols and ensured that they had powder in the pans and shot rammed home in the barrels. He kissed his wife on the forehead and set off for The Star Inn, in the centre of the village. He took a seat by the window, drank a tankard of ale and watched as the villagers went about their business.

After about half an hour, he saw what he had been waiting for, one of his gang members leading a covered packhorse along the road towards the Inn. This was the sign that George would be along in a few minutes. Brian stood up and walked out into the road.

He didn't have long to wait before George Styles and some more of the gang appeared. They were each leading packhorses with covered loads strapped onto their backs.

"What are you doing with my goods?" bellowed Brian.

George was taken aback, firstly he hadn't expected to see Brian and secondly the fact that Brian was asking such a question, so openly and loudly, in the main street.

"I'm just moving, um to a safer place." George replied.

"And where would that be, your house?" Brian asked, accusingly.

"Don't be daft Brian, um are your goods, I was just thinking ..."

"You appear to be doing a lot of thinking nowadays, don't you George?" Brian cut in, not giving him a chance to finish.

"It looks to me as if you're stealing from me and these men are helping you. Are you setting up on your own now, George?"

George was beginning to feel uneasy. What was Brian up to? The one thing he had always admired about George was his level headedness and his insistence on secrecy. To be out here on the street with a raised voice, shouting about their business was most unlike him.

George turned and saw the look on the faces of the men around him. They were also puzzled but not in the same way as George.

No one had seen Brian for some weeks now and had started to consider that George was their leader. Here was Brian back in their life again and belittling George. Some turned and looked at George, awaiting his response.

"Brian, I'm not. I was just moving it to a safer place."

"You are a thief. You are stealing from me and the rest of the men with you. Only they are too stupid to know it."

George suddenly realised that Brian had him in a corner. He had to either capitulate, or take up the challenge that Brian had thrown down. He looked Brian in the eye and realised that he had little choice.

If he chose the first option he would find that he would be demoted within the gang and his life in the village would be unbearable or he could choose the second option and take up the challenge and fight Brian for control of the gang.

George reached for his cutlass and drew it from his belt.

This is what Brian had been hoping for, he knew George well enough to expect him to opt for a fight, to defend his reputation.

Brian hadn't led the gang for as long as he had, without being one step ahead of his men and the Law. As soon as he saw George's hand move towards the cutlass, Brian brought his right hand from under his coat. In it he held a loaded flintlock pistol.

He cocked back the flint, over the pan and raised the pistol pointed it towards George's chest. He then reached under his coat with his left hand and returned it holding his second flintlock pistol.

Again Brian drew back the flint with this left thumb and also levelled this pistol at George's chest.

What Brian hadn't counted on was that George's wife, Beth, was coming out of a house across the road from The Star Inn. Although she was a foreigner, having been brought up in Horam, She was a formidable woman and so was taken notice of.

In Beth, George had a woman that no one messed with. She may only be four foot eleven inches tall but she was full of spirit and punched her considerable weight. As George had found out, on many occasion.

Seeing the two men she ran between them.

"Brian." She shouted. "NO."

Beth was not only George's wife but a distant cousin of Brian's.

"Put down those pistols this minute." She ordered.

There were very few men who could expect to get away with such action, let alone a woman. But it brought him to his senses. If he shot George, like this, how would he get the respect of the men? No he would fight him, George may be stronger but Brian had the experience.

It would be seen as cowardly, shooting a man who only held a cutlass. It may be sensible when confronted by a rival gang or the Riding Officers, but not now.

Both Brian and George looked at Beth and then at each other.

"Put away your cutlass and fight me like the man you always pretend to be." Brian ordered, as he lowered his pistols.

This remark was a direct challenge to George's manhood, not only in front of the gang members but his wife as well.

George handed his cutlass to one of the men who had been helping him move the contraband. He then removed his pistol from his belt and handed it to the same man.

Brian looked around and found that his old friend Neal was approaching, to see what all the fuss was about.

"Neal, come and hold these for a few moments while I sort out a little business with George."

Once Neal was at hand Brian passed over his brace of flintlocks and his own cutlass.

Beth could see that these two men were about to get into a fight that only one of them could come out the victor. There was no purpose in this at all. Foolishly she decided that she would try to stop it before it started, so she stepped between the two men again, putting out her two hands to hold them apart.

Brian was in no mood for this and with his powerful right arm he brushed Beth aside, sending her sprawling onto her backside.

George was not known for his sentiment but couldn't stand by and have, his wife handled in this way. George lunged forward and threw a punch at Brian's head, but Brian was well prepared and he stepped one pace back to allow George's fist to sail past his chin, without contact.

Brian brought his left fist forward very quickly and made contact with George's chin, sending him backwards against the leading packhorse. It wasn't long before both men were exchanging punches, both to each others faces and body.

Blood was soon strewn all over their faces and fists. Brian sustained a cracked cheek bone during the initial exchanges which caused the right side of his face to swell considerably, partly obscuring the sight of his right eye.

The fight went on for twenty minutes, by which time the two men had fought their way into the Village Square. The upper hand had changed many times. Neither man could claim to have taken control of the fight, at any time.

George was younger and very large but Brian had experience to count on. Where George was able to throw many more punches and possibly hit harder, Brian had the knowledge on how to evade the more telling punches and ensure that the ones he throw, reached their target.

On reaching the Village Square everyone around saw that both men were very tired, their faces were bruised and bleeding but still neither man would give in. By now it was obvious to the on-lookers, that this was a fight for power rather than pride.

As far as George was concerned, that he was a better man to lead the gang, than Brian. George thought that being younger and fitter than Brian, was all that was required to run a gang of Free Traders.

As they circled each other for the umpteenth time, the whole village was now gathered around them, many were supporters of Brian and some, mostly family and drinking pals were supporting George.

The punches were getting fewer and lacked the strength and fury of earlier. Brian was using what energy he had left, to defend himself from the blows being thrown by George, rather than in striking back.

Brian needed to bring this fight to an end, as soon as he could. He needed to demonstrate, to the whole village, that he wasn't only the leader of the Free Traders but was strong enough to exert his will again. Defeating a big and strong man, such as George, would allow him to do just that.

Brian saw that one of the men in the front of the crowd was carrying a stave. He turned as quick as his body would allow and grabbed the stave from the man's grip.

George was not slow to take advantage of his opponent standing there with his back to him, so he advanced quickly to attack an apparently defenceless opponent.

Brian was no fool, he knew that George would take his chance and attack whilst his back was turned. George had only taken two paces when Brian spun around to face him.

George hadn't realized that Brian had been arming himself, while his back was turned. As such he ran into a full strike from the swinging stave. It caught him a heavy blow against his upper right arm, knocking him sideways.

Before George had recovered his balance Brian came in quickly and hit him again, only this time across the left side of his head, sending him tumbling to the ground.

George's friends didn't think that this was right. So before Brian could take up a position to land the final blow, Fred Cannon shouted "Catch."

George looked through his blurred eyes and saw something heading his way. He didn't know if his reaction was to protect himself from another blow or what but he put out his large hands and closed his fingers around the object heading his way. He recognized the shape it was a flintlock pistol.

With Brian standing above him, preparing to deliver the *coup de grace*, with the stave raised above his head, George had to act quickly. He adjusted his grip on the pistol, cocked back the flint hammer and pointed it in the general direction of Brian.

He had no time to check if the pan still held any firing powder or not, time was against him. If he had a flash-in-the-pan or no flash at all, Brian would finish him off anyway. George fired at the shape towering above him.

The pistol exploded into action, there was no flash-in-the-pan but the smoke associated with a correctly discharged pistol. The shot went directly into Brian, up through his chest and struck his left shoulder blade, sending him spinning backward onto the ground.

Brian had not expected George to go to such lengths to win the fight. Both men had originally discarded their own pistols and swords when the fight started, so why had he done this? The fact that he, Brian, was about to attempt to end George's life with the stave he had taken from a man in the crowd, didn't seem to cross his mind.

The pain from the shot travelling through Brian's body was intense. He couldn't feel his left-hand side and his left arm would not obey his commands. He needed to get up, if nothing else so he could leave here before George could administer even more punishment. Brian felt like a wounded animal.

George struggled to his feet and realized that he would have no time to reload the pistol before Brian got to his feet.

It would be no use turning to Fred Cannon, as he only carried one pistol. The flintlock pistol he held was of little use to him though. He quickly turned it around in his hands and held onto the warm barrel, with his large right hand. He now had a weapon he could use.

Brian was having difficulty in rising himself from the ground. He had managed to get himself onto his knees and was supported by his one good arm. The shock of being shot and the pain running through his body made thinking and acting difficult.

George, on the other hand, was not befuddled any more, he now found himself in a position to end the fight once and for all. As Brian turned his head to see where George was.

George brought the butt of the pistol down on to Brian's head, leaving a gaping wound on the left temple, sending Brian crashing to the ground again. George was about to repeat the assault when the constable came running up, calling that a troop of Dragoons had entered the village. This brought about the end of the fight and George was shepherded away to one of his relative's homes, so that they could repair the damage he had suffered.

From being an important member of the community, a person who could count on the support from nearly everyone in the village, Brian was alone, lying there in the mud of the Village Square. All those who had called themselves his friends had turned away and returned to their homes. Not one person had come over to see if he was even alive.

The patrol of Dragoons was soon upon the limp body of Brian Cockburn. Sergeant Greaves dismounted and checked if Brian was still alive. Finding that he was, he ordered one of his men to put Brian across the saddle of his horse and detailed off two others to accompany them to Battle hospital.

Sergeant Greaves didn't know if Brian would make it to the hospital alive and if he did, whether there was anything that could be done for him. The hospital was run by monks with some knowledge of medicine.

If Brian did survive, then Sergeant Greaves knew he would be well rewarded. Over the last year Brian had given the Sergeant many half-ankers (small kegs) of Genever and Brandy. These were payments so his patrol was not around when Brian was moving contraband.

The Sergeant had no interest in trying to discover what had happened here today. This was Sergeant Greaves last patrol in the Cuckmere Valley. His troop was being reassigned to the Pevensey Bay area, from tomorrow.

Sergeant Greaves looked around for the constable but he, also, was no where to be seen. With Brian on his way to hospital and his patrol reduced to just the three Dragoons, it was time for them to return to their barracks in South Bourn and make his report.

Once George had been patched up, washed and rested he could reflect on what had happened today. It was now obvious to him that Brian had engineered the fight to re-establish his authority on the gang and the village. George hadn't wanted to kill Brian and he hoped that this was not the case. He was pleased to have won the fight and with Brian out of the way, was able to take, what he saw was his true position as the leader of the Free Traders in the Cuckmere Valley.

George was familiar with organizing the gang, getting the men in the right places to land the contraband, hide it out of sight of the authorities and ensuring that the goods were available for the customers, when needed.

What he was soon to discovered, was that he didn't know how to find the customers and ensure that the money flowed, as it should. He also found that it was not just brawn that was needed to run a gang of Free Traders but a great amount of brains as well.

Free Trading operations that are successful are those where its men didn't get arrested. If they were unlucky enough to let any men fall into the hands of the Customs men's, it was the leader's job to ensure that the men were not convicted. This gang hadn't had a man convicted for some five years now.

This was down to Brian's knowledge of people and what makes them operate in the way they do. Some you can frighten and others you buy with either gold sovereigns or contraband.

In areas, such as Hastings, local Magistrates ran gangs of Free Traders. In those gangs none of their men were ever convicted.

In other areas the Magistrates received substantial payments to ensure the same results. A jury, made up from locals, rarely found a Free Trader guilty of any offence connected with smuggling. The economy of the villages, near to the South Coast, relied on the money that was generated from the activities of the Free Traders.

CHAPTER 2
Watch it burn

The Free Traders considered themselves to be business men. They were bringing goods into the country that bypassed the excessive taxation that the Government was imposing, on these items. Without paying the taxes, they could sell their goods at a good profit. Their customers got the goods cheaper, than through proper channels, which allowed them to also make a good profit.

To try to stop the smuggling, the Customs services stationed teams of Riding Officer, under the control of Comptrollers, at various towns, along the coast line, particularly in the South of England. Aldfriston came in the area controlled by the Comptroller at Newhaven, Mr Williams and in particular the area patrolled by his Riding Officer, Graham Johnson.

Graham was about thirty two years old, five foot six inches tall with a pleasant face and a deceptive smile. He was lucky in that he didn't have to do much exercise to retain his relatively slim figure. He carried a pair of flintlock pistols and a cutlass.

He had been with the Customs Services since he left the Army, after the war against France. He had been a Sergeant and couldn't find it in himself to work directly for anyone, so he chose a job that would give him a certain amount of autonomy. He had been brought up in Kent. In these times if you were from a village only three miles away, you were considered to be a foreigner. Kent was a lot further than that.

One night, about two weeks after George Styles had taken control of the Aldfriston gang of Free Traders, Graham Johnson, had been out on one of his night time patrols.

He rode his horse, Stan, to White Bofthill on top of the Downs. He then used the tracks, made by the sheep, who pastured on the Downs, to take himself down to the farm land below.

At the bottom of the hill, his narrow track met up with the main track coming from Aldfriston, via Winton Street, bypassing the village of Berwick, skirting Alciston and heading towards West Firle.

Across the track was a lane leading to Tilton farm. Just off this cross tracks was a small coppice and it was here that he decided to lain in wait.

Graham was an experienced Riding Officer. He knew that the smugglers used this track to move their illicit goods to their customers. He would wait for an hour at this spot, to see if the smugglers came this was, tonight. If not he would move on to another place and try his luck there.

From just inside the coppice he could see along the track, back towards Alciston. It also sheltered him and his horse from anyone coming upon him by chance, from any direction.

It had been some time before he heard the slight sound of someone coming along the main track. As they drew nearer he could detect the sound of two ponies and the footsteps of a man, with them. This was what he had been waiting for.

At this time of day, nearing dusk, you were not likely to find people about on foot with ponies. It was important that he didn't spook the ponies.

If the man coming towards him was a smuggler, it would be no good just getting the illicit goods, when he had the chance of catching the man with them. So he gently stroked the neck of his horse to signal him not to make a noise that could be picked up by the ponies or the man.

Gradually a man with two pack ponies, carrying half-ankers slung across their backs, came into view.

A half-anker was a small barrel containing about 4 gallons of high proofed spirits – brandy or genever (Gin). They were strung together in pairs to allow for easy handling by the tub carriers. The spirits would be in the High Proof state and were dangerous to drink. They would require diluting before the spirits could be sold for drinking.

Graham waited until the man had just gone past his hide, then rode out from the coppice and, with one of his flintlock pistols to hand. He quickly brought his horse along side the man.

"Stop in the Name of King George." He ordered.

"What have you there?" Graham challenged the man.

"I was just taking these ponies back to the farm, for my Uncle."

"What are they carrying?" He asked.

"They have nothing of interest to you Sir."

"Stand still while I dismount, if you run I'll shoot you." Graham said.

Graham soon noticed that this was no man but a youth. He made no attempt to flee and stood and retained the reins to his charges, while Graham dismounted. As he got down Graham slipped some rope from a bag he carried, strapped to his saddle.

"Come here young man." He ordered.

The youth let go of his ponies and joined Graham.

"Hold out your hands." He ordered.

The youth had no intention of being shot so obeyed Graham. In a deft movement Graham had slipped a noose of rope over the hands of the youth and tightened it to ensure that they couldn't be released. The other end of the rope he tied to the straps securing the load on the nearest pony. Graham intended to ride his horse and lead this leading pony, using the rope that the boy had already been using for the same purpose.

Having secured the youth, Graham proceeded to examine the ponies load. He found that each was carrying six pairs of half ankers; four were brandy and the other two were genever.

"Where were you taking these?" He asked.

"No where Sir."

"I'm sorry son but these look very much like smuggler's contraband and that makes you a smuggler. I'm taking you back to Seaford. Tomorrow morning I'll put you in front of the Magistrate."

As he was not far from the route that brought him to this spot, it didn't take Graham and his prisoner long to climb back up the hill. Using the various tracks over the Downs he would be able to get his prisoner back to Seaford, without the chance of being seen.

His only difficulty would be when he rode through Blatchington, just outside Seaford. Up to that point he could avoid any form of habitation but in doing so it brought him directly into this village.

By the time they reached Blatchington everyone was at home. The occasional dog barked but they were quickly hushed up, as the people inside thought that the ponies were those of Free Traders. It was not wise to be to aware of their goings on.

Having passed through Blatchington, Graham headed for Seaford Gaol. The gaoler was not at all happy being disturbed, at that time of night.

"Alfred, lock this young man up for the night. I'll be back for him in the morning to take him before the Magistrate." Graham ordered.

"I can't feed him." Alfred protested.

"If he's with you tomorrow, send word to his family to provide his food."

Having untied his prisoner and handed him over to the Gaoler, Graham needed to ride on to Newhaven, with the ponies and the captured contraband. There he could deposit it at the Customs House and give his report to the Comptroller.

The trouble was getting the contraband over the river, as the Customs House and the home of the Comptroller, were on the opposite side of the River Ouse. The Ferryman wouldn't work at night but Graham was sure that he could persuade John Ferris to make an exception tonight.

He took the two ponies into the Ferryman's barn and tethered them up, together with his horse. He walked over to the Ferryman's house and banged on his door. It took some time before anyone came to the door.

"What's the rush? I don't start work until tomorrow morning at seven o'clock." Came a call, from within the house.

"I need to get some contraband over to the Customs House tonight John." Graham called. "There's a guinea in it, if you do it now."

A guinea was a lot of money so it didn't take long for John Ferris to get his clothes back on and be ready for a late night row. The trouble with doing this at night was that John couldn't see the exact flow of the river.

He knew the tides and as such knew which way the river would be flowing. The other problem was that he wouldn't be able to see any debris in the water, which could hole his boat.

While he was getting ready, Graham went back to the barn and, after several journeys, brought all the pairs of half-ankers of spirits and placed them on the quayside, where the ferry boat was moored.

With Johns help they soon had the ferry loaded. John Ferris took the oars and got Graham to untie the ferry. Then he started to row across the river. The flow was quite fast and going upstream so John headed towards the harbour mouth, inching over the river as he went.

When he was just over half way over, he could turn the ferry upstream and let the flow of the water take him back towards the other side of the river. All he had to do was steer it towards the quayside and his mooring.

John tied off the ferry and helped Graham get the half-ankers up on to the quay. As Graham put it, if he had to wait until Graham had finished his business, he might as well earn his money and help to get the half-ankers to the Customs house.

Within the hour Graham, with John's help, had got the contraband over the river, into the Customs house, given his report to the Comptroller and returned back over to river, to his horse.

Graham rode back to Seaford. Instead of returning to his lodgings he went to the Magistrates house to inform the Magistrate about the prisoner and arrange to present him before the Magistrate at a time convenient to him, the following day.

Seaford was a small town but a classic 'rotten borough' (A town that had more Members of Parliament than the number of people warranted).

As such if the Magistrate wanted to keep his job he needed to be on the right side of the local Members of Parliament, thus he too was also against smuggling.

Mr. Maxwell, the Magistrate for Seaford, was not in the pay of any of the smugglers in the area, but had been known to accept 'gifts'.

It was the patronage of the local Lord of the manor that Mr Maxwell courted. The Lord of the Manor was courting favours with the King, who was losing revenue because of the smugglers activities.

Graham arrived at the Magistrates house quite late in the evening. He took his horse around to the back of the house, so as not to be seen by any town's folk that may be in with the smugglers. He walked around to the front of the house and had trouble in getting Mr. Maxwell to answer the door. Once inside he gave Mr. Maxwell his report and asked what time he should bring the prisoner before him, at the court house.

Unfortunately for Graham, as he, his prisoner and the ponies carrying the contraband were starting off up to White Bofthill, they had been seen by one of the farm workers, from Tilton Farm. This man occasionally helped out the Free Traders. He had recognized Stanton, the youth leading the ponies, and realised what he had been doing. He quickly went back to the farm and borrowed one of its ponies and rode off to Aldfriston, to rout out George Styles. He reported what he had seen and was rewarded with a shilling.

Having one of his men arrested was going to be the first real test of George's ability to protect members of the gang, from the law. Loyalty is a fickle thing and as he had seen after he took over the gang, many of Brian's staunchest supporters had quickly switched their allegiance to George. He believed, rightly so, that they could swing just as quickly away from him. This put him under tremendous pressure to ensure that his man was not convicted.

Brian had never carried out any negotiations with any official, himself. He would send others, they carried the full authority of Brian and made it known for whom they were making the call.

To be seen in actual contact with a Magistrate could mean arrest and the gallows.

George, on the other hand, had decided that, on this occasion, he would personally visit this Magistrate. George was not yet versed in what was required or more importantly, what was prudent.

It was late at night when he arrived at the front door of the Magistrates house. He knocked, using the butt of his pistol to ensure he was heard.

After a few minutes the door opened and there before him was Mr. Maxwell and just behind him stood Graham Johnson, the Riding Officer who George was told had arrested his man.

"What can I do for you?" Mr. Maxwell asked.

George had been caught off guard. He hadn't expected to see Graham there. He could hardly ask Mr. Maxwell to let off his man with the arresting officer stood behind him. After a moment of feverish thoughts George had his answer,

"One of my friends has gone missing and I was wondering if you could advise me how to find him. His name is Stanton Collins from Aldfriston."

Mr. Maxwell turned to Graham.

"Is that not the man you told me about, the one in gaol, the Smuggler?" He asked.

"It is Sir, the very man. He was arrested near West Firle with twelve pairs of half-ankers of Brandy and four of Genever, Contraband Brandy and Genever." Graham said, addressing George not the Magistrate.

"There must be a mistake Sir." George said.

"Stanton is a good young man, the son of the local Butcher. I've never known him to do such a thing."

George looked at both men for a reaction but none came.

"It is possible that he found the ponies wandering, unattended and was taking them to the nearest farm to find their owner. Not knowing what they were carrying?"

George was addressing the Magistrate, trying to put some doubt in his mind as to whether Stanton was actually breaking the law and so give the Magistrate reason to release his man.

"I doubt if the owner would want the brandy or genever returned. They could be disposed of in a manner the Magistrate may decide." George said.

It was obvious to all three men that George was offering a bribe to Mr. Maxwell and if necessary, the Riding Officer as well. He waited to see if his offer was to be taken up.

"The contraband is in the hands of the Customs and is King George's property now." Graham said, with certain authority.

He was letting both the Magistrate and George know that the bribe being offered was not on the table.

"Stanton's family would be more than pleased to recompense the loss." George said, quickly.

"Sir, I think you should go. Mr. Collins will be before me tomorrow morning and I fear that he will not be returning to his family for many years." The Magistrate said.

With that he turned away from George and closed the door.

George wasn't happy. On previous visits, this Magistrate had been willing to accept brandy, genever and lace for his wife. It must have been because Graham was there, that he had turned him down.

George couldn't go back to Stanton's family and tell them he hadn't succeeded in securing their son's release. To do so would have weakened his hold on his gang and made him open to challenges from Brian's friends, who would be only to ready to take over the gang until Brian was fit again.

He had two choices, one was to wait until Graham had left, then return and threaten the Magistrate with his life, if Stanton was not released the next day or, the more dangerous option. Going to the gaol and forcing the gaoler to release Stanton.

The later option would then have Stanton and himself open to arrest warrants being issued. Even in these times, rewards of up to one thousand pounds were not uncommon to secure the arrest of smugglers.

Stanton had great potential, within the gang. Although he was young, he was strong, had a quick mind and was good at planning routes, hiding up and evading detection.

It is for this reason that George had been surprised that he had been arrested. Once he knew Graham Johnson had arrested him, George understood.

Graham was a very clever man and had out foxed many a Free Trader in the area. To be arrested by him was no shame. Stanton would learn from this experience and George doubted if he would be arrested again, even by Graham Johnson.

George only had a few minutes to wait before Graham came out of the house and walked off to collect his horse. He watched until Graham rode off towards his dwellings. Once he was out of sight George walked out of the shadows, crossed the road and approached the Magistrates house. This time he went around the rear of the house and entered, without knocking, by the kitchen door.

There was a lit lantern standing on the table, so George took it up and walked into the hallway. He stood still for a moment and listened for the sound of the Magistrate's voice. There was a sound coming from the room to his left. George took out his Flintlock pistol, drew back the flint and checked that there was powder in the pan.

When he was ready, he opened the door and stepped into the room. There were two people in the room, Mr. Maxwell and a lady, who George recognized as Mrs Maxwell. Mr. Maxwell was stood by the fireplace lighting his pipe with a match.

"Your wife can leave us now Sir." George said, with the authority of having his pistol pointing directly at the Magistrate.

Mrs. Maxwell gave a muffled scream and looked at her husband to see if he was going to protect her. Mr. Maxwell was not a fighter.

Although he owned a pistol he was not proficient in its use. He was not going to put his life in danger; the very thought of trying to protect his wife never crossed his mind. All he could think of was to motioned her to do just as she had been told.

"What do you want now? I told you that Collins will be going away for a long time. With this intrusion into my home I might sentence him to hang." The Magistrate said.

"If Stanton is not with his family by night fall tomorrow, I will be back and burn your house to the ground, with you and your family inside." George snarled.

"I'll have you watched from now until Stanton is released, where ever you go, I'll know." He let that sink in for a moment.

"If he's not back with his family tomorrow ..."

He didn't think he needed to repeat his threat. Mr. Maxwell had beads of sweat running down his forehead. Whether it was from what he had said or the fact that the flames from the match had reached his fingers.

With that said George turned around and walked back into the hall. He felt that he had nothing physical to fear from the Magistrate. He left the house the way he had entered, after placing the lantern back on the kitchen table.

Mr. Maxwell sat down in his chair and reached for a large glass of contraband Brandy. He couldn't remember being so frightened.

As George had travelled to Seaford, alone, he wasn't actually in a position to carry out his threat, unless he did the watching himself. He decided to return to Aldfriston and send one of his men back, before daylight tomorrow morning, to watch the Magistrate. Luckily as he rode through the hamlet of Sutton he saw one of his helpers standing just outside his doorway.

"Fredrick, I need you to go into Seaford, first thing tomorrow and keep an eye on the Magistrate, Mr. Maxwell. Make sure that he knows you're watching him."

"Won't he have me arrested?" Was an obvious question to ask.

"No, he has other things to think about, but with you there it'll focus his thoughts. Here are two florins and if I get the result I want, there'll be two more for you." He said, as he dropped the two coins into Fredrick's outstretched hands.

By dawn Fredrick was stood outside Mr. Maxwell's house. Following Georg's instructions to be in full view, he stood across the road, in front of the house, so that the Magistrate could see that he was being watched.

Mr. Maxwell was having his breakfast when his wife said that there was a foreigner standing over the road and looking at the house. A cold shiver ran through his body when he realised that George had kept his word. He had assumed that George was all bluster. The fact that his house was under observation made him understand that George Styles was very serious.

Mr. Johnson had done him no favours saying that the contraband couldn't be returned. He would now have to make a judgment to release George Style's man without any financial benefit to himself. If he didn't release Collins then, from the fact that the man was watching his house, George was sure to carry out his threat.

It was nearly ten thirty before Mr. Maxell left his house for the short walk to the Courthouse. George's man was still standing across the street. Mr. Maxwell took no more notice of him, as he turned in the direction of the courthouse.

He hadn't gone far when a voice, from behind him, broke into his thoughts.

"Good Morrow Magistrate."

Mr. Maxwell turned around and there, sat on a horse, was George Styles.

"Away with you or I'll have you arrested." He shouted.

"I've done nothing." George replied.

"You're trying to intimidate me and that's against the law."

"If you do what's right, no harm will come to you or your family Sir." George said.

Before the Magistrate could answer, George urged his horse to move off, taking him quickly out of reach of Mr. Maxwell.

After a few more steps towards his destination Mr. Maxwell turned around and found George's man still following him.

"Leave this place." Mr. Maxwell ordered.

The man was more frightened of George than ever he was of these hollow threats from the Magistrate. Seeing that the man was not going to leave him alone, Mr. Maxwell continued to the Courthouse.

Once he was sat behind his desk, Mr Maxwell felt that he was invincible. This was his Court; he was going to administer justice in the best way he knew. He instructed the constable to bring the prisoner before him. Graham Johnson had arrived a bit before the Magistrate and was seated to the left of the Magistrates desk.

Young Collins arrived between two men, each holding one of his arms. Mr. Maxwell had expected an older man than the youth stood before him. He was about sixteen years old, four feet ten tall and with piercing blue eyes. The eyes seemed to drill into Mr. Maxwell's, looking right into his soul, making the Magistrate feel very uneasy.

"You are charged with being in possession of contraband Brandy and Genever, What have you to say for yourself?" The Magistrate asked, trying to establish his authority over this youth.

"I found the ponies wandering in the lane. I was taking them to the next farm to see who they belonged to." Collins said.

The Magistrate now had no doubt that George Styles was intent on getting his man released. It was obvious that Collins had been told by Styles what to say.

With this blatant disregard to the law, Mr. Maxwell now realised that his house would be burned to the ground if Collins was not released.

Having heard his defence, he could let him off the charge. After all it was one mans word against the others. He couldn't justify, in this instance, why he should punish this boy for doing a good deed. The fact that Graham Johnson was an honest pillar of the community and an Officer of the King's Customs services, skipped his mind.

Mr. Johnson may not be happy but it wasn't his family who would suffer. The Customs man would have to be consoled that he had stopped the Brandy and Genever being delivered to the customers and was now in the Customs House in Newhaven.

"Stanton Collins, in this instance I am going to release you. It's a criminal offence to trade in contraband goods. If you stand before me again, on a like charge, you will be transported to the colonies for a minimum of five years. Do you understand me?" Mr. Maxwell said.

Collins was surprised at this turn of events. He had expected to be locked up, transported or hung.

"Aye Sir, I understand. You won't see me again."

Graham Johnson was not so pleased. He knew that young Stanton was a member of George Styles gang of smugglers but he could see, from the look on the Magistrates face that he was going to release him.

"Sir, May I remind you that the ponies were carrying contraband and that this is now the property of King George." Graham said, after he had stood up and faced the Magistrate.

"I am aware of those facts, thank you Mr. Johnson."

Looking at young Stanton. "You must be more careful of how you help out other people young man. The next time you may well come across a Dragoon Patrol, they shoot smugglers without asking any questions. You were lucky to be arrested by Mr. Johnson, here." He said, indicating towards Graham.

"You may go now but remember if you come before me again I'll not be so lenient."

"Thank you Sir, I'll follow your advice." He said and smiled.

Having been released, Stanton left the courthouse and headed for home, accompanied by the man used to watch Mr. Maxwell.

Graham was not happy with the outcome of the trial but knew that it was of no use protesting, as the Magistrate had made up his mind.

What he was sure of was that young Stanton would be out there again and Graham was sure that next time he would get a conviction.

Just as Graham was leaving the courthouse, some ten minuets after Stanton had departed, a man came running passed him.

"Is Mr. Maxwell here?" He shouted, as he rushed into the building.

"Yes." Graham replied, turning to see what was so important that this man should be running in this fashion.

The Magistrate was just getting up from his desk, after noting the details of the case in his journal. He looked up and recognized the man rushing into his courtroom; it was the constable who lived two doors from him.

"What is the hurry Mr. Wells?" Mr. Maxwell asked.

"There is a fire at your house Sir."

There was not time to put his books away, he just left them on the desk and ran out of the Courthouse and down the street towards his home. He rarely showed any affection towards his wife but he was concerned for her safety and this made him move quicker than was usual for him.

Before he arrived at his home he could see the smoke above the street and the smell of it in the air.

As he neared his house he could see the flames coming from the windows, at the front of the house. To his relief, his wife and servants stood well away from the burning house.

At his wife's foot was the chest that held all their documents and money. She had organized the recovery of this by her servants, before she ordered them out of the house. If they were to rebuild the house then they would need the money to pay for it and for their clothes.

As Mr. Maxwell stood, with his wife, watching their house burn to the ground, the Magistrate looked around and, back up the street, was a man he recognized sat astride a large black horse. The man raised his three cornered hat, turned his horse around and rode off. It was George Styles.

CHAPTER 3
It's not that easy

It was four weeks before Brian Cockburn returned home from Battle hospital. His shoulder blade had been completely shattered by the bullet fired by George. As a result he had lost the use of his left arm. It hung beside him like an empty corn sack.

As a result of the clubbing he had also received from the butt of George's pistol some of his facial muscles had been damaged, leaving skin drooping on his left cheek. Brian realised that he was a broken man and taking back control of the Aldfriston Raiders would be impossible. Even with support from his friends, they were not strong enough to usurp George Styles.

Brian had tried to contact some of his trusted friends but only David Prosser came to see him and he did so in the dead of night, so as not to be seen.

David reported that George had made it clear that he was now the boss and if anyone disagreed they could leave the gang. Two did and within a week they had left the village, being driven out by the other villagers, who depended on the income from Free Trading and couldn't chance these men going to the authorities.

One other man, Neil Simpson had tried to remove George from this earth but missed his shot and died from the volley of shots from George and his friend Ned. There have been no more challenges to his leadership.

One glimmer of hope came from this conversation. David told Brian that although George was running the gang, the number of trips had fallen to one a week, from the two to three while Brian was in charge. This was causing some disquiet as the earnings of those who helped to land the consignments, had dropped considerably. Some men were stealing to keep their families in food.

George was aware that Brian had returned but his pride was stopping him from calling on him to ask for his help.

A few days after David's visit, Brian received a visit from George. At first he thought that may be George had come to finish off the job he had started or order him out of the valley.

These fears were far from the truth. By now George realised that he didn't have all the knowledge to operate a gang of Free Traders. What he needed was Brian's business brain George had come to ask for help in selling the contraband.

George had made contact with one merchant, from London, but he felt that the man was robbing and as he had no other outlet for his stock he had to go along with him. This brought about a big smile from Brian.

"Not so easy, is it George?"

"No it's not, I didn't realize just how hard you must have been working to keep the goods moving and money coming in."

Before Brian could say anything George's face changed from one of benevolence to one of authority.

"Brian, the gang is mine and there's no way I'll let you back in." George snarled.

"I need your help and for that you will be well paid. If you try to swindle me I'll finish of the job I started."

Brian realised that George meant every word and he had no wish to get back into the gang anyway.

"I do have a few friends who will buy your goods and give you a good price. I'll expect a cut for arranging this." Brian said.

Brian's wife had been able to feed their children and pay for Brian's medical help from money she had been able to put by but this wouldn't last forever. His actual wealth was in a bank, hidden from his wife and anyone else who may look for it.

George had hoped for a favourable reply but was surprised at Brian's willingness to help out the man who had nearly killed him and left him for dead.

"What I need is for you to arrange the collection and payment for the goods and take orders for future consignments. For this I'll pay you fifty guineas a consignment." George proposed.

Brian took a deep breath before he answered; he hadn't expected George to be quite so generous. With this amount of money he would be able to replenish his wife's dwindling funds and then continue to put money aside, to secure their long term future. In a few years they could move away and set themselves up in a big house with land.

There would be many opportunities for development of this arrangement but didn't wish to push things to quickly or he would frighten George away. After all George had only just entered the realms of business, to suggest other ventures may be too much.

"OK George, I'll find you your customers and take orders for you. Fifty guineas are acceptable. It's no where near what I made before but that is old hat now. Yes we have a deal." Brian agreed.

With the agreement made they shook hands and Brian called to his wife to bring out some brandy and biscuits for them to celebrate their new relationship.

Mrs. Cockburn wanted to kill George for what he had done to her husband but that could wait until later. Having Brian back at home was what she had dreamed of over the last month. He was not only home but now appeared to be in a good mood. His happiness was all that she and the children wanted.

Now that George had the support of Brian, he was able to increase the amount of contraband he could move, thus increasing his income. With Brian renewing his contact the orders came flooding in.

George had been planning for his first really large consignment for some weeks now. He had learnt never to leave anything to chance. If you did, then you were inviting disaster. He had been particular as to the day and time the Lugger was to bring over this consignment of contraband.

The most important job was to make sure that the Riding Officers and Dragoons wouldn't be in the area on the night this large consignment was landed.

The Dragoons generally patrolled without an officer, normally in fours or sixes, lead by a Corporal or Sergeant.

George had spent some time and a considerable amount of money cultivating good relations with the Sergeants and Corporals in charge of the various troops that patrolled this area. In this way they could be relied on not to be around when landing his contraband.

George's gang was not the only one operating in the Cuckmere Valley. There were two smaller gangs working out of West Dean and Lullington, on the other side of the valley. George had been quick to realize why Brian had allowed them to exist as the Dragoons were more than satisfied with the small seizures they were able to get from these gangs. Together with the 'presents' of brandy and genever he left for them, they left his gang alone.

Unlike the Riding Officers and Navy, the Dragoons got very little in way of bounty for the capturing of contraband. Any money that did go their way, found its way into the pockets of the officers, rarely down to the Dragoons.

He learned to be careful never to hand over the coins or the half-ankers to the Sergeants. He arranged for them to look in certain places to collect their 'presents'.

Dragoon patrols were not sent out every night and there was little formal planning of the areas to be patrolled or what they were actually looking for.

It was unusual for the Dragoons to ever catch any smugglers and when they did come across them it was generally by luck.

On occasions the Regiment would receive a notice, from a Riding Officer or the Comptroller of Customs, asking that they sent out a patrol, when they had information that contraband was expected to be landed in their area.

If the troop leader was in the pay of the smugglers, they would arrive late or make such a noise that the smugglers were so alerted to their presence that they would either run away or stand and fight. Being that the large gangs of smuggles would have at their disposal one to two hundred men. They could outnumber the Riding Officers and Dragoons ten to one, in a fight. Although not so well armed, the weight of numbers would win the day.

As well as ensuring that the Dragoons were paid not to be around, George had also applied himself to the Riding Officers, especially those stationed in the Seaford area. Seaford, being a rotten borough, had men in the Customs service who were given the posts, so that they would have a vote. They were not expected to actually have to carry out any duties, which the appointments should require of them.

The exception to this was Graham Johnson, he wasn't one of the rotten borough lackeys, he actually believed in the job he had, so carried out his duties as best he could.

The pay, for a Riding Officer was not good so, occasionally, he would availed himself of the generosity of the Aldfriston gang and like the Dragoons he ensured that he had some successes by capturing contraband from the smaller smuggling gangs in the area.

The Riding Officers who patrolled from South Bourn, across Beachy Head, Birling Gap and down to Excet were most certainly in the pay of the smugglers.

They didn't come this far west unless they were keeping out of the way from the gangs, whose pay they were in. Even so George had made arrangements so these men also kept away from his area.

This next delivery was to be special. A very large quantity of contraband was due so to ensure that any of the Riding Officers, working for the Comptroller at Newhaven, were not in the Cuckmere valley, George had sent one of his men into the village of Piddinghoe, in the River Ouse Valley.

This river was of national importance. Within the Weald area, they produced the best cannons, used by both the British and many foreign Navy's. They also produced the best quality gun powder. All this was transported by sea, from Lewes. So when, a century earlier, a storm closed the river mouth at Seaford, a new channel was dug, to allow this trade to continue. A new port was named – Newhaven.

Because this was to be his biggest consignment yet, he sent one of his men to Piddinghoe, along the River Ouse. This man's main task had been to see if he could recruit half a dozen men and three horses to help land a cargo at Newhaven harbour and move it to Lewes.

Even though Piddinghoe was less than eight miles from Aldfriston, George's knew that his man would be considered a foreigner and they couldn't to be trusted. George also knew that the local Free Traders would not be happy with him moving into their area and as such they would make sure that his cargo didn't get landed.

George had a reputation of handing out severe punishment to those who stole from him. Because of this he knew that they would not try to seize the cargo for themselves. The only alternative they had would be to inform the local Customs Comptroller. The Riding Officers would gather in Newhaven, in the hope of capturing George's cargo, thus leaving the Piddinghoe smugglers alone.

With the surety that the Dragoons would be patrolling on the Marshes at Pevensey and not over the hills, above South Bourn and Beachy Head, George felt reasonably confident that his men wouldn't be disturbed.

Additional precautions had been made to ensure that any Riding Officer coming over the Hills from Birling Gap, could be dealt with.

Twenty batsmen would be sent up to Cliff End, to watch out for anyone coming along the Seven Sisters cliffs. This spot also gave a good vantage point down into Cuckmere haven, where most of the activity of the night would be happening.

The batsmen had instructions to either capture inquiring people, to make them unable to continue their journey or if the necessity arose, to kill them. George knew that such action would bring about feverish activity to capture anyone involved in the killing of a Customs man.

Some years earlier one of the Riding Officer, from South Bourn, had been lured to his death along the top of Beachy Head. The culprit had deliberately moved the white stones, which marked the path along the edge of the cliff. When the Riding Officer rode along this marked path, his horse walked over the edge of the cliff and into a 600 feet fall to the base of the cliff. It was reported that the Riding Officer was able to grab on to the grass but that he couldn't retain his grip and fell over the cliff to his death.

The search for the perpetrator, of this deed, was still going on and a reward of £1,000 had been posted for information leading to their arrest.

CHAPTER 4
We need you tonight

A knock on the bedroom door startled Graham. He looked at his watch, hanging from the chair by his bed. It was only eight o'clock! Mrs Jefferies knew he was not to disturb this early, especially after he had been out late the previous night.

The wind was blowing across the roof, above his head. Although sunlight was trying to force its way into his room, through the gaps in the curtains, he had no intention of getting up for a while yet.

Graham took his duties as a Riding Officer very seriously. He was stationed in Seaford so that he could patrol the Sussex coast from the River Cuckmere valley, to the east, to the River Ouse, in the west. As well as patrolling the coast he was also responsible for covering up to ten miles, inland. This was so that he could check that no sheep fleeces were being illegally shipped over to France. Because this problem only happened for a couple of months a year, it was only then that he would venture more than four miles from the coast.

Graham had been out late last night, on his horse Stan, patrolling some of the more discreet highways and paths that he knew were frequented by the smugglers. Most of their activities were carried out under the cover of darkness but hopefully with the help of a certain amount of moonlight. Over the years Graham had gradually found many of their secret routes. The paths and tracks they used to get contraband from their landing places to safe hideouts where they could store the contraband, out of site of the Riding Officers, to await collection by their customers.

Last night Graham had patrolled along the villages between Seaford and Newhaven. He had waited at track junctions and stood by the edges of some woods, listening for men their ponies but he heard nothing. Last night he thought that there should be a landing of contraband. He hadn't heard of one arriving for the last few days so one was due, very soon but not last night.

It was well after he had sent Mark, his trainee, back to his lodgings, at the Comptrollers House, in Newhaven, that Graham walked up onto Seaford Head. He wanted to get a bit of air and clear his mind. Life had been quite boring recently, he had captured nothing for a while and he thought it was time he received a bounty. Mrs Jefferies could do with her treat of Genever as well.

Graham sat down on the grass edge of the cliff and looked out to sea. He listened to the waves breaking against the shore and returning back to the sea, dragging the pebbles with it. It was then that he thought he saw a flash of light, coming from a point about half a mile, off shore. He strained his eyes to see if he could see if a boat was out there but he could see nothing. The light did not reappear, either. Were his eyes playing up or just him being hopeful?

If it had been a signal, then he might be able to catch the smugglers by surprise. He knew that the smugglers, working between Seaford and Newhaven were just small gangs or about ten men, at the most. As a result the consignments were generally quite small.

At the most only about forty pairs of half-ankers, split between Brandy and Genever. Together with a couple of cases of Tea, the occasional bale of lace or a bag of tobacco. Even if he only captured half of that, he would have done well.

Yes he would go out and see what was around. By heading along the coast, even if he saw no one around, he would be able to read the signs if anything had been landed in the last couple of hours. He rode along the coast to Newhaven but saw nothing. Either they were not about or they had already moved their goods inland. If he rode back through the hills, he may have found a few men and ponies, carrying the illicit goods.

Realising that he had been out on a wasted trip, after visiting the village of Denton and the hamlet of Newton, he rode on to Bishopstone. Here he called in on his friend, the village constable. After a tankard of ale with him and his wife Graham rode on to Blatchington and then home.

Finding no Smugglers activities at all, surprised him. Even without a run taking place, there was normally someone around with the odd half-anker of genever or brandy on their shoulder or slung across the saddle of their horse. It had been on one of these types of patrol that he had arrested Stanton Collins, a few weeks earlier.

Many of the smugglers used sacks tied around the hoofs of the horses to muffle the sound of their hooves striking the flints, which made up much of the surfaces of the roads and tracks in this area. They carried hooded lanterns to light their way, when there was no light from the moon. Not everyone supported the smugglers and there was money to be made by informing on them. Because of this the smugglers needed to keep their movements as silent as possible.

Graham lodged with Mrs. Jefferies ever since he moved into this area. It was not easy for a Riding Officer to get lodgings in these days. No one trusted them, whether or not they were part of a smuggler gang. These were men entrusted by King George to gather taxes and arrest anyone not paying what was due. A lot of people had things to hide, when it came to taxes.

Because much of the economy of the Sussex and Kent coast relied on the trade of the smugglers, it would be very brave of a person to take a Customs Officer into their home, especially one who believed in doing his job contentiously. They would run the risk of being ostracized by the local community.

Mrs. Jefferies was not someone who could not be ignored and when she and her late husband decided to take Graham in, it was because Lionel Jefferies wanted to know the whereabouts of this specific local Riding Officer. He needed to be able to send him away from areas he wasn't wanted, a task he did very well, for Lionel was, himself, a smuggler.

Since Lionel had perished at sea a few years earlier, leaving Mrs Jefferies a widow, in her mid-thirties. She now needed Graham there even more as by letting out the room. It brought her in the money she needed to survive. In return for his rent Graham received a good roof over his head, good wholesome meals and while Lionel was alive, some excellent Brandy and Genever, of which he asked no questions.

Graham knew that he was being used at times and that Lionel was distracting him from where he might get some good pickings but Graham was no fool, he was aware that Lionel was part of a very small gang of Smugglers and having a roof over his head was more important than the small pickings Lionel's gang would give him.

Graham used his time to go after the bigger fish, those with a hundred men at their disposal and who were bringing in two 300 ton Lugger's full of contraband each week.

Graham wasn't the only Customs man, in Seaford. There were four others, only these were paid, not to work but so that they could vote. This was a classic 'rotten borough'. For a very small town, they had three Members of Parliament. Provided that the other men turned up and voted for one of these men, they were paid. Graham had made it clear, right from the start that he was here to do the job he was paid to do and would vote for no one.

CHAPTER 5
We need you tonight

Mrs. Jefferies was not in the habit of disturbing Graham until at least mid day, when he had been out on patrol the night before and it was now only eight o'clock.

"What is it Mrs. Jefferies?" He called.

"Young Mister Mark's in the kitchen. He has an important message for you. Shall I send him through?" She asked.

"No, I'll be there in a few moments, can you give him a drink and something to eat?"

Mrs. Jefferies was ahead of him there.

"He already has a tankard of ale and is getting through a few biscuits while we talk."

Tea was an expensive commodity at this time. In France you could get a kilo of tea for just 1 shilling and 4 pence. In England, once the tax had been added, it would cost 8 shillings. This made it the subject of much of the smuggling along this coast line. Because of its price, for people like Mrs. Jefferies, what little she could afford was only used for entertaining guests. For day to day entertaining, people were offered ale.

"You spoil that young lad; he'll not be able to ride his horse if he gets any bigger." Graham joked with his landlady.

Mark Downer was a trainee Riding Officer. He had been assigned to Graham Johnson to teach him what is expected of a Riding Officer.

Mark was the sixteen-year-old son of Mr. Downer, the Customs Comptroller in Chichester, further along the Sussex coast. His father wanted his son to follow in his footsteps but Mark was a stubborn boy. He didn't mind the work but was adamant that he would not work for his father.

This was the reason his father had apprenticed him to Mr. Williams, the Customs Comptroller at Newhaven. In his wisdom, Mr. Williams sent Mark to work with one of his most experienced men.

Because of his age and the extra money he would receive from Mark's father, Mark lodged at Mr. William's house, in Newhaven.

It was recognized that Graham was a good Riding Officer, with many arrests behind him and the respect of both the Customs Comptrollers and the smugglers alike. There was no one, in the Customs community, who knew more about the smugglers in this area and how they worked, than Graham.

Graham had his flaws, in that the pay of a Riding Officer was not as much as it could be. As a result, it was not unknown for him not to be around when the smugglers were landing their cargo.

Graham was, in his own mind, able to balance this with the fact that he was able to capture more than his fair share of illegal goods, landed in his area, along the coast. This brought him some nice extra income in the form of bounties as a reward for his work.

Mark had only been with Graham for about three weeks and hadn't yet been shown over the whole area Graham was responsible for. He had kept Mark to the villages that were only a few miles from the coast, along the Downs and between Seaford and Newhaven.

In this way Mark hadn't far to go, at the end of a patrol, to reach the ferry, that took him over the River Ouse, to Mr. William's house.

Allowing Mark to travel alone at night could be very dangerous, especially for a young Riding Officer. There were quite a few smugglers who would reward anyone who was able to put a Customs man out of action. It would soon be time for Graham to take Mark on longer patrols, along the Cuckmere valley into Aldfriston and West Firle, but that could wait until next week.

Graham got dressed in his outside clothes, as he thought that Mark would be bringing a message for them to go somewhere to arrest someone or other. He put on his stockings and trousers, then his blouse over a thick under vest. Graham always left his riding boots by the back door, along with his riding coat and three-cornered hat.

His pistols and cutlass were on the small table by the bedroom door. These he picked up as he left his room.

He clipped the pistols to his belt, just to the left and right of the buckle. He liked them there so he could walk comfortably as well as ride his horse without having to move then. This position also gave him access to them when the need arose.

Mark hadn't been out with Graham last night, as he had been sent off home for an early night. Had he have been with Graham, to the end of his patrol, he would have known not have come to Mrs. Jefferies home this early. This was one of the first things Graham had told him.

Graham arrived in the kitchen soon after being called.

"Mark, what brings you here at this time of the day? Has Mrs. Williams told you to tidy your room or something?"

"You jest Mr. Johnson, my room is always tidy." Mark replied.

Graham had always insisted that he be addressed properly by Mark. Time would come, when he was fully trained, that he could consider himself an equal to his older officer. Then he would only allow him to call him by his Christian name, when they were alone.

"It's Mr. Williams who sent me over to see you, he also told me to send Mr. Trigger to him as well."

"What is this message then? That has caused Mr. Williams to get me up and about at this time of the day?" Graham asked.

"I can only tell you. It's not for others. Is what I was told." Mark said, looking in Mrs. Jefferies direction.

"Would you mind leaving us Mrs. Jefferies, Mark has some secrets to tell, men's things." Graham said.

This brought a flush to Mark's face and Mrs. Jefferies chuckled.

"Girl troubles again then Mark? You should pay Barbara with coins for cleaning your room."

Mark had confided in Graham that the Newhaven Ferryman's daughter had been paying him attention but, he hadn't reciprocated her advances.

Mrs. Jefferies put down her mixing spoon and left the kitchen. She had been around Mr. Johnson for many years now and knew that sometimes he had to talk business that she shouldn't be party to.

This had also applied when her husband was alive and he needed to talk to others about his business.

In some instances it would be dangerous for her to know, although when her husband was alive she would do her best to find out anything Graham was talking about, that may be of use to Lionel.

Once the kitchen door had closed Mark told Graham that Mr. Williams had received information that there was to be a big landing of contraband tonight. It was said to be happening in Newhaven harbour at about 10 o'clock. Mr. Williams was gathering all his men up to surprise the gang and capture, hopefully, the biggest consignment of Brandy, Genever, Tea and Lace anywhere this year.

Mr Turner said Mr Williams was also hopeful that this would get him a better position in the Customs service and allow him to move up to a more lucrative positions in London.

"I haven't heard of any such cargo for tonight." Graham said, more to himself than addressing Mark.

Graham looked through the window and out to sea. On the horizon he could see dark clouds and with the wind blowing in off the sea he summarized that the clouds would soon follow.

"It looks as if we'll see some heavy seas tonight. I don't see how anyone could try to enter the harbour at night, not in those seas."

"But Mr. Williams said it came from a very reliable source." Mark insisted.

"I know of some of his 'Reliable sources' and they are generally smugglers who want him and us, to be somewhere else."

"Mr. Williams told me to tell you that if we didn't come tonight, that we could both say goodbye to our jobs. You know how my father would react to that. He'd have me back home working as one of his Riding Officers."

"Don't worry about that I wouldn't wish that on anybody, even you."

They both sat back and drank their ale and with Graham's help, finished off the plate of biscuits. Graham took this opportunity to think things over; he didn't like to be threatened, even by his boss.

He needed to get a perspective on this. Once they had finished Graham had decided what to do. He suddenly stood up.

"Mark, meet me here at 4 o'clock, with your horse. Make sure those pistols of yours are loaded and you have plenty of shot and powder."

"Do I need my cutlass as well? I would much prefer to use that in a close fight." Mark said, with an air of excitement.

"You in a close fight, you'd run a mile if George Styles came at you. This is no barroom brawl we get into out there you know, people die." Graham didn't like to dampen Mark's bravado too much but he needed him to realize the dangers they could be in.

"Yes bring your cutlass."

Graham remembered when he was young and ready for a fight but he was in the army planning to fight the French. That was a much less dangerous encounter than coming up against two to three hundred Smugglers, on your own.

"I'm not planning for a fight this afternoon, just a ride out to look around and see what is going on out there." Graham said.

"Then why are we going so well armed, if you don't expect a fight?"

"Because it is what is expected of us. That's why." Graham said.

With that Mark rose, put on his coat and hat.

"Thank you for the ale and biscuits Mrs. Jefferies." Mark called out.

A voice from the depth of the house, 'he was welcome'. Mark left through the front door and headed to where he had tied his horse.

A man, whom Mark hadn't seen before, was standing by his horse, with his back to him. The man's hand was running down the horse's rein, which was tied to the gate post. His right hand was smoothing the horse's neck.

Mark owned a magnificent mare, she had been given to him by his father, on his fourteenth birthday and they had been inseparable ever since. She was full fourteen hands, black with a white star on the forehead and four white feet.

The man was several inches taller than Mark, about three stones heavier and appeared to be about to walk off with his mare.

Mark looked around to see if the man had any friends about, if so he would have to take extra care. There was no one else about so he decided that if he was to gain control of the situation quickly, he needed to frighten this man enough, so that he didn't have time to notice the age of the person confronting him.

Mark reached onto his belt with his right hand and unclipped the pistol hanging to his left side. With the pistol in his hand he raised it ready to thrust it into the neck of this man.

As Mark took a step neared his horse, she turned her head around towards Mark and looked at him. She gave out a loud whinny of recognition, which startled both Mark and the thief. The man took a firm grip of the rein with his left hand and brought his right hand over to rub the horse's face to keep her quiet. He didn't want to alert its owner. Having quietened the horse down, he looked around.

To his right there was no one around but as he turned his head to the left he found himself looking down the barrel of a flintlock pistol. He heard the click, as the flint was taken back, to half cock. He froze, the colour drained from his face and his jaw dropped open.

"If you want to live, move away from my horse." Mark ordered.

The man moved his eyes away from the pistol and into the eyes of the person holding it. This was just a lad. He didn't frighten him, even with a gun in his hand. Who was he to stop him stealing this horse?

One of the early lessons that Mr. Johnson had taught Mark was how to recognize when a man was about to attack. 'This is just as important when you are in an Inn, enjoying yourself, as it is when you are arresting someone.' Graham had told him.

This was true now. Here was a man ready to fight for the goods he wanted to steal. Mark was much quicker than his adversary. He had noticed the change in the man's face and the way he had released hold of the horse's rein. This man was about to attack, thought Mark.

With a sudden move, which caught the thief by surprise, Mark took two steps back and brought the second pistol from his belt and fully cocked this new weapon and brought the first one to full cock.

The man now found that instead of one held cocked flintlock pistol pointing at him, there were two.

"Do I shoot you or do you leave now?" Mark asked, before the thief could think of his best move.

"Stealing a Riding Officers horse is a hanging offence and that horse belongs to me." Mark snapped.

"You're no Riding Officer." The man snarled.

"Do you want me to call Mr. Johnson out here?" Mark asked.

"This is not one of his horses. He would never let anyone ride any of his horses, especially someone as young as you." The man said, still standing by Mark's horse.

"I said that this is my horse and you are to move away or I'll shoot you as a horse thief. I'll count to four and then my left hand pistol will speak for me" Mark ordered.

"One," "Two," "Three." Mark counted slowly. As he was about to reach four he lowered the barrel of his left-hand pistol to point at the thief's right foot. He did this without moving his eyes from the man's.

By the time he had reached 'Four' the man had made no move; in fact he smiled back at Mark. 'I called your bluff' was what he challenged. The smile soon disappeared when Mark fired his left-hand pistol and a shot hit the man's boot, just missing his toes.

The man looked down and then back at Mark.

"The next one is between your eyes." Mark snapped.

The man was now realizing that this boy was not afraid to use his pistols. They were not expensive toys, they were deadly weapons.

From behind Mark's left shoulder, came a call from the house.

"If I was you John Badger, I'd leave now while you still have your life." Graham Johnson called.

"I was just admiring his horse, that's all." John answered.

"Like the ones I caught you with last year, I expect." said Graham.

"Now be on your way before I let my fellow officer kill you."

This was enough for John; he'd been caught out, so he turned to leave. Before he took a step, he received a stern warning form Mark.

"Come near my horse again and I'll kill you without warning."

John moved away and returned back to the town where he could find someone much easier to steal from.

Mark watched John go before turning around and looking up at the upstairs window, where Mr. Johnson's room was.

"Thank you Mr. Johnson."

"You be careful how you use your pistols, if there had been some of his friends around, you would have had two empty pistol now." Graham warned.

"I didn't injure him, only shot his boots." said Mark "and I did look around before I approached him." Mark reassured him.

This brought a smile to Graham's face. This young man will make a good Riding Officer and should live for a long time.

Before he joined his horse, Mark reloaded his discharged pistol; he then untied her and sprung into the saddle. His journey back to the Comptrollers house, at Newhaven, would only take him half an hour if he kept to the road along the coast. He would veer off to reach Horfe ferry crossing, on the eastern side of the Rover Ouse.

On reaching the Horfe ferry crossing, Mark took his horse into the barn behind the ferryman's house. He had an arrangement with the ferryman to use his barn to stable his horse on this side of the river.

To get his horse over to the other side of the river was not only time consuming but costly. He would have to ride further inland, to Stock Ferry, where the ferry man there had a special ferry to move animals across the river. The only other way was to ride up to Lewes, cross over the river by the bridge, then ride back down the far side of the river into Newhaven town and to Mr. Williams stable.

As he would need his horse later that day, neither were valid options. It would not be until 1793 that a bridge would be built, across the river, in Newhaven, so then traffic could cross here without using the ferry or the long diversion.

Having seen to his horse, ensuring that it was wiped down, fed and watered, he went to the quayside to see if Mr. Ferris was about.

If not, he would have to call at the house. There was no need for this, as there, on the far side of the river, was Mr. Ferris and his boat.

"Can I have a trip across the river please?" Mark called.

Mr. Ferris turned around and saw it was the young Riding Officer.

"Be with you in a few moments Mister Mark. I'm just waiting for Mrs. Ferris to come back with her chattels."

Mark was not in a hurry. He had about five hours to kill before he had to return to Seaford, so he just sat on the quay side, with his legs hanging down towards the flowing waters below.

He was enjoying the silence and letting his mind just go blank and drift like the river flowing below his feet.

"Good morrow Mister Mark."

He recognized the voice of the ferryman's daughter Barbara,

"Good morrow Barbara." He replied.

She sat down beside him and dangled her legs down beside his.

"Waiting for my father are you?" She asked.

"Yes, but I'm in no hurry. I have a few hours to kill before I've to do anything else today."

"I expect you'll be seeing a girl later?" Barbara enquired.

"No I don't have a girlfriend. I've work to do with Mr. Johnson."

"Oh" was all that Barbara said.

Barbara was about seventeen years old. Five foot two inches tall. Her shape can only be described as womanly, even for her young age. She had fair hair, a round face with delicate features. Her lips were full and whenever she looked at Mark there was a sparkle in her hazel eyes.

They both sat there in silence for some five minutes until Barbara saw her mother walking towards her father's ferry.

"I'd better get back to my chores before my mother catches me." So she quickly swung her legs back onto the quay and stood up.

"See you later." She called, as she ran back to the house.

With the water flowing down to the sea, Mr. Ferris started off by rowing up the far side of the river, against its flow. After twenty yards he headed across the river, pulling hard on the oars, against the tide.

He had built up considerable strength and knowledge of the river, over the years. In this way he used up the least energy, to achieve the desired result – crossing the river with his cargo.

By the time he had manoeuvred his boat across the river it was close to approaching where Mark was seated. Mark always found it interesting to watch Mr. Ferris at work. He stood up and waited for Mr. Ferris to throw up the rope, so that the boat could be anchored to the quayside.

Mark helped Mrs Ferris up, from the ferry, onto the quayside. He then climbed down the ladder, into the ferry.

After crossing the river Mark arranged for Mr. Ferris to collect him at three o'clock, this would give him time to cross the river, saddle his horse and get to Mr. Johnson's house by four o'clock.

CHAPTER 6
I see no boats

There was one thing Graham did admire about Mark and that was his punctuality. At 4 o'clock there was a knock on the cottage door and Mark stood there, his two fine flintlock pistols hanging from his belt and his cutlass slung from his left hand side.

"Ready, as ordered, Mr. Johnson." Mark said.

"That's what I like to see, a sign of respect." Graham said.

He turned back, picked up his coat and hat, put them on. Before he left, he turned his head and called back, into the house,

"Good bye Mrs. Jefferies. We'll be back at about six thirty. Could you have a hot meal ready for the two of us? We're going out again later and young Mark will need some proper food inside of him."

Mark was the kind of boy who all the women wanted to mother, so the request to feed him was never refused by Mrs. Jefferies. It was a slur to say that Mark was not well fed by Mrs. Williams but it was not the good country food that Graham liked.

Graham had been over to the stables, at the farrier's, earlier to saddle his horse, ensured that it was rested and ready for a busy night's work.

Mark had been taught, from an early age, that looking after a horse was very important. If you relied on your horse for getting you around or as part of your work, then a well kept horse was an important asset. This showed in the way his mare was prepared for the nights work. She had been washed down and brushed, the bridle was clean and the saddle put on with an under blanket, to protect the mare from pressures transferred through the saddle to its back. He had feed and watered her, earlier, then allowed her to rest.

As they walked out to collect their horses, Mark asked.

"What are we doing this evening then Mr. Johnson? I don't want to tire my mare out to much, if we'll be busy tonight."

"Don't you worry none young Mark, we're just going for a ride down to Excet Bridge and see if there are any signs of activity at the river."

"What do you expect to find at this time of day? You've always told me that George Styles only brings his men and boats out at the last minute. This is far too early for that, isn't it?"

"I'll show you a thing or two about how we'll know what they'll be up to tonight." Graham said.

With that they both untied their respective horses and mounted them. Graham led off, towards Seaford Head, Mark followed.

"You're right, George and his men won't be around yet but there are always signs that they will be around later. If they are going to land a consignment tonight, I want them to believe I won't be around."

Mark was not at all happy with this, he didn't want to shy away from a fight with the smugglers but he didn't relish the idea of riding into them unprepared either.

"Are we not being a little open in doing this Mr. Johnson? If anyone sees us they may report us to George Styles and he'll either send some men out to tackle us or change their plans for tonight."

"Don't you worry none about us being seen, we sorely will be and George will be told about it." Graham reassured him.

"I still don't think this is wise. If Mr. Williams were to find out and tonight's exploits in the port was not to come off, he'll be very angry."

"Mark, you worry too much about other people. What you need to do is learn some of the tricks of the trade. That's why you're here."

"I'll show you how you can spot what the smugglers are up to. How well prepared they are, for their next delivery."

This young man needs to trust him more, thought Graham. Still he had only been with him for a few weeks. In time he'll learn to trust his judgment. Mark's main trouble was that he was in fear of Mr. Williams, in the same way as he feared his father.

Mark's father was a good Customs Man, he had served his country, used his wife's money and family influence well, to secure himself a profitable area to control.

On the other hand Mr. Williams had been given his position more because he would vote for the right man and could be trusted to get his men to do the same. His inability to do the job was not considered an issue.

By this time their horses had brought them to the end of Seaford Head. Graham told Mark to get out his telescope and to view the scene, from the river mouth back along the river to the bridge. He did the same.

Mark put his telescope to his eye and quickly scanned the scene he was told to look at. When he had reached the bridge he lowered his telescope and looked at Graham. Graham was still viewing the river mouth.

"I couldn't see anything that says the smugglers are here."

"In that case you had better look again young man. There are at least three boats moored near the river mouth and I would guess a few more closer to the bridge."

Mark always thought he had good eyesight and with the aid of the telescope could see well, for a very long way. He had also learned that it was no use in arguing with adults, even if you're right. On each occasion he had questioned Graham's guidance, he had found himself in the wrong.

He raised the eyepiece back to his eye and adjusted the telescope so that he was correctly in focus on what he was looking at. This time he took his time, scanning both river banks carefully and not rushing to see who could reach the bridge the quickest.

"There's one boat on this bank and there is another just by it." Mark said gleefully, "and another, how did I miss them? I'm sure they were not there a moment ago." He said excitedly.

"You must always take great care when you look at anything in the distance, not everything is what it seems." Graham said.

"If you look further along the river, just past those two large bushes by the bend, you'll see that a boat has been brought up onto the river bank and covered up with some reeds." Graham instructed.

Mark looked along the river, found the bushes Graham had described but couldn't see the boat that Graham was pointing out. Mark rubbed his eyes and refocused his telescope but to no avail,

"I can't see a boat Mr. Johnson. Are you sure there is one there?"

"You won't see the actual boat but if you look at the reeds on this side of the bank you'll see the way they are laying with the wind."

"Aye I can see that." Mark confirmed.

"Well if you look at the reeds between the bushes you'll see they are leaning different ways, the pattern gives the outline of a boat."

"Oh I see it now. I would've missed that one completely. I'll remember that in the future." Mark said.

Graham knew that these lessons wouldn't be wasted on Mark. He was a good student and would be a credit to the service in later years. He just hoped that he would have him, by his side, until that time came.

"Let's go and look around a little closer to the bridge. I think you may find something interesting there." Graham said, as he urged his horse forward.

Mark quickly collapsed his telescope and put it away in its leather case. While doing this he urged his horse forward with a squeeze of his knees.

His horse was well trained and had been his constant companion. They covered many miles together and got used to each others ways.

That was one area Graham couldn't teach Mark, he was a far better horseman. In fact Graham had learned a few things from Mark, not that he let him know. Graham was Mark's teacher after all.

When they reached the bottom of the hill they turned, firstly towards the beach. Graham wanted to see exactly how heavy the sea was today. Their horses didn't like the sea or walking on the beach. The sea breeze was not to their liking and the pebbles under their hoofs could get lodged in them. It was alright once they reached the sand but Graham was not going that far. He stopped at the high tide mark and looked around.

The tide was on its way out and if he didn't miss his guess the tide would turn at about 7 o'clock that evening and reach high tide at about 10 o'clock.

This would be just right for the lugger captain. He would be able to bring his craft in close to the shore, if he ran aground on the way in he would be able to refloat as the tide rose and his boat became lighter.

"You see the tide, Mark? When will it return to high tide?"

Graham was always testing Mark and so far he had always come up with the right answers.

Mark thought about it for a few moments and tried to calculate just how far the tide was from its last high tide. Although they had ridden this way many times before Mark had never really taken much notice of the tide. His mind had always been on whatever mission they were on and not on the peripheries. That was Graham's area, so he thought.

"I would think that as the tide is going out now, it will turn at about, say 8 o'clock and reach high tide again at about 10 o'clock."

Mark looked at Graham to see any reaction to his estimations.

"Well I think you're right about the high tide but if you look at the current high tide mark you can see that it has not long turned. As such it will reach low tide until about 7 o'clock."

Mark felt good about reading the high tide timing but was disappointed that he had got the low tide wrong.

"Why's it important to know about the tides, if we're in Newhaven tonight. The Lugger will come in there at any tide?" Mark asked.

"You should always be aware of the tides if you work near the sea Mark. It is them that decide when the smugglers will be working and I don't believe that there will be any landing in the harbour tonight. It'll be here between 8 and midnight." Graham said

"By the time we've been to the bridge, I'll show you the proof."

With that said, Graham turned his horse around and, followed by Mark, rode up the valley towards Excet Bridge.

When they reached the bridge Graham told Mark to dismount and tie both of their horses up on the bush by the side of the track. Once Mark had secured their horses, Graham led the way across the track and instead of heading to the top of the bridge he turned to go down the bank to the river.

"Why are you going down there Mr. Johnson? I thought you said that we were going to the bridge."

"Aye but I also said I would show you proof that the smugglers will be out tonight, come on down Mark and I will show you something."

Mark slipped and landed on his backside, as he descended the riverbank, much to the amusement of Graham.

"You had better keep your feet along here or you'll land in the river. With the tide going out, it will take you down to the sea before you know what is happening. How'll I explain that to your father?"

Mark regained his feet and followed Graham towards the bridge. As they reached it Graham stepped aside and beckoned Mark forward.

"Look under the bridge and see what's tucked away in between the struts. If there are half-ankers of brandy and genever, then we'll be in for a run tonight. If not, we'll go to Newhaven and keep Mr. Williams company."

Mark carefully passed Graham and, holding on to the struts so that he didn't fall into the river, worked his way to the middle of the bridge. He couldn't believe it, there, as Mr. Johnson had said, were two pairs of half-ankers of brandy and two more of genever.

"They are here as you said Mr. Johnson, four pairs of half-ankers in all." Mark reported.

"Well done, now look over to the other side of the river and under the bridge struts, what can you see over there."

Mark carefully turned around, keeping one hand firmly holding on to one of the crossbeams. There before him were a further two pairs of half-ankers but he couldn't see if they were brandy or genever.

With this information at hand he worked his way back to Graham and reported what he had found.

"Those two pairs will all be genever, Sergeant Sampson much prefers genever to brandy." Graham said.

This statement shocked Mark. Mr. Johnson saying that these items of contraband were awaiting collection by the dragoon's Sergeant, who patrolled this area.

"Who are the others for then?" Mark asked.

"Us" Graham replied.

Mark was shocked, he had always been led to believe that Riding Officers were not allowed to take bribes and if they did then they were no better than the smugglers themselves.

He understood that the reason why he had been assigned to work with Mr. Johnson was that it was thought that he was the best and one of the most experienced Riding Officer around.

Mark heard that Mr. Johnson's honesty was above reproach. All this showed was that he was clever. He could carry on with his Customs duties without his superiors really knowing what he was doing.

As far as Graham had been concerned, as long as he was able to seize as much, if not more, contraband than the other officers in the area, he would be left alone to feather his own nest, much like the Comptrollers did theirs.

"George leaves us 'presents' so we'll find somewhere else to be this night. He knows that if the 'presents' are not taken we will be active in the area that night."

"You mean it is a sort of signal to the smugglers not to go out that night?" Mark inquired.

"Well not exactly, I've never known the smugglers to cancel a run. He is more likely to enlist the help of more men to fight us off."

"So what are we going to do?" Mark asked.

"We'll not be here anyway tonight, so we don't have to take his bribe." Graham swung around his arm and struck young Mark full in the back and sent him into the river.

"Don't you ever use that word in my presence." Graham shouted, as Mark's head reappeared above the water.

"Help me out, I'm drowning." Mark called, as he was pulled along in the current, towards the sea.

"You fell in, you get yourself out." Graham called back.

While Mark was being washed down to the sea, Graham swung himself down under the bridge to retrieve his 'present'.

If Mark couldn't get out soon Graham would take his horse and a rope, ride down stream and help him out. He was so outraged by what Mark had said; he would leave him to his own devices for now.

Mark was not a good swimmer, he had been in the sea before and fallen out of his boat but he hadn't been required to swim far.

The river was flowing quite fast, with the tide going out, the speed of the river increased. He found himself drifting to the middle of the river as the water flowed around the left-hand bend, drawing him with it.

Had he fallen in about ten yards further down stream the water was quite still and he would have been able to climb out where he went in, as it was he would have to get himself to the river bank somehow. With riding boots and his coat now full of water he was finding if very difficult to just stay afloat let alone swim in any given direction.

Mark had strong arms and legs so with a form of doggy paddle he managed to make way, using the flow of the current, to edge himself towards the bank, some hundred yards downstream after the bend.

Graham helped him self to two pairs of half-ankers of brandy and one pair of genever and manoeuvred them from under the bridge and onto the river bank. He looked along the river bank to see if Mark had got himself out yet and saw that he had just reached the side of the river and appeared to have a secure hold of some grass or reeds growing on the bank.

Not having to ride to his rescue, Graham could see about loading the half-ankers on the horses, before he went to collect Mark. Once he had completed that task he thought it time to collected Mark, before he fell back in again. He untied the two horses and walked them along the riverbank until he came across Mark pulling himself onto the top of the riverbank.

"Why you oaf, there was no need for you to have done that. I nearly drowned myself. What would you have told my father?" screamed Mark.

"I'd have said you died in the course of duty chasing Smugglers and he would have buried you as a hero, instead of a fool,"

"Now get up here and dry your self off, before you catch a cold."

Mark took off his clothes, revealing a young, but very muscular body. His upper arms showed that many years riding good horses had developed his muscles well, his chest hadn't yet grown any hairs and his stomach was very flat and showed strong muscles. Like his arms, his legs were also muscular.

Between them they wrung out Mark's clothes until they held only a fraction of the water they had when Mark reached the river bank.

"Now get dressed and clean your pistol and cutlass, you may need to be ready to fight. Even if you get wet, your weapons can't suffer."

Mark shook out his clothes to remove even more water and then dressed while Graham sat down on the top of the riverbank and explained to him that it was all a game with the Smugglers. There couldn't be winners and losers, if there were, many men would die and families would suffer.

Many farm workers had to steal from their employers just to find food to keep their families alive. If caught they were more than likely to find themselves before a Magistrate. Most of which were landowners or farmers themselves. If this wasn't their first offence they could be transported to Australia for a number of years, leaving their families in a far worse position. Moore often than not they would be ejected from their cottage, ending up in the village poor house and reliant on the local villagers, who paid a local tax to support the needy of their community.

Mark understood this but was now frightened to ask why Graham had taken the 'presents' from the Smugglers. Just being dressed, from the first swim, he had no intention of having a second trip into the river.

"You're now wanting to ask me why I took the brandy and genever. Aren't you Mark?" Graham said, braking into Marks thoughts.

"Well, yes I was. I didn't think you're the kind of man who behaved like that." Mark said, reluctantly.

He wanted to understand the man he had been trusted with and who, up until now, had shown him only the most honest side of the Riding Officers job.

"On occasions I'll take the gifts. We aren't that well paid and occasionally I like to give Mrs. Jefferies a present for looking after me so well. Since her husband perished in a storm she hasn't had many opportunities to have her beloved genever."

This still didn't answer questions that were still going unasked.

"There is also another reason for us taking these tonight." Graham continued. "If George found that none had been taken, he will bring out an army of men to protect his goods. He can call on about two hundred men."

"Two Hundred!" exclaimed Mark.

"Yes, he can call on men from all the villages in the valley and go as far inland as Berwick and Selmeston for even more. Don't ever under estimate the smugglers ability to outnumber you."

Graham then continued in explaining that by taking some of the half-ankers, George will be aware that at least one of the Riding Officers had visited the bridge and wouldn't be in the valley that night. It was the usual practice for a Riding Officer to cover likely landing areas, each day.

With several gangs working out of the Cuckmere valley, sometimes two Riding Officers would visit the bridge and so the smugglers would leave sufficient for each one.

"I though you said that we should be here tonight, with such a landing taking place and not going over to Newhaven?" Mark said.

"Boy, you have a lot to learn about this game. There are no rules and as such you can't be accused of breaking any. I don't intend to be in Newhaven tonight, now we have discovered all this. It is about time we got you your first bonus for capturing a consignment of contraband"

This brought a smile back onto the face of Mark.

"I had to take the half-ankers so that George will believe he is free to carry out his work, undisturbed. I'll see if I can find the Dragoons later on and if they have taken theirs we'll be able to ride in and really surprise George and his gang."

"I still don't understand how this will help us?" Mark said.

"If he believes we'll not be around, he'll only bring out about fifty men; otherwise he would bring many more, does that answer your questions?"

Yes, thought Mark, there was sense in what Graham was doing but Mark still didn't like being bribed by these gangs.

All the time they were talking, Mark was working on his pistols and cutlass. It was important that all the wet powder and shot in the pistols were removed and then the barrel dried out and the outer parts wiped clean from the salt water, which could cause the pistols to rust. Being a tidal river, there was no fresh water, this near the sea, just sea water.

Graham had taken one of the pistols and was working on that one while Mark worked on the other. They both finished the pistols at the same time. Mark then took his cutlass and cleaned this off with his saddlecloth and the handle, with his neck scarf.

Graham took up both pistols and felt them, one in each hand, this had been the first time he had had the opportunity to hold Mark's matching pair of flintlock pistols. They were perfectly balanced and fitted well into Graham's hands.

As he held them he noticed that they were always pointing in the direction he was looking at and as he raised them, he found that they would be pointing at the exact spot he was 'aiming' at. What he would give to have such a fine pair as these.

He turned them over in his hands and there, on the lock plate was the inscription of 'Heylin'. This was then a pair of pistols made by H. Hadley of London, one of the finest gunsmiths in the country. How Mark had come into possession of such fine weapons he couldn't imagine but he would make it his duty to find out, at a later time.

"You keep saying 'I', where will that leave me?" Mark asked.

"You will have to go into Newhaven and join Mr. Williams and his little gang of officers. Your job will be to explain to Mr. Williams why I'm not there."

"If I tell him about what you're doing, he'll have you on charge."

"Don't worry, you'll only have to give him a little lie, I'll think one up later for you to tell him."

Before Mark could reply, Graham stood up,

"We had better get back to Mrs. Jefferies and her hot meal now. We'll both need to get it inside us before tonight's work." Graham said.

They both mounted their horses, after Mark had refitted the saddle cloth and adjusted the sets of the half-ankers that were slung on their saddles, two on Graham's and one on Mark's.

"Let's get going, if you've got that one secure?" Graham said.

When Mark said that he was ready they proceeded down the track and turned back up towards Seaford Head. As they started across the Head Graham steered his horse towards a large group of gorse bushes. Mark's horse followed without any instructions from its master. It had quickly learned that where ever Graham went, its master was sure to follow.

"We'll put these half-ankers deep in here for tonight. I don't want Mrs. Jefferies to know that we are aware of the goings on in the valley tonight. She has to believe we will be in Newhaven." Graham said.

"Are you saying that Mrs. Jefferies is in with the smugglers?" "Her husband was a smuggler himself and she still passes on some information on my comings and goings. In that way the local people don't shun her." Graham realised he was deep in thought, most likely about Mrs. Jefferies.

"Don't you worry about Mrs. Jefferies; she wouldn't let anything really nasty happen to either of us. She has sometimes warned me not to go somewhere, in case I ran into trouble she thought I couldn't get out of. I sometimes pass her information to put the smugglers on the wrong foot so that I can capture a cargo or two. It works for us both. In a silly way we look after each other."

Marks education had gone on in leaps and bounds this day.

Graham dismounted and lifted down the two pairs of half-ankers of brandy, from over his saddle. He went into the gorse bushes, pushing them apart with his legs.

Gorse is a very sturdy plant with sharp thorns all over the branches, around the leaves and flowers. You need good protection if you aren't to suffer scratches, when you enter such bushes. This is why Graham had chosen them as his hiding place. He moved into the bushes for about six feet and put the half-ankers down.

"Pass me the one you have Mark."

Mark urged his horse forward to the edge of the bushes and lifted the half-ankers off his saddle and reached, using the rope that held the pair together, he passed them into Graham's hands. He then moved his horse away so as to leave a route of escape for Graham.

Graham put the third pair down with the others and returned to his horse. On leaving the bushes he carefully ensured that the branches went back into their natural lay, so that no one would be aware that they had been disturbed.

"We'll collect them in a few days and give Mrs. Jefferies a surprise."

As they come over the top of the hill and started to head down to the cottage Mark looked up over towards the downs.

"Mr. Johnson. Who are those riders, in the distance?" He said, pointing to a spot away to their right.

Graham took out his telescope and focused it on the group of riders Mark had pointed to. Mark followed and they both came to the same conclusion.

"It's a Dragoon patrol I believe Mark."

"Where are they going? I thought they kept to the coast most of the time." Mark asked.

"That is true but if Mr. Williams is trying to capture smugglers in the harbour, he'll want the smugglers to believe the coast is clear. So he'll have asked the Dragoons to patrol away from the coast and into the country side."

On approaching Mrs. Jefferies cottage they could smell the meal she was cooking, drifting on the wind for some hundred yards or more away. She always gave Graham a hot meal if he was going out at night. A habit she got into when her husband went to sea.

She was aghast to see that Mark was in wet clothes, when he walked into her kitchen. She laughed heartily when he said he had slipped and fallen in and Mr. Johnson had left him to float down river. Even so she sent him into her bedroom and told him to get out of those clothes and put some of her late husbands on. She could put his by the fire and dry them.

After Mark had left the kitchen Mrs. Jefferies turned to Graham,

"You look after that young man, you hear me. He'll be your master one day and won't forget how you treated him." With a change in tone she continued.

"I've grave forbearing about whatever you are at tonight. You take great care of both young Mark and yourself. I don't' want to bury either of you."

There was genuine concern from Mrs. Jefferies. She saw Graham as her responsibility and Mark like the son she and Lynal never had.

"Don't you worry any Gladice; I've taken care to get Mark out of the danger that's around tonight. His battles will come soon enough. When I think he's good enough to not get him self killed." Graham reassured her.

Graham had only used her name twice before, once when he first moved in and she soon put him in his place. The second time was when he came to tell her that her husbands boat was missing and all those on board were thought to have been lost to the sea.

Mark soon returned with his wet clothes in his arm and Mr. Jefferies very large clothes hanging off him. Graham nearly burst out laughing but received a dig in the ribs from Mrs. Jefferies before he did.

"Give me those clothes and sit down for your meal young Mark and don't take any notice of what Mr. Johnson says, we'll soon have you back in your own clothes."

With that she went over to the cooking stove and using the rope she had strung above the stove to dry her own clothes. She hung Mark's clothes so that they would dry out, from the heat of her stove.

Mrs. Jefferies then served up the meal of stew and vegetables with a side plate of home cooked bread to help fill them up.

They were all deep in thought through out the meal and although Mrs. Jefferies tried to engage in some conversation she was unsuccessful, so eventually gave up trying.

At the end of the meal she asked if they would like to take a tankard of ale into the parlour, while she cleared away the dishes and washed up. This they both accepted, with Graham leading the way through. He took up his usual seat and Mark took the seat on the other side of the fireplace.

"You'll have to give that one up when Mrs Jefferies comes in. That's her favourite seat. Not even Mr. Jefferies would sit in that one."

Mark didn't want to have to move again so he rose and pulled up another seat, between that of Graham's and Mrs. Jefferies.

"What are we going to do tonight Mr. Johnson? I don't like the idea of George getting away with his caper. On the other hand if we disobey Mr. Williams we'll be in so much trouble." Mark was very concerned.

He had taken up this life to catch smugglers but had always been brought up to obey orders, he was in a quandary.

"I've been thinking about that. You will go to Newhaven and join Mr. William's party. I don't see why both of us need get into trouble"

Mark was about to protest at being left out but Graham put his hand up.

"I know how you feel, young Mark but I'm going to have to travel many miles tonight. I'll be going over hills and tracks that either you, or your horse, are familiar with. If the Dragoons aren't where I think they'll be I may have to abandon the whole scheme and come and join you in Newhaven. It's important, for us both, that one of us is with Mr. Williams, to give out the story of the others absence."

Mark could see the sense of this and noticed the emphasis Graham put on 'young'. In other words he wasn't yet experienced enough.

"I'll do as you ask." Mark said, reluctantly accepting the order.

"Don't you worry none, Mark. There'll be many more chances for you to join in and had it not been for Mr. William's orders for tonight, I would willingly take you along with me, but I can't." Graham lied.

Mark smiled at this and noticed that this time Graham had left out the word 'young', when addressing him.

Mrs. Jefferies entered the room with small tankard of ale and took up her seat by the fire.

"Your clothes are nearly ready Mark, you can get changed when you like. Use my bedroom and leave Mr. Jefferies clothes on my bed."

"Thank you very much Mrs. Jefferies, I'll change nearer the time to leave. Then I'll have some warm clothes on, to set me up for the night."

"What are you two up to tonight then, more riding over the hills chasing those nice Free Traders?" Mrs. Jefferies teased.

"Oh no Mrs. Jefferies, Mr. Johnson..." here Graham quickly cut in to what Mark was saying. He had no intention of Mrs. Jefferies being aware of what they are really up to.

"...and young Mark has been ordered over to Newhaven tonight to help Mr. Williams on some job. We don't really know what we'll be doing or when I'll be home. If you will leave a light on in the kitchen, I'll come in that way so as not to disturb you." Graham put in.

Mark looked over to Graham and suddenly realised what he had been about to say and remembered what Mr. Johnson had said about Mrs. Jefferies and her connection in the town.

After they had finished their ale, Graham said it was time that they started out to Newhaven. Firstly he sent Mark to get changed and then thanked Mrs. Jefferies for their meal and for drying Marks clothes.

"That's no trouble Mr. Johnson. You just be careful tonight and look after young Mark, he hasn't got your nous for when to go in and when to hold back, so you take care."

Having been warned of his conduct, Graham rose and went into the kitchen. He put on his riding coat, three-cornered hat and a good scarf that Mrs. Jefferies had made for him.

Just as he finished dressing Mark came into the kitchen, now dressed in his own clothes.

"Come on young Mark we have much riding to do tonight."

Mark took his riding coat and his hat from Graham, which he then put on. Mrs. Jefferies entered the kitchen. So Mark wouldn't have to search the cottage for her to thank her for the meal and drying his clothes.

Having said their thanks and good byes they left the cottage and went out to their horses. They checked that their saddles were correctly fitted and fastened, the reins were fitted properly and that the horses were ready for their nights work.

On their way over towards Newhaven, the two Riding Officers discussed the night ahead and thought that they would be unlikely to have any success at the harbour.

"I can't see anyone taking a boat into Newhaven harbour tonight, with the sea so rough. I don't know of a captain who would risk his boat on such a night." Graham said.

"I agree, this is more of a night to land goods offshore than the harbour" answered Mark.

"I'd put money on it that this is a set up and we're being deliberately pulled away from where the actual cargo is being landed?"

"From what we found at Excet, that is were the landing will be but what can we do about it? Mr. Williams has ordered us to join him and I hear he can be very nasty if we don't obey his orders."

"I haven't had any bonus lately. I think it's time for us to get one. All we need to do is get the contraband into the Customs House at Newhaven and we'll get paid." Graham said.

"But we'll be tied up until well after midnight at Newhaven, by that time they will have landed their goods." Mark observed.

"You go and tell Mr. Williams that my horse has thrown a shoe and that I've had to take him back to Seaford." Graham said.

"What if he says that we'll all have to wait for you, before we set about our business? How'll I deal with that?" Mark asked.

"Tell him that I could be some time and that they should leave a message for me at the Comptroller's house. That should suffice."

Mark wasn't happy. He heard how angry Mr. Williams can get. If Graham wasn't careful he could loose his job and so might Mark.

"Be careful Mr. Johnson. George Styles and his men can be very violent. If you are on your own, your life could be in real danger."

"Don't worry. As long as I meet up with those Dragoons we saw earlier, I'll be alright. You take care yourself and mind you don't fall in and get wet again."

With that they parted company, Mark continuing on towards Newhaven and Graham heading up towards High and Over.

CHAPTER 7
Hand over the money

It was a cold dark night on the coast, the sea was running high and the rain was beating down but this was perfect, as far as George Styles was concerned. Tonight he was expecting a lugger to anchor just off the coast at the mouth of the River Cuckmere.

Only a mile inland there were no clouds and a full moon was illuminating the countryside. This gave more or less the effect of daylight over the village of Aldfriston and the surrounding area.

George was not sure if this was good or bad, good because his men could work easier as they could see what they were doing, but bad as any patrolling Dragoons or Riding Officers could also see what his men were doing. George was a careful man that is why he had never been arrested. Tonight, like any other such night, George had ridden up to Cliff End to ensure that Geoff had the signal to send to the Lugger Captain when the time was right and that the batsmen were ready.

With each consignment he used a different signal. This ensured that no one else brought the lugger in to shore, before he was ready. Also, if the customs men took over the lugger, in an attempt to capture him and his men, they wouldn't give the correct signal. George and his men would then disappear into the night.

George made his way back to Excet. He waited to receive the signals from all his outposts. He would signal Geoff, at Cliff End, to signal the Lugger Captain.

Although it was a dark night at the coast, all the smugglers were able to see sufficiently to carry out their tasks. Their eyes had got use to working in such poor light, over the years. To them this was nearly as good as daylight. Geoff could see the Lugger bobbing about in the waves, about a mile off shore, waiting for its signal to come in closer to shore.

Once the lantern signal had been given, the Captain of the Lugger responded with a signal of his own, to acknowledge Geoff's.

Now George could signal to his men, in the rowboats, at the mouth of the river, to start to row out to the Lugger. The unloading could begin quicker and the Lugger could be away and be back in its port in France before daylight.

There were about eight small boats heading out to the Lugger. Each one about three hundred yards behind the other, In that way they wouldn't have to stay out, in these high seas, for longer than necessary.

Once he could see that the first boats were underway, George told Geoff that he and his men were to keep as quiet as possible.

Geoff knew what was expected of him and his men. They had preformed this task on many occasions and as yet killed no one.

George used Excet Bridge as his base, when consignments were being landed. Here he could control his men and could make good his escape if things went wrong. All this had to be planned well in advance.

The men in the rowboats were well on their way out to meet the lugger. Each boat had eight men on the oars and four others who acted as lookouts, guards and loaders of the cargo.

As the first boat reached the Lugger, George's most trusted gang members, Harry, jumped up into the Lugger and greeted the Captain.

"Good evening Captain Saviour. You have the cargo we ordered?"

"Yes Monsieur, everything is here for you tonight." The Captain said.

"It had better be. George was very unhappy last time. I'm under orders to stay on board your boat and ensure that we get what we are paying for."

"That is alright by me. Can I have the money now?"

The Captain was chancing his arm. Especially after the last trip where he had been short ten pairs of half-ankers of brandy and five of Genever.

"I'll pay you after the last half-ankers is loaded." Harry said, sharply.

He was aware that the Captain could kill him there and then.

"The money will come over with the last boat." Harry said.

The Captain was paying dearly for his silliness on the last trip. He was new to this area and thought he was doing these English men a favour. Because of what he had done, no other French Captain would bring their boats here until Captain Saviour had put things right. George was a very good customer, one that any of them could afford to lose. His reputation was well known by those used to trading along this part of the coast.

Each of the rowboats could take up to two hundred pairs of half-ankers on a good night but tonight they were restricting themselves to one hundred and fifty pairs each.

The sheer hard work, to row the boats through the high seas would exhaust any oarsmen; even the trip out to the lugger had tired some of them. They were glad of the rest while the boats were loaded or while they stood off the lugger awaiting their turn to come along side.

On nights with lesser seas they would put a boat on either side of the lugger but on nights like this they only loaded on the leeward side. This lessened the chances of losing the cargo over the side and roaming loose in the seas, to wash up on the shore later, for any Tom, Dick or Harry to collect and either sell or have for themselves.

With the four men on the rowboats taking and passing each half-anker onboard, it would take fifteen minutes to load each boat, with eight boats this meant it would take well over two hours to complete.

The Captain was well aware of the dangers that he and his boat were in. He was not at all interested in the safety of the Englishmen. He knew that he would be paid for any goods delivered, even if he had to wait for the next trip.

His worry was of any Customs boats or Navy ships that may be around. He put three of his men on watch, one on the bow, one on the stern and one on the seaward side of the boat. This man's job was to watch the horizon and see if he could see any other ship out there and if so, where they a danger to them.

Being that the Captain had brought his lugger in as close as he could get, to the shore. The length of time they would be there and the changing tides, it was not easy, for him, to see if any ship were coming along the coast.

With the cliffs, leading to Beachy Head and towards Seaford, obscuring any chance of getting an early warning of the Navy or Custom cutters approaching, especially if they chose to sail close to the shore. If this happened their chances of getting away wasn't good.

The Lugger's, used for delivering to the Free Trading, were very well armed and were a good match for any Customs or Navy Cutters that they encounter. All had at least one swivel gun on the bow and in most cases they would have some along each side and at the stern. These guns gave them a good advantage.

They didn't need to be broadside to their target to engage them. As a result few of these boats had been captured or for that matter sunk as a result of their engagement. The risks of actual capture were not high, if they were prepared to fight their way out.

The men at the bow and stern would watch the sea close to the cliffs and also up to the top of the cliffs, where George's men were stationed. These men would signal to the Lugger if they saw any danger, so it was important that those on the lugger kept watch for such signals.

'So far so good' thought George as he stood on the bridge, waiting for signs that all was well.

It was not long before he was informed that the first boat was now coming up the river, with its cargo and the second boat had left the lugger. Each crew knew what they had to do and where their landing point was.

There were men and horses waiting at various points along the riverbanks to unload the cargo and take it off, either directly to the customers or to a hiding place, to await collection. It was important that the cargoes were moved far away from the coast quickly.

The Riding Officers and Dragoons only operated within ten miles of the coast and so it was important to get the goods out of their reach.

Other than the sound of the waves breaking against the beach, there were no other sounds to cause George any concerns. He kept watching up to Cliff End for any signal that anything was going wrong.

It was Geoff's job to not only organize his men but to ensure that he was in contact with the lugger, the batsmen over towards Seaford Head and George on the bridge. There was only one time where Geoff was to use anything other than the lantern and that was if he noticed that they had walked into a trap. He was told to fire of both his pistols, leaving five-second between each shot.

Before the first boat had reached the bridge, Geoff signalled that the third boat had left the lugger. In a few moments George could hear the sound of the first boats oars bringing the boat up the river. The tide was working with the boats and helping them along.

As the boat came up to the bridge George called out
"Is everything OK Dan?"

He knew that Dan was on the third boat but he needed to know if the lugger was full of Dragoons or Customs men, trying to trap them.

"Dan's not on this one he'll be along later." Came the reply, much to the relief of George.

"Take it easy, you have a long way to go. Be careful as you pass Aldfriston, I've tried to ensure that the constable is not around but you never know with that slimy old fox."

"Don't worry we'll be as silent as we can and the boys will have their pistols at the ready, just in case." John replied.

"Will the tide be with us by the time we reach the village?" John asked.

George though and realised that it will take them half an hour to reach the village and the tide was due to turn about them.

"If you want to float by the village, row quickly, the tide will turn in half an hour." George said, urgently.

John and his boat went under the bridge. George could now hear the urgency in their rowing. They had been able to relax once they entered the river mouth, after the tiring work they had put in to bring the boat back from the lugger. Even though they were carrying a lighter than normal load, the effort to reach the river had been greater and as such they needed to be able to take it easy until they reached the bridge.

This boat was headed the furthest up river, to just below Endelwick Farm. They couldn't expect to reach there for an hour or more, so needed their reserve of energy. There they would unload the goods into special holes under the bridge. It would be collected later the next day, by their customers.

As much as possible George tried to get his customers to move their own goods as it put him and his men in lesser danger. One of his men would be there to ensure that they took what was theirs and paid the correct dues. If the Riding Officers came into view they would disappear, leaving the customer to take the consequences. If George didn't get paid for that consignment, the profits were so good that he could afford to lose one consignment in three and still make money.

George had become a very cautious man and not one for allowing trouble to land on his doorstep. Like Brian, before him, he never actually used Aldfriston as a landing point for his wares.

With such hamlets as West Dean, Tullington, Frog Firle, Littleington, and Milton Street all along the tidal stretch of the river, he had many places to land his goods.

This also kept the Riding Officers and Dragoons guessing. By going even further up stream, George had even more places to hide his cargo's, away from prying eyes.

The Cuckmere River valley not only took the main flow of the river but has many tidal ditches running from it. These irrigated the fields and in places, were more marsh than fields. This also gave George places to hide his boats. If you didn't know the right paths across this marshland, you could sink, much like in quick sand.

Any boat with more than 6 oars could be confiscated and either taken into the service of the Customs men or destroyed to stop them being used again by the Free Traders. These ditches also gave him even more ways of bringing his cargo ashore. One such ditch ran all the way up into West Dean village.

The bridge that ran over this ditch, near to West Dean Village, had been specially altered so that the boats could go under it. With bushes growing on either side of the ditch, by the bridge, once the boats had gone under the bridge, they were invisible to anyone travelling along either the road along the valley or the track into West Dean village.

The ditch only came in view again, once it was in the village and even then it was protected from view by a low flint wall.

As well as the ditch and cover being special, the two boats that were used along it had been especially adapted. They were much narrower than normal boats; they had no mast and only two sets of oars. They also had poles that some of the men could use to push the boat, very much like a punt.

George had decided that as this was to be a large cargo he would need to land it in several extra locations. He only told a very few of his men where they were to take their particular load and then only just before they set out in their boats. In this way George was sure that no one could double-cross him.

The only other person who knew the full plan was Norman. They had gone over it together, days before the cargo was due and each would take responsibility for various aspects of the landing.

Today had been no different but his normal men were surprised that he had brought in men from Crowlink, Gayle's and Fox Hole farms. The reason given was that it was important for the boats to be unloaded, as soon as they arrived at their landing points.

The second boat, commanded by Sam, was designated for the West Dean landing point so just after it had passed under Excet Bridge, it drew into the right hand bank. Two men were waiting for them.

On the other side of this bank was one of the special ditch boats, ready to receive its cargo. The second one had been taken out of the water, laid upside down and covered by reeds. It would be put back into the water after the first boat had been loaded and moved off.

The first thing the crew, in the riverboat, had to do was to secure the boat to the bank. Once done they could start to unload the cargo onto the top of the bank. The men from the ditch boats then started to load this into the first of their boats. When done the crew of this boat set off towards West Dean.

The second ditch boat was uncovered by its crew and manoeuvred towards the ditch. They started to tip it over so as to land in the ditch the right way up, ready to be loaded. Unfortunately they had pushed the boat just that bit to far over the edge of the ditch. Instead of being able to tip it over, it slid down into the ditch and landed upside down.

"You fools" Sam yelled.

"You've done this so many times, have you lost your minds."

"Now get down there, get it out of the ditch and do it again." Sam said.

"We can turn it over in the ditch Sam." Tom said.

"Don't be daft Tom. You'll get water in the bottom of the boat. The cargo of tea will get soaked and ruined. Will you tell George if he loses this cargo?"

There was no need to say more. Tom and two of his crew jumped into the ditch, one each at either end of the boat. They lifted it back up onto the bank, then clambered out, turned the boat over to empty it off the ditch water. This time they took more care as they tipped the boat back into the ditch, the correct way up this time. All this took 10 minutes and was putting the river boat out of its schedule.

"Tom you'll have to load your own boat. We've to get back out to the Lugger and collect Harry before the lugger sets sail." Sam called.

With that Sam and his crew carefully went down the bank and into their boat. The third boat had just gone upstream so they were running about five minutes behind schedule.

"OK men we will take it in turns to row back to the Lugger. George would never forgive us if anything happened to Harry." Sam said.

With that the main oars men took a firm grip of their oars as they manoeuvred the boat around and headed out towards the sea again.

The reason why they had been assigned the West Dean cargo was so they could return to collect Harry. This landing point was the shortest from the lugger. When they went under the bridge Sam called.

"Have you got the money for Harry, George?"

"Yes, catch," George called back, as he dropped a heavy leather purse over the bridge and down into Sam's ready hands.

"Now go quickly, I don't trust that Captain and if he doesn't get his money before the last of the cargo leaves his boat, he may well kill Harry and run back to France with the rest of the cargo."

All the men knew that time was important. The lugger would not wait for them to return. Their timetable was the tide not the clock. If they waited too long they could find themselves high and dry on the shore until the next tide.

While all this was going on Harry was ensuring that the correct goods were being loaded into the appropriate boats. This meant that there would be no need, later, to move items from one location to another. As well as doing this he also kept an eye on the cliff tops for any signal from his men

Sam's boat would keep to the left bank, allowing the full boats the right banks, in this way they were not likely to collide with each other. Sam counted that they had passed four other boats by the time they had reached the mouth of the river and were into open sea.

While moving down the river he had changed oars men twice. The first was to give the normal oarsmen a rest. He would need all the experience and strength they could muster to reach the lugger.

The second change had been before they left the shelter of the river mouth and were affected by the waves coming in from the heavy seas. He now brought the experienced men back onto the oars.

Harry was in the process of watching the last boat being loaded with the remaining cargo from the lugger.

"I think you are ten pairs of half-ankers of brandy short again this trip Captain." Harry said.

"That is not possible, you haven't counted correctly." The Captain said, as he turned to his First Mate

"What did you make the count?"

"Five hundred half-ankers of brandy, four hundred of genever, ten cases of tea and six bails of lace, Captain." The First Mate answered.

Well Harry knew that wasn't right. The order was for six hundred pairs of half-ankers of brandy, five hundred of genever. The tea and lace were right.

He himself had counted these off the Lugger but, there was supposed to be the ten pairs of half-ankers extra, which were missed of the last order.

"George said he told you that unless you brought over what you missed off the last trip. I wasn't to pay you for this cargo." Harry said.

The Captain was not use to being talked to this way on board his own ship. He was in sole charge and ran his ship on very strict discipline, so as to ensure that the lugger was a safe ship to sail.

"You have miscounted. The First Mate has confirmed the count as correct." Captain Saviour insisted.

"I'm sorry Captain but that count he gave was for your last load, not this one. I've counted that you have unloaded six hundred pairs of half-ankers of brandy tonight, not the five hundred he said." Harry could see the Captain was getting very angry and didn't intend to give over the extra ten half-ankers.

The captain turned away from Harry to face his first mate. If Harry missed his guess, when he turned back both he and his first mate would be holding pistols in their hands and he was not mistaken. The Captain turned around a few moments later and the first mate took a pace to his Captains left so that they were both facing Harry, each holding a pistol.

"Hand over the money or we'll kill you where you stand and feed you to the fishes." The First Mate ordered.

"I don't have the money with me Captain. It's coming over in the last boat. I told you that when I first came on board." Harry replied.

"There have been eight boats. The one below can leave now without you. I want my money now, not later. If you don't pay up immediately, you'll be shot." The Captain said.

"Captain" The stern lookout called.

"There's another boat coming, do I engage it with the gun?"

The Captain looked into Harry's eyes to see if this was a trap.

"This boat has the money, so I wouldn't advise you giving the order Captain." Harry said, before the Captain could answer the lookout.

"No. Keep your gun on it, in case it's a revenue boat." The Captain called.

"Alright Harry, you appear to have the upper hand this time but you can tell George that this matter is not over. I know that he received the correct cargo last time." Captain Saviour said.

"If you are relying on your first mate to do your counting, I believe that you may be wrong. If tonight's count was anything to go by you could lose a lot of money if I only paid you for what he said was unloaded." Harry said.

The Captain looked at Harry but the first mate made a steep forward to avenge the insult that had been levelled at him. In time, the Captain put out his arm and arrested his mans progress,

"Not tonight John."

Before any more could be said Sam called up from the rowboat.

"Harry I have the money, do you want it now?"

Harry leaned over the side to see who was with Sam. Then he looked back at the Captain.

"I'll get your money now Captain but I'm not paying for the ten pair of half-ankers you haven't delivered."

With that he turned back towards the side of the lugger from where he had seen Sam. Leaning over he called

"Bring it up with you. Young Sam may like to come aboard and see what a lugger is really like." Harry called.

Both Sam and young Sam were good fighters, proficient with both pistols and cutlasses. Harry wanted them to guard him as he paid the Captain.

In the meantime the ditch boats had been making their way along the ditches and under the road bridge.

This was a tricky manoeuvre, as the men propelling the boats could no longer stand and push the boats along with their staves, against the ditch banks.

They now would have to lie down, along the sides of the boat, with their backs against the cargo and use their staves against the underside of the bridge. There was only room for two men on each side. The others got off, cross over the road and wait for the boat to reappear.

They only had three hundred yards to travel, once they had negotiated the bridge. On arriving at the end of the journey they tied up the boats, behind a low flint wall which acted as a guard against people, animals and carts from falling into the ditch and, as far as the Free Traders were concerned, it hid the presence of their boats. On the other side of the wall, stood two wagons, one for each boat load. The cargo would be unloaded into the wagons and they in turn would spend the night in the barn, just opposite.

The men acted quickly to unload their respective boats into the wagons. This was a spot where the Dragoons often rode to bring them from the next valley into the Cuckmere valley. This gave the smugglers the incentive they needed not to hang around. There was just the crew from the boats to fight off any Ridding Officers or Dragoons. The odds would not be in their favour as their opposition would be better armed and closer in numbers.

The wagons were ready but not yet harness to the horses. Two of the men ran over to the barn, collected the horses and brought them over to the wagons. It was their task to harness the horses by the time the wagons were loaded.

The horses had been left with their harnessed already fitted, all that needed to be done was them to be connected to the wagons staves.

It took twenty minutes to unload the boats and this was how long it had taken the two men to collect and harness the horses to the wagons. Another two men then ran over to the barn and opened the doors wide so that the horses and wagons could be driven in.

After they had completed their task, the men would all make their own way home. Most of them lived on this side of the river, one lived in West Dean so had only yards to go to reach his home. The rest would be home within the hour, provided that they didn't run into any of the Dragoons or Ridding Officers.

In the mean time Harry had finished paying the Captain for the cargo and then handed him an order for the next trip. The list specified the quantity and quality of the goods required. It also said the day and time the delivery was to be made. Harry then handed him a separate piece of paper, which showed the signal to be used for the next trip.

Having completed his task, Harry and the two Sam's climbed down into the rowboat below and headed back into the safety of the Cuckmere River.

CHAPTER 8
The Dragoons patrols

Having left Mark to his errand, Graham rode hard. Passing through the hamlet of Blatchington and along the tracks that lead him up to the Beacon, from here he could look down onto West Firle.

He couldn't see any sign of the Dragoon patrol. The village was fairly well surrounded by trees houses, so this didn't completely surprise him.

If they would be anywhere in West Firle, it would be in one of the four Inns that dominated village life. West Firle was set on one of the pilgrim's routes and being the seat of Lord Gage. He encouraged travellers to rest in his village, partake of the hospitality and accommodation that they provided. It allowed him to get to know prominent figures and find out what was going on around the country.

Graham would enter the village from the western end. In this way he hoped that, as he swept along the main street, he would come across the patrol. Time was on the side of the smugglers, not his. He had to find the patrol and then get back to the Cuckmere valley before the smugglers could unload the contraband.

The Dragoons patrols were reasonably predictable. They had more or less set patrol routes, which was alright for them, as it allowed them to know how long each patrol would take but it also allowed those wishing to evade the patrols, to do so.

Before Graham left the Beacon looked over towards Excet and thought that he saw a small signal light shinning out from Cliff End. It was only visible for a very short time and with the wind blowing so hard it could have just been his eyes playing tricks with him.

He turned away to clear his eyes and lowered his hat closer to his eyes to give them a bit of shelter from this wind. Graham then turned around again and looked at where he had thought the light came from but this time his eyes caught a glimpse of light coming from out at sea. He had been right.

George was landing contraband at Excet tonight, not Newhaven.

This made finding the Dragoons even more vital. By midnight all the goods would have been landed and hidden away from view, he would never get at them then.

Graham urged his horse on. They headed down the hillside, towards the village. It took him ten minutes to reach the outskirts. Now he had to find the inn that the dragoons were drinking in.

The Beanstalk Inn was the first inn he came to but there was no sign of the Dragoons there, so he rode on, passing the Woolpack inn, where there was also no sign of the Dragoons. Neither of these inns encouraged the Dragoons to dally. They were far more interested in the pilgrim travellers and the trade they brought.

Graham began to think he had been wrong about their destination. Were the horses, he and Mark saw, a Dragoon patrol at all? He was getting quite despondent at this point but he continued on to the Ram inn and as he rounded the bend in the road he could see that his search hadn't been in vain for there were the Dragoons and their horses, his spirits lifted immediately.

His appraisal of the situation had been correct; the troop he and Mark had seen earlier had gone to an Inn, before they returned to their barracks at South Bourn. To his delight another troop had stopped off there for a drink and they had an Officer with them.

Graham recognized the Officer. He'd only met him once before but knew he was a trustworthy man, the son of one of the local land owners. So he had a vested interest in ensuring that the area was safe.

Several of the Dragoons looked up as Graham approached. Most knew Graham and so returned to their talking and drinking. Seeing that Graham was stopping and about to dismount, an older dragoon called to one of the young men and told him to take care of Graham's horse.

Graham nodded his thanks and moved over to where he saw the leaders of the patrols gathered.

"Mr. Hill I believe, I'm Graham Johnson, Riding Officer from Seaford. Can I get you a drink?"

Although he was in a hurry, he knew it was no good trying to bully the Dragoons into action. Graham would have to work on their base instinct, that of the bounty money and the chance of some of the goods for themselves.

"That's good of you Mr. Johnson, I'll have a brandy."

Graham parted from the Lieutenant and went into the Inn and walked up to the small bar.

"Hello Jim, I'll have two brandies please."

Without turning to see who it was. Jim scolded at the newcomer

"Wait your turn I've to look after the soldiers first."

Graham was not in the mood for this. His time was short so he took action which he knew would get Jim's attention,

"Riding Officer" He shouted, "I'm seizing all the liquor in this Inn, for investigations concerned with smuggling."

There was sudden silence in the bar room. Jim turned, like on a top, to face the source of this interruption to his business. He was just about to go into a rant and rave about all the liquor being honest and above board, when he recognised who he was addressing.

"Mr. Johnson, what a pleasure to see you after such a long absence, two brandies' I believed you ordered."

Jim drew off the two glasses of brandy from the barrel.

"Have them on the house." He said, with a smile.

The signs that the innkeeper knew the intruder relieved the tension that had come about when Graham announced who he was. As a result the dragoons returned to their drinks and the sound of their talking filled the barroom again.

"That's kind of you Jim. Mr. Hill will appreciate your kind gesture."

With that Graham left the barroom and rejoined the Lieutenant at a table. By this time the two Sergeants had also joined their officer.

"Long time no see Sergeant Kelly, you seem to be keeping well, is that yet another stone you've added to your poor horse's burden?"

"Away with you Graham, My horse will out run yours any day." The Sergeant retorted.

"I don't doubt that but not with you on board it won't."

Graham then turned his attentions to a much more familiar figure.

"Ah Sergeant O'Riley, how did you fall in with this old rough neck? I thought you'd more sense then let your men mix with his rabble."

"It's not my choice. Mr. Hill decided that we would come along and surprise him. May be get some drinks out of him, so that he wouldn't be put on report. Until you came it was working well."

Graham had known both the Sergeants for some time. They were trustworthy men to have on your side, in a fight. He was also aware that they were quite willing to turn a blind eye, if the price was right.

"You haven't met up with us by chance Mr. Johnson?" Mr. Hill said.

'God an intelligent Officer', thought Graham. Most Officers in the Dragoons were there because 'Daddy' bought them their commission, many were not that well educated and few had any military nous at all, relying on their Sergeants to get them through such tiresome tasks.

"You're right Mr. Hill. I was going over to Newhaven when I thought I would take a ride up to High and Over, before setting off. Whilst up there I noticed some signal lights coming from Cliff End."

He then went on to explain that he had earlier seen one of the Dragoon patrols heading for Firle Beacon and he had heard that they were sometimes known to stop off at one of the Inns in the village before resuming their patrol. After all it was taxing riding for hours at a time over the hills and could become quite thirsty work, at that.

He chose not to tell them of the patrol he and Mark had undertaken that afternoon, in Cuckmere haven. They may think that they were being used and that this wasn't a chance meeting.

"You'll be wanting one of us to give you a hand, then Graham?" Sergeant O'Riley asked.

"That was my initial intention Pat, but with both patrols here, I would like to ask for both of you to help. You see if this is as big a cargo as I suspect, there will be plenty for all of us."

Mr. Hill was not sure what Graham meant but the two Sergeants did. Before Mr. Hill could say anything Sergeant Kelly replied

"What'll be our cut tonight then Graham, half each?"

They had never got this much before but it was his starting point.

"You know better than that Shamus. You get a quarter of the Brandy and Genever and a crate of Tea we get to the Customs House."

Mr. Hill sat there open mouthed. He hadn't realised that the men would get anything from this. He thought the officer got the bounty.

With Graham's unofficial agreement they could take a proportion of the contraband, as payment for their work and risks, and the Regiment would get the payment due for the contraband in the Customs House.

This was Graham's normal payment, which had always been accepted by the Sergeants. They knew that none of it was any good to Graham unless they helped him get it away from the smugglers.

The Dragoon officers would then get money as a reward for the work of their men. The Officers didn't think the men deserved any reward, so it would be divided between them. Mr. Hill was, tonight, learning the men had their own way of getting their share.

"How will we do this tonight, we're normally, already in the Cuckmere valley, when the smugglers are at work and we are prepared to strike at prearranged spots. We'll have to fight our way to the cargo this night." said Pat, the more astute of the two Sergeants.

"I was thinking about that on my journey over the hill. I'd put my money on them landing the bulk of their cargo near Frog Firle. As there are two patrols I believe that if we go in there, from two directions, we can get them before they realize what is going on." Graham said.

With that he drew a quick map on the table showing them how he thought it should go. Both the Sergeants looked at the plan and agreed that it had a good chance of success. Pat thought that they would have trouble passing through Aldfriston but thought of a way around that.

"If Mr. Hill went with your troop, Shamus, and took half the troop directly into the village and stopped there for a drink at the market cross. Shamus, you could take the other half of the troop and slip quietly by, using the track around the back of the houses."

Mr. Hill was not to sure that him going with the other troop and then splitting it in half could serve their purpose.

"I don't see how splitting up the troop will allow us to capture the smugglers? Surely we'll need everyone we can get, at the landing site."

Pat had expected that question from his Officer. This young officer had potential. He was smart and was learning well under his tutorage.

"Sergeant Kelly will explain it to you as you ride, Sir. Don't worry you and your men will be in the thick of it, before the night is out."

Pat had worked and fought with Shamus on many an occasion so there would be no need for him to explain the benefits of the plan; Shamus could do it as they rode.

"Pat you bring your men with me over the Beacon, while Mr. Hill takes his troop along the base of the hill to Aldfriston." Graham asked.

"I'll get my men together, as we have a longer journey than Shamus and his poor old nag." Pat moved away quickly, before the heavy arm of Shamus connected with his shoulder.

"Shamus, I'll fire a shot into the air when we start to move in. That is the signal for you to take up your place and Mr. Hill to start his nights work."

"OK Pat, see you at the Frog Firle later and take care of Mr. Johnson, you lost the last Riding Officer you were protecting. I wouldn't want Graham to suffer the same fate."

With that they all rose from the table and went about gathering up their men and horses.

Sergeant Pat O'Riley hadn't actually 'lost' one of the Riding Officers, he was accompanying two weeks earlier, but the officer was still off duty, due to his injuries. They had been over at Bulver Hithe, near Hastings and come across many men unloading a lugger pulled up on the shore.

They tried to arrest the smugglers but were hopelessly outnumbered, being only ten of them and about one hundred and thirty smugglers.

The Dragoons did have the advantage of surprise and although they were better armed than the smugglers, the sheer weight of numbers was too much for them.

They had to withdraw and wait their chance when the smugglers broke up into smaller groups, to take their cargo inland to sell.

They tracked one such group for several miles until they were in a position to move in on the smugglers, their horses and carts, near the village of Netherfield. This group was about twenty five strong and few were armed with much more than a stave, so they decided to attack.

The Riding Officer hadn't been on many actions like this. He had mostly fought on foot and understood how this was done. He hadn't gone into a fight on horseback before. The one thing that the Dragoons were well trained to do. As a result of this and the lack of training, his horse had thrown him when it was surrounded by the smugglers swinging their staves. Once on the ground, he was beaten and had to be rescued by Pat and one of his men.

Pat and Fred O'Sullivan had ridden into the smugglers at full speed, swinging their swords around the heads of the smugglers, on a few occasions connecting with some part of their bodies. Neither of them was interested in killing or maiming the smugglers but they did intend to get the Riding Officer away and if this meant that people died then so be it.

With the smugglers making a gap, to save them selves, the two dragoons put their horses each side of the Riding Officer and with other dragoons now taking an interest in what was going on, rode in to join the foray.

Pat reached down from his horse

"Take my hand." He shouted.

The Riding Officer looked up and to his relief saw a friendly face looking back at him. He reached up and with the little bit of strength remaining, and with the help of Pat, he raised himself to his feet and reached up to hold on to Pat's saddle.

By now the other Dragoons had reached them and so Pat rode his horse out of the encircling smugglers. Still swinging his sword around and, on the side that the Riding Officer was hanging on, Fred rode his horse close by to ensure that he was protected from any smugglers revenge attacks. Once they were away from the smugglers and one of the dragoons had captured and brought the Riding Officer's horse over to them, Pat and Fred helped him to mount his horse and ensured that he was fit to stay on board.

The Dragoons had to retreat with their wounded and let the smugglers go on their way. Pat and his men then took the Riding Officer to the hospital in Battle and the last that anyone had heard, he hadn't yet returned to Duty. Every one knew that he owed his life to the quick action of Pat and his men but Shamus was not going to admit this, especially to Pat.

CHAPTER 9
Look what I found in the barn

The journey for Pat and his troop was quite easy but they had a long way to go, the first part was to ride up to Firle Beacon. This would put quite a strain on the horses, not something you wanted to put your horses through before a fight, but it had to be done.

The first half a mile towards the beacon was not too steep, so they rode at a trot. Later, as the track got steeper, they brought the horses down to a walk. Eventually the track got steeper so Sergeant O'Riley ordered his men to dismount and suggested that Mr. Johnson did the same.

"The horses can rest as we ride along to High and Over." Graham protested. But he was overruled by the more experienced horsemen.

"I want my horse fit when we reach the top, not fit to drop and yes they can rest as we ride but we want them ready for a fight at the end of it, not just rested."

With that, the conversation stopped and all the riders, including Graham were on foot and walking beside their mounts. Once the troop had reached the top, Pat ordered the men to walk for a further hundred yards, to allow their horses to get their breath back. This done, they all remounted and set off at a steady trot towards High and Over.

Graham drew his horse along side that of Pat's.

"What do you think our chances are tonight Pat? I know we have two troops but Mr. Hill is not experienced, he may fluff his part?"

"Don't you worry non about Mr. Hill. Shamus will brief him and if he puts Corporal Jones along side him, he'll learn more tonight than his officer training gave him and we'll achieve our aim." Pat replied.

Even though he said this, to relieve Graham's concerns, Pat had been thinking the same himself. The problem would be to ensure that Mr. Hill kept to the plan and not to jump off to quickly. If he did, then the whole night would be wasted and lives could well be lost.

Graham had been worried that all the law officers and Dragoons, that were usually about were not in the Cuckmere valley. Had bribes been paid or was it just coincidence. He didn't know how to broach this with Pat. To offend him at this point of the operation would finish any chance of a successful night.

Before Graham could say anything, Pat interrupted his thoughts,

"I don't understand why none of us were in the valley tonight. I was told to patrol up to Firle Beacon and then go to Horsebridge and circle back to our barracks at South Bourn."

"Shamus had told me that he was taking his troops up to the Eight Bells in Jevington and then over to West Dean and back over through Birling Gap and Beachy Head, before reaching the barracks. He would have been in the valley at about this time and would have seen any goings on, so why was he in West Firle?"

"I was wondering the same thing Pat. Mark and I were ordered over to Newhaven tonight, leaving no one to watch over Excet."

They rode on in silence for a while longer.

"Look Pat, I don't know what is going on but are you and your men with me in this? Can I rely on your full support? If not we may as well call it off right now, before anyone gets hurt."

Pat thought for a moment and realised what Graham was really asking. He pulled up his horse and turned it around to face his men. Had it been any other man, who had questioned him in this way, Pat would have taken offence, but Graham and Pat had worked together for sometime now and there was considerable respect between them so there was no disrespect in this question.

"Look men. We'll be going into the unknown tonight. This operation was not planned before Mr. Johnson arrived in West Firle. As such we don't know what we are going up against, nor does Mr. Johnson. The two things we have going for us is surprise and fact that Mr. Hill and Sergeant Kelly will be coming to our aid, blocking off any reinforcements the smugglers may try to bring in from the village." Pat said, addressing his platoon.

He let that sink in for a moment and then asked.

"Are you all behind Mr. Johnson and myself? If not we'll call this off right now and return to the inn in West Firle."

Pat didn't expect anyone to oppose their plan but he wanted Graham to be sure of his men's support. For the rest of the troop of Dragoons, as far as they were concerned, if Sergeant Kelly was behind the plan then it was good enough for them.

The younger members wouldn't speak up against their Sergeant and the older members knew that Pat would have thought this out well before allowing them to come along with Mr. Johnson.

There was a short silence and then one of the men said.

"Mr. Johnson, do you think this will be a big load that we're going to capture and is our split the usual one?"

There was a murmur of agreement from the other dragoons.

"'I believe we've all been drawn away from the valley because it's a big load. Sergeant O'Riley and Sergeant Kelly and I have all agreed on where we can best get the largest haul and, on how best to protect ourselves while we do it. Yes the split is the usual one." Graham replied.

"Are you ready to get us some brandy and genever for my birthday celebrations on Saturday?" Sergeant O'Riley asked.

"Aye" came the reply from his troop.

"There we have it then Mr. Johnson. Your troops await your every order." Pat said, with a smile.

"Let's go then or Shamus will be there before us." Graham said, as he turned his horse back towards High and Over and urged it on.

As they neared the road, that lead over the hill and down towards Aldfriston, Graham pointed out the spot where he had see the signal lights. Pat took out his telescope, which he had confiscated from a smuggler in an earlier skirmish. Putting it to his eye he scanned the area of coast that Graham had pointed out.

"I can see a boat out there and I believe there are still some small boats rowing away from it, in towards the river mouth."

"Good we're not to late then Pat. I think we need to get down to Frog Firle and set ourselves up for when they land their cargo."

"When we get to the bottom of the hill we'd better go to the river on foot as the sound of the troop approaching on horseback will be heard." Pat said.

He turned around and told his men to be as quiet as they went down the hill. He detailed off the two youngest men to hold the horses at the bottom.

As Graham was about to move, Pat took hold of his horse's bridle,

"Patrick will lead the way from here Graham. This is a military operation from now on. You can arrest people, if you want, later but the Dragoons will get you there."

Graham hadn't expected this and was about to object when he looked into Pat's eyes and saw that there would be no argument with him. The incident, when he had to rescue the Riding Officer at Netherfield, a few weeks earlier, was still on his mind and he had no intention of allowing his men or anyone else, to be put in danger again.

Patrick was an experienced soldier and Pat used him to go in front of the troop to check the ground and ensure there were no surprises.

He rode past his sergeant and Mr. Johnson. Two other dragoons followed and they would gradually fall further back from him as the troop processed down the hill.

"I'll go now Graham, I want you to follow up at the rear. When we've dismounted you can come forward and show us where the landing will be. We will take over again from there." Pat said.

Graham didn't like this one bit. This was his plan and he wanted to see it through, from the front. He had known Pat for long enough to know that if he wanted his support he would have to go along with him, well at least for the moment anyway.

The troop moved down the hill off the road, following the tracks that the sheep used rather than that of the carts and horses. This was because the sheep tracks were over the grass and the ground was much softer, with fewer stones to injure the horse's hoofs.

It also had the advantage of being quieter and with sound travelling so much further at night, this was the major factor why Patrick had chosen this route.

Graham would just have ridden down the main track and with so many horses moving together the sound would have been heard as far away as Berwick or Wilmington, he learned something new today..

Patrick reached Tile Barn, at the bottom of the hill and pulled his horse up. As the first horse and rider of Dragoons reached him, he dismounted and handed his reins over to the rider. He took out his flintlock pistol and walked forward to the end of the barn and peered around the corner. He was looking to see if any of the smugglers were about, as this was a likely hiding place for tonight's consignment of contraband.

There were no sounds coming from the barn so he moved forward towards the barn door, which was ajar. Just as he reached the door he heard the sound of someone approaching from inside the barn.

He took two steps away from the actual entrance, so that he would not be hit by the door, as it swung open.

Out of the barn came a man wearing boots, coat and three-cornered hat but he was not carrying any weapons, which gave Patrick a very big advantage.

Fred Cannon and the men with him had already taken the two carts and teams of horses down to the river. But Fred had realised that he hadn't prepared the barn to receive the goods, later on. George was very adamant that even though the half-ankers were under cover, he didn't want them to be easily found, if the Riding Officers came by.

This barn had a secret chamber, under the grain storage area, where they would be hiding the brandy, genever and tea but Fred would have to clear away some grain sacks first to leave the chamber cover free. Having done this he was now going back to his men. It was this that was on his mind as he left the barn. He didn't expect to be confronted by an armed man, especially when the man was a Dragoon.

"Say a word and I'll kill you." Came the quiet, but firm, voice of Patrick.

Fred froze in abject horror, George had said that there would be no Dragoons or Riding Officers in the valley tonight and here was a Dragoon.

"That's a good boyo, now let's go and see my Sergeant then shall we."

He waived his pistol towards the corner of the barn, indicating that Fred was to lead the way.

"No funny business now. I'm a good shot and haven't missed yet."

Actually Patrick was known as the man who would miss a barn door, even if he was inside the barn but Fred was not to know this.

While this was going on, the rest of the troop had arrived behind the barn. Sergeant O'Riley had gone to see what was going on, by riding up to the lead man, who was holding Patrick's horse.

He left strict instructions that Mr. Johnson was not to be allowed forward unless he specifically passed word.

Just as he reached Patrick's horse a stranger came around the corner of the barn, followed closely by Patrick. Pat dismounted and also passed his reins over to the lead man and walked over to Patrick's prisoner.

"Well who do we have here then? Out for a late night walk, are you?"

"That's right Sir, I just popped into the barn to get myself a pocket full of grain, when this man stopped me." Fred replied.

"Do you really expect me to believe that pack of lies. My children could come up with something better than that." Patrick said.

Try as they might the dragoons couldn't keep Graham from going forward to see what was going on. Graham was no kid, fresh out of training, he had years experience in Customs duties and had been a Sergeant in the army himself, so was not going to be put off by these men. He also dismounted but did so at the rear of the troop, handing his reins to one of the young men who was, later to look after all the horses.

"Who have we here, then Pat?" Graham asked.

"Good evening Mr. Johnson." Fred said.

He realised that any pretence of an evening walk was over now.

"Well done Patrick, you've brought Fred Cannon to us. For those of you who need the introduction, He is George Style's brother-in-law. He oversees the landing of consignments in this area."

"No one has ever arrested me for that Mr. Johnson." Fred said.

That was not really true, he had been arrested on three previous occasions but as his sister was married to the local magistrate, each charge was dismissed as soon as it got to court.

"What are we going to do with you tonight Fred? I can't let you go but if I keep you your men will get suspicious and call off the landing." Graham said, as much to himself as to Fred.

"I won't say a word; I'll just go off home and say I've hurt my leg."

"I say you let me take him back into the barn and kill him. That will solve two problems, first no trial will be needed and the second is that he can't tell about us" said Patrick, thrusting the barrel of his pistol into Fred's face.

"Patrick, that may be a good idea but you'll have to be silent. May be there's some rope in the barn we could use to string him up." Graham said.

Pat was surprised at this cold blooded approach that Graham had to solving their problem. He had never thought that Graham was this kind of man. Graham walked back to his horse, followed by Pat.

"What are you doing, we can't do this, it's against the law and I'll not let my men be part of it." He said, in a low voice.

Graham said nothing but just strode off until he reached his horse. Here he stopped and turned around, to confront Pat.

"Look I'm in charge of this operation, you said you could get us close and that I was to keep out until we were there. Well things have changed now. Your men have captured a smuggler." Graham said.

"I agree things have changed but you can't kill him like this."

"I have no intention of killing him. I want his co-operation, so if he believes that we are prepared to kill him, he's more likely to help us."

"Now where's that rope?" Graham said, delving into his bag.

Sergeant O'Riley returned to Patrick and the prisoner, stopping off to instruct two of his men to follow him. On reaching Patrick he told him and the two others to take Fred into the barn and tie up his hands and gag him. The look on Fred's face was one of sheer horror. He had heard that Mr. Johnson was a fair man and one that could be trusted to treat you fairly.

"Please, I'll do anything you want." He pleaded.

Graham returned to Pat's side, carrying his rope,

"Let's get us a way into these smugglers shall we?" Graham said, with a smile on his face.

Both of them followed on behind the dragoons and their prisoner, into the barn. When they reached Fred, his hands were already secured behind him and one of the dragoons had removed Fred's scarf ready to make a gag.

"Now Fred you're between a rock and a hard place. You have me, who is prepared to string you up here and now and then you have George who would kill you if he thought that you had betrayed him." Graham said.

These same thoughts had also been going through Fred's mind, since he had been captured.

If George lost his cargo tonight and he found out that Fred had been arrested then let go, Mr Johnson was right, he would be killed.

"Mr. Johnson, we can't just string him up here without a trial, can we?" Sergeant O'Riley asked.

"Oh yes we can." Patrick responded.

"This scum was part of the gang who killed Joseph and I vowed that I would kill every man who took part in that nights attack."

It became very clear to Fred that there were at least two men here with a very good reason for killing him. The Sergeant of the Dragoons appeared to be the only one against it.

"Please Sergeant, don't let them do this. I have a wife and three children who rely on me, they will starve if I am not around."

"There's not much use in trying that one, son." Patrick growled.

"Joseph had four children who are now without a father, so I don't think his brother Patrick here, will feel much like letting you go." Pat said.

Fred saw that his position was now hopeless and sank down onto his knees and started to cry. He had never thought that being a Free Trader would bring about his death.

Pat turned to Graham, took his arm and led him away, outside the barn.

"You can't kill him in cold blood Graham. I'll not allow it." Pat said sternly.

"I told you I had no intention of killing him but I think Patrick may well do so if we're not careful."

This shocked Pat. He was so busy watching Graham dealing with Fred that he had forgotten Patrick's words. He had fully fallen for Graham's act.

"You'll have to talk to Fred and get him to show us where his men are landing the consignment tonight. Full details, strength of his party and how many boat loads he is expecting." Graham said.

This was better; thought Pat.

"Will we let him go after he tells us this?" Pat asked.

"Only if he promises not to tell his men and that he escapes as soon as we attack. Otherwise I'll find a way of letting George know how we found his goods. That will put more fear in him than anything we can do." Graham said.

Still outside the Barn but facing into the doorway, so the sound would not be heard to far away Pat raised his voice.

"You can't kill this man. I'll ask him to help us. If he does then I intend to set him free."

"And if he doesn't I'll string him up." Graham said.

Fred was still crying but he heard what was being said in the barn doorway and was relieved that the Sergeant was trying to save his life. Pat strode into the barn and ordered his men to leave and not to let Mr. Johnson in until he gave the order.

"Right now Fred, you have just a few moments in which to decide your fate. Both Mr. Johnson and Patrick want you dead. I, on the other hand, want information about what is going on at the river."

"If I tell you what you want to know, you'll save me them?"

He could now see a way out of his situation and how he could return to his men, later to his wife and children.

"It's not as simple as that. If you're released and then go and tell your friends that we're here, it'll put my men in great danger. I can't have that happening. If you say a word to your men, you're dead!"

Nothing was as simple as Fred had thought. He was just going to spin them a yarn and get the hell out of there, to warn his men.

"You can keep your life on three conditions. One, you show me where your friends are and tell me how many men you have. Two, how many more boats will be unloading there? Three, you go back and join your friends, act normally, not giving away the fact that we're here. Provided that you escape and our raid is a success, word won't get back to George that you helped us."

Pat let this sink in for a moment and then asked if Fred understood what was required of him.

"I don't know if I can do this for you Sergeant. If George even suspects that I've met you he'll kill me."

Ever a good tactician Pat worked out how he could cover Fred's back.

"You show me where your men are and I'll assure you that my men will attack from another direction."

Fred realised that the Sergeant was determined to get his co-operation and safeguard him at the same time.

"OK, I'll help you but keep those two away from me."

At that moment there was a small commotion by the door which appeared to be Graham trying to get at Fred, with the help of Patrick.

"Don't you worry Fred I'll keep them away from you but, double cross me and I'll join them in finding you and stringing you up at the Cross in Aldfriston."

"Mr. Cannon has decided that he's going to help us on our mission tonight men. I want you all to forget you've seen him and his name. If I hear of anyone of you talking about this incident, I'll have you posted to the worst area there is and you know I can do that, remember John Dobson?"

Pat let that sink in before detailing off his men for the rest of the mission. Graham went up to Fred and putting his face very close to his said.

"You can be assured that I'll remember tonight and if you don't help me out at other times I'll let George know of tonight's little escapade."

Oh my God, thought Fred, not only has he got one of the Dragoons gunning for him but now Mr. Johnson had recruited him as an informer. He now very much regretted not clearing away those few sacks earlier, before taking the carts down to the river.

Patrick untied Fred's hands and helped him to his feet, while Fred rubbed his hands back to life Patrick put him in no doubt what would happen to him if he double crossed his Sergeant, as he owed the Sergeant his very life.

Sergeant O'Riley came over to Fred, after talking to Graham.

"Right now Fred, you go with these two Dragoons and show them where you're landing the cargo. You can then return to your friends. You'll be watched from now until we've captured the cargo. If you try anything; my men have instructions to kill you, without any further warnings."

Pat detailed off David, who was an excellent shot with the carbine and big Paddy to escort Fred Cannon back towards the river.

"If he gives us away, shoot him. I don't care if it's in the back or any where else but make sure he's dead." Pat ordered David.

This brought a shudder down Fred's spine as he looked at the second of his two minders; Paddy was a good six foot tall and very broad. Paddy smiled down at Fred and clamped his very large right hand onto his shoulder.

"Now then sir, my Sergeant tells me I'm to look after you, we're not going to have any trouble with you now, are we?"

That smile hid a very determined man who, if Fred didn't miss his guess, would do anything his Sergeant asked. He reminded him of George.

Fred was beginning to wonder who he should be afraid of. Had he misjudged Mr. Johnson's actions as just bravado, to frighten him in to helping them? Were the stories about him true? Was he a fair man. It had been difficult to tell tonight.

He had no doubt that the Dragoon called Patrick would kill him, given the opportunity, with or without the blessing of his Sergeant.

Now he realised of all the men present, it was the Sergeant who would kill him without a single thought, legal or not. He had been surprised how young Sergeant O'Riley was but he saw that he commanded the respect and complete obedience from his men. George's obedience came out of fear.

Fred and his two minders left the barn and moved down the small valley leading to the river. It was at the river bank that the two carts were to be loaded with brandy, genever, tea and lace.

As they began to turn the corner Fred stopped and asked the Dragoons to be very careful not to be seen by his men at the river. As they proceeded around the corner they could see men by the river bank hauling half-ankers up over the bank from a boat.

There were about twenty men, of which about eight were from the boat. The dragoons estimated that once the boats had left they would be up against twelve men and from past experienced they would not expect more than three of them to be armed with pistols. The rest would have staves or a cutlass or two to fight off any Riding Officer who may chance on them.

"Now remember what the Sergeant said. David will be staying around and watching you. He is a good shot. If you make one wrong move He'll shoot you where you stand and believe me, he can do that without any problem, from this range." Big Paddy said.

"Now go and join your men." Paddy told him.

Fred believed Paddy, so left them and joined his men at the riverbank.

As soon as he had gone David, slipped away and went up the side of this valley to where he had spotted a small group of trees and some bushes. He was going to put himself up there so he would be in a very good spot to see what the smugglers were up to and especially Fred.

Big Paddy returned to the barn and reported the strength of the smugglers and layout of where they were doing their nights work.

"Right we had better split into two parties then. One will stay here to receive the first consignment and the men with it and the others will come with me down the river a bit and we'll ride in, once the last boat has unloaded." Sergeant O'Riley ordered.

Having detailed off his men, he turned to Graham.

"No disrespect Graham but you're not a good enough horseman to go with us. I'd like you to take charge of the party I leave in the Barn. Corporal O'Sullivan will be with you and he can be totally relied upon. It was he who was with me when we rescued Mr. Turner the other week."

This was a good recommendation but Graham would much have preferred to have been riding down onto the smugglers, by the river. He did understand why he was being asked to stay.

To get to where Pat wanted would require very skilled horsemanship, far better than Graham possessed. If Mark was here, he would have gone with the Dragoons for the experience.

Pat separated off his troops into the two parties and gave explicit instructions as to what should be done and when.

No one was to make a move until they heard his pistol shot, if the party in the Barn needed to move, they were to do so with as little noise as possible.

His party consisted of his best horseman, not necessarily the best fighters but the level of surprise that they hoped to have, would mean that fighting would be unnecessary.

Having done this, he left the barn with his men and disappeared into the night leaving Corporal O'Sullivan and Graham to set the men out so that they could catch their pray.

While Graham and Sergeant O'Riley had been setting up their end of the operation, Sergeant Shamus Kelly and Mr. Hill had brought their troop along the base of the Downs, below Firle Beacon and in behind Aldfriston village.

It was not so important, as they passed by the village of Alciston as there were no houses for two hundred yards from where they rode. This was very much the same as they rode passed Berwick but they did stir up a dog or two, which did start barking. Their owners appeared to take no notice, so they rode on.

Just before they reached the hamlet of Winton, Shamus called a halt to the troop and instructed them to close up around him so that he could explain what they would be doing tonight.

"Right men, tonight we are going to show Mr. Hill that he had chosen the wrong troop to command and that he should be in charge of the best troop in the regiment, this one."

This brought a murmur of agreement from most of the men, not that they were unhappy with their own officer but in agreement that they were the best. There had always been a rivalry between the troops of Sergeant O'Riley and Sergeant Kelly on which was the best, encouraged by the two Sergeants. In that way the men worked better and made their Sergeant's lives easier.

Sergeant Kelly addressed his second in command and a man he would trust with his very life.

"Corporal Jones, I want you to take your section with Mr. Hill and, making a fair bit of noise, go into the market square and make out to have a few drinks at one of the Inns and be showing off to Mr. Hill as to how good his protection is tonight."

He made it clear they were not to drink, just give the impression of doing so. They had to be able to ride hard and fight off any reinforcements that may leave the village, when the time came, later.

"Remember there are only six of you and Mr. Hill. Pat would not be very happy with us if we lost him an Officer he had just broken in." That brought a laugh from the whole troop, including Mr. Hill.

"Sir, I know you're an Officer and a good one at that but, I don't think you have been in such a battle as we'll have tonight, so I would be grateful if you follow Corporal Jones's lead and you'll be able to drink out on tonight's work for many months to come."

"Thank you for the advice Sergeant, I think Sergeant O'Riley would be very angry if I got myself killed, so I'll do as you advise."

"Don't forget men, no one moves out, from the village, until we hear shoots coming from Frog Firle. Then we move quickly and trap these smugglers in our net." Mr. Hill said, before Sergeant Kelly could open his mouth and give the same warning.

Mr. Hill knew his limitations but he also needed to get the respect of the men around him, as his life and theirs would depend on each other this night. Having said this he gave Sergeant Kelly a broad smile and wished him luck, promising him a drink at the end of the night if everything went well.

"OK Corporal Jones lets go and cause a distraction."

"You do realize the drinks are on you Mr. Hill." The Corporal said, as he rode off, before Mr. Hill could answer.

"What have I got my self into now, I'll take this out on Sergeant O'Riley for leaving me with such a band of brigands." He said over his shoulder to Sergeant Kelly and waved as he rode after his troops.

Sergeant Kelly knew that both his men and Mr. Hill were all in good hands. Pat would never let his officer out of his sight if he didn't trust him fully. With Mr. Hill's party heading straight into Aldfriston he gathered his men together and they rode off on the track which would take them around the village to meet the road for Frog Firle, at the end of the village high street. His men rode on the grass verge so as to make as little noise as possible.

Shamus hoped that the locals may think that they were smugglers passing by and wouldn't look out and raise the alarm.

This proved to be what happened. Shamus and his men reached the road undetected and so rode off around the corner and away from the village. They found a spot to get off the road and await the signal. Here they could ride out and stop any villagers from joining the smugglers, at Frog Firle.

Corporal Jones and his men made no effort to hide their entrance into the village. While eyes were on them Sergeant Kelly and his men would be safe to slip by. On reaching the market square, in a loud voice, Mr. Hill asked the Corporal if his men wanted a drink? There was a cry of agreement, from the Dragoons, so they all dismounted and leaving a man to hold the horses, Mr. Hill led the way to the Star Inn and ordered a round of drinks for his men.

Slapping a sovereign down on the bar and offering drinks for everyone in the bar, he instructed the innkeeper to keep the ale coming for his men, for as long as they could stand.

The innkeeper was so interested in the sovereign that he failed to recognize Corporal Jones. Had he done so, these actions would have raised alarm bells. It was well known that Sergeant Kelly may like a drink or two but he never allowed his men to get drunk on duty.

As the Sergeant and Corporal were like two peas in a pod, he would have known that none of the men outside would be allowed to get as drunk as the officer had intermitted. Corporal Jones realised this and took up his drink and staggered out of the inn before the innkeeper realised his mistake.

With the troop outside the inn, all apparently drinking heavily, the inn keeper saw no reason to get a message to George Styles men; he couldn't see this bunch of dragoons being any threat to tonight's smuggling run.

What he didn't see was that on the arrival of each round of drinks, the horse trough received a fill up. Mr. Hill instructed that the horses were kept away from the horse trough; the last think they wanted was for the horses to be drunk.

After half an hour the men started to give the impression that they were very much the worse for wear.

One or two got up onto their horses and lay out with their arms around their horse's necks. It was their intention to be the first to go into action, when the signal was given. They would go directly to the inn doorway and stop anyone from leaving, by blocking the exit with the bodies of their horses, while the rest of the troop mounted and rode passed them towards Frog Firle.

So far so good, all the parts of the plan were now in place and thanks to that extra piece of luck of coming across Fred Cannon, they knew exactly where the smugglers were, how to take them and their consignment of contraband. Now all they had to do was wait for the last boat to unload and then they could strike.

CHAPTER 10
Is there anything I can do for you Mister Mark?

Mark hadn't wanted to journey to Newhaven by himself, for two reasons. Firstly he had agreed with Mr. Johnson that the smugglers would be landing their contraband at Excet and this is where the action would be. The second reason was that Mr. Williams was sure to blow his top as Mr. Johnson was not with him.

How would he be able to convince the Comptroller that Mr. Johnson's horse had come up lame, he didn't know. Mr. Williams had been very explicit in his instructions. All his Riding Officers would meet up at Newhaven.

Mark had ridden with Graham until they reached the track led to Blatchington. Here Mark waited as Graham rode off to White Bofthill.

Having waved a final goodbye to Graham, he rode through Blatchington village, where he was asked, by several of the villagers the whereabouts of Mr. Johnson. Whether this was in concern for his welfare or for some ulterior motive Mark couldn't be sure.

On each occasion he gave the same story that he intended to give Mr. Williams. The more he repeated the story the more believable it became. Mark soon even believed it himself. He was sure Mr. Williams would as well.

When he left the village, he branched to the right at the junction of two tracks. This track would lead him into Bishopstone and on to the nearby hamlet of Norton. Here again he was asked about Mr. Johnson,

"Left you on your own tonight, has he?" John Knight, the bailiff asked.

"No his horse went lame. As I've to get to Newhaven before six thirty, he sent me on ahead." The lie was just tripping of his tongue now.

"Go carefully and take the right hand turn through Norton. It may not be safe for you, on your own, to go straight." Mr. Knight said, in a veiled warning.

It had been Mark's intention to take the right turning to lead him on to Denton anyway but this warning reinforced his decision. Had Mr. Johnson been with him they would have taken on whoever was along the track.

Denton was another small village or some may call it another hamlet in the hills above the River Ouse. Mark was not accosted as he rode through the village but several heads did turn in his direction. After leaving Denton he headed to the road that would lead him to the river and the ferry crossing.

It took Mark fifteen minutes to ride to the ferry crossing and a further ten minutes to stable his horse. Once he was on the ferry it would only take him another ten minutes to reach the Comptrollers house.

As he stabled his horse, the side door of the barn opened and with what light was available from outside the barn, he could see the silhouette of a young woman. The only one he knew, this side of the river was Barbara, the ferryman's sixteen-year-old daughter.

She walked over to where Mark was tending to his horse.

"Good evening Mister Mark." She said, with a smile on her face.

"Good evening Miss Barbara, what brings you out at this time?"

A silly question really, as Mark knew that Barbara had her eye on him and flirted with him whenever the opportunity arose, which appeared to be whenever he was around.

"I saw you riding up so thought I would come and give you a hand stabling your horse."

"That's kind of you but she doesn't take kindly to strange hands on her."

"Are you intending to cross the river Mister Mark?" She enquired.

"Yes, as soon as I've finished here."

"Well my father has only just set off for the other side, with a load of wool sacks. I don't expect he'll be back for at least a quarter of an hour."

This annoyed Mark as he had hoped to get to Mr. Williams in plenty of time to tell him of Mr. Johnson's delay.

"Is there anything I can do for you then Mister Mark? Before my father comes back and you go back to the lonely room of yours."

Mark was not sure what she meant by this, was she inviting him for a meal or what?

"I'm working tonight Barbara. I won't be in my room for a long time yet."

By this time he had finished tending to his horse and as he turned around, ready to head for the side door of the barn, he found himself face to face with Barbara. Not more than three inches separated their faces.

The lantern that he had hung up, while he had been settling his horse down, was still alight and its rays were shining on Barbara's round face, her eyes sparkled in the light and her lips appeared to be slightly open and tilted up towards his.

Mark didn't know what came over him but he found his lips drawn towards hers. As his head tilted down he noticed her eyes closed and her lips came close to his. Mark felt a stirring, as their bodies closed together.

Their lips met and it seemed forever that they held each other by just their lips. No other parts of their bodies were touching. This sent a tingling throughout Mark's body, a feeling he had never experienced before.

His had completely forgotten what he should have been doing that evening. The stirrings were taking control of his thoughts. All he wanted to do was to get very close to Barbara but he had no idea of how to go about it. He had never had a girlfriend, well not one that he had kissed quite like this.

Barbara, on the other hand was experienced at entertaining men. Before Mark had come on the scene, she had been involved with three Newhaven boys, all of whom lived on the other side of the river. This barn had been a regular 'play area' for her and these boys. She was very familiar with the best areas of the barn to use to enjoy Marks body. Places they could roll together with the least chance of being discovered. There was less chance of that at night than in the daylight. She was aware of her father's belief that sex was for married people and anyone experiencing that before they were married would be branded for ever, with her father across the river, she was safe.

Barbara moved her hands forward and rested them on Marks stomach, pointing the fingers upwards. The palms of her hands were just resting above his belt. Slowly she moved her left hand up to his chest, slightly angling her fingers in towards his flesh so that he could feel each and every one of her fingers travelling up his body. Mark froze, his lips dried up and he found himself out of breath. Had he been breathing, he couldn't remember. He wanted to draw himself away from her, so that he could take a breath, but he felt that if he drew away, she wouldn't allow him back again.

The fact that her hands were touching his body hadn't registered with him fully. Had he tried to pull away she would have pulled him in much closed. Like the reaction he was getting below, breathing is also a natural process and without realizing it, he found that he had started breathing again. Not via his mouth but through his nostrils. Once his brain had cleared he felt Barbara's left hand gripping his right chest and then moving up, under his coat and finding its way onto his shoulder and down, inside his sleeve, onto his right upper arm.

Barbara moved her head back a little so that their lips parted.

"You have very good muscles Mister Mark, are they only on your arms or do you have any others?"

Mark didn't know what to say, this was all very new to him. The last time his body was touched by a woman was by his nanny, when he was about five years old. He just stood still and looked into Barbara's eyes.

Her right hand started to move downwards from his belt and was heading down between his legs. What should he do? If he tried to stop her, would she walk away and laugh at him or should he let her continue?

Barbara was in control of the situation now. She guessed he'd never been with a woman before, so she'd have to be careful not to scare him away. She removed her hand from his arm and brought it down his arm, carefully took his right hand in hers and moved it upwards onto her left breast.

Mark was stunned, he'd never felt a woman's breast before. He had no idea of what he should be doing, what did she want him to do, what if he hurt her, what if he didn't please her, how would she feel about him then? The questions were racing around his head.

"Barbara I..." was all he could get out before she put her lips back to his and this time she was pressing forward with her lips. He then realised that her right hand was now firmly between his legs.

Barbara's other hand was still on top of Mark's hand and it started to move his hand to encourage him to take hold of her breast. Everything was going at such a pace that Mark didn't know if he was coming or going. He wanted to use his hand to remove Barbara's hand from between his legs but his body was saying not to, what was he to do?

In his mind shot the fact that he was here on business not as her plaything but then she moved both of her hands to his belt, removed his pistols and threw them into the straw, below the lantern.

Moving her hands back to the centre of his belt she untied it. Her hands then moved down as she undid the buttons that held the front of his trousers together, all the time she kept her lips firmly against his.

His father would have wanted him to be doing all this with one of the young ladies being lined up for him to marry. On the other hand, Mark was more than happy with the girl who appeared to be leading him in this adventure. After all, every time he had been in close contact with Barbara something would stir. Even if he didn't realize, his body was attracted to her.

Once her hands had reached the last button and undid it, there was nothing to keep him penned up any longer.

"I see you brought me a present Mister Mark." She said, as she removed her lips from his.

"I didn't realise what I was doing, I'm sorry." Mark spluttered.

He didn't think that Barbara was happy to have him between her fingers but he soon got the message that she was more than pleased.

Before very long, seconds in fact, he felt a real stirring and a sudden release of pressure. His eyes closed as he realised what had happened, Oh my god what have I done, he thought, she will not want me after this.

Barbara hadn't been at all surprised. She already thought this was Marks first true encounter with a girl. As such he didn't know how to control himself. She had experienced this with other boys, so was prepared for it.

"Why don't we go over here in the straw and lay down?" She said.

Mark didn't expect this. He thought that after what he had just done she'd leave him and not want to see him again.

Mark pulled up his trousers and followed her over to the area where the straw was heaped up in a pile about two feet high. Barbara looked at him and told him to lie down on this pile of straw. Mark climbed onto the pile of straw and laid down on it, turning to face Barbara was now above him.

The light from the lamp was not so bright over here but he could still see Barbara well enough to watch her bend forward and raise the hem of her dress up over her head. She had nothing on, under her dress and as such her naked body came into view bit by bit. Firstly her shapely legs, then her tummy, followed by her breasts and, as her dress fell behind her head, her smiling face looked at him.

"Do I have to take off your trousers as well?" She asked.

Mark didn't answer, nor did he remove his trousers, his eyes and mind were fixed on Barbara's breasts. He had never seen anything so wonderful as this before, he had imagined what a woman's breast were like but never in his wildest dreams had he envisaged a sight as good as this. There before him were two perfectly shaped breasts with a central area that stood out.

As Mark made no movement to either reach up to her or to remove his trousers Barbara knelt down between his feet and ran her hands up his legs until she reached the top of his trousers. Her hands then separated and, following the line of the waist, she moved around his body until she had a grip of his trousers just at the start of his buttocks.

"Raise yourself up or I'll never get these off." She told Mark.

This brought him back to reality; his eyes left the line of her breasts and up to her eyes, which were looking into his. He raised his bottom off the straw and felt Barbara pull at his trousers until the waistline reached his knees, there she stopped pulling and ran her hands back up his, now naked legs. As her hands reached his loins they didn't stop and hold him but continued up his body.

Over his firm stomach, onto his rib cage and up to his chest, her hands rode. Barbara was nearly at full stretch at this point so she moved her hands back to the lower part of his rib cage and used this area as a pivot. By transferring her weight to her hands she could take the weight off her legs.

Barbara was fully in control and this is what she liked. She would be able to get the type of pleasure she wanted. Knowing that she'd not have to wait for her partner to get their pleasure first, as Mark had already reached that point, she could enjoy herself.

Until now, only one man had considered her pleasure, before his own, but he was a married man, she couldn't rely on him for her future happiness.

Barbara moved her feet so she was astride Mark's legs and then she lowered her bottom down so she could rest her warm body against his.

Mark was lying very still. He didn't know what to do. It was all so very new to him. He was both excited and terrified at the same time. Here he was in a few moments he would be making love to a beautiful girl but what if he got things wrong. Would she ever want to see him again or maybe tell her friends how bad he was. His hands were still by his side, he wanted to touch her breasts again, now there was no material between his hands and the soft flesh of the breasts.

"They won't burst if you touch them." Barbara said, interrupting his very thoughts.

He licked his lips, nervously and placed both his hands on her breasts. He now felt like he was in heaven, not the wicked sins he was lead to believe he would descend into, if he did such things before he was married.

With her weight now transferred Barbara took her hands away from his ribcage and rested them on his shoulders. Mark looked into her eyes and saw what he thought was heaven shinning back at him. He was completely under her spell and just followed whatever lead she made.

Mark could feel the beat of her heart and every breath she took, but what was she expecting of him?

He could feel himself straining to reach even larger proportions but with no where to go. He believed that where it should be was between her legs but no one had ever told him of this or how to achieve it. Once there he had no idea what he was expected to do, did he just keep still, did he move about and if so how, would he hurt her if he got it wrong, he was so confused.

Barbara wanted to teach him so much tonight but she realised that Mark was here on business and before long he would remember this and may well throw her off and return to his work. While she had him in a state of confusion she decided to press ahead with what she really wanted, sex with this handsome young Riding Officer.

She transferred some of her weight onto her hands and raised her bottom whilst at the same time moving forwards against his manhood, until she felt the warmth inside her. With this achieved she stopped her forward movement and began her ride of pleasure. She looked Mark full in the face and smiling at him with her eyes and lips.

Mark really didn't know what to expect. What he felt was the warmth of her body as she lowered herself over him. He smiled back, still not knowing what to do next but he presumed that Barbara was going to remain in control of that as well. So he decided just to lay there, in the straw, hold her breasts and enjoy the experience. All thoughts of what he was here for had completely gone out of his mind now.

Barbara moved at a rhythm that she felt easy with. This was her time, hers to enjoy. By keeping upright, with his hands on her breasts, she ensured that he was touching the area that gave her the most satisfaction.

Women were not expected to enjoy sex. This was a man's domain, with the women there to provide the facility for the men to get enjoyment.

Few men were aware of the areas of a woman's body that would allow her to get as much, if not more, enjoyment than their partner.

She closed her eyes, knowing that Mark would be watching her, in the limited light was available from the lantern. Seeing Marks face in her mind, she could concentrate on getting the satisfaction she desired from her lover.

His muscles were strong and as she moved, these muscles brought about an even greater feeling. Never had she felt so at one with any of her previous lovers.

Her fingers took a firm hold of the flesh of Mark's chest, not that there was much to take hold of. Neither of them could see, but she had broken the skin and blood was weeping out around her fingernails and across his chest.

Mark had no recollection of this. The warmth of her body and the feeling of her around him, teasing him to greater expansion, were all he could cope with right now. He had no idea what, him being with her, was doing to her or how she felt. All he could see was a beautiful girl above him moving at an ever-increasing rhythm.

Although Barbara had had sex before, she had never instigated it on her own account. She had been the girl that boys flattered into bed, so as to enjoy themselves and boast about it to their mates. Tonight she was doing this for herself. She didn't believe that Mark would be talking about this afterwards, to anyone.

The faster she moved the greater the pleasure she was experiencing. He was not moving around so it was easy for her to ensure he hit the same spot every time. Her breathing became shorter and her mind started to swim. As she was starting to lose control she felt an enormous warmth come all over her body and a shudder travel from her toes to her fingers, her arms gave way and the weight of the top half of her body transferred onto Mark.

Mark hadn't expected this, but there again he had never made love before so he didn't know what to expect. His hands slipped off her breasts, down to her ribcage, where he was able to regain his hold on her, as her body lowered itself towards his.

He lowered her gently so that her face rested against his cheek and her head was on his shoulder. He gently pulled her closer to him.

They lay like this for some minutes before either of them reacted. It was Mark who made the first move. He had never felt the body of a woman before and here he was with a naked woman lying on top of him. His hands had been holding her breasts and he had made love to her. If heaven was better then this he couldn't wait to enter.

He slowly moved both of his hands down Barbara's back, his right hand following her back bone and his left hand following the contours of the right hand side of her body.

His right hand reached the dip in the small of her back and then it rose up the other side onto her bottom. He was nearly at the fullest extent of his reach now and he wished he was just a few inches taller so that he could take a full grip of her cheeks.

The left hand was now sliding up onto the top of her right cheek. He again squeezed her closer to his body, this time feeling himself entering her again and causing a little moan close to his right ear.

"Not again Mister Mark, I'm tired now and need my beauty sleep." Barbara whispered into Marks ear.

He turned his head slowly towards her, to look into those twinkling eyes of hers and to kiss her soft lips. Although she had said she was tired this didn't stop her kissing him again and running her hand over his face and into his hair. They were both very much wrapped up in feelings for each other at that moment. What Mark was there for this evening had gone out of his mind.

"Mister Mark, did you want to cross the river tonight?" A call came from outside the barn.

'Oh my god', thought both Mark and Barbara, this was her father calling. If he came in the barn and found them they would both be in trouble. Her elder sister had been caught and her father had marched her and the young man straight to the church and insisted that the vicar married them.

Mark could just hear that her father was still rowing across the river, so he had a few moments to get to the riverbank. There was no time to act like a gentleman and wait for Barbara to get off him. He needed to dress very quickly so with all the energy he could muster; he heaved her over on her back, beside him. This completed, he sprung to his feet and tried to run to the barn door, forgetting that his trousers were secured just below his knees.

He fell flat on his face in his rush, which Barbara thought very funny but was not silly enough to laugh out loud, in case her father heard her. Mark scurried to his feet and pulled up his trousers to his waist and again started forward to the barn door, attempting to secure his belt as he went.

On reaching the door he stopped, realizing that he was not in a fit state of dress to be seen outside, just yet.

"Just coming." Mark called. "I'm just cleaning my pistols."

"Be quick Mister Mark, I saw the other Riding Officers gathering at Mr. William's house some ten minutes ago and you know how angry Mr. Williams gets when people are late."

Everything was coming rushing back to Mark now, why he was here and what he had to tell Mr. Williams about Mr. Johnson's non-appearance. Then again, as he turned to go and collect his pistols he viewed Barbara standing there with her dress above her head. She was about to let it slide back to cover her supple young body. If Mr. Johnson had come along with him he wouldn't have enjoyed the company of Barbara for the last quarter of an hour and he would still not have experienced the pleasures of making love to a beautiful woman.

Barbara looked towards the barn door and saw Mark turn to retrieve his pistols, just as she had raised her dress above her head, all her desires said for her to let it fall back onto the floor and take Mark in her arms again. But to do so now would be stupid, she was sure that Mark would be around for quite a number of months and with the way they had held each other just now, he would want her again.

Even so she held the moment for a few more seconds, allowing Mark to view her one last time that evening, in the lantern light and to ensure that her body was etched into his mind.

After Mark had taken about four steps across the barn, towards his pistols, Barbara let her dress fall over her body, covering it from his view.

He now needed to collect his pistols, coat, cutlass and hat, as quickly as he could, or her father may get suspicious and come up to the Barn.

Barbara went over to the stall and collected his coat and hat as he picked up his pistols and thrust them into his, now tied, belt. She put his hat onto her head while she helped him on with his coat. This made her feel part of him, part of his world. It made her feel really good and warm inside.

Mark turned around, after putting on his coat and looked into Barbara's eyes and saw love shinning out from her dark pools. He reached up and lifted the hat off her head, bent forward and kissed her fully on the lips.

This time his mind was on what he was doing and the fact that he needed to make a quick exit from the barn and onto the ferry boat, as such he only lingered about a second before drawing away from her arms and lips.

"Will I see you again?" Barbara asked. What she wanted to know was would they share each others bodies again.

"I'll see you again soon, all being well." Mark replied.

He now felt he had a reason to live and a reason to be careful when he was tackling the smugglers.

Mark was now fully dressed and had with him all his weapons for the night's work. As he left the barn he looked wistfully back towards Barbara and then returned to his work and get to the ferry before Mr. Ferris came looking for him. He hopped that Barbara would stay in the barn until after they had started off across the river or Mr. Ferris may well guess what he had actually been doing in the barn.

Mark reached the quayside just as the ferryman was about to climb the ladder and come looking for him.

"I don't have much time Mister Mark; I've a lot of cargo to move tonight."

"Sorry Mr. Ferris." Mark said, as he climbed down into the boat.

He moved passed the two oars men that were helping Mr. Ferris this evening. He took up a seat at the bow of the boat and upon instruction from the ferryman he untied the rope securing the bow to the side of the quay.

As the boat reached the middle of the river, Mark looked back towards the barn and thought he could see the silhouette of Barbara leaving the barn. She had returned to turn out the lantern, which Mark had left alight, in his rush to leave the barn before Mr. Ferris came and found him with his daughter.

Mark smiled, as he remembered what had gone on in the barn.

"A penny for your thoughts?" Mr. Ferris asked.

This brought Mark up sharp. Who was talking to him, what did they mean? Oh lord what had he done to get this comment. Mark looked up and could see Mr. Ferris looking at him with and inquisitive look.

"Sorry Sir, what do you mean?" Mark asked.

"You appear deep in thought tonight, not the talkative young man you usually are. I thought you may like to share your thoughts, that's all."

There was no way he could tell Mr. Ferris what he was thinking. These thoughts were to be shared with only one other person, this mans daughter.

"Just trying to remember what I had to tell Mr. Williams as to why Mr. Johnson isn't with me tonight."

Was all he could think to say. Not fully a lie either, he had to remember the story he had been telling others.

"Another lie he's getting someone else to tell for him, is it Mister Mark?"

It would appear that he was renowned around here for this, so he saw no need to lie to Mr. Ferris.

"Not a real lie, just stretching the truth a bit." Mark smiled.

By this time the boat had reached the far side of the river, Mark bid Mr. Ferris farewell and climbed the ladder unto this quayside, waving to the ferryman and his helpers as he strode off towards Mr. William's house.

CHAPTER 11
Oh what a farce

As Mark approached the Comptrollers House he could see several other men, on horses, gathered around the entrance, waiting for Mr. Williams to join them. Mr. Climpson greeted Mark as he walked up.

"Where's Mr. Johnson then Mark? Slept in again I see."

This brought a chorus of approval from the other four Riding Officers, for Graham had a reputation of liking his bed, when there was work to be done.

"No, his horse went lame as we set off, so he had to go to see the farrier and get another horse. He'll be joining us as soon as he can." Mark replied.

Saying it this time had nearly convinced Mark that Graham had a lame horse but would he be able to repeat it to Mr. Williams?

With those thoughts going through his mind Mark didn't hear Mr. Williams approaching.

"Well Mark, where is he then? None of those lies he makes up when ever there's work to be done." Came the stern request for information, from Mr. Williams.

"His horse went um, lame." Mark spluttered.

"He, he told me to say that he'll be along, as soon as he gets back to the furrier and gets himself a fresh horse."

There was less conviction in the lie, this time. It was coming out with more splutters than when he said it to the inquiring villagers and Mr. Climpson just a few moments ago. He hoped Mr. Williams didn't notice his hesitation.

"In that case we will wait for him. If he'll not be long." Mr. Williams said, probing Mark's story.

"He may be some time. We were a mile out of Seaford when the horse got lame." Mark put in quickly.

Was it too quick? If so Mr. Williams would know he was lying?

"Also, Mr. Ferris is moving cargo across the river, so he takes a long time to make the return journeys. I had to wait twenty minutes myself."

Mr. Williams was not sure whether to believe Mark and this fairly plausible story or call his bluff and wait for Graham. If Graham wasn't coming then they may miss out on capturing the smugglers.

"We won't wait for Graham Johnson tonight. Let's get over to the harbour and get ready for the smugglers and their cargo." Mr. Williams ordered.

Without a horse Mark would have to walk to the harbour but Mr. Climpson came along side him and told him to jump up behind him. He had a big horse and it could easily take the extra weight of young Mark. Graham and Mr. Climpson had been friends for a long time and he saw it as his duty to take care of Mark in Graham's absence, especially as he didn't expect to be seeing Graham this evening.

Once Mark was seated behind the big Customs Officer, Bob asked.

"Well young Mark, now you've given Mr. Williams the story of Mr. Johnson's disappearance, where is he really?" Talking in a low voice, so that it wouldn't carry as far as Mr. Williams.

"I don't know what you mean Sir." Mark said, in a hurt tone of voice.

"Mr. Johnson will be along as soon as he can."

Bob Climpson wasn't put off by this feint of hurt, in Marks voice.

"Look young man, I've known Graham for many years now and I smell a rat. Has he found out where the real landing point is and he's out to capture it for himself?"

This shocked Mark. He now hoped that Mr. Williams hadn't come to the same conclusion. If he had they would both be in big trouble. Mr. Johnson had told Mark that if ever he was in trouble, he could always turn to Bob Climpson. Was this such a time?

"Look Sir, if I say anything and Mr. William's hears, both Mr. Johnson and I will be in big trouble, Please don't ask, then I don't have to lie to you as well."

Bob now knew the answer and realised what he and one of the other riders had thought. Tonight was going to be a waste of time and the old fox, Graham, was going to see all the excitement tonight.

Mr. Williams sat proud on his black stallion. He was leading his men into a battle against the smugglers, enemies of King George and his Government. Mr. Williams had never been in the army or navy so had never led any men into a real battle before, this was his moment for glory.

It didn't take them long to reach the Customs House. At the far end of the building was a covered space where a large rowboat was kept. The wall, at the far side, had half a dozen rings set into it so that the Riding Officer's horses could be tethered.

Stood by the corner of the Customs House, just in front of the boat, was a group of seven men all dressed in what, to Mark, looked more like Navy Seaman's uniforms than the dress of the Customs Officers.

He was right in the style of dress, these were the uniforms from the Navy but they had been adopted by the Customs service to be used by any sea going men, such as these.

"Good evening Mr. Williams, we are all here as ordered." George Ellis, their leader said. He was a man whom had many years experience in the Navy, as showed by his weather beaten face.

"Good evening Mr. Ellis." Mr. Williams replied.

He had never fully trusted George Ellis. He suspected him and his men, to be in with the smugglers.

"Right men let's get the boat into the river ready to arrest the smugglers." Mr. Williams ordered. He was not including himself in this work.

He had told George Ellis, earlier, that he just wanted a drill to see how quickly his men could gather and get the boat ready, he hadn't told him about going after any smugglers.

"You said this was a drill Mr. Williams." George said.

"We didn't bring our arms, to do any fighting." One of the men said.

"I don't need to tell you everything and any way the Riding Officers will do any fighting that's needed." Mr. Williams replied.

There was a murmur of disapproval from the seaman at being duped; they felt that they were not trusted.

"I won't forget this." One said, in a low voice, two of the others agreed.

"Come on Mr. Ellis let's get this boat in the water." Mr. Williams snapped.

"OK men lets get the boat into the water, David go and get the oars."

With that said they set about their allotted and well-practiced tasks.

"Lift." George called, as those around the edges of the boat took up their places. It was a heavy boat but they were all strong men, well practiced at this. By working together, the boat rose from its resting-place. The men started to move forward but they were not working together.

"Steady now!" Came the call, as the bow dipped a little.

As the bow came up and level George called for them to advance towards the quayside. Once the men reached a spot, about one boats width away from the edge, they turned along the quay side and walked towards the sea, so that the stern could be brought around to be level with the edge of the quay. When this had been achieved George called a halt.

"Down." Was the next instruction he gave.

Mark was watching this with interest. He had never seen the Customs boat launched. Before he could say anything Bob told him to dismount so that they could tether the horse under the cover. Mark quickly jumped off the horse and moved to the quayside to watch what the boat crew was doing.

Had he been with Graham he would have been called back to tether Bob's horse for him but Bob realised that Mark hadn't seen this before so it would do his education good to watch what was going on.

David arrived with the oars across his arms, together with coils of rope.

"Let's have the ropes then David." George said.

David lowered the oars to the ground, picked up the ropes and walked over to those by the boat. He handed out three coils, keeping the last one for himself. The seamen took up positions each end of the boat and bent to grip the edges of the bow and stern.

"Lift and Turn." George called.

With that all the men lifted the boat and rolled it over onto its keel.

"Tie on your ropes."

Mark was so engrossed in what was going on that he hadn't noticed that Mr. Williams had gathered the Riding Officers around him, so he could brief them on what was to be done that night.

Mark couldn't see how they were going to launch the boat from the quay. There was quite a drop from the quayside to the water below, even though the tide was coming in, there would be a long wait until high tide, even so the boat would still have quite a few feet to drop. George was not going to let a little drop to the water upset him in getting the boat in the water.

Once all the ropes had been tied on, the four men with the ropes went to the port side of the boat and held on the ends of their ropes.

"Don't just stand there looking, come and help." George said to Mark.

"I don't know what to do Sir." Mark said, as he approached the boat.

"You just stand by me and do what I do young man and you'll not go far wrong." George said, in a fatherly manner.

I bet Graham wouldn't have let me do this, thought Mark. Graham's not here so he couldn't stop me, was his second thought. So he took up his position to the right of George.

George looked around to ensure that the men were in their positions.

"Push" He called.

With that they all pushed the boat towards the quayside, with the extra man helping, the boat moved over the quayside easily.

As the keel reached the edge, those holding the ropes took up the strain of the ropes and held the boat still. No one had told Mark to stop pushing so it came as a shock to find himself with the whole weight of the boat resisting his push. He looked around and found that George was standing up, so was the man to Mark's right. He wasn't sure what was going on so he stood up.

"What do we do now?" Mark asked George.

"We wait until those two have got into position and then we push the boat over the side of the quay." He was told.

The two seamen each took up their positions by the side of the quay and held on to the ropes that were secured to the port side of the boat.

"Pull." Was George's next order.

The two men behind Mark and George started to pull at their ropes and bring the boat up onto its side. George and the man to Marks right were stood close against the boat and with their legs, protected by their boots, stopped the boat from sliding back from whence it came.

"Are you helping us or what?" George snapped, at Mark.

"Sorry Sir."

He quickly moved back to the boat and took up a position to hold the boat with his legs, like the others. The boat rose up but before it could get upright George called a halt to the pulling.

"OK, now we launch the boat. Steady now we don't want this young man in the harbour, do we?"

"Don't we." Came the call from the two men behind Mark.

"Young man, you push when I do and you stop when I do or they'll have you into the harbour before you know it."

"Ready, push." George ordered.

The three men, George, Mark and the seaman to Marks right started to push whilst the two men slowly walked forward, keeping the boat in its same position, in relation to the ground. As the boat reached the quayside George called a halt and told the two men behind him to start lowering away.

"Keep hold of the side Mark or the boat will come back at us and break our legs." The man to his right said.

Mark could see the logic to this so took a better grip on his part of the boat. The starboard side of the boat started to be lowered over the quayside, as the men slowly fed out some of the rope they were holding.

As the starboard side of the boat came to nearly level, with that of the port side, George called a halt. This would allow the two men with the other coils of rope to move around to take up their position against the port side of the boat, but not in the way of the others holding the other ropes. Once every one was in position George called for a final push over the edge.

As the port side of the boat fell away from the quayside the four men, holding the ropes now had the full weight of the boat.

"Steady." George called, as he manoeuvred himself away from the side of the quay and went around, so that he could watch the lowering of the boat.

"Lower away." He called.

Mark could see that this was a well-drilled manoeuvre, the boat was now making a rapid but controlled decent into the harbour. Splash, the boat had reached its resting-place.

"Tie it on." George ordered.

The two men with the port side ropes tied theirs onto the rings set into the quay whilst the other two moved forward and carefully dropped the ropes into the boat, they would secure them properly when they boarded, later on.

Mark turned to George, after thinking for a few moments.

"Sir, how do you get the boat back onto the quay?"

George smiled back at Mark.

"A lot of hard work and a high tide." He answered.

Mark thought again and asked,

"Wouldn't it be easier if you had a gibbet and pulley system so you could launch the boat quicker, not having to rely on the tide to get it ashore again?"

George hadn't thought of this, although he had used such a system on board the Navy ships he had sailed in.

"What a good idea young man, I'll put that to Mr. Williams."

There were also nods of approval from two of the seaman who Mark had just help in launching the boat.

Before Mark could get carried away with his popularity, with the boat crew, Bob Climpson shouted over to him.

"Mark now you have finished playing with your toy boat, come over here and do what you are paid for, being a Riding Officer."

Mark realised that he had got himself involved in something he wasn't here to do but he found it a useful experience. Mr. Johnson had told him that every new thing you learn would stand you in good stead, as a Riding Officer.

"Sorry Mr. Williams." Mark said, as he ran over and joined the others and the Customs Comptroller.

"Keep your mind on your work young man, hasn't Mr. Johnson taught you that yet?" Mr. Williams asked.

It was obvious that Mr. Williams was going to take out his frustration that Graham wasn't there, on Mark. He decided to keep quiet and not inflame Mr. Williams any more, by answering back.

Bob put his arm around Marks shoulder and whispered

"Don't worry Mark, nothing much has been said, so you haven't missed anything important."

"Mr. Ellis is the boat ready yet?" Mr. Williams called.

"In a moment Sir, we just have to load the oars and then we'll be ready."

"Then let your men do that. Come over here." Mr. Williams ordered.

This upset George, he knew that Mr. Williams was the boss but that is no way to treat the coxswain of the Customs Boat.

When everyone was around him, Mr. William's then outlined what he expected to happen tonight and what he planned to do to capture the contraband. All the men looked at each other, in disbelief.

"Sir," Bob said, "I'm not saying what your plan won't succeed but what if there is no lugger coming in tonight?"

"Of course there will be. My information is reliable." Mr Williams replied.

"What if they make a run at us, our small boat won't stop them."

"It won't happen. No skipper will deliberately run down a Customs Boat."

All the Customs men knew that was not true. Smugglers will do anything to get their goods ashore. The death of Customs men wouldn't put them of.

"Mark, you can take my horse to ride up to the harbour entrance. Old John will look after you." Bob said, referring to his horse by name,

Normally he didn't let others ride his horse but Graham had told him what a good horseman Mark was, he felt that his horse would be in good hands.

"Thank you Sir." Mark said, glad not to have the long walk from the Customs house, to the harbour mouth. Mark reached out and took the signal lamp from Jack, the keeper of the Customs House.

"Is it fuelled up?" Mark asked.

In reply he received a stony glare that told him that it was. Jack was not use to being questioned in such a way and by a boy as well, was an insult.

"Sorry Sir." Mark said, realising his error.

Knowing he had to keep on Jack's his good side as later tonight, after midnight if he didn't miss his guess, he would have to wake him up to receive all the contraband that Graham would be bringing in. Jack smiled back and handed him a tinderbox, to light the lamp.

There was not much of a harbour wall jutting out to the sea, so the boats had to be very careful as they approached the harbour mouth. Mark would only be able to reach the headland to watch and see if any Lugger's were approaching the harbour.

After handing the lamp and tinderbox back to Jack for a moment, he mounted Bob's horse and quickly realised that Old John was a full stallion with plenty of spirit.

The horse decided that it didn't want Mark on board, so tried to rear up to dismount him, he tried this three times with no success. Bob decided that he would not interfere. Either Mark was as good a horseman as Graham had said he was, in which case he would get control or he wasn't and Old John would throw him off. All the Riding Officers were looking on, all had heard Graham boast of Mark's horsemanship and wanted to see if it was true. They were expecting to have to come to Marks rescue but still he sat there.

Old John next decided to drop his left shoulder, to dislodge this new rider. As this didn't succeed he then dropped his right shoulder but the result was the same. Mark had been thrown many times, when he was first learning to ride, so he was ready for these tricks.

Having not succeeded with the simple tricks he then decided that he would swing from side to side as he galloped off down the quayside, still the rider would not budge. Nearing the end of the quay, Old John stopped quickly, hoping to throw Mark off, over his neck and head.

This also failed, as this young man had, again, anticipated the move and sat well back in the saddle. As the horse stopped and lowered his head, Mark brought his feet, still in their stirrups, up and crossed over the horse's neck to give him leverage from being shot forward and flying over into the river. As soon as the horse started to raise his head again Mark uncrossed his legs and lowered them by his side again and sat up.

Just as Old John was about to turn to his right, Mark pulled the reins to the left, holding him facing down the river. With his right hand he patted Old John's neck and spoke to him in a quiet manner. He wanted to yell at him for what he had done but knew that this was not the way to get control of this spirited animal.

After a few moments the horse relaxed under him so Mark let him turn to the right and he urged Old Jack into a walk back along the quayside. Bob saw what had happened and realised that Graham had underestimated this young mans horsemanship, he was the best he had seen in his many years with horses and horseman.

Before Mark could see him watching, Bob turned around and headed for the Customs Boat. As Mark and Old John reached the corner of the Customs House, the other riders shouted their approval at what he had done.

"Bob always said that no one else could ride Old John but him. Well done young Mark." Mr. Tucker said, with a sound of admiration, echoed by others.

Mr. Williams was not impressed at all. This was his night and he was not intending to share it with anyone else.

"Now you have at last got control of that old horse, you can now get yourself over to the river mouth Mark and watch out for our Lugger."

Yet again not impressing his men with his leadership qualities but Mr. Williams was not here to win a popularity contest; he was here to capture contraband. Jack handed up the lamp and tinderbox to Mark and waved him off, with a smile of respect.

It only took Mark a few minutes to get to the harbour mouth, on this great stallion; it was a pleasure to be in his saddle. Mark had tried out a full gallop at one stage and been surprised at the speed they reached. This was a horse that could take on anyone in a chase. I wonder how much he would take for it. Mark's father was a wealthy man and he was sure that if he asked him, he would put up the money to purchase Old John.

That could wait for now, Mark dismounted and found a bush where he could tether Old John while he took up his station to watch for any boats that may be trying to enter the harbour.

It was very difficult for him to find shelter from the wind and sea spray that was covering this part of the coast. The waves were about five feet high, breaking against the shore. The wind was blowing from the east and with the combination of the waves and the wind; even a landlubber like Mark could see it would be hard for a boat to navigate safety into the harbour.

Mark could also see the waves were driving up the river, but at a lesser height than out to sea. This would cause Mr. Williams and his crew problems if they set off to intercept any luggers actually venturing up the river.

Even though Mark had brought along his telescope, he couldn't see as far as the Cuckmere River mouth at Excet. There were cliffs obscuring his view so he was unaware that there was a lugger anchored off shore and unloading its goods into George Styles boats.

While Mark was watching for the non existent lugger to arrive, Mr. Williams had all his men board the customs boat, in readiness for their interception.

Bob pointed out that they couldn't see if Mark gave a signal from in the boat. Wouldn't it be wiser for someone, him preferably, to remain on the quay side, to watch for Mark's signal.

Mr. Williams didn't like someone finding fault in his plan so decided that they would cast off and row into the middle of the river and wait for both the signal and the lugger.

The wave power had diminished a little, by the time they had come as far as up the river as the Customs House but they were still powerful enough to severely rock their boat. Even a large row boat as the Customs boat, still was thrown about quite considerably. The ballast of all those men on board made little difference.

Other than the seamen, who were there to row the boat, all the others were not sailors and found the experience very bad. Every one of them spent most of the time with their heads over the side, bringing up what ever meals they had had that day. For some it felt that they were trying to bring up meals they had had for the last week.

Even Mr. Williams had been sick but he tried very hard to keep his dignity and thus control of the situation whilst all his men were so ill. He was sitting at the stern of the boat and watching towards the place where he expected to see the signal from Mark. The seamen were sitting with their oars in their hands facing Mr. Williams and smiling at the fact that these 'important' Customs men were all being sea sick, even in the river.

CHAPTER 12
Knock, Knock, Knock

Graham was annoyed being left in the barn with three dragoons, when all the action was going to be by the river. He did understand why Sergeant O'Riley hadn't taken him along but he didn't have to like it.

"Mr. Johnson, I'll walk down to the bend with you if you want. You can see what's going on, but as soon as the first wagon moves off we'll have to return to the barn or we may well spoil the whole thing." Paddy said.

The Sergeant had left Paddy behind, to look after Graham. He knew that Graham wouldn't stay where he was put for long. He was more likely to take advice from an old soldier than one of the young ones.

"I'd like that and you're right, we mustn't let my silliness get in the way of what we are hoping to achieve tonight." Graham said, with a smiled.

With that said the two men left the barn, but not before Paddy had told the others not to venture out of the barn while they were away. They walked on down the track, to where Fred had departed from his escort.

"We can see enough from here." Paddy whispered, as he put his arm out to halt Grahams advance towards the smugglers.

How much Graham would have liked to have been on a horse at this very moment and charged down on the smugglers but that action could well lose him his life, as the other dragoons would not be in place yet.

The two of them stopped and stood by a tree, at the side of the track. If anyone looked towards them, they wouldn't stand out but would be moulded into the shape of the tree. Paddy pointed out the spot where Danny, the other dragoon, was hiding and keeping an eye on Fred Cannon.

On returning to his men, Fred Cannon had explained that there were more sacks over the trap door than he had thought. He realised he should have taken someone else with him.

He now wished he had done so. With two of them they could have overpowered the Dragoon and got away before the rest of the troop arrived.

The first of the three boats, that were expected at this landing point, had unloaded its cargo and was rowed away to hide up. Fred helped to load the half-ankers onto the first wagon and secure them so that they didn't make more noise than necessary, even though they only had a few hundred yards from the barn. By the time they had secured this load the second boat was pulling into the bank. Fred didn't need to tell his men what to do as they had all done this many times before. The locations may have been different, the wagons may have replaced pack horses but the tasks were all the same.

Fred looked up to the trees, where he watched one of the dragoons go, when they let him return to his men. Was this man still there, could he really see what he was doing, was he as good a shot as the other dragoon had credited him for?

All these questions were running around his head. He didn't want to let George down but his life was precious to him. He believed Mr. Johnson would let him escape, if he said nothing. Within a short time Fred was so engrossed with what he was doing that he had completely forgotten about the dragoons and the Riding officer waiting to strike.

The smugglers worked on for half an hour, unloading the second boat and completing filling up the first wagon. The driver of this wagon started to move it off towards the barn, when Fred called him back.

"Wait until the last boat is here. I want to see how much there is, before you go. The second wagon's not big and you still have room left at the back."

This was unusual, thought the driver, but the second wagon was a lot smaller, so he saw the sense of what Fred said.

Sometimes the later boats would come in with much greater cargoes than anyone expected, because the Lugger Captain had brought over more than was ordered and no Free Trader would let the chance of a bigger profit slip by. They didn't have long to wait before the last of their boats came up to them and tied up at the bank.

"How much are you carrying?" Fred asked the first man onto the bank.

"Just the normal. George is taking the overflow up to Milton Street."

With this information Fred let the first wagon go up to the barn but he warned the driver to take care and not go to fast. He wanted his men to have a bit of a rest before they helped to unload the wagon. Fred was not thinking about the Dragoons or Mr. Johnson. Fred returned to the river bank to help unload the boat.

Sergeant O'Riley had taken his troop back, half way up the hill, towards High and Over. From here they headed towards the coast so that his men could arrive, down river from the smugglers, when they made their attack. He knew it wouldn't be easy, that was why he only took his best horsemen.

Once he believed they were far enough down stream, for their progress he swung his horse around and headed it diagonally down the hill. First to the left and facing towards Aldfriston, then after one hundred yards, he turned his horse around to the right to face back towards the coast. He continued with this zigzag movement until the troop nearer to the river.

It had taken them twenty minutes, from leaving the barn, to reaching the bottom of the hill and forming up again.

Pat made no attempt to move forward towards the smugglers. He wanted t his men and the horses to rest up. He needed their minds on the fight that was to take place soon. Pat manoeuvred his horse over to that of young John.

"Well done John you rode well down that hill. Now I want you to lead us forward, towards Frog Firle, keep away from the river bank." Pat whispered.

"When shall I stop, we don't want to get to close too early, do we?"

"About two hundred yards should do it, no closer. If you feel we should stop earlier then you call it."

John was very conscious that his Sergeant had put a lot of trust in him. This was a dangerous mission and if he made a wrong call the whole troop could be put in danger. John led off, taking the troop in single file, along the base of the hill and well away from the bank of the river. He had realised that if they went too close to the river any smugglers boats coming up the river might spot them and the whole element of surprise would be lost.

John could see the smugglers, about four hundred yards away, by the river bank. They were hard at work and, as far as he could see, none of them had seen or heard the troop approaching.

He proceeded slowly, watching for any sign that they had been discovered and also watched for a point where he could take the troop away from the hill and down towards the river, in readiness for their attack.

When he led off, John hadn't looked back, so was unaware that his Sergeant was on the next horse, behind his. That would have bothered him had he known. He intended to show his Sergeant that the trust put in him was not misplaced.

At about three hundred yards from the smugglers he drew his horse to a halt and checked the lay of the land. About twenty yards ahead of him was a hedge row, which lead towards the river. It was just after a dyke and so he believed that there wouldn't be another dyke on the other side of the hedge.

As the hedge neared to the river, it got higher. If he was right it would hide both men and horses from the view of the smugglers, as they would be in the shadow of the hedge. This would allow them to advance much nearer to the smugglers without being seen.

Riding up alongside John, Pat asked, in a whisper, why he had stopped. In whispered voices they discussed what John had seen. Pat agreed with him the hedge would make a good cover during their initial advance on the smugglers. John was pleased that his Sergeant liked what he had seen. Now it was time for him to move aside and let his leader take them around the hedge and into position for the attack.

Pat moved his horse forward towards the corner of the hedgerow that John had pointed out. As John had suspected, there was no dyke on the other side of the hedge, so they could keep close to the hedge, giving them less chance of being seen. All Pat had to hope for now was that none of the smugglers heard or saw them, before they had got into position.

Pat stopped before he actually reached the river bank, partly because the hedgerow didn't go that far and in case another boat came by. He turned the horse to face towards the smugglers. They were still hard at work, unloading the third of the boats cargo onto the bank and then into the wagon.

He looked along the hedge and could see that his entire troop had drawn up their horses and turned them to face the smugglers. As well as keeping an eye on the smugglers, his men were also keeping an eye on him. They knew that Pat would lead them off in the raid and would signal the attack.

There were about twenty smugglers working by the river and only ten dragoons. Pat had worked out that with the element of surprise, and the advantage of being on horseback, they could disperse the smugglers with one charge into their ranks. If they made plenty of noise the smugglers would believe them to be much larger troop than they actually were.

Now all they had to do now was to wait for the smugglers to finish unloading the last boat into the second wagon.

Pat and Graham wanted to be able to move the captured contraband off, as soon as possible. By letting the smugglers load the second cart, they could move it up to the barn and beyond before the smugglers could regroup and attack them, regaining their goods and in the process injuring his men.

At about the same time as Pat and his men were turning round the corner of the hedge, the first wagon with its driver and four of the tub men started off from the river towards the barn.

Although Graham would have liked to have stayed and joined in with Pat and his men, he knew that the whole plan would be scuppered if the men in the barn didn't capture the first of the wagons, so he reluctantly followed Paddy back to the barn.

On reaching Tile Barn they set about laying the trap for the driver and men, with the wagon. Again, surprise was the main advantage they had over them but Graham was also aware that silence a major factor. It would be of no benefit to them if they raised the alarm and spooked the smugglers at the river, before Pat and his men were ready to move in.

Two of the young dragoons were sent to hide just around the corners of the barn, with the instructions that as soon as the wagon had disappeared into the barn, they were to come up and close the barn doors behind.

One of them was to remain outside, to raise the alarm if the barn was to be attacked. The other would join in with the capture of the driver and men accompanying him.

Graham and Paddy took up positions behind some corn sacks, stacked on the floor. One on each side of where they had thought the wagon would stop. In that way, one of them would quickly get control of the driver and wagon and the other, with the three dragoons could capture the tub men.

Sergeant Kelly and his half troop had now reached the point where the river and the road were at their closest. They had been lucky in that the smuggler's boats, going up river, had passed without anyone seeing or hearing the Dragoon moving along the road.

This was expected, because the noise of the rowing would drown out the sound of the horses but it would not stop the chance of one on the non rowers seeing the men on horses. Shamus believed that had they done so, in the moonlight, it is more than likely that they would have thought they were some more of the gang going to another pick up point along the river, so not raising the alarm.

If Shamus and his men stayed here once the fighting started they would be in a very good position to capture many of the smugglers. This spot was a natural funnel for any smugglers running away from Pat's troop, when they attacked. It could also cause them problems, if the smugglers turned and run back towards Pat's men to regain their contraband. Shamus believed the best course for them was to hold this spot and stop any men from the village joining those by the river, at Frog Firle. All Shamus and his men had to do now, was to just sit and wait for Pat's signal.

Mr. Hill and the other half of Shamus's troop were busy giving the impression that they were in the village just to get drunk, before returning to their barracks. They had been at this for half an hour when Mr. Hill passed word that he thought it was time for some of them to remount their horses, in preparation for the end of the night patrol. Gradually one by one the men finished their drinks and returned to their horses. Two of them were arm in arm with girls from the village.

"You're not taking them back to the barracks." Corporal Jones called.

"Why not?" One of his men asked, already sat on his horse.

"Pass one up here, there's plenty of room up here with me my lovely." The same man said, to the little blond, big bosomed girl stood nearby.

Mr. Hill realised he had to stop this short or the noise that was ensuing could well drown out the sound of Pat's signal shot.

"No women are allowed in barracks so there's no point them coming with us. Next week we'll come back and you can spend more time getting to know these ladies." Mr. Hill said firmly.

The men realised, from the tone of his voice, they were here for a purpose and so raised no objections.

By the time the dragoons had said goodnight to the girls and remounted their horses, Mr. Hill hoped they would get the signal soon. If they moved off towards Frog Firle, instead of heading towards Wilmington, the most common route back to South Bourn, it might raise some concerns among the villagers who had gather about the inn.

Among them were about twenty young men and a few older ones. Some of whom had been questioning his dragoons why they were in the village and where they were going after they had finished their drinking. The men were out to impress the new officer, as well as obeying the orders from their Sergeant, not one of them gave anything away.

Once Pat had seen the last of the half-ankers being loaded onto the wagon, he started his horse forward. He had worked out that by the time the smugglers had secured the load, his men would be in a position to start their attack, provided they were not spotted before hand.

The rest of the troop, prompted by Pat's movement, started to move, line abreast, across the area that separated them from the smugglers. Pat drew his pistol while the rest of his men drew their cutlasses.

It was their experience that the smugglers would keep well away from Dragoons if they were swinging their cutlasses around the smuggler's heads.

Pat would fire off his pistol, to signal their attack, when the moment was right. He would then thrust his pistol back into his belt and draw his cutlass, as they rode into the attack.

Fred Cannon had completely forgotten about the Dragoons and the Riding Officer. He had been so concerned in ensuring that the boats were unloaded as quickly as possible and that the consignment was moved back to the barn and safety. With only half a dozen half-ankers left to load, Fred told most of his men to head for the barn, ready to unload the wagons.

Eleven of the men broke away and started to walk up the track towards Tile Barn, leaving just six men to finish off loading the contraband. While Fred and the driver checked that the load was secure, he allowed two more of the men to head for the barn.

When Pat fired off his pistol it brought the full horror of it all rushing back to Fred. 'Oh my God' he thought, what have I done? If any of the men put two and two together he would be a dead man as soon as George found out.

He decided he had two options. The first was to stand and fight. Second he could run. Both of the options held out a hope in that he might well survive the night. If George found out about his encounter with Mr. Johnson and his Dragoons, well his life would be over.

Fred had never been one to run away from a fight, so he decided that his best option would be to fight and then call for his men to withdraw once the Dragoons were upon them.

With only twenty men in his party and many of them were now about sixty yards away, near the barn, there was no way he would be able to protect this wagon and its load. Of the few with him only he was carrying a pistol and two were armed with staves.

He believed that those heading for the barn would run to the barn, to protect the first wagon, leaving him and his men very vulnerable. It was time to turn and run, even before the Dragoons reached them.

The Dragoons came in shouting and calling, as they rode towards the smugglers. How they managed to get that close to the smugglers, without them noticing them, Pat couldn't guess, but he knew that any closer and their horses wouldn't be able to reach a good speed to frighten their quarry.

Pat didn't want blood shed, it was his intention that the smugglers would run away, leaving them the consignment. If the smugglers did stand and fight then Shamus and his men would be coming in from Aldfriston to add support and numbers to the fight. With that many Dragoons, against only twenty smugglers, he was sure they would run.

Everything was going the way of the authorities that night, for just as Pat fired off his pistol Tile Barn doors were slamming shut behind the first wagon.

The driver didn't know what was going on. There wasn't a high wind, so why had the doors shut behind him? He hadn't told his men to close the doors. None of the men, from the river, would have reached the barn yet. They would just be finishing loading the second wagon, what was going on?

The area of the barn that the driver was standing in suddenly became full of light. Neil looked around for the source of the light and found he was looking into at a Dragoon's pistol. He looked up and found himself face to face with a big smile on the owners face.

"Make a sound and it'll be your last." Corporal O'Sullivan said.

He then heard a sound of someone coming towards them, from his right. He relaxed as he thought his men were coming to his rescue.

"One down, all we need now is Sergeant O'Riley and his men to capture the other wagon and we'll have the pair." Graham said.

Then his men were shepherded along, behind him, with Dragoons behind them. It appeared his rescuers also needed rescuing.

This was not what the driver had hoped to hear. He now realised that he was also the Dragoon's prisoner. Neil wasn't worried about any trial. The local Magistrate was due to get four pairs of half-ankers of brandy and two of genever, from this consignment, so he wouldn't be best pleased with the Dragoons and Riding Officers taking his goods.

"Harry, get back to the barn door and stop any of the smugglers from entering." Corporal O'Sullivan shouted.

Mr. Johnson, will you go and help out at the door. Will and I will secure our prisoners and then join you."

Graham did as he was told. There would be plenty of time for him to question their prisoners later.

Mr. Hill must have had a guardian angel with him because just as the last of his men had remounted there was a distant sound of a pistol shot. This was the signal he had been waiting for, now the fight would begin and he would have his first touch of action.

Corporal Jones led the way out of the village, followed very closely by the rest of the troop and Mr. Hill. Corporal Jones knew the lay of the land around here and was well aware of what they were here to achieve.

By the time they had gone four hundred yards passed the last of the houses Mr. Hill rode up beside Corporal Jones.

"Shall we stop here and hold off any reinforcements. I think we're far enough out of the village to hold them off."

"Not a chance Mr. Hill. They could surround us very quickly here, there is a spot nearer Frog Firle which will offer us better protection and make it harder for the smugglers to get past and help out their friends."

Corporal Jones was talking about the spot where Sergeant Kelly had been holding his men in readiness. It would allow them to protect the rest of the Dragoons, who would be taking control of the contraband.

It also ensured that they could call for support, if the villagers launched an attack, greatly outnumbering the Dragoons.

Mr. Hill didn't question the Corporal's judgment. This man was far more use to this countryside than him and also in what was required in fighting the smugglers. Mr. Hill was learning a lot about the men under his command tonight. The other officers had led him to believe that the men were ill-educated, badly disciplined and had no sense of what was required of them.

Tonight had so far taught him different. These men might not have been educated, couldn't read or write but they were very aware of what was required of a Dragoon in the field. There had been no question as to what was expected of them. They had followed all the orders they had been given. Even when told not to drink the ale that had been served by the innkeeper. Much against their better judgment they poured much of it away, so they didn't get drunk and would be ready for the fight.

As soon as they arrived at the point, in the road, that Corporal Jones had decided on, they pulled up and all but one of the Dragoons dismounted. He took the reins of the other horses and stood by to have them ready if the troop needed to remount and move out.

Mr. Hill was impressed with the actions of the men. Each one of them took up a position facing the village, with their carbines in their hands, pistols in their belts and a cutlass hanging by their side. These appeared to be a formidable bunch. He wouldn't like to come across them.

"Now remember men, we are here to stop or slow down the progress of any of the villagers who try to get to Frog Firle." Corporal Jones called.

"Once they come into view I'll give the order to fire your carbines, Shoot to kill. If we can kill just one of them, that should stop them for a while."

Turning to Mr. Hill he said.

"Sir I realize that this is your command but I'd be grateful if you could just stand over there." He pointed over to a point by the road and about ten yards away from the men.

"Will you watch towards Frog Firle and tell us if any of the smugglers are coming this way, we don't want to get caught between the two groups."

Mr. Hill did as he was asked and kept an eye on the ground that he had been sent to observe. He was also interested in what Corporal Jones and his men were doing.

None of this had ever been taught him as military tactics, especially for Dragoons. They were horse soldiers not foot soldiers and what they were doing was more the tactics of infantry.

While Mr. Hill and his men were riding out of the village, it became obvious to those older villagers that they had been duped. The Dragoons were really here to capture the Free Traders and their goods. The majority of the village knew when large consignments of contraband were arriving, as most of them or their relations were involved, in some way or other, in handling or protecting the goods, until they were moved off to be sold.

Bill Jefferies ran into the Inn.

"The dragoons are attacking at Frog Firle, we must help them."

All the men in the bar put down their drinks and left the inn on the run, they followed the ones that were already leaving the square and going down the road towards Frog Firle. There were about forty villagers chasing after the Dragoons, the young and fittest, leading the way. This brought about a long line of disorganized men advancing on well trained Dragoons.

With the front of the line of men being young and inexperienced they didn't realize that they might be running into an ambush. The first three young men were about a hundred yards from the position of the dismounted dragoons when they heard Corporal Jones issue the command "Fire."

Not one of the three had ever been the target of carbine fire before and as such didn't realize what was happening. There were six flashes of light from one hundred yards ahead, followed by the sound of four gusts of wind as four of the bullets rushed passed them.

The other two didn't pass by but struck home in the chest and right leg of second of the villagers.

The sound of the bullets hitting a body was not pleasant for anyone, especially for the one on the receiving end of the bullets. The velocity of the combined force of the two bullets hitting him took him off his feet and up into the air, pivoting in the air and landing face down in the road.

The other two young men kept running towards the Dragoons, not realizing that their friend had been killed. As they came nearer to the Dragoons Corporal Jones gave the order for three of his men to draw their pistols while the other three continued to reload their carbines. With the two villagers just twenty yards away and with his pistol in his hand, Corporal Jones gave the order for the right hand pair of Dragoons to aim at the right hand man and he and the other Dragoon would aim at the man on the left.

Again the villagers heard the order "Fire."

Only those standing by the body of the first man to fall registered the words. The two young men in front of the Dragoons stood no chance as they were hit, at very close range, full in the chest, with two shots each.

From hearing Corporal Jones issue the first order to fire, Mr. Hill had turned to look at what his men were doing and not on his assigned task. The sight of the first villager falling had disgusted him.

This was the first time he had been in the vicinity of a killing. Seeing the other two men still advancing on the troop, the horror of what was about to happen, struck him dumb. His whole body was shouting out for his men not to shoot these two but no sound would come out of his mouth.

He started to move forward, hoping that he could intervene with his presence but he was too late. Just as he reached Corporal Jones shoulder the order to fire was given and all he could do was stand and watch as these two young men fell at his feet, stone dead.

Mr Hill turned and faced his Corporal, his voice had now returned to him.

"Why, Why did you kill these boys, they couldn't harm us?" Was all he could find to say.

He didn't get an answer only a rebuke.

"Mr. Hill, Sir, who is watching our backs, you may see some more of these boys coming to kill us, if you look that way."

Turning his head towards Frog Firle, Mr. Hill suddenly saw that he had neglected his duty. There were men running towards them, with what looked like carbines in their hands. In fact they were staves but this illusion served to bring him to realize that they were fighting for their lives. Being compassionate would only serve to bring about their own deaths and he was not here to have his men killed, on his first patrol.

He turned his eyes back to Corporal Jones and all the Corporal could see was a very big question coming from his officers eyes - what do we do now?

"Join your horses." Corporal Jones ordered.

"After you Sir" He said.

He and one of his men took up station to protect the rest of the troop as they retreated into the track where their horses were waiting. The Corporal and the Dragoon walked backwards towards their horses The Corporal and his companion were keeping their eyes on the advancing smugglers.

When they reached the point where the track met the road, Corporal Jones looked around to see if his men had remounted and where his horse was. The men remounted and the young dragoon, in charge of the horses, was at the side of the track holding the reins of the Corporals horse.

"What do we do now?" One of the dragoons asked.

"Are we going to fight here?"

"If so I don't like it one bit." Another said.

Corporal Jones was not sure what they should do; the villagers hadn't moved since the killings, they had just gathered around the first body that fell. The men from Frog Firle were only forty yards away but they seemed to be more interested in reaching the village than taking revenge on the Dragoons.

"Let them pass by and we'll go and join Sergeant Kelly. If they come this way we'll draw swords and ride out. " The Corporal replied.

There were a few moments of tension, while the Dragons waited to see which way the smugglers were going but as soon as they passed Mr. Hill gave the order to ride out to Frog Firle, at the gallop.

Mr. Hill and Corporal Jones left cover last, allowing their men to ride out first, so that they could cover them. As they followed, Mr. Hill asked.

"Why did you order the killing of those men Corporal?"

"It was not a conscious effort to kill the first men Sir but to cause injury so as to deter the rest of them from following." Came the reply.

"We had to stop the other two as they would distract us from the rest of the villagers and we would most likely have been over run. Then where would we be now?" He asked.

Mr. Hill thought for a moment.

"We'll have to talk this over with Sergeant O'Riley and Sergeant Kelly later. I didn't like it one bit but I see why you gave the orders."

That was the last that he intended to say about the incident that evening. The next morning, in barracks, he would sit around with the two Sergeants and Corporal Jones and discuss these actions before he put in his report to his company commander.

On the sound of Pat's pistol shot Shamus gave the order to advance towards Frog Firle. It was his intention to travel at walking pace, line abreast, so as not to get entwined in the fight between Sergeant O'Riley's men and the smugglers.

If what they had planned came off the smugglers would be retreating back this way and so his men could sort them out, if the need be. As they got closer to the landing point he could see that the smugglers had given up any fight they may have put up and were advancing towards him and his men.

Shamus could see no point in capturing any of the smugglers. This would only hamper the next stage of the night's operations, the movement of the contraband to Newhaven Customs House.

"Turn to your right, in line." Sergeant Kelly ordered.

The troop swung their horses to the right and urged their horses on.

"Form up on the road."

Shamus shouted as he let his men go passed him. He wanted to be in a position to see what the advancing smuggler would do? Stop and form up for a charge back at the Dragoons or continue to the village. If they decided to fight then his men would ride them down and cut them to ribbons.

Just the sight and sound of yet another troop of Dragoons charging at them should be enough to take the fight out of the smugglers, so the need for ribbons of flesh and pools of blood were hypothetical. He hoped.

By the time that Shamus and his men had reached the road and formed up, the smugglers, with Fred in the lead, were running by and heading for the village and Mr. Hill's troops. Shamus hoped that Mr. Hill was letting Corporal Jones direct the men tonight.

With the smugglers running home and the villager's, most likely coming to their rescue, then they could very well be caught in a trap of their own making. Mr. Hill hadn't been involved in any form of actual fighting before so might not realize all the problems that can occur in such incidents.

Shamus decided to take his men back across the fields to the landing point and Sergeant O'Riley's men. There was no need to hide their presence now, any boats still coming up the river will either, stop and wait for the Dragoons to leave or pass by on the far side of the river, outside their reach. By the time they reached the river bank, he heard a volley of shots coming from back towards the village. He recognised the sound of the shots coming from a trained force. Shamus didn't think he needed to worry about his men, back towards the village.

Pat and his troop had reached the fully loaded wagon and not a smuggler willing to stand by to protect it. He knew that they still had more work to do.

"John, Shamus, Mark, you three bring the wagon up to the barn, the rest of you follow me." He said.

"Shamus, you and Mark chase them, I'll get the wagon." John called.

He realised that if the six smugglers fleeing towards the village looked back and saw that Pat had ridden off and left only three of them to take the wagon, they would return and fight for their property. There was no question as to John's authority to give them orders; Pat had taught them all to take charge, if the need arose and not to question the one giving the order.

Shamus and Mark rode of after the fleeing smugglers, taking their horses in a zigzag fashion to make out that there were more horses following them than there actually were, shouting as they rode. Fred had no intention of turning around, in the distance he could see, what looked like another troop of Dragoons, spread out in the field in front of them.

Just as Fred had realised that they were in a trap the horses ahead turned and headed towards the road. There may only have been about half a dozen Dragoons but then again there were only six of them.

"Head for the village and home" Fred called, "We can come back and get our goods when we've rounded up some men." he shouted, not knowing what had been going on and if there were any more surprises awaiting him.

The two Dragoons perused their pray until they reached the spot that Fred had observed the Dragoons, lead by Sergeant O'Riley. Here Shamus called a halt to their pursuit. The two turned their horses around and went back to the landing spot.

By this time Sergeant O'Riley and his men had now returned across the field, from the road, and they all met up and went forward to the landing point.

In the mean time Pat and the rest of his troop were perusing the smugglers headed for Tile Barn. The first of the smugglers reached the barn doors only to find them firmly closed and apparently locked from the inside.

"Neil open up, the Dragoons are after us." The first man called, but there was no answer.

Pat and his men were advancing quickly on the smugglers, shouting as they rode. All this was to keep the smugglers from turning and fighting. Pat wanted them to remain in a state of turmoil and a disorganized rabble. If they stopped to think they could well have decided to fight, then blood would be spilt and it may be some of Pat's men who would be injured.

He could see the first man had reached the barn and couldn't get in. This brought relief to Pat. If they had managed to get holed up in there, especially with the Riding Officer and three of his men, they wouldn't be able to capture the consignment.

With no answer coming from inside the barn, the first smuggler turned to see the Dragoons riding up towards them, swinging their swords in the air and catching the moon light, giving an impression of there being more swords than there were Dragoons.

"Head for home." he called to his companions, as he himself turned and headed off to the road and back to Aldfriston.

Pat slowed his horse and called for his men to do the same, he saw no need for bloodshed if the smugglers were running for home.

They had secured their objective, in capturing the two wagons full of contraband. As he reached the barn he waved three of his men to follow the smugglers to ensure that they didn't return to recapture their goods.

"Graham, it's us, open up." Pat called. "We've the second wagon now so we can get away from here."

The barn doors swung open and out walked a beaming Graham Johnson. He went over to Pat's horse and patted it on the neck.

"We did it, we did it Pat." He said with relief.

"Were any of your men hurt?" He asked. There would be no real celebrations if any of the Dragoons had been injured or worse, killed.

"I'll have to wait a few minutes before we know. When Shamus and Mr. Hill join us we'll know then." Pat said.

With that he turned to see Shamus O'Riley riding up to the barn, with some of his troop, escorting the second wagon up the slope.

"How did it go Shamus?" Pat called.

"Fine Pat, the plan worked well but there was a bit of firing going on with Mr. Hill and Corporal Jones men, we'll have to see if they're alright."

Mr. Hill and Corporal Jones and their men rode along the road, back from Aldfriston to Frog Firle, they saw no need to go along the river as Sergeants O'Riley and Kelly and the rest of the troops were all in that area. As they came over a brow they saw the fleeing smugglers running towards them, away from Tile Barn, followed by three Dragoons. Corporal Jones ordered the troop to advance in line and let the smugglers go past on the other side. They had no need to fight them and no intention of capturing them either.

"Draw your swords and defend yourself." Mr. Hill ordered, as they came closed to the fleeing smugglers. Corporal Jones was pleased with the order given by the officer, he could see this man was learning fast and would make a good officer.

The smugglers ran passed the dragoons, with no attempt to fight them as they were happy to just get away from all these military men. They had never had to encounter such a large force before. On other occasions there had only been one troop of dragoons and about fifty to sixty smugglers. This meant that they nearly always had beaten them off, with not to much trouble. Tonight they were down to just twenty men and it appeared that there were at least that many Dragoons, not a fair fight, in anyone reckoning.

As the three men from Pat's troop reached them, Corporal Jones said for them to follow the smugglers up to the top of the brow. They were to watch to see that the smugglers didn't return. He would send one of his men to fetch them when they moved out to Newhaven.

CHAPTER 13
The shot came from Frog Firle

George Styles was busy watching out to sea, through his telescope, He wanted to ensure that the last of his boats was loaded and was heading safely back to the river mouth.

The last boat had just pulled away from the lugger when George heard what sounded like a distant pistol shot. Had it come from the lugger or from down the valley, he wasn't sure. His companion called from the other side of the Excet Bridge.

"George there was a shot from up towards Frog Firle, I think."

This brought his attention away from the safety of his men out at sea.

"Are you sure Norman?" He asked.

"Yes, it wasn't far enough to be from the village and in the wrong direction to have come from West Dean."

George thought for a moment and decided that as there was no follow up sound, it must have been Fred instilling discipline on his group.

"Leave it Norman, let's see if they are clear of the lugger and get into the river before we worry about what's going on at Frog Firle." George said, as he turned back to his observation of the lugger and his boats.

The last boat was now some hundred yards away from the lugger and heading, with the tide, in towards the river mouth. The lugger was raising its sails, pulling up the anchor ready to head out into the channel and back across to France.

George lowered his telescope and looked up towards his men at Cliff End. He expected to see a signal to say that all was well and that the boat was now in the river. After a few minutes the signal came and George could now concentrate on the next two boats that were due at the bridge.

The first one should be here in a few minutes and the second and final boat wouldn't arrive for at least twenty minutes.

The men at Cliff End would remain where they were, until the last boat reached the bridge and they received a signal from George. In turn they would signal the men at Seaford Head to stand down for the night.

George wouldn't be fully relaxed until all his boats were safely up the river and unloaded, with their cargoes tucked away in the hiding places, well away from prying eyes and especially those of the Riding Officers.

At each of the landing points he had put one of his most trusted men, either close friends or relatives, such as his brother in law Fred Cannon at Frog Firle.

As they each completed their allotted tasks they would head for George's cottage and report on what they had received and how well it was hidden. Within two days of the consignment arriving, it would be well away from the valley and off to the various markets and customers.

Both of them were now concentrating on listening for the first of the boats when they heard, what sounded like a volley of carbines firing.

"What the hell was that?" George asked.

"Did you see where that was from, Norman?" George demanded.

Norman was just a shocked as George.

"No, it sounded as if it was from up near the village to me." Norman said.

It was still raining at the bridge but they could both see that near Frog Firle, the fields were basked in full moon light. The rain masked any detail so they couldn't see anything and the landing point was round a bend from where they were, so even on a clear night they wouldn't have been able to see what was going on there.

They both concentrated to listen for any sounds they could pick up along the valley. Both could just make out the sound of many men shouting and calling but they couldn't make out what was being said.

When the sound of this second volley reached them it sent panic through both of them. The only people who had the discipline to shot in that way were the Dragoons, not a gang of Free Traders.

"What are the Dragoons doing down there?" Norman asked, coming to the same conclusion as his leader.

"I don't know but you'd better go and find out before we let the other two boats up along the river." George ordered.

Norman ran to the end of the bridge, where his horse was tethered and mounted it with just one bound.

Few gangs of Free Traders would dare to try and take away a consignment from George Styles and the Aldfriston Raiders. The last one large enough and brave enough to do so were the Hawkhurst Gang but they had stopped operating ten years ago and many of their members had either been killed, jailed or transported to the colonies. The few remaining members were too old for something like this.

As Norman started his horse moving, George called out "Don't hang around, find out what's going on and then get straight back here, I don't want these last two boats stuck out in the open for too long if there's trouble about."

"Okay George, see you soon." Norman said, as he urged his horse on.

Norman was a good horseman and with the light improving as he went further inland, he could increase the speed of his horse.

By using the fields along the riverbank, Norman could reach Frog Firle far quicker than taking any of the tracks around the area. It took him about four minutes to reach the spot where the Dragoons, lead by Sergeant Kelly, had waited before making their attack on the smugglers landing party.

As Norman rounded the corner of the ditch and hedgerow he could see that the smaller of the wagons had started on its journey to Tile Barn. To his horror the wagon was being driven by Dragoons and not their men.

What George and he had dreaded was in fact taking place, the Dragoons and presumably the Riding Officers had captured their goods. In the distance he could see men running and being pursued by Dragoons.

Norman had to decide what to do. Should he return and report to George what he had seen? But he realised that he hadn't seen much. How could he be able to explain the two volleys of shots, they had heard. He needed to go further, at least to the landing point, to see if there were any bodies there? Norman waited for a few moments, until the wagon had passed the corner and headed up towards the barn. Now he could move forward without the chance of being seen by the Dragoons. He urged his horse forward, but kept it at a walk.

He was a bit worried that the departing Dragoons might return after they had chased their quarry away. He made sure that he was able to turn his horse and flee, before they realised that he was about. He was half way from the hedge, to the landing site, when those very Dragoons, accompanied by six others, appeared back along the riverbank. His heart missed a few beats as he reined in his horse.

Norman turned his head and saw that behind him was just a wall of blackness. If he stayed still and his horse was quiet there should be no reason why he would be discovered. He thought that they would follow their colleagues up to the barn. Norman had read the situation correctly, that is precisely what the Dragoons did. Once the last horse had rounded the corner, towards the barn, Norman urged his horse forward at a walk.

As he crossed the landing site he could see there were no bodies lying around, or for that matter, signs of a fight. He did see discarded staves scattered over the field, in the direction the men had fled. He needed to see where the men had gone and see what had been going on. May be they were the ones firing the volleys of shots.

After crossing the field, Norman came to the opening where the smugglers and Dragoons had passed earlier. As he got to the far side of this gap, he reined in his horse and looked at the scene ahead of him.

Still running towards the village were the group of Free Traders, from the landing site but to his left he could see two groups of villagers on the road. The nearest group was about five in number and two of them appeared to be kneeling down to see to two injured men. The furthest group was much larger in number, about twenty he guessed. Two of them were cradling a young man who appeared to be lifeless. On the drift of the wind he heard a voice calling to the fleeing Free Traders

"Fred, Fred Cannon, come here, your boy's been shot."

Norman could see that there was no point in following Fred and his men. If Fred's son had indeed been shot none of the Free Traders or villagers would be willing to take on, a large contingent of Dragoons.

They didn't have the arms, training or discipline to have any hope of success. It was time for Norman to head back to Excet Bridge, but first he wanted to be sure what the Dragoons were doing with the wagon and did they also have the first, much larger wagon.

He turned his horse around and rode back towards the landing point but instead of crossing the field, he followed the base of the knoll, towards the corner that the second wagon had disappeared around, a few minutes ago. His horse seemed a bit jittery but he took that as just signs of being disturbed by the shouting coming across the field, from the villagers.

He was only about fifty yards from the corner when a shot rang out from the knoll. Norman felt a pain in his right leg. The shot frightened his horse, which meant he needed to regain control of it, so he could ride away from here, before any more shots rang out, in his direction.

The horse started to head for the corner and up towards Tile Barn. That was the last place Norman wanted to go. Riding into the Dragoons on an out of control horse was not a good idea. It was then that he realised that his leg was hurting, when he tried to put pressure on his right stirrup.

He pulled the left-hand rein hard and managed to gain a certain amount of control of his horse. It swung to the left and raced off across the field and back to the safety of the darkened area, towards Excet. Norman had no mind for his wound, if it was a Dragoon firing at him, he needed to get as far away as possible before he could reload and take a second shot. Although he knew the ground, he couldn't see much ahead of him.

The Dragoon was thinking how had he missed such a good target, at such close range? He was quickly into his practiced routine to reload the carbine. First the powder down the barrel, carefully ramming this home, followed by the shot and wadding, also rammed home. He didn't have time to put the ramrod back in place so discarded it on the ground. He quickly turned the carbine around and poured a small amount of powder in the tray and pulled back the flint.

Having reloaded the carbine, he looked about for his quarry, he had heard the sound of the horse galloping across the field in front of him so he scanned the field and there, about two hundred yards ahead and slightly to his right, he spotted his target. All the time he was searching the area in front of him, he had been raising the butt to his shoulder and bringing up the carbine barrel ready to aim and fire.

If he got off a shot, he would be lucky to hit such a fast moving man but he had his reputation to maintain. He was the best shot in the troop and if they found out that he had missed, at such a close range, he would be mocked un-mercifully.

Norman rode like the wind and bent forward along his horse's neck, trying to keep his profile as small as possible. He felt a sharp pain in his left shoulder just as his horse was in the middle of its jump over a ditch. He didn't understand why this was and was in the middle of this thought when the sound of the Dragoons second shot reached him.

Norman had been very unlucky. The dragoon hadn't been able to see the ditch and the possibility of the horse needing to jump. David had fired for greater range than was actually necessary, which meant that he had fired over the head of Norman.

Had the horse not jumped, Norman would have been riding free, with just the shot in his leg. Now he did have problems, he was finding it difficult to use both his legs to control his horse. With the left arm now going numb, the control with the reins was also difficult.

This made riding at speed very dangerous. He had to try and get his horse down from a gallop to a more controllable trot. It took him about two hundred yards to achieve this but once done, he knew that he'd be able to get away and report to George.

Sergeant O'Riley had just reached the barn when the first of the carbine shots rang out. He and three of his men turned their horses around to face the oncoming, but unseen enemy. All drawing their pistols ready for a fight. All they could hear was a horse moving quickly, firstly getting nearer and then moving fast away from them, across the field.

"Let's get them men." The Sergeant called, as he urged his horse forward into a gallop, followed by the three dragoons, who had reacted quickest, to the danger.

As they reached the corner of the track at the edge of the field the second shot rang out from the knoll. Sergeant O'Riley looked across the field and could just make out the shape of the fleeing horse and rider jumping over a ditch at the edge of the field. His trained eye saw that the rider's body made an involuntary jump as the shot hit home.

"Whoa." The Sergeant called.

He could see no point in pursuing the lone rider and anyway he was injured and was unlikely to be coming back for a fight. Pat pulled up his horse and his men did likewise. Turning and then riding them back to the barn, at a walk. Just as they passed the corner, young David walked down from the knoll, carbine in hand and the ramming rod now safely secured in its place, under the barrel.

"Good shooting there young David." Pat said.

"Do you think I got him Sergeant?"

"Oh yes you got him. I don't think you killed him but I would be surprised if he lasts the week out."

Medicines and surgery were very primitive at this time, those available were of local origin and bore as much from folklore as to actual remedies which would work. A rough poultice would be the most likely help he would get, to put on the wound, to bring out any poisons. Few survived serious wounds. Norman would likely have gangrene set in and then there was no hope for him.

"You didn't miss him when he was so close to you, did you David?" called one of the Dragoons,

"And you call yourself a good shot, even the Sergeant could have got him, close up."

This brought laughter from the other men, for everyone knew that their Sergeant was not the best shot, with a carbine, in fact he was near on bloody useless with it.

"He caught me by surprise. I saw him go along the riverbank and follow the other smugglers back towards Aldfriston. I was just standing up to join you loafers when he suddenly appeared in front of me." David said.

"I only had time to get off a hurried shot but I got him in the leg." David said, as they continued up to the barn and joined the rest of the Dragoons.

"We appear to have a small problem Pat" said Shamus O'Riley as he and the rest of his men reached the barn,

"One of the smugglers arrived from Excet to see what was going on and young David put a couple of shots into him."

Pat looked at young David with pride but he didn't think Shamus had finished his report yet,

"And!" he enquired.

"He got away and was heading back to Excet."

"Was it George Styles?" Graham asked.

"No he didn't seem to be that big to me." Shamus said, after a moments thought. It was then that he realised that he hadn't tried to identify the man. If it had been George Styles, then young David would have done them all a big service tonight.

"I think it was a man known as Norman Turner." David cut in.

113

Graham was pleased at this information. Norman was one of George's most trusted men and so this would weaken his gang.

"If he's gone to report to George we had better get this consignment on its way as soon as we can. Once Norman gets to him George will want to round up as many men as he can to get these goods back and inflict revenge on us for tricking him tonight." Graham said.

By the time Mr. Hill and his men had reached the barn. All the Dragoons gathered by the barn door and were all talking amongst themselves, about their particular roll in what had been achieved that night.

"Mr. Hill, you have good men here, I hope you appreciate the fact." Graham said, as he strode over to greet the officer.

"Yes they did well, didn't they?" He said, with some pride.

"Sir, we have a problem. George Styles sent his man, Norman, from Excet Bridge, to see what had been going on here. David put a couple of shots in him but he escaped, back to Excet." Sergeant Kelly reported.

Mr. Hill thought for a few moments. There was nothing he could do about that man. To send a section of men after him would be a waste of resources and they would likely run into a band of the smugglers.

The best plan would to get the hell out of here as quickly as they could, but first he needed to address the men.

"Sergeant Kelly let's get the men together quickly, I just want a quick word and then we'll have to get off to Newhaven, before George Styles organizes a rescue mission." Mr Hill said.

Pat didn't need telling twice, he had already realised the possibility of George trying to recapture his goods and had detailed some of the men to bring the first, larger of the wagon out of the barn.

When the men were gathered around, Mr. Hill addressed them.

"I just want to say what a privilege it's been for me to be with you tonight men. Sergeant Kelly had told me that the most activity I could expect tonight was to see Sergeant O'Riley's face drop when we rode into West Firle and found half of you resting."

This brought a few jibes from Pat's troop at Shamus's men.

"Now for the serious part." Mr. Hill said, in a raised voice.

"We have done well so far. No one injured and our horses still fit. Mr. Johnson says we have to get our spoils to the Customs House and that means getting these wagons up the hill behind us and to Newhaven."

This brought a few calls such as 'Why not take it all back to barracks, Graham won't be able to stop us,' and the like.

Mr. Hill hadn't forgotten the three men Corporal Jones had sent to guard their backs and realised that for the whole journey to Newhaven they would need to maintain this ability.

"Sergeant O'Riley can you spare Corporal Jones and two of your men to join me to bring up our rear and ensure that we can protect you all."

Corporal Jones was surprised that he had been requested, especially after Mr. Hill's reaction to the killing of the villagers, earlier. Sergeant O'Riley looked at the Corporal to see his reaction to the request, had the officer grown up this quickly and could he be trusted to guard their back, even with his right hand man by his side. Corporal Jones didn't wait for the answer

"Harry, get your horse and make sure your carbine and pistol are reloaded and join us. That'll be enough men, with the other three Sir." Corporal Jones addressed his officer.

Shamus could see that his Corporal was more than happy to stand along side Mr. Hill and fight with him. The fact that he only took one man showed his respect for the officer.

"Sergeant Kelly, will you organize getting the first wagon up the hill and Sergeant O'Riley, will you get your men to take the second."

With that, they all went their separate ways, Sergeant Kelly with the first wagon, Sergeant O'Riley following with the second and smaller one. Mr. Hill and the two dragoons rode back towards Aldfriston, to join up with Pat's three men. They would follow at the rear and defend the wagons. Graham Johnson just looked on in disbelief at what had happened.

"Let's go then, my troop will take the largest wagon up the hill and the men you have left, can bring up the smaller wagon Shamus." Pat said.

There was no argument from Shamus. It would be better if each man took command of their own men, as they knew their strengths and weaknesses.

The problem, that none of them had realised, was that the first wagon had been loaded for just a short and relatively level journey to Tile Barn. The wagon hadn't been loaded to go up the very steep hill to High and Over.

Although the four horses, pulling the wagon, were strong and rested, there was no way on earth that they alone would be able to drag this very heavy load up this hill. Pat Kelly realised this as soon as the wagon had cleared the end of the barn. He had to think quickly to ensure that they didn't lose this precious load, 25% of which would belong to the troop, if they could get it to Newhaven.

"Hold it there John." Pat called to the dragoon who had been detailed to drive the wagon.

"Shamus is there any room on your wagon for some of this load?"

"No this wagon is full and anyway I only have two horses to draw it Pat."

Well that was it, he would have to unload half the load here, take the first half up to the top, unload them and then return for the second half. The problem with this is that the wagons horses would be too tied to pull the second load and the smugglers may have got reinforcements, by then.

The only way up this hill would be to use the troop's horses to help pull the wagon up the hill. It took them a short time to fasten ropes to their horses saddles and then attached them to the harnesses of the wagon's horses. Provided that they maintained a steady pull, with all the horses, they should make it up to High and Over with no trouble.

"With your permission we'll move off now Sir." Sergeant Kelly said.

"Let's get going, the quicker we move off the quicker we can get back to barracks, Sergeant." Mr Hill replied.

CHAPTER 14
What the hell has gone on?

George had stopped the two remaining boats from going up the river, until he understood what was going on up there. He was waiting for Norman to report back.

The first of the boats to arrive was the last loaded boat. It carried fifty pairs of half-ankers of Brandy, forty of Genever, 10 cases of Tea and 7 rolls of Lace and was destined for Crow Lane. There the goods would be unloaded and transported, by ponies, to Berwick village, to await collection by a merchant coming in from Sevenoaks.

The last of the boats was the one that George sent out to pay the Captain of the Lugger and bring Harry back. Being lighter than the other boats; they had been able to row up the river much quicker and so came in just behind it.

George leant over the bridge and explained what they had heard and he had sent Norman to investigate. Until he returned he wasn't prepared to let the two boats go any further.

Although the men weren't happy at being left here, exposed to both the elements and a chance of the dragoons catching them, they understood George's reasoning.

After only a few minutes George could hear the sound of a horse galloping across the fields and heading his way. He guessed it must be Norman. He called Harry, Sam and Luke, to get up onto the bridge and listen to whatever Norman had to report. The three men were quick to obey and arrived on the bridge at the same time Norman's horse arrived.

George was the first to react, when he saw that Norman was laying, slumped along his horse's neck and holding on as best he could. He grabbed hold of the horse's reins and brought it to a halt. Norman slid from the saddle and landed, with a thump, on the boards of the bridge.

Sam was the next to arrive. He took hold of the horse's reins from George and walked the horse off the bridge. He walked it around to calm the animal and cool it down.

Harry and Luke joined George at Norman's side. They bent down to see how he was. George rolled him over, onto his back, so that he could see if he was even alive.

"Norman, Norman," George called.

"God what hit me?" Norman asked.

George, Harry and Luke gave an audible sigh. They all thought that Norman was dead. To hear his voice and realise that he was asking questions meant that he was alright.

"What happened to you?" George asked.

"I was just riding by the knoll, near Tile Barn, when a shot rang out and hit my leg. The horse bolted and I had a job to get it under control but once I did we headed off, over the field, to come back here. Just as I was jumping the ditch, I felt I'd been kicked in the shoulder and the pain was terrible. I then heard the sound of the carbine shot and realised that they had shot me again." Norman reported.

George turned to the men around him and with their aid, lifted Norman up and carried him to the end of the bridge and sat him up, leaning his back against the bridge support. They gathered around Norman, including Sam, still holding Norman's horse's reins.

"Right Norman, tell us what you saw." George ordered.

Norman explained that when he got there, he had seen the second wagon being driven towards Tile Barn, by Dragoons. Men were running along the field, near the river, and heading towards Aldfriston. He said that he didn't want to follow the Dragoons as he thought there may be more, near the barn.

"What did you do then?" Harry asked.

He continued to explain that he had followed their men, but after a while he saw that there were a lot more Dragoons, on the road. He saw two groups of villagers along the road, towards the village and what appeared to be some bodies lying on the road. Fred Cannon was being called over to one of the groups. He realised that if he broke cover he risked the chance that the Dragoons would chase him.

It was then that he returned to the field and went along, under the knoll. His intention was to get as near as he could to the barn and see what was going on and how many Dragoons there were? Once he was shot in the leg, it was obvious to him that he had been seen and the best thing for him to do was to get back here. It was his bad luck that the Dragoon, on the knoll, was such a good shot.

"Well done, Norman. We'll have to get you home and get those wounds fixed up." George said.

"Sam, get some of your men and get Norman into the boat. Then row as fast as you can and get Norman home. See that he is fixed up. If anyone tries to stop you, shoot them. Do you understand?"

Sam understood. He could see the risks to everyone but Norman was important to the gang and was an old friend. He quickly brought three of his men up from the boat. They helped Norman into the boat and set off, up the river.

"Luke, you follow Sam's boat. Before you get to Crow Lane, let off a couple of your men and send them ahead to ensure that there's no Dragoons waiting for you. If all is right, then continue there and unload. If not, go on to Endelwick Bridge and hide the goods there."

"Harry, you can take charge of Norman's horse and wait with me while we get the men off Cliff End and Seaford Head." George said.

The two of them went back onto the bridge. George picked up the lantern and sent a signal to Cliff End. They would signal Seaford Head and the men from both sides of the river mouth would come back to the Bridge. They would have to wait about twenty minutes before the men arrived, so George and Harry discussed what had happened and what they could do about it.

It soon became obvious to them that there were a lot of Dragoons, to have been able to overpower all their men and take control of the two wagons. A single patrol wouldn't have had the manpower for this. How had Graham arranged this?

If so, then there would be no point in chasing after them, particularly at this time of night. George decided that they would wait until the morning, get all the details of what happened and then plan what should be done.

The men from Seaford Head arrived, first. George told them what had happened and that they were all to go home. Those from near by were to go straight home, from here. Those from Aldfriston were to take the road up past Charfione, Clapham Farm and Littleington. He realised it was a longer way home, but if the Dragoons were still around, they could get arrested.

George and Harry got on the horses and headed for the road that he had just described to these men. It was his intention to wait at the junction for the men coming down from Cliff End.

They didn't have long to wait. The men arrived in dribs and drabs but once the main party had arrived George explained what had happened, then sent them off home.

George and Harry rode off, with the intention of getting home as quickly as they could. Tomorrow would be a very busy day and they needed to get plenty of rest before then.

CHAPTER 15

High and Over

"Every one, dismount and get ropes on your horses and tie the other ends to the wagon. We are all going to pull this damn thing up the hill." Pat ordered.

"Sergeant, our horses aren't built for this, it could kill them." One of his troop called.

"Don't you think I don't know this? We have to get this load up to the top, as quickly as possible. We can all rest once we reach the top."

"Paddy, David, I want you two to get some poles to use in the rear wheels to stop the wagon moving down hill if we come to a stop." Pat said.

Shamus had been listening in to what Pat was doing and made a quick judgment as to the needs of his wagon.

"Pat you can have two of my horses if it'll help, but I need the men."

"Thanks Shamus, get your men forward to tie them on the cart and I'll detail my men to look after them."

It took about ten minutes for Pat and his troop to get the wagon ready before ordering them out.

"John you take control of the wagon, everyone listen out for John's call, when he says move or stop you all obey. OK John, when you're ready."

Pat wanted just one voice controlling the wagon and who better than the man driving the main carthorses.

"Take up the slack in your ropes." John called.

He didn't want to start moving if some of the ropes weren't tight or the weight of the load would not be evenly distributed between the horses.

John was aware that the main weight would be carried by the carthorses but they would rely on the others to make it to the top. Once he could see all the ropes were tight he gave the order to move.

"Shamus you had better keep your wagon here at the bottom, at least until we have negotiated that first bend, I don't want you to get up my arse, if we get stuck on that bend." Pat said.

"Don't you worry none Pat. I'll wait down here until you are clear. That'll give me time to get these extra horses tied on to this wagon." Shamus said.

Each man took hold of the horse or horses they were detailed to control and urged them forward. Paddy and David took up station each side of the rear wheels of the wagon, strong poles in hand, ready to thrust them into the spokes, if the wagon stopped. One spot where they could find trouble would be after they had been going about fifty yards. The road turned sharply to the right and the string of horses would have trouble keeping a weighted pull going through that corner.

Pat and John had also seen that problem, so they discussed how best to negotiate this obstacle. After this corner, although, towards the top of the hill, it got very steep, the rest of the journey would not be too bad, as there were no more corners to take.

"John I think we should call a halt just before we get to the corner what do you think?" Pat asked.

John thought for a few moments, the horses were all pulling well at the moment so he didn't want to stop the momentum they had. To do so would put a greater strain on all the horses and Pat's idea would mean stopping again once they got around the corner and re-positioning the horses again.

"I say we go for it. Take the corner as far to the left as possible. Be ready to slip the ropes of those horses on the right, if necessary." John said.

John looked at Pat to see if he agreed, it was a more risky strategy but it should get them around that corner.

"If you think it'll work, let's do it. If you're wrong what then?" he asked.

"If I'm wrong, then the wagon will tip over and everything will roll down the hill and flatten Sergeant O'Riley and his men. There will be something good to come out of it. My brother, Corporal Jones, would be promoted."

This brought laughter from those around, but no one, not even Corporal Jones, would wish harm to come to the Sergeant.

"You heard what John said. We go for the corner. You three, on the right, draw your swords and be ready to cut the ropes if the horses are in danger of getting under the wheels."

The cargo may be important but for a dragoon his horse ranked before a drink, just.

Graham was walking up behind the first wagon. His horse was roped to the head of the wagon and was being controlled by one of the Dragoons. He heard what was being said and could see what they were planning. Graham would keep back, not that he was trying to skive out of some hard work but because, from a few yards behind the wagon, he would be able to see what was happening and hopefully be able to shout a warning, if he noticed a problem.

All the men around the wagon were good horsemen and so were keeping control over their charges. It surprised Graham just how much of an even pull the horses were giving the load. There didn't appear to be any horse having an easy time.

John ensured that they didn't try to move to quickly. He wanted to be able to stop quickly, if need be. He manoeuvred the wagon over to the left side of the road, as they neared the corner. By the time that the carthorses had reached the corner, the lead horses from the troop had already gone around the bend.

The timing, as to when he ordered the carthorses to turn, would be critical. Too early and they would not get around the corner at all. To late and the lead horses, of the troop, would have to stop pulling or their ropes would cut into the carthorses and stop them from pulling.

At what John thought was the right moment he gave a tug to the bridle of the lead carthorse, to put it over to the right, not too far, to quickly, but a gradual turn.

The lead horse followed his lead and all the other three large horses followed their leader. John saw that one of the ropes, from a trooper's horse, was moving in very quickly towards the lead carthorse,

"Paddy," yelled John, "Get your horse over to the right, NOW."

Paddy was day dreaming of the tales he'd be telling and how drunk they were all going to get, at the weekend at Sergeant Kelly's birthday bash.

John's call had brought him back to the reality of what still had to be done tonight. He pushed at the neck of his horse and reached under its neck to pull his head over to the right and in the direction he needed to go.

"Sorry John." Paddy called back, "That won't happen again."

"Make sure it doesn't and the rest of you keep your mind on the job." John shouted.

The offending rope quickly moved away from the carthorse's head. This allowed it to concentrate on its job in hand. The wagon was very close to not getting around the bend. Sergeant Kelly saw that if the two men with the poles got by the right hand rear wheel, they may be able to lever it around the final bit of the bend.

"Paddy, David, get around to the right rear wheel and use your poles to move the wheel past that rock, at the corner." Pat said, pointing at a large rock that was the corner stone to the bend.

Pat and David moved along the right side of the wagon so that they could place their poles down into the track and against the rock so that they could lever the wheel past it. The wagon wheel came into contact with the poles but with the load on board it had no intention of being persuaded to pass the rock in front of it.

David and Paddy tried with all their might to lever the wheel but it would not move. They were lucky that the poles, they had picked up by the barn, were very stout and didn't show any signs of giving way.

"We need some help." Paddy called, when it became obvious that the wheel was not moving. Pat ran forward from the rear of the wagon and Fred let go of the reins of his horse and ran back to the corner, to lend a hand. All four men took up the strain of the poles and started to push, but not together.

"Let's get it together." Paddy called,

"On three. One, Two, Three. Push." Paddy called and the other three took his lead and after three they all put a big effort into it. You don't move a load like this in an instant, first there was no movement at all, despite the four men leaning fully into their task.

"Harder." Pat called. "Get your weight behind it."

They were not actually on the side of the bank that fell away behind them. If the wagon didn't get past the corner, even with the effort of the horses pulling, the lay of the land, together with the weight of the load, would most likely topple the wagon over on its side. The load would roll over the bank and into the valley.

The major incentive, for these four men, was that if the wagon did tip over, it would come their way and not all of them would escape. With an almighty push, there was a slight movement of the wheel towards the corner.

"Keep pulling John." Pat called, "make it quick, I don't know how much longer we can hold this wheel."

John had seen what was going on but hadn't urged the horses forward too fast, in case they couldn't guide the wheel around the rock. Now he was sure that the poles and the men could hold the wheel in place, he urged the horses forward, to pull the rear of the wagon around the corner.

Everyone held their breath, as the wheel approached the rock, would it jump the poles and all their efforts be in vain or would it round the rock.

Inch by inch the wagon moved forward and the wheel turned slowly but the poles and men were holding. With a big effort from the horse, the rear of the wagon suddenly jumped to the left a few inches and rolled passed the rock.

This sudden movement caught the four men, on the poles, by surprise as the pressure they were exerting suddenly had nothing to push against and the four of them shot forward. Pat and David fell face down onto the road. Fred and Paddy both shot forward into the side of the wagon and bounced backwards, landing on their backsides.

This was not the image Pat wanted to present to their local Riding Officer but with Graham walking up the hill behind the wagon, leading Sergeant Kelly's horses, there was nothing he could do about what Graham saw.

"Resting while your men do all the work Pat." Was the first thing Pat heard, as he began to rise from the road.

"I'll show you about work when we get to Newhaven." Pat snapped, at Graham.

"Well done boys, now get back to your posts, this hill has not finished with us yet." Pat said, to his three helpers.

Paddy and David picked up their poles and took station each side of the wagons rear wheels, while Fred went forward to his horse.

A smile returned to Pat's face, as he turned back to his horse and Graham, "nearly lost it there Graham." He passed by both Graham and his horse and went down the hill a few yards,

"Shamus." He called

"Aye Pat."

"Start up the hill now and keep to the left, as you approach the corner, there is a nasty rock on the right." Pat said.

"OK, but I may need some of your horses when we reach the steep bit at the top. My horses won't make that part of the hill."

Although Shamus's wagon was smaller and carried a lighter load, they only had two carthorses and four of their own, to get the load up the hill. If they took it easy they would be able to get around the sharp bend. They would also be able to pull the wagon along the rising and straight part but the sharp rise, two hundred yards from the top of the hill, would be beyond the capability of this horseflesh.

Mr. Hill and Corporal Jones heard Pat's call and so they prepared to retreat, firstly back to the barn, where Shamus and his men were. All the time Shamus was at the barn, there was no need for the rear guard to worry about them being cut off by smugglers coming up the track from the landing point. Now they needed to ensure that this didn't happen.

"Let's move back to the barn Corporal." Mr Hill ordered.

"OK men fall back to the barn and wait for Mr. Hill and myself."

With that the four men turned their horses around and rode between the Officer and Corporal and headed the two hundred yards back to the barn.

Once they were on their way Corporal Jones moved his horse forward a few yards to take a good look down the road. He ensured that the smugglers and villagers were not following them.

"All clear Sir, I think they'll leave us alone tonight." He reported.

"Thank you Corporal, lets get back to the barn and the men."

With this he turned his horse around and rode beside the Corporal until they reached the barn.

"I think I can look after our rear if you want to see what's going on with the wagons Sir." Corporal Jones said, as they reached the barn.

"Thank you Corporal, if there's trouble I'll come back to help."

The Corporal smiled as his officer rode up the hill. They will have a good officer there, if they can train him right.

Shamus found that the journey, up the hill, wasn't as bad as they had expected, due partly to the fact that they had six horses and Pat had warned them about the corner and the large boulder.

Pat and his men didn't have to work too hard, once they had rounded the corner, the rest of the journey was straightforward. The horses were more than able to cope with the steeper part, to the top of the hill. When they had reached the top and moved a hundred yards on, Pat called a halt, so that the horses could be rested.

"Graham, will you see if Shamus wants those horses." Pat called.

Graham acknowledged Pat's call and shouted down to Shamus but received assurance that, like the first wagon, his horses could cope with this last part of the hill.

Once both the wagons had reached the top of the hill they drew up behind each other and the men released their horses from their pulling duties and walked them around, to ensure that they hadn't suffered any harm.

Corporal Jones and his detachment had also reached the top of the hill but they didn't join the others, they dismounted to give their horses a rest but kept watch down the hill, in case anyone was following.

"Sergeant Kelly, Sergeant O'Riley, Mr. Johnson." Mr. Hill called. "Come over here please."

Those summoned handed the reins of their horses to the nearest Dragoon and walked over to Mr. Hill, who was stood some fifty yards along down the road.

"What is the plan from here on Mr. Johnson? I know that you have to get this contraband over to the Customs House but do you need all our men?"

"I need sufficient men to ensure that we can get the two wagons to the ferry and protect us as we do." Graham replied.

Mr Hill looked at the two Sergeants and enquired how many men would be needed for this.

"I think just one of the troops will suffice." Shamus said.

"As I'll need to report all this to the Colonel, I think that my troop will return to South Bourn, whilst you go with Mr. Johnson." Mr. Hill said.

"Okay Sir but can I keep John to drive the large wagon? He's the best man in either of the troops to handle this." He didn't really address Mr. Hill but was addressing Pat.

"No trouble Shamus, you can have him for tonight but I want him back in the morning." Pat said, slapping Shamus on the back.

"Right let's get this lot home." Mr. Hill said. They all broke away and organized their respective men, for the journeys they had this night.

"Corporal Jones." Shamus called, "Get your self over here."

Corporal Jones recognized this as an order to get there quickly so mounted his horse and rode with haste to his Sergeant. On arrival he didn't dismount as he suspected that he was about to be given a job to do, which usually meant riding into danger.

"Take young Daemon and lead the way to Newhaven, don't get too far in front, I don't want the locals to be roused. Keep an eye out for anyone with an interest in what we're doing."

"What about the rear." Corporal Jones asked?

"Don't you worry non about that, there will be enough of us here to cope with anyone following us." Shamus said.

By now Mr. Hill, Sergeant Kelly and their troop were all mounted and ready to head out.

"Good luck Sergeant and thank you for the experience Mr. Johnson." Sergeant Kelly had far more important things on his mind. He wanted to ensure that they got their cut.

"Don't forget our 25% when you come back to barracks Shamus, I've counted what was loaded." He joked.

"Mr. Hill, if you're going by Excet Bridge, take care that George Styles and his men have departed first. He'll not be too happy if you turn up, after spoiling his party." Graham called.

"Noted" Mr. Hill replied.

After a few more exchanges between those leaving and those escorting the wagons to Newhaven, the troop moved away and headed off towards Excet Bridge and South Bourn.

After waving them good bye, Shamus and Graham got ready to move off. They had discussed the route earlier and Shamus had told Corporal Jones where to lead them. If he thought there was danger, he would take them on a different route, but they must arrive at the Ferry before daylight.

They would go along the top of the hill towards the beacon, overlooking Firle, but would turn off and head down to the hamlet of Norton. This would bypass Blatchington and Bishopstone. By going through this hamlet, it had the most supportive constable. Someone they could rely on to give them assistance, if need be. He also passed on information of the smugglers activities, if he thought there would be any trouble between the two groups.

It took them about three hours to reach the outskirts of Norton. Shamus hadn't pushed them along. He wanted to ensure they could be called upon to move quickly, if the need arose, tired horses couldn't do that.

They came into the hamlet on the eastern side, between two farms and their cottages, Graham had ridden up to join Corporal Jones and Daemon as they reached the village. He wanted to be there as it was not unusual for the Riding Officers to be accompanied by two Dragoons and this fact wouldn't go unnoticed by anyone looking out. By the time the main party arrived it would be too late.

On reaching a 'T' junction they turned westwards towards Denton and rode out of the village. As they reached to out skirts, Shamus and the wagons were negotiating the road junction. Graham didn't continue with his two companions but waited for the main party to catch up with him. Before parting from Corporal Jones he said,

"You'd better get the ferryman up when you reach the river. That will save us time when we arrive."

Although they headed towards Denton they turned off this track. By missing out Denton they shouldn't meet up with anyone, until they reached the ferryman's house.

"Good morning Mr. Johnson. I understand you have a big load for me."

"Yes quite a bit but I'll get some of these Dragoons to help you row it over, if you like."

"That'll be good of you, my men are not up yet and it would take half an hour to get them here anyway. The Corporal says you want to get this into the Customs House as quickly as you can."

"Right then men." Shamus said. "You three get over to the ferry boat and help load it and row it over to the other side."

There was no question to what they had to do, they handed over their horses to their companions and did as they were bid. Shamus then turned to four of his men, who had just dismounted.

"You four unload the wagon and get it down to the ferry."

"Daemon, you take all the horses into the barn and look after them, we will need them fed and watered when we have finished."

"Yes Sergeant." The young Dragoon said.

"I'll take John over on the first boat Shamus." Graham said,

"I need to get a cart and horse from the farrier's yard and your best skilled at harnessing the horse to the cart." He said to John,

"You heard what Mr. Johnson said John, go with him and leave the wagon, we'll look after it."

"OK Sergeant."

It took them about fifteen minutes to load the ferryboat with its first load. When all the passengers were on board they set off for the other side of the river. Whilst they were rowing across the river Shamus ensured that the wagon was unloaded at the side of the quay and then set about bringing up the smaller wagon ready to unload this as well.

On reaching the far side of the river, Graham and John climbed up onto the quayside but didn't wait to help unload the boat, they needed to get off and commandeer the farrier's cart. This would ensure they could get the contraband down to the Customs House quickly. Graham didn't try to wake the farrier; instead he and John went into his stable and picked the biggest horse there.

John collected the harness and while John harnessed the horse Graham went around the back and manoeuvred the cart so that the horse could be backed up and connected to it. Once this was done, John took the cart back to the quayside.

Graham went off to Mr William's house to fetch Mark. Mark hadn't tried to sleep. He sat up, in the kitchen and waited to see if Graham had achieved their aim. He had nodded off and his head was rested on the kitchen table, when Graham opened the door.

"No time to sleep now Mark."

"Did you manage to capture anything?" Mark asked.

"Yes, two carts full." He said, with pride.

"Where is it?"

"It's coming over the river, as we speak. You need to go and get the Customs House open. The first load will be with you soon. Graham said.

By the time Graham arrived back at the quayside, the ferryboat had gone back over the river and the next load was being put on board. Two of the Dragoons had remained on this side of the river to guard the Genever, Lace, Brandy and Tea. They helped John load it into the Farrier's cart. It took ten minutes to load and by this time Graham had rejoined them.

"You're counting what's coming over Shamus?" Graham called.

"Aye I am and I'm keeping one in four half-ankers for the boys."

"What I can't count, over this side, wasn't captured." Graham replied.

Graham could trust Shamus. The Dragoons weren't interested in the tea or lace so would just take 25% of the brandy and genever, this would satisfy both him and Pat and their men. It was worth it for Graham, without their help none of this would have reached the Customs House.

Once the farrier's cart was loaded, from the second boat, Graham told one of the dragoons to stay there and help to unload and guard the next boat full, while the rest of them took the cart load off to the Customs House.

John was a good horseman and was able to guide the horse and cart safety along the quay to the Customs House. Mark was waiting with Jack, to unload the cart and stack it in the warehouse.

With the five of them working hard, they had unloaded the cart within ten minutes. Graham told Jack to guard it well and the four of them set off to get the next load. Graham thought Mark could work for his share now as he had done it all so far.

An hour after they had arrived with the wagons, at the ferryman's house, all the consignment, destined for the Comptroller, was under lock and key.

"Mark, you stay over here, I need to talk to the Sergeant before they set of for South Bourn. I'll tell you all what went on over breakfast, if you can arrange that with Mrs. Damson."

"You bet." Mark said excitedly, he also had something to tell Mr. Johnson as long as the cook wasn't listening in.

John and Graham took the horse and cart back to the farrier's stable and Graham placed a half-anker of brandy just inside the door. That completed, they returned to the ferry and crossed over the river.

"Shamus, have you got what you needed?" Graham asked, as he stepped up onto the quayside.

"Yes and we have it all loaded into the small wagon so it'll be easy to take it back to the barracks."

"Did you leave the half-anker of Brandy and Genever in the barn for Mr. Ferris?" Graham asked.

"Yes, it's under some hay, just inside the side door." Shamus replied.

"Thanks." Graham said, as he shook his hand.

"Tell Mr. Hill and Pat how grateful I am. This will help me out a lot and we've hit back, for once."

"Will you be coming to Pat's birthday party?" Corporal Jones inquired.

"No I don't think so, I've work on Monday and I'd never make it, if the last party is anything to go by." Graham replied.

CHAPTER 16
Sorry I didn't get here last night.

Now that the Dragoons had departed, with their wagon load of goods Graham could now go to Mr William's house and enjoy one of Mrs Damson's breakfasts.

He walked into the back door of the Comptrollers House and the kitchen, where Mrs Damson was preparing breakfast. Mark was seated at the kitchen table, already eating his breakfast.

"Good morning Mrs Damson." Graham said.

"A good night, I hear, Mr Johnson." She said, with a smile that lit up the room.

"Yes a very good night and I couldn't have done it without the help of young Mister Mark, here." He said.

"What did I do? I just came here and sat out there, by the harbour mouth, catching a cold." Mark rebuked.

"You made sure that I could go and capture the goods, without either Mr Williams or the smugglers realising that the Dragoons and I were about, that is what you did." He said, with a big grin.

By this time, Graham had removed his hat, coat and weapons and hung them up and laid the weapons on the side table. He then joined Mark, at the kitchen table.

Mrs Damson came over and spread out an array of food in front of Graham, together with a large tankard of ale. She then gathered up her breakfast and joined the men.

Once they had all finished their meal, Mrs Damson cleared the table and then went into the dining room to make it ready for Mr and Mrs Williams breakfast.

As she was about to leave the dinning room, Mr Williams arrive and he was not in a very good mood. Last night had been a failure. He had had such high hopes of capturing a large cargo of contraband, last night, which could have meant promotion.

"Didn't Mr Johnson do well last night?" Mrs Damson said.

"How did he do well, he never arrived." Mr Williams snapped.

"Oh I mean the contraband he and the Dragoons captured over at Frog Firle, last night. It took them an hour to stack it into the Customs House, this morning." She reported.

It took Mr Williams some moments to comprehend what Mrs Damson had just told him. How could Mr Johnson have captured such a large consignment without him knowing? Was that why he hadn't joined the rest of the Riding Officers here last night and did Master Mark know about this?

"Mrs Damson, send for Mr Johnson and get Master Mark to report to me now." He ordered.

"They're both in my kitchen." She replied.

"Then send them here, this instance." He shouted.

While Mrs Damson was out of the room, Mark gave Graham an account of his evening. Starting from his encounter with Barbara.

What Graham needed to hear about was what went on, once he joined the other Officers. Mark told him about watching the boat being launched and then his ride on Mr Climpson's horse. After that, he was sent to sit near the mouth of the harbour. There he sat watching for the lugger.

The only good thing about this was that he wasn't in the boat, like all the others. They were in the middle of the river, being tossed about by the waves, which were coming in from the sea. Most of the men were very seasick, including Mr Williams. They called it a day, about ten o'clock.

Mrs Damson arrived back in her kitchen. She looked at the two men.

"Sorry, I told him about your adventure, last night. He's not at all happy. I don't know why. I thought he wanted to capture the contraband."

"Ah yes, but he wanted to be the one who captured it." Graham replied.

"Well you had better go to the dinning room, both of you." She said.

The two stood up and headed out of the kitchen and made for the dinning room. As they reached the door, Mrs Williams was approaching the door, so the men stood aside and allowed her to precede them into the room.

Mr. Williams was striding about, at the far end of the room. He turned when he heard the door open but was, at first, disappointed to see that it was his wife entering the room. The two Riding Officers enter the room, behind her.

"Mrs Williams, please leave us alone." He ordered.

"I'm here for my breakfast. If you want to talk business, then take them into the drawing room or invite them to join us for breakfast." She retorted.

She then headed for the side table, where Mrs Damson had laid out the breakfast meal.

Mr Williams was not happy with all the people in the room with him but he knew that his wife was right, so stormed out of the dinning room and expected the two men to follow him. Graham indicated to Mark that they should follow Mr Williams.

"Nice to have seen you again, Mrs Williams." Graham said, as he left the room.

Mr Williams went into the drawing room and sat down by a small table to the right of the main window. He didn't invite either of the men to sit.

"Sorry I didn't make it here last night." Graham said, but Mr Williams ignored him.

"Well what is this I hear about you getting a big consignment of contraband, last night?" He said, looking directly at Graham.

"Sir, Mark and I thought that you were being brought away from where the contraband was really being landed. There was no way that George Styles would be using Newhaven Harbour, to land any of his goods."

"I had reliable information." Mr Williams snapped.

"That may be so Sir, but when we rode out, in the Cuckmere Valley. We found evidence that they were ready for a consignment, last night."

"Why didn't you come and report this to me?"

"With all respect, Sir, you had made up your mind that it was to be here and nothing I could've said would have changed your mind." Graham reported.

"We saw a troop of Dragoons riding over the Downs, towards West Firle." Mark put in.

"I don't care if you saw a regiment of Dragoons, you report to me first." Mr Williams shouted.

"Sir, it was my idea to go after the Dragoons and see if we could attack the smugglers, not Mark's. I used him to allow me to ride after them. Had I not found them, or they were not willing to join me, I would have ridden here and joined up with you, Sir." Graham said.

It took a few minutes for Mr Williams to calm down but he realised that Graham had, in fact achieved what he was trying to do last night. His mind was working overtime, how could he turn this to his advantage, how could he get all the glory?

"Tell me what happened, in detail. I'll have to report to London."

Graham went through his ride over to West Firle, the luck in meeting up with not one but two troops of Dragoons and Mr Hill, their Officer.

How they had agreed to join in his plan and they worked it out, between the two Sergeants and the Officer, exactly what they would do and where they would attack the smugglers.

They had split into two main groups and how one of the troops had then split into two smaller groups, to get around Aldfriston. How they had found Fred Cannon and got him to show them the landing point.

For Mark, the most interesting part was the plan to attack the landing point, once all the cargo had been landed and loaded onto the second wagon. Graham told how the Dragoons had fought off the villagers, who were trying to come to the rescue of the smugglers and that they think three villagers were killed.

Mr Williams was not happy people had been killed but he could put the blame, fully on the Dragoons and their Officer, so he would be clear of that.

Graham then went on to explain how they managed to get the two, fully loaded wagons, up onto High and Over and then bringing them here to Newhaven, crossing the river, this morning, and getting all the contraband safety into the Customs House. Jack was making the count of what they had brought in and would have it ready by lunch time.

Mr Williams thought for a moment and then dismissed the two men. There was no thanks or well done. He had too much on his mind. He had a report to write, to show this was his plan. He had to come out of this shinning brightly.

Graham and Mark returned to the kitchen. Graham picked up his hat, coat and weapons. He headed back across the river and off to Seaford. It had been a very long night and he needed his rest.

Mark sat back down at the kitchen table. He was still trying to take in all that Graham had said.

"A good night for the both of you, Mister Mark?" Mrs Damson said.

Mark was not sure what she meant. Graham had done all the good work. Then he realised that she may have overheard him telling Mr Johnson about Barbara.

"It was Barbara's fault. I didn't chase after her." Mark said.

Mrs Damson smiled at Mark, to him, it was a knowing smile.

"Really Mrs Damson, it was her who undressed me and then got me on the hay. Then she took off her dress and sat on top of me. None of it was my idea." He protested.

"Did you enjoy yourself with Barbara?" She asked.

Mark didn't know how to answer this. He had never done this before, so had nothing to compare it with.

"I don't know Mrs Damson. That was the first time." He said and blushed.

Before Mrs Damson could enquire further, Mark got up and went up to his room, as quick as he could.

In the mean time, Mr Williams was busy getting his thoughts together. He needed to be able to write a report to show that it was his plan and it was he who arranged for the Dragoons to be available. Most importantly, that it was he who led the attack on the smugglers and it was under his orders that they got the contraband back to the Customs House.

He had forgotten he hadn't yet had breakfast, but had greater things on his mind. He went to find paper, pen and ink and set about writing the report. He intended to deliver this in person, to his superiors, in London.

The report took him an hour to write and read through. He was happy with what was said. It mentioned nothing about the roll that Mr Johnson had or the fact that Master Mark had duped him. There was nothing about the wild goose chase he had been sent on. He did mention he had sent his men into the harbour, as a diversion, to show the smugglers he had fallen for their trick.

Then, believing the success of his report would rest on the fact that the Dragoons were not likely to send in a report of their own. He felt happy.

If the Dragoons did, there would be some glaring differences but it was a chance he needed to take, if he was to get promotion, away from this small town.

After he was happy with his work of fiction, he called Mrs Damson and ordered her to get some clothes ready for him to change into for his journey up to London. Prepare a small bag, with a change of clothes, to take with him. He also ordered her to send Barbara to the Farrier and collect his horse, so that he could ride to Lewes and catch the mid-day coach to London.

CHAPTER 17
Does anyone know where they took our goods?

George Styles was furious, when he got the full details of how much he had lost to the customs men, the previous night. Three hundred pairs of half-ankers of Brandy, Two hundred pairs of half-ankers of Genever, fourteen cases of tea and ten bails of lace, this was a loss of about One Thousand pounds to him alone.

Although the profits he would be making from the sale of the rest of the consignment would make up of this loss, he was not at all happy.

The previous evening he had tried to find out what had gone wrong. Why were so many Dragoons in the area? How did they find out about the Frog Firle landing point? He didn't use it often and last night he had only chosen it because he had a big order for these items, from along the coast at Brighthelmston and towns beyond. No one should have been aware that he would be using it. Other than himself only two men knew of it, Norman and, Fred, his brother-in-law. Neither of them would say a word.

Last nights enquiry had drawn a blank. He hadn't been able to call on Fred, with his son being killed by the Dragoons. He had sent for him but George's sister sent back word that he was not coming.

Again, George had sent for Fred and again he didn't arrive. Instead Fred's right hand man, William arrived. George quizzed William at great lengths on what had gone on, at Frog Firle, but was no wiser at the end of it. William had told him they had all been unloading the boats into the wagons.

Fred had been there and, to his recall, no one had left the landing site until the first wagon had been loaded. Even then Fred had held it back until the last of the boat arrived.

William went on to describe the panic that ensued when the Dragoons attacked and how Fred had tried to hold everyone together before, like the rest, he withdrew. He went on to tell how they had been called over to the road, as they crossed the field and discovered that Fred's son had been shot.

George sat back and thought for a few moments. No one in the room, not even Ned spoke. To interrupt George during one of his thinking secessions, could bring about a fit of rage which had left one man dead and another with a limp, for daring to interrupt his thinking. George was better left alone to his thoughts.

Five minutes went by then another five and still he said nothing. Then he started to murmur to himself, not exactly talking. No one could understand what he was saying, not even the odd word was distinguishable. This went on for another ten minutes, all the time he was engrossed in whatever it was his mind was working on.

They could all have left and he wouldn't have noticed. Had they done so, when he was ready to talk to them, he would have been very angry not to find them there waiting his every word. So they just sat there and waited.

"Right, I don't know what caused this but we're going to do something about getting our goods back." George said. "Does anyone know where they took our goods, Newhaven or Lewes?" He asked.

"I meet a man, from Norton, this morning." Luke Smith said.

"And?" George asked.

"He said last night he was woken by the sound of a lot of horses going by and what seemed like two wagons." Luke said.

"Yes but where were they going?" George snapped.

From Norton they could well have gone on to Lewes or Newhaven. This wouldn't be a chosen route, by the smugglers. It is a long way to Lewes from there. You're on the wrong side of the Downs to have an easy time, with loaded wagons.

Luke continued. "He told me that he had spoken to his brother, who lives in Denton but they heard nothing."

Luke let that sink in for a moment. "I'd say that means that they have taken it to Newhaven, especially as Mr. Johnson reports to the Comptroller, Mr. William's, there."

"Good work Luke." George said, as he took in this information.

"That makes things a little more difficult but not impossible." George said.

Ned suddenly realised what was in George's mind.

"You can't be serous George, we can't attack the Customs House, it would mean the gallows for all of us."

Ned was possibly the only one, of two men, who could have said that to George and got away with it. The other one being Norman.

"We will do it and we'll get away with it, mark my words and I'll have nothing said against me."

George was angry that anyone had spoken out against him and his plan.

"The Hawkhurst Gang may have got away with it some years ago but they've improved their Customs Houses and have resident guards in them whenever they have anything to guard." Ned insisted.

"Then we kill the Guard." George said, looking Ned straight in the eyes.

This brought an end to the discussion; Ned could see that George had made up his mind, so that was it.

"Right, all of you can go, Peter, Luke, and Ned. Stay." George was short with everyone, when he was upset,

All the others left the house without saying another word. They would receive their instructions later on, so there was no need to ask anything.

Once the others had left George beckoned his lieutenants around the table so he could go over his plan to get his goods back. It took an hour to go over everything and ensure that everyone knew what their tasks were.

Unlike earlier, where no one questioned George, during these discussions, all those present had an equal voice. As long as they all understood that George had the last word. There was no question of George not getting his goods back.

"Let's go to the Star and have a few ales, to wash out the thoughts of last night and drink to our success tomorrow night." George said.

On the walk to the Star Inn George took Ned to one side, "How is Norman today? I didn't like the look of his leg or shoulder last night."

"I saw his wife earlier; she has cleaned up the wounds and put poultice on them." Ned replied.

"She also said that had you not put the cobwebs on his shoulder he may not be with us now, she sends her thanks."

For some reason or other the people in Sussex would use spider's webs to stop the bleeding. It formed a type of skin over the wound and this allowed the blood to catch on to something and form a scab, stopping bleeding and the chance of infections.

"Did you give Mrs. Simms some money so she could get Norman to a doctor?" George asked.

"Aye, I gave her three sovereigns."

"Good, let's put that behind us now and get on with what has to be done tomorrow night." George said, bringing that chapter to an end.

After they had sufficient ale to put them in a good mood, they left the Star. Headed out to find the men, that each of them would be taking tomorrow night.

They would need to be briefed what to bring and where to be. No one was to be told what they were going to be doing. Those who were at the earlier meeting wouldn't be saying anything, if they knew what was good for them. George would think whoever talked today was the same person who told on them last night.

Luke went to his house and collected his pistol and cutlass, kissed his wife farewell then left for the furrier's barn, to collect his horse. He was to use his contacts in Norton and Denton to get a few men who would be able to do some of the hard work in emptying the Customs House.

He needed eight men in all to load the fishing boat, with the contraband. George had decided that they would get a fishing boat from Seaford. His brother worked on a fishing boat and they could use that to bring the contraband back to Aldfriston.

Luke needed to ensure that the ferryboat would be manned. Some of the men would help the ferryman to row men across the river and wait, with the ferryman, to ensure the ferry was ready to take them back over the river, once their work was done.

With the use of the fishing boat they should be able to complete their task within an hour and then be back into the hills before reinforcements could be summonsed by the Comptroller of Customs. George didn't know very much about Mr. Williams. He expected him to be around gloating over his haul. He had no idea that he would be in London and leaving the way virtually clear for George and his gang to retrieve their goods.

It took Luke half an hour to reach Norton, where he went to seek out the man he had met earlier in Aldfriston. There was no Inn in the hamlet, so he just stopped and asked around until he was pointed to a small cottage at the edge of the village. Luke knocked on the door and was met by a young lady of about seventeen years old,

"Is your father in?" Luke asked.

"My farther lives in Blatchington Sir, my husband's in if you want to see him." She replied.

The man Luke was seeking was about thirty seven years old, his face was potted with scars from some disease or other and suffered from a limp that he got in the war against France. Could this buxom girl really be that man's wife?

"If your husband's in then I wish to speak with him." Luke said.

She asked him to wait whilst she went to find her husband. Luke wondered what this man had, to get a wife like this. He had found it very difficult to get a wife of his own age. Had he not been for the beerbaby (*one conceived due to drink*), she wouldn't have married him at all.

Still stood outside, Luke was looking around the hamlet and noticed that there weren't many houses here and from what he had seen, not many able bodied men either. It was possible that they were in the fields working but he hadn't seen any as he rode into the hamlet.

"Good day Sir." Mike Adams said, from behind Luke.

This brought Luke around to the business at hand. He turned to face the voice that had interrupted his thoughts.

"Hello, my name's Luke, I need some help, is there somewhere quite we can talk?"

"I can't see how I can help the likes of you. My leg stops me from doing very much." Mike said.

"I need to find some men who'll be willing to earn themselves some money, for a nights work." Luke replied.

"Come in to the house and I'll get my wife to fetch us tankards of ale and biscuits." Mike said, as he stood aside and waved Luke into his house.

Luke found himself in the parlour with three seats, a small table and a fireplace against the far wall. There was not much room here and there was a cloth hanging across the room, from the ceiling, to the left of the fireplace. This separated this part of the only room on the ground floor of the house, from the cooking area.

"Take a seat Luke." Mike said. "Wendy, bring us some ale and biscuits." There was no need to raise his voice, as the cloth didn't stop much noise from passing around the room.

Mike took up a seat facing Luke, "What can I do for you?" He asked.

"Well first I'd like to give you something for the information you gave me this morning, it proved very useful." Luke said, as he put his hand into his coat pocked and drew out two florins.

"I didn't tell you much and certainly not to be rewarded in such a way." Mike said, as he looked at what Luke had just placed on the table.

"My boss decided what such information is worth and he instructed me to give you that, but he also needs something else from you."

There always has to be a catch, this sort of money doesn't come without a price attached to it, thought Mike.

"What is it that your boss needs then Luke?" He asked.

"I need to find two men, in this area who can row a boat and another six who are strong and hard workers. Can you help?"

Mike wanted to ask what this was for but chose not to. To know too much might get him into trouble, people handing out the sort of money Luke was, were not involved in legal employment.

"Let me think, I know of four men in Blatchington, Wendy's family, who are good in the water and my brother and his son are good with a boat, they have one over at the harbour they use for fishing."

"How big is his boat," asked Luke.

"Oh not that big, just enough room for them and their nets."

"What about six others, can you think of any men who will fit this bill?" Luke asked.

"No sorry I can't, there aren't many in this village and those that are, are law abiding." Mike said.

Luke was not pleased to hear this but the most important task was the oarsmen and it appeared that he had found them.

Wendy came in with tankards of ale and a plate of biscuits. She placed them on the table and picked up the coins, smiled at her husband and left the two men to continue talking.

"Can you get a message to these men to meet me here, tomorrow night at about six o'clock?"

"I can't guarantee they'll come." Mike said. Luke didn't need to hear this. He drew his pistol and put it in front of Mike's face.

"They'll be here or I'll find your young wife and pass her around my men, before I kill both her and you." Luke let that sink in for a moment,

"Do I make myself clear?" Again he paused and then put away his pistol.

"There'll be two florins for each of the men and a further two for you if they are here."

With that said he turned and strode out of the house and mounted his horse, urging it off towards Denton village before Mike had regained his composure.

Little did Luke know that the young wife of Mike's wouldn't be an easy prey to him or his men. When he had threatened her husband she had been looking through a gap in the cloth and as a result she had found Mike's pistol, which he always kept loaded. She had it ready in case Luke hurt her husband. This young woman wouldn't take anyone hurting her or her husband, without putting up a fight.

After Luke had gone, she came from around the cloth and, with the pistol still in her hand, went up to her husband and put her arms around him.

Although he had guns in the house he never handled them, after his experiences in the war he had vowed not to touch one again. In fact he was positively frightened of the very sight of them.

"Its all right dear, I'll go and find the men, they'll be here tomorrow night."

She held him close and then kissed him gently on his left cheek as she rose and went back behind the cloth and put the pistol in its hiding place.

Luke needed to find the six men for loading the fishing boat. If he couldn't find them in Denton he'd have to go on to South Heighton, a hamlet half a mile further up the River Ouse valley. On arriving at Denton he noticed that the Constable was around and it was common knowledge that he kept the Riding Officers informed of what was going on. Luke decided that he would continue on to South Heighton instead.

Luke had no more luck in South Heighton than he had in Denton. He hadn't wanted to bring over men from the Cuckmere valley if he could help it, as they wouldn't know the lie of the land. They would be easily noticed as foreigners to the locals in and around Newhaven.

His plan was to get men who knew the area and were known hereabouts. Some who would not ask too many questions as to what they would be asked to do for their florins.

As he left the village he started to head home. He looked down into the valley, towards Newhaven, and started to pan his vision towards Seaford when he noticed the Mill at Tide Mill.

Of course, he thought, who would be more use to moving heavy items around and working as a team than the workers at the mill. So instead of heading home he changed the direction of travel and headed down into the valley and towards Seaford.

It took him twenty minutes to arrive at the Mill and to his delight there were a group of men just leaving the mill. They appeared to be heading to their homes, a short distance from the mill.

"Good day." Luke called, as he approached the men.

"Good day to you." The leader of the group said.

Luke drew his horse to a halt in front of the group, blocking their way to their cottages. He smiled at the leading man

"I was wondering if you men would like to earn a couple of florins each."

He believed in being direct, he needed their attention quickly and to see their reaction to such an offer. If they were dismissive, he would go no further. If there was too much interest he would have to be careful how much he said. They could well be informers to the authorities.

"That's a lot of money to be offering strangers, Sir." One of the men to the rear of the group said.

"Aye, what would we have to do to get this money then?" asked another.

Luke saw that they were not jumping up and down to get his money. They appeared to be cautious men and that pleased Luke.

"I need six men to help me move a cargo one night this week." He said, trying not to give too much away but telling them what they would be expected to do.

"There are seven of us and for that money we wouldn't want to leave anyone behind." The group leader said, testing the water with this stranger.

"Seven would be as good as six." Luke replied.

"And the price would be the same, two florins for each man." He asked.

"Yes." Luke said.

"Then come to my cottage and we'll talk about it while I have my meal." He said, inviting Luke to follow him.

Luke dismounted his horse outside the man's cottage and tied the reins to a post. He followed the man into his cottage and was introduced to the man's wife.

There was no offer of any drink or anything to eat from this household. It was obvious to Luke that these were very poor people and his offer of money was the equivalent to about a week's wages for this man and his family.

Luke took a seat, offered to him by the man, who then asked Luke what is it he wanted the men for?

Luke saw that this man was a very hard-hitting person. He was not one of those who believed in pleasantries, he came to the point.

"I need men to load and unload a cargo I'm moving across the river at Newhaven, at night." Luke said. There was a short lull while the man thought of the next question,

"Why at night?" He asked.

"Because its goods I don't want others to know about, trade secrets you might say." This prodding was getting on Luke's nerves.

The man continued to eat his meal, keeping Luke waiting for either his answer or the next question.

"Two florins is a lot of money just to move some goods, are they legal?" He eventually asked, but with his mouth still full of food, spitting some of it across the table towards Luke.

"Sir, if the goods were legal and I could do it in daylight I wouldn't be offering you two florins each. I'd only be offering two florins for the group of you." Luke said, with a firm voice.

"Now can I have your answer? I need to find these men today and I appear to be wasting my time talking to you."

Luke stood up, before the man could answer

"And it's not that you appear to need any extra money for your family. I expect your fellow workers are living the same way that you are." With that he turned to leave the cottage.

"Don't be too hasty Sir; I'm sure we can do what you want of us. I'll ask the others." The man said.

"I thought you spoke for them, if I'd known you didn't I wouldn't have come to your cottage but spoken to you all outside."

To clinch the deal Luke decided to throw in a further offer,

"There will be a further two florins for the leader of the group, the person who delivers them and organizes them for the work." Luke said, turning back to look at this man again.

Luke could see this man was now with him. The extra money for him was enough to get him in favour of the scheme, irrespective of the risks to either him or his group.

"I'll get the men to agree and I'll bring them along to the spot in the river you want us." He said.

"Good, I'll send a message to you tomorrow to tell you the day, time and place. You are to tell no one of this and not even your men where they are going. Do I make myself clear?" Luke said sternly.

"If word gets out, George Styles will come around and see you."

That brought a look of real fear from this man, George's activities and ruthlessness was well known, for miles around.

Luke had no intention of staying around here any longer, he had his men and he had put the fright into this man. He would deliver his men and say nothing to anyone, other than to let his men know that the deal was agreed. He strode out of the cottage, leaving the door open as he walked through the group of mill workers, standing outside awaiting news of what was on offer and if they were going to get this money.

"Are we working for you Sir?" One of the younger men asked.

"Ask your friend." Was the only reply Luke felt like giving.

Rejoined with his horse, Luke rode off towards Seaford but took the turning off to Bishopstone and from there, to High and Over. Now he felt safe, he would soon be back in Aldfriston. He felt he had been lucky so far today, in not meeting up with any Riding Officers or Dragoons, especially after the activity of the previous night.

On arriving in the village he went straight around to George's house and reported on his progress.

"Good work Luke, will they all turn up?" George asked.

"Oh yes they will. Your name was enough to ensure that once they had agreed there would be no going back on their word." Luke confirmed.

"You make me out to be an ogre Luke." George said, with a smile.

"You are." Luke said. He was quick to move out of arms length.

"Be off with you. See you at the funeral tomorrow."

Peter Gibbons was in charge of the horses and ponies needed to transport the consignment away, once it had been liberated from the Customs House and delivered back here, in the fishing boat. It wouldn't take him long to organize sufficient stock to do this part of the operation.

Being the local farrier he had a good knowledge of and reason to visit the various farms and tradesmen. They would hire him their horses and ponies whenever they were needed.

Anyone from outside may have thought that these animals were possibly the best tended in the county, due to the amount of times they visited the farrier. Those in the know knew what they were up to during the nights they were in his care.

With the help of his boy he was able to get messages around the area for the people to have their animals ready for use in the next few days. He would send word when they were needed and where to bring them.

Once he had ensured that he had the numbers he needed he went back to George's cottage and told him that his side had been arranged.

"Right, I'll see you at the funeral tomorrow, be ready to move soon after that." George said, giving the first indication of how soon he intended to retrieve his goods.

Like Peter, Ned sent word around to twenty of his most trusted men, those he would always prefer to have beside him in a fight.

They were to be ready to leave at a moments notice. There was no going to the George or Star Inns and getting drunk, they could leave that until they had completed this next assignment. Ned would then buy them the ale they needed to get drunk.

George had complete faith in Ned and if he was given anything to do he would do it. They had grown up together and were more like brothers than friends. They had fought together as children, had fights against other groups of boys from the local villages, such as Berwick and Milton Court. Had chased the same girls and made love to each other's sisters and married girls from the same village - Chidingly.

George and Ned finished the day off with three pints of ale in the Star Inn.

"We have everything in place now, tomorrow we'll teach the Customs men that they don't steal from me and don't kill boys from our village." George said, as they walked out of the Inn.

"Aye we will. See you tomorrow George." Ned said, as he turned the opposite way to George, as they both went their separate ways to their cottages.

CHAPTER 18
I'll make a Virgin's Wreath

Fred Cannon and his wife had an early caller the morning after their son had been killed by the Dragoons; it was Reverend Simpkins, the village priest.

He was an old man who had been the village priest for more than thirty years and was well versed in the goings on of his parishioners. He received many an half-ankers of brandy and genever, over the years, so would bless the Free Traders adventures.

"I'm sorry for your tragic loss Fred." He said and turning to Ann Cannon "and your sad loss as well, my dear."

"Thank you Reverend Simpkins." Fred said.

"Would you bless our son?" Ann asked, handing him a florin.

"Take me to him and I'll commend his soul to heaven."

Ann led through to the room that young Fred shared with his three brothers and two sisters. He was laid out on the centre bed, covered over with a blanket.

Reverend Simpkins went up to the boy's head, removed the blanket from his face and made the sign of the cross on his forehead, saying a few words to commend him to God. Having completed this he covered his face and left the room.

"Has the Constable been to see you?" The Reverend asked.

"Yes, he came last night." Ann answered.

"Good, then we can plan the funeral. I would say tomorrow afternoon would be best, it gives the grave digger time to prepare the grave."

This surprised Ann and Fred; they had thought they would have a few days with their son, before he was finally taken from them.

"Reverend. Why so soon?" Fred asked.

"I'm going to Chichester. I have to see the Bishop the day after tomorrow, so I won't be back for a week or more."

"As he was so young, could he have a virgin's wreath?" Ann asked.

The Reverend thought for a moment, this was an unusual request for such a wreath to be made for a boy. They were usually only made for the young girls of the village.

"Had he been with a girl?" The Reverend asked.

Not a usual question for one so young but if they wanted his permission to have such a wreath, to take into church with his coffin, then this was an important question, all would depend on the answer.

"No he hadn't." Ann said. Hurt that they should be asked such a question of a boy only thirteen years old.

"In that case he can have a Virgins Wreath." Reverend Simpkins said.

This brought a smile onto Ann's face, for the first time since she had found out that her son had been killed.

"I'll get his sisters to make one for him and they can carry it into church for him" Ann said. Talking more to her self, than the others in the room. With that she left the room and set out in her search for white paper, to use to make the wreath.

It was a tradition in Aldfriston to make wreaths of white paper flowers that were carried, before the coffin, into the village church of St Andrews. After the service they were then left inside the church, around the side walls. The name of Virgins Wreath came about because it was tradition for only young girls, who hadn't yet lost their virginity. In certain circumstances this was also extended to young boys. This honour had been extended to Ann's little boy.

Ann called her two daughters, Carol and Jane, to her and instructed them to go around the village to collect as much white paper as could be spared and bring it back to the house.

"Why so much paper?" Jane, the youngest asked.

"To make paper flowers. Then we'll use them to build a wreath for young Fred." Her mother replied.

Jane didn't fully understand but chose not to question her mother any more. With that they set off on their task. On leaving the house they split up, one going to the left towards the church, the other right towards the village square. They called at each house and requested white paper, just as their mother had instructed them to do. Four of the houses, they called at, said that they would make flowers and bring them around in the morning, but all the other houses found at least one sheet of white paper for the girls.

The girls had circled around the village and meet up at the far end.

"I got lots of paper." Jane said.

"And so have I." Carol said.

"We should be able to make lots of flowers from this."

Jane told her sister of the three houses who said they would make flowers. Carol said that one, she called on, would do the same. Their mother will be pleased with what they had done and Fred will get a large wreath.

When they reached home and presented the paper to their mother she was very pleased with what they had done. Ann had a lot to do to ready the family for the funeral. First she taught the girls how to make the flowers.

At the start the girls took ages to complete each flower but as they got more practiced they were turning out flowers quite quickly.

Ann set about finding something clean to wrap her son in, for his coffin. Although Fred had his income from the Free Trading, by the time they had paid their rent and found food and clothing for the family there was not much left for savings or having spare clothes.

All the children had 'hand me downs' so young Fred's clothes would now pass to his younger brother, with the exception of the blouse he was wearing when he was killed. That was so covered in blood that Ann had fed it to the fire. Every time she looked at it, she would remember this time and she didn't want that to follow her.

Ann had lost four children in the last six years, three to ague fever, which took many people in the villages in the Cuckmere Valley. The average life expediency for children was just four years. If they passed this point then they could be expected to reach adulthood.

Ann was busy ensuring that her husband and all the children had suitable clothes to wear to church. Those that were dirty were either brushed clean or for the very dirty ones were washed in the pail and hung out to dry. All she hoped was that they would be dry in time for the funeral tomorrow.

Fred found that his son's death kept him away from George and his questions about the previous night. How much longer he could hide behind this he didn't know. It was time to face George. He had heard that there was a meeting at George's house earlier and that William had gone in his place. It was reported that George was planning something but only the closest lieutenants were in the know.

"Ann. I'm going to see George." Fred shouted

He put on his coat and hat, then walked to the cottage door and left Ann to sort out his son's funeral.

The walk to George's house took him longer than he had expected. At every house someone came out to offer sympathy for his loss. At times the comments about his son brought tears to his eyes but he tried to hide these as best he could. Eventually he found himself at George's door.

Fred hesitated, for a moment, before he knocked. He needed to compose himself. If he went in there full of emotions he could find he said things about what went on at Frog Firle, which he needed to keep to himself.

"Come in." Came the call, from within the house,

Fred recognized George's voice. He braced himself once more before he entered the house. As he entered he took off his hat and found himself standing face to face with his brother-in-law. George put out his arms and drew Fred towards him,

"I'm so sorry for your loss Fred, how's Ann taking it?"

This action surprised Fred. He'd never thought of George as an emotional or caring man.

"She's working her way through it. The problem will be tomorrow, at the funeral."

"You take care of her for me won't you Fred and I'll take care of those responsible for this deed." George said.

This sent a shiver through Fred's body but luckily, although George was still holding him, George thought it was just a reaction to the loss of his son not guilt or fear.

"Thank you George." Fred said, as they parted from the embrace.

"I heard that you're planning something, is there anything I can do?"

"No, you just look after Ann and the children. I'll look after the business. If I need you I'll send for you but that'll not be until after the service."

Fred would have chosen to have been in the middle of things. To see what George had found out about last night and keep him self busy.

"The Reverend has allowed us to make a virgins wreath for young Fred." Fred said, with a tear running down his right cheek.

"That's good of him; young Fred was a good boy." George replied.

"Now you get off home to Ann and I'll see you at the service, what time is it?" He asked.

"About two o'clock I believe." Fred said. He put his hat back on and left George's house.

Stepping into the street Fred gave a sigh. This had been a very hard meeting for him. He was expecting George to question him about last night and how the Dragoons and Riding Officers had found them and gone off with his goods.

As he hadn't said anything about it, Fred assumed that Will had given him sufficient answers that didn't point, in any way, towards him. Had he done so then death of his nephew or not, George would have killed Fred without a second thought.

When he got home, Fred found Ann in tears.

"What's up dear?" He asked, putting his hands on her shoulders.

She turned and fell into his arms sobbing uncontrollably.

"Why, Why, Why." She repeated time and time again.

There was no answer to this that he knew would placate her.

"It's one of those things my love, he always wanted to join in with the big boys games. Only this time the boys found the men were not playing the same game and paid the price for it."

Fred held her tight for a quarter of an hour, until her tears were all cried out. She drew back a little and looked into his eyes,

"How do we keep them safe Fred? If it's not the Argu, from those blessed midges in the fields, it's the soldiers killing our boys. What are we to do for the rest?" She asked, with tears still running down both her cheeks.

There was no answer he could give. Their income came from Free Trading and the patronage of her brother, if they moved away then what would he do.

"I've kept some of the money you've been giving me and I've about one hundred sovereigns." Ann said.

Fred looked at her in surprise, he'd never thought she been putting away their money; he thought that she had spent it all, keeping them fed and clothed.

"What do you mean one hundred sovereigns?" He asked, pushing her away to arms length.

"Let's leave here and go to some town where you could get a job and the children could get proper schooling and medicine. The money will give us a start." Ann said.

Although Fred liked the idea, there was no way he could allow this, not at this time. If it were seen he had so much money, questions would be asked how he came by it. Especially so soon after the customs men had captured George's consignment. Informers were known to be well paid, for information leading to the capture of contraband. Fred didn't want anyone pointing a finger at him, not at the moment.

"I'll make some enquiries about a suitable town. You mustn't tell anyone, not even your brother, about this." He insisted.

"But I'll have to tell my family where we're going, at some time." Ann said, not understanding why Fred wanted to keep this matter a secret.

"Not until I tell you, woman." Fred said, angrily, as he removed his hand from his wife and moved away.

Fred didn't want to continue this conversation so he picked up his hat.

"If you want me for anything, send one of the children over to the Star, I'll be there."

With that he left the cottage and strode over to the Star Inn, ignoring any messages of sympathy that came his way. Fred's mind was on how he was to keep George from suspecting that he led the Dragoons to Frog Firle.

Ann was distraught that Fred didn't appear to take her plan seriously and as he opened the door, to depart for the Inn, she picked up a plate and threw it after him. By the time the plate had reached the spot where Fred was standing, he had moved through the door and closed it behind him. This resulted in the plate hitting the door and it fell to the ground. The door didn't reopen so it was obvious, to Ann, that he hadn't heard the plate hit the door.

Ann had no time to be angry with Fred now. There was so much to do. Sorting out clothes for young Fred to be dressed in for his burial had caused her to collapse and had it not been for Fred arriving home, when he did, she would most likely still be distraught. Now she had recovered, it was time to get back to what she had been doing.

Having found the clothes she wanted, she ensured that they were clean. The blouse, she had chosen, was stained so she quickly washed it in a bucket of water and hung it onto the apple tree, at the back of the cottage. With luck the wind would dry the blouse before the day was out and it would be ready for young Fred to ware.

Carol called out to her mother, as she heard her return to the kitchen after hanging out the blouse.

"Mother, how many flowers are we to make?"

"How many have you made already?" She asked.

"About twenty." Jane called.

"That's not enough yet, have you got more paper to use." Ann asked.

"Yes there are about five sheets left." Carol said.

"Do all of them and with the ones that you said others are making, there should be enough for a really big wreath for Fred, he deserves that."

Both Carol and Jane continued with their work and once they had finished, their mother sent them out to collect some willow sticks, so that they could build the wreath to support the flowers.

The Reverend Simpkins was having a busy day, not only had he called on Ann and Fred but he had to call on the other two families, of the other boys killed the previous night. These boys were older than Fred so there was no question of them having the virgin wreaths but their funeral had to be planned as well.

To maximize his income, from these tragedies, he persuaded all the families to have just one service. He had no intention of charging them less, because of a joint service, but he would only pay the wardens for one service.

The one thing he would have to pay extra for was another man to help out Henry, the gravedigger, to prepare the three graves. There would be no trouble here, as there was always someone in the George Inn who would do anything for the price of a couple of pints of ale.

The village was a very quiet place this day, there were not many people in the Inns and the women folk were helping out their friend, who had lost loved ones, in preparing the funeral.

It was quite noticeable that there had been no sign of the usual pairs of Dragoons, who rode through the village on two or three occasions each day.

By the time the evening had come, all the arrangements for the funerals had been completed. The graves had been dug and the bodies removed to the barn that was used by the village undertaker.

The village closed down early that night, there were no drunks wandering the streets. Everyone was indoors still reeling from what had happened to their village. Hopefully they would be able to lay that to rest when they all gathered at the church, the next day, and celebrated the lives of the three boys who had been so tragically struck down.

The day of the funeral was a bright one, the sun was shining and the birds were singing. Ann was up early. She wanted to ensure that all her family had eaten early and that they knew exactly what they would be doing later and what time they were to be dressed and ready for the church.

Fred, Carol and Jane arrived in the kitchen together. The girls were being comforted by their father. An unusual sight, Fred had never been the comforting type. He was generally a hard, unfeeling man. When their other four children had died he didn't even attend the church services, he would go out and drink himself into unconsciousness, coming around several hours after his children had been buried.

"I want you all here washed and dressed at one o'clock, and that includes you Fred. You're not missing this one, if you do, I'll send George to find you and if you don't come I'll tell him to ensure that it's your funeral tomorrow."

All those present knew that Ann meant every word she said. Fred knew if she asked her brother to kill him, he would do so without a second thought. Anyone hurting his sister hurts him and everyone knew what that would mean.

"I'll be here, I've to find three other men to carry Fred's coffin." Fred said.

Ann was just about to say that they needed four when she realised that her husband, his father, would be the fourth man and that pleased her. She circled the table and coming up behind her husband she gave him a hug to show she understood and approved. Ann was a very proud wife this day.

When they had all eaten Fred left the cottage. He needed to find the other pallbearers, leaving the girls to help out their mother.

"Now which one of you is going to carry the wreath for Fred?" She asked.

Carol's face became red as she replied,

"I think it would be best if it was carried by Jane."

Both Jane and her mother looked at her but for different reasons.

"Why, you're the eldest?" Jane asked.

"I don't feel it is right for me to carry such a wreath." Carol said, not wanting to go any further with the explanation.

Before her mother could say anything Carol left the room running and went up the stairs to the children's room.

Jane was confused about what was going on with her big sister but her mother just smiled at her.

"You have a big honour today, not many girls get the chance to walk in front of their brother in church and you'll be the focus of the whole service."

"I know but Carol is upset, why can't she do it with me? She's Fred's sister as well."

"I'll go and talk to her dear." Her mother said.

Ann went up the stairs and into the children's room and found Carol face down on her bed, crying. She went over and sat on the bed, placed her hand between her shoulders and rubbed her gently.

"What did you mean down stairs, that you don't think its right for you to carry the wreath?" Ann asked.

Carol continued to cry for a few minutes longer, then raised her head and turned towards her mother.

"I'm not a virgin. I didn't think it was right for me to carry the wreath for Fred, it seemed wrong to me." She said, sobbing slightly as she spoke.

Being a village and knowing everyone in it, Ann was surprised that she didn't know about this before. Word of when a girl was 'plucked' soon got around the boys in the village and the women soon got to hear about it. The story would be around to their mother within hours of it happening.

"And when did this happen?" Her mother asked, in a smooth voice. She didn't want to frighten her by putting her under some inquisition.

"The night Fred was killed. I'd met up with his friend Eric, by the church gate and we had gone into the church grounds for a talk. One thing led to another and before I realised what was happening we were laying on one of the tombs and he was entering me."

Ann said nothing. She now understood why she had heard nothing of this. Eric was one of the other boys who had died that night. The very night he had taken away her daughters virginity.

"Mum was I a bad girl, to do it with someone who was then killed? Was that Gods punishment for what had happened in his grounds?" She asked, with tears streaming down her face.

"No my child it was no punishment. It may seem that way to you now but it was not." She said, as she reached down and pulled her daughter up into her arms and held her to her breasts.

Oh what a mess, thought Ann, I only hope that she's not pregnant.

"We'll not tell your father or Eric's parents of this." Ann said.

"You can walk beside your sister as she carries the wreath, she wants it and I think it will do you good."

"But I'm not a virgin." She insisted.

"Only Eric, you and I know of this and none of us are going to tell anyone. What the rest don't know, won't hurt them, will it?" She said.

"Boys always tell, although he said he wouldn't I bet he did and I bet Fred knew before he died." Carol sobbed.

A little lie wouldn't hurt at the moment, thought Ann.

"He'd only just reached the Inn when everyone went running off after the Dragoons. He wouldn't have had time to tell them anything." She said.

This seemed to comfort Carol and she sunk deep into her mother's breasts and slowly her crying subsided.

As Carol pulled away from her mother, Jane walked into the room.

"Have you asked her mother?" Jane asked.

"Yes I'll walk with you, in the church." Carol said.

This brought a big smile from Jane and she came up to her big sister and put her arms around her.

"Are you better now?" She asked.

"Yes thank you."

Ann left the room and let the sisters talk and comfort each other.

One o'clock came and there, stood in front of Ann, were her husband and her children. All were dressed and clean, ready to leave for the church.

The service was at two o'clock but Ann wanted to be in the church well before that. She wanted to have the choice of the aisles, for her family. After all George Styles was her brother, so that must stand for something in this community, especially today. This service would be for the Free Traders families, families not connected with smuggling were not likely to attend.

Once she had inspected her family she moved to the door.

"Let's go then shall we?" She said.

Fred ushered the children out of the door and followed his wife through the door. Carol was carrying the wreath of white flowers that Jane would carry down the aisle, in front of her brother's coffin.

Ann was right to get to the church early. Already the first row of seats, on the right aisle, had been taken by Eric's parents, brothers and sisters. Ann led her family to the first row, on the left side.

Once the family had taken up their seats, Fred left them and returned to the entrance to the church. Here he would await the arrival of his son's coffin. The church soon filled up, with all the expected people there, including her brother George.

Ann heard the cart approaching the church, so sent the girls out to join their father, taking the wreath with them.

"Don't run." She said, as they scurried away.

At two o'clock the undertaker arrived at the church gate, with his cart. On it were the three coffins of the boys who were killed, by the Dragoons, the other night. There were twelve men stood at the church door. Reverend Simpkins indicated for the men to go to the church gate and take up their respective coffins.

Reverend Simpkins moved forward, with the girls at his side.

"Fred, we'll have your son's coffin to head the procession, Eric will follow with James Felon to bring up the end."

While the men organized themselves, ready to follow the Reverend's orders, he turned to the girls.

"You two will walk in front of your brother's coffin. When it is put on the stands, you put the wreath onto his coffin." Both girls nodded that they understood what was expected of them.

When all was ready Reverend Simpkins turned back towards the church and as he started to walk slowly back into the church and the waiting congregations he started the service.

"I am the resurrection and the life, saith the Lord: he that believeth in me, though he was dead, yet shall he live: and whosoever liveth and believeth in me shall never die."

By this time the Reverend had reached the church door, followed by the coffins of young Fred, Eric and James, all in line.

He continued as he walked slowly into the church and down the aisle.

"I know that my Redeemer liveth, and that he shall stand at the latter day upon the earth. And though after my skin worms destroy this body, yet in my flesh shall I see God: whom I shall see for my self, and my eyes shall behold, and not another."

Reverend Simpkins was now in the nave and turned around to face the congregation and the three coffins that had been behind him. The coffin bearers had placed Fred's coffin on the centre stands, with Eric's to his left and James to his right. The two girls now stood behind their brother's coffin.

"We brought nothing into this world, and it is certain that we carry nothing out. The Lord gave, and the Lord hath taken away: blessed be the name of the Lord."

Ann found this hard to accept, it had been the Dragoon's and Riding Officers who had taken her beloved Fred, not the Lord.

Ann was very much into her own thoughts as the priest led the congregation through Psalm XC.

It was not until half way through the reading of St Paul's epistle to the Corinthians that she came back to join those around her. "... for the trumpet shall sound, and the dead shall be raised incorruptible, and we shall be changed..." read Reverend Simpkins.

Once the lesson had been read Reverend Simpkins waved forward the pall bearers to take up the coffins. This time the coffins were to head the procession out of the church and over to the recently dug graves.

After the men had adjusted their loads, they turned and headed back to the church door, Fred's coffin was preceded by his sisters carrying the wreath. Behind were the coffins of Eric and James. Reverend Simpkins walked behind James coffin and the mourners filed out from the pews and followed on.

On arrival at the gravesides, the sisters placed the wreath onto the head of Fred's coffin. Once everyone had arranged themselves around the various graves, Reverend Simpkins said "Man that is born of a woman hath but a short time to live and is full of misery..."

Again Ann lost whatever was said after that, tears flooded from her eyes and her heart was full of distress and she sobbed uncontrollably. This was echoed around the other two grave sides.

As young Fred's coffin was lowered into the ground, Ann reached forward and took off the wreath and handed it to Carol.

"Go and place this in the church, with the others." Ann said.

Jane went with her sister and it was not long before they were back, beside their grieving mother, after placing the virgin's wreath along side those already lining the wall.

While the girls had been away, Reverend Simpkins had concluded the service, with the girls arriving back as he was saying."... the love of God and fellowship of the Holly Ghost, be with us all evermore, *Amen.*"

The other families were stood around the graves of their lost ones, each waiting for the Reverend Simpkins to commit their loved ones to the ground.

George Styles stood back from all of this, his mind was on how he was going to wreak his revenge on the Customs men for what they had done.

George had noticed a foreigner, at the back of the church, as he left to follow the coffins out of the church. He had instructed Henry to bring the man to him, in the churchyard, whether he wanted to join him or not.

Henry joined George and with him was the stranger.

"He says his name is Jethro and he's looking for you." Henry said, introducing the foreigner.

"What is it? What do you want with me then Jethro?" George asked.

"I've been asked contact you and ask you to meet with someone who has something he wants delivered." Jethro said.

"I'm not a delivery boy." George snapped.

"I'm told that my contact will offer you a good payment for the delivery, if you agree to it." Jethro said.

"Why've I been selected for this honour?"

"It's because of the location of your village and where the item is to be delivered to, is what I'm told." Jethro said.

"What's this item?" George asked, looking directly into Jethro's eyes.

"I haven't been told. That's why the meeting is requested."

"Where do you live Jethro?" Henry asked.

"Pevensey" He replied.

"And where does the person, I'm to meet, live?" George asked.

"He's a Frenchman. He delivers contraband to my area but asked to meet the leader of the smugglers of this village." Jethro said.

"Go wait by the church door." George ordered Jethro.

"Henry what do you think, is this a trap or an opportunity?" George asked, as much to himself as to Henry.

"I've heard of Jethro, he's a smuggler and runs a small band of men, about twenty I've heard." Henry said.

After a few minutes more discussion George turned around and waved for Jethro to rejoin then.

"I'll meet your Frenchman, but not here, At the Eight Bells in Jevington. There'll be just you and him. If there are more, I'll kill you and anyone with you. Do I make myself clear?" George asked.

"Yes that's what I was told to arrange, just the three of us." Jethro said.

"I'll bring with me whom I want. I don't like traps and I smell something bad here." George said.

"This is no trap, I can assure you. This man needs to do business. His life is at stake to ensure that the delivery is made." Jethro said. Giving away far more than he should.

"When is this meeting to be?" asked Henry.

"On Wednesday, next week, at eight o'clock in the evening." Jethro said.

"I'll be there." George said.

Then he turned away from Jethro and walked across the churchyard towards his sister and her family.

Henry looked at Jethro.

"You're not needed around here my friend."

Jethro took this as his time to leave and so did just that.

CHAPTER 19
Dereliction from Duty

Mr William had wasted no time in making sure his version of events, on the capture of the contraband in Frog Firle, was reported directly to his superiors, at Customs House in London. Once his horse had been brought from the farrier's and Mrs Damson had packed his bag, he rode into Lewes and caught the stage to London, report in hand.

He had left instructions for Mark to remain at Newhaven and to spell Jack, with the guard duties, at the Customs House, until he could arrange for the contraband to be moved to a more secure place.

The first night was quiet. Jack and Mark talked about all sorts of thing. Mark found it very interesting to listen to Jack telling him about how the town had grown up since he was a boy and the work that was being done to have a bridge built over the river. He said that it appeared that the main problem had been that the river was in regular use by coasters going up the river, as far as Lewes. They would still need the use of the river but traffic coming along the coast also needed to cross. So the design had to cope with both forms of traffic needs.

Mark was happy not to be working with Mr Johnson. It was a cold night and he didn't like riding over the Downs when it was cold. His room, being high up in the rafters of Mr William's house, got very cold at night. Jack would have a good fire going in the Customs House.

Mark's room was small, with just his bed, a dressing table, chair and wash stand. He had few needs, there was space to hang up his clothes and he used the dressing table to clean his weapons. At the end of his bed was his trunk, where he kept the few possessions he had.

He would need to go out later. He was to relieve, Jack at the Customs House, at about 10 o'clock tonight and stay there until 8 o'clock tomorrow morning. But first it was nearly dinner time. Mrs Damson was always punctual serving her meals. She could be quite sharp if people were late and the food, she had spent time preparing, was allowed to get cold.

Tonight Mark had been told that dinner would be at 8 o'clock and instead of having it in the kitchen, with Mrs Damson, he was to have his meal with Mrs Williams. He didn't understand why she'd invited him that night. Mrs Damson said that Mrs Williams had wanted some company tonight. She didn't want to eat alone.

Because of this invitation, Mark decided that he would look in his trunk and find some better clothes to wear, instead of his usual working clothes. He found a good blouse, a finer pair of trousers and a pair of shoes, instead of boots. Once dressed, he looked him self up and down and was pleased with what he saw.

It was nice to be wearing something special. He remembered that he had told his mother, when she packed these, that there would be no reason for him to need such clothes. She was right, he was wrong!

Mrs Williams was a fine woman, a few inches taller than Mark and well built but shapely. Mark had started to notice such things since a few nights ago, when he was in the barn with Barbara.

Mrs William's hair was brown and her face had sharp features but not ones that gave her face any lack of pleasant character. She had blue eyes, a pair of thin lips around a largish mouth, which hid gleaming white teeth. He thought that she was about thirty five years old, a couple of years older than his mother.

A bell sounded in the hallway, at five to eight. This was the warning that dinner was about to be served. He left his room and walked down the narrow staircase, leading to the next floor. Here would be found the main bedrooms, some guest's bedrooms and a sitting room, used by Mr and Mrs Williams. In this room they would either retire, after the day ended, prior to going to their respective bed rooms. Or it was here that they would entertain guests, after a meal.

As he walked along the corridor, towards the main staircase, he found himself passing Mrs Williams bedroom just as she was coming out.

"Good evening Mark." She said, greeting him with a smile.

"Good evening Mrs Williams." Mark replied.

He moved aside to let her move in front of him, towards the stairs. Instead of passing by she stopped and took his arm.

"You can be the man of the house tonight, as Mr Williams is away on business." She said, as she squeezed his arm.

This surprised Mark, Mr Williams had been away on business before and on those occasions he had never been invited to join her for dinner. In fact she said that she preferred to eat alone, if he was away, often turning down invitations to eat with friends.

They reached the top of the main staircase as Mrs Damson was crossing the hallway, at the bottom of the stairs. She was carrying plates for their meal. As she passed she looked up the stairs and saw the two of them starting to descend. She smiled, as much to herself as to them.

"Your dinner will be ready very soon Sir." She said, addressing Mark rather than Mrs Williams.

Had she mistaken him for Mr Williams? No she was present when he left for London this morning. She would have known if he'd returned. Mrs Williams looked at Mark and smiled.

"You appear to be the man of the house already Mark, I'll have to ensure that you keep up your end, won't I?"

On reaching the bottom of the staircase they stood aside to allow Mrs Damson to return to the kitchen. Mark reached the dining room door and stood to one side to allow Mrs Williams to enter before him. When she reached her chair, at the end of the table, Mark took hold of the chair back and pulled it out so that she could be seated.

He had watched his father's butler do this for his mother, many times. Once she had sat on the chair Mark gave the seat a push so that she was closer to the table and her place setting.

"Thank you Mark, my husband never does that for me." She said, as she turned and looked into his eyes.

He noticed that there was a sparkle in her eyes and a smile across the whole of her face. Marks eyes strayed down to the expanse of Mrs William's abundant cleavage had was now well in view.

Mark started to move to the place he sometimes sat at when he had been invited to dine with Mr and Mrs Williams, mostly when his parents had visited. The place setting was not there.

Mark looked along the table and there was a place setting at the head of the table, the place normally reserved for Mr Williams.

"Take your seat Mark. You're a man now, so you can sit at the man of the house's seat." Mrs Williams smiled.

As Mark walked back along the table to his seat, he was wondering what she had just said – 'you are a man now'. He still had many years to go before he could be considered to be a man, in anyone's eyes. Still pondering that point he sat down and looked along at Mrs Williams.

It was only now that, in the candle light, he could see that Mrs Williams was a very pleasant looking woman. Tonight she had dressed in clothes that showed off her figure and especially her full cleavage. There was not much being left for his imagination. He found himself going red.

Mrs Williams smiled, picked up a small bell by her side and rang it a few times, to summons Mrs Damson to serve their meal.

"I presume that you're ready Mark." She said teasingly.

Mrs Damson came into the dining room, carrying another covered dish and placed it on the side table. She picked up one plate and brought it over and set it before Mark. She then returned to the side table, picked up one of the covered plates and returned. She lifted up the cover and looked into Mark's eyes.

"Help yourself to whatever you fancy tonight." She said.

Mark looked at the plate and saw rough cuts of mutton. He looked back at her and thanked her. Using his fork, he took a couple of pieces of the mutton.

Mrs Damson looked at him, "You'll need more than that if you are to keep your strength up tonight." She said.

"That's alright, Mrs Damson, I've a sleeping duty at the Customs House tonight, nothing taxing." He replied.

"You never know when you'll require your strength, isn't that right Mrs Williams?"

Mrs Williams just gave a knowing smile, "You never know what is around the corner these days?"

Mrs Damson looked at Mrs Williams and they both smiled, she then replaced the cover and walked up to Mrs Williams and repeated the process with her, without the need to ask her to take more to build up her strength, she knew what she wanted tonight.

Once this was done she returned to the side table and picked up the second covered plate. Again she served Mark first. She removed the cover, offered the contents to him. This plate consisted of various vegetables, carrots, swedes and parsnips. Mark took a few and thanked Mrs Damson.

After she had served Mrs Williams she placed the plate on the small table and left the room. She closed the door behind her, leaving them to enjoy their meal

Mark was not sure how to make small talk with Mrs Williams. He had never had a conversation with her on any subject. In fact he had only previously spoken to her a few times, twice to ask Mr Williams whereabouts and twice to ask about how the household works and what was expected of him. For this, he had been referred to Mrs Damson.

"Mrs Damson does cook a good meal." He said, after finishing this first mouthful of food.

At the evening meals, when Mr Williams was at home, the meal was generally taken in silence, only broken when Mr Williams wanted to chastise those present.

"I only employ staff who can satisfy the men in my house."

This again brought redness to his face. He was thinking of Barbara and how she had satisfied him. Surly Mrs Williams was not aware of this? He lowered his face in the hope that, from the length of the table, she couldn't see the colour of his face.

"Did I embarrass you in some way Mark?" Came a teasing remark, from his table companion.

"No, not at all Madam." Mark lied.

"I felt embarrassed for talking during the meal, that's all."

There was a gap now in the talking, as they both devoured their meals. Each time Mark looked up and along the table towards Mrs Williams she seemed to be picking up a carrot or parsnip, with her fork, and taking it, tip first into her open mouth and smiling at him as she did so.

Mark didn't understand what was happening but, for some reason, he felt stirring, very much like when Barbara laid him on the hay. What with his face going red and this, he felt very uneasy.

Mark knew that he would have to get up to serve himself to the pudding. He was worried that what was stirring, would show out against the thin material of his trousers.

He tried not to look in her direction anymore or think of what had been happening tonight or with Barbara the other evening. In this way he hoped that he could control himself.

Mrs Williams realised what effect her actions were having on Mark. She hadn't had so much fun, with a young man, since she was a teenager herself. In those days she led on the boys but backed away before she went too far. Tonight she intended to go all the way and have her way with this handsome young man

With Mr Williams it was just a routine. Every Friday night he would ask her to come to his room at nine thirty. She would undress, lay on his bed and he would do as he wished.

"Did you enjoy that Mark, even the carrots?" Mrs Williams asked, in a playful manner, as Mark laid down his knife and fork, after taking the last mouthful of the food.

"Yes, thank you. That was a fine piece of mutton." Mark replied.

"And the vegetables, how did you find them?" She enquired, looking him straight in the eye.

"Satisfying I hope?"

"They were fine as well." He replied.

The way she was looking at him and the sight of her breasts, pushing against the thin material of her blouse, started up all his thoughts again. His face reddened but he hoped that she wouldn't notice.

To his horror she asked if he was alright, his face seemed to be red. He reassured her that he was alright.

Just then Mrs Williams reached out and picked up the bell again and rang it to summons Mrs Damson so she could clear away the plates.

Mrs Damson arrived a few moments later and brought with her the pudding, an apple pie. This was Marks favourite. He had enjoyed this many times and commented on the fact, each time. She placed it on the small side table, then came over to Mark, to clear away his plate.

She had also noticed that his face was red, but said nothing about it. It appeared that Mrs Williams dress, with no doubt her actions and what she had been saying was having its desired effect on Mark.

She looked down at Mark, as she gathered up the plate, and noticed that there were stirrings down below. This brought a smile to her face and a bit of the devil arrived.

"Have you dropped something down you trousers Mr Mark?"

Mark had no reason to look down. He knew what she was referring to.

"Nothing to worry about, thank you Mrs Damson."

"Don't be shy Mark." Mrs Williams said, "I'm sure that Mrs Damson would be pleased to wipe it off for you, won't you Mrs Damson?"

"It would be my pleasure." She said, holding a cloth in her hand, so that she could use it for the purpose.

"That's very kind of you but it's not necessary." Mark insisted.

Having had her bit of fun, Mrs Damson went to the other end of the table, after placing Mark's plate on the side table. She leant forward and whispered something into Mrs William's ear.

"That big?" She exclaimed.

"Oh yes." Mrs Damson replied, as they both looked in Marks direction.

If he hadn't got a red face by then he sure as hell had now. He didn't know what to do. He felt like running out of the dining room and back to his bedroom. His mother had always told him that a gentleman never left the table until the ladies had left the room. He didn't feel much like a gentleman at that moment.

Mrs Damson finished picking up the plate in front of Mrs Williams, then she gathered together any of the used plates and cutlery and set out the plates, forks and spoons for the pudding. She left the two of them together to finish their meal. Only once they had both gone upstairs would she come back and cleared the room.

"That was a fine meal, thank you Mrs Damson." Mark said.

"Thank you Mister Mark, I hope you enjoy the rest of the evening as much." She said, with a knowing smile, that Mark didn't understand.

Once she had left the room and closed the door firmly behind her, Mrs Williams got up and went to the side table to serve her self with apple pie.

"Mark, are you coming up for the apple pie?" She enquired.

Mark started to rise from his chair but as he did so he felt himself brushing against the edge of the table.

He glanced down and saw that his trousers were very much distorted and it would be obvious to Mrs Williams what was causing it, as Mrs Damson had done a few minutes earlier. He sat back down, but not before Mrs Williams had noticed what had occurred.

She smiled to herself, the carrots and parsnips had had their desired effect on Mark, she thought. She had also undone a couple of buttons, at the front of her blouse, while she stood at the small table, without him being aware of her doing so. What extra they would reveal will play their part now. After serving herself to a slice of the apple pie she turned towards Mark.

"Are you not having any pie today?" She enquired.

"I think I'll give it a miss today. That meat was more filling than I'd expected." He replied.

She turned her head back to the small table.

"I find meat quite filling as well but I always have room for Mrs Damson's pie. Would you like me to service you Mark?" she asked, without looking around at him.

He was grateful for this and accepted her offer.

She cut him a slice of the pie, put it on a plate and brought it over to him. Mrs Williams manoeuvred her self so that she was able to stand sideways towards Mark's shoulder, before she lent forward to place his plate in front of him. Being a polite young man he was sure to turn his head to look at her, as he thanked her. His eyes would be so close to her chest he couldn't but get a full view of what she had on offer.

Mark did turn his head, towards her, as she lent forward to place the plate, in front of him. What he saw, right in front of his face, was the sight of Mrs William's right breast nearly falling out from her blouse. Having seen Barbara's he could now see that they came in different shapes and sizes. The one he was observing, right now, was larger than Barbara's but was it as firm? He asked himself. Not that he expected to find out, after all this was his boss's wife. As his eyes eventually met hers she smiled at him.

"There you are. I'll make a man out of you before the nights out." She said in a low, sultry voice.

This gave her the opportunity to look further down, as she moved back a bit, to see what Mrs Damson had described to her earlier. Yes, there was a man down there waiting for her.

As they eat their apple pie, they kept their thoughts to themselves. Mark didn't look up once and Mrs Williams decided to keep her own council. If she wanted to follow through with her plans, for this night, she had to let his trousers subside, so he felt comfortable leaving the room.

Eventually, at the end of the meal, they both looked up and faced each other, eyes meeting eyes. In some way Mark had the idea that Mrs Williams knew exactly why he hadn't gone to serve himself with the apple pie, but this fact didn't stir him again. He found that he appeared to be able to control himself now.

Again Mark noticed how pleasant Mrs Williams appeared, as she sat in the candle light.

"Shall we retire now Mark?" she asked and held out her hand for him to take and lead her out of the dining room.

"I'll gladly escort you upstairs Mrs Williams, this has been a very good evening but I'll soon need to change for my duties at the Customs House." He replied, as he rose from his chair.

"Who'll guard me in this big empty house tonight?" She asked. "With Mr Williams away in London, I'm sure that he wouldn't want me to be left completely alone tonight."

Mark could see the reasoning behind what she was saying but he had his orders from Mr Williams to guard the Customs House, he had said nothing about looking after his wife's safety.

"When Mrs Damson goes home I'll ensure that all the windows and doors are secure. When I leave you can secure the main door behind me. You'll be completely safe then." He said, reassuringly.

Demurely she replied "I do hope so Mister Mark or you'll feel very bad if harm comes to me, in my bed."

Mark walked along the table and took Mrs Williams hand. He didn't notice her glance down towards his trousers. Taking his hand she rose and put her arm into his, ready for him to escort her upstairs.

They left the dinning room and entered the hallway. Mark looked over to the clock, standing by the main door. It showed nine thirty. This surprised him as it hadn't seemed an hour and a half ago since he came down for his evening meal. He had thirty minutes to prepare himself for his duty and ensure that the house was secure.

They both climbed the stairs to the first floor, Mark taking the left hand side and Mrs Williams the right, still holding firmly on to his arm. When they reached the top of the stairs Mark started to guide her to the left to take Mrs Williams into the sitting room, where she normally retired after the evening meal. The room was just to the left of the top of the stairs but it appeared that Mrs Williams had different ideas. She held his arm tightly and instead guided Mark to the right. They walked down the corridor leading to the bedrooms. She had given him no indication that she was tired, she seemed in good spirits.

"I was thinking of letting Barbara go. What do you think Mark?"

This was very much out of the blue. It took Mark a few seconds to gather his thoughts and find a suitable answer to her question.

"I'm sorry; I don't understand what you mean?" Was all he could think of to say.

By this time they had arrived outside Mrs William's bed room and she let go of his arm and turned so that her back was against her doorway. She looked into Mark's eyes and smiled.

"I don't want Barbara to work here anymore. Her mind isn't on her work and she is becoming sloppy in her cleaning."

"If I talk to her and she improves will you keep her on?" Mark asked.

Mrs Williams had reached behind her back and opened her bedroom door, pushing it open so that Mark could see inside, for the first time.

"Do you want her to stay then Mark? If so we can talk about it."

She reached out and took his hands and backed into her bedroom.

He had never been into a ladies bedroom before, not even his mothers. The smells were different to that of any other of the rooms in the house. There was a smell of flowers and scent wafting lightly around.

Her voice brought him back from his muddled thoughts.

"Close the door behind you." She said, as she released his hands.

Mark obeyed, turned around and closed the door. He turned around and found Mrs Williams sitting at the foot of her bed. She indicated he should come and sit beside her.

Mark felt very nervous. Barbara was a woman of his own age and she frightened him the other night, gave him much pleasure but still frightened him. Mrs Williams was as old as his mother, although at the moment looked younger.

"I'm alright stood here." He said, about three feet from her.

"Barbara was telling cook about how she found you in her father's barn the other night. When you should have been over this side of the river, helping Mr Williams."

What had she just said? He didn't believe Barbara would be telling anyone about what they did. Now, here he was being told, by his boss's wife that not only did she know what had happened but she was in a position of being able to tell Mr Williams why he was delayed. If she did this, he would lose his position here and more than likely be sent back to continue his training in his father's area. He decided to bluff it out and pretend that nothing had happened.

"She came to tell me that her father had just set off across the river and that he wouldn't be back for some time that is all." He said, but he realised it lacked sincerity.

She smiled back at him, "Your friend down there is telling me a different story." She said, indicating with her index finger, the bulge was back in his trousers.

Mark instinctively placed his hands across the offending area, hoping that out of sight, out of mind, for both of them.

"According to cook, you laid down in the hay, allowed Barbara to undress you and then ride you like a fresh young filly, on its first gallop in the spring. Or is Cook lying to me Mark?" Her face was more stern now, challenging Mark, making him understand that she held the lives of both Barbara and his in her hands.

"I don't need a girl here who is only interested in getting into my men's trousers." She said.

"That only happened once and then not in your house Mrs Williams." Mark pleaded.

"I only have your word for that, Mark." She said sternly. "How do I know that she hasn't been undressing my husband whenever she cleans his room?" She asked.

Mark thought quickly, "She's not like that Mrs Williams. She would never betray your trust in her."

"Come here Mark." She said gently, with the smile returning to her face. She reached out both her hands towards him.

He didn't know what to do. If he disobeyed her, Barbara would loose her job, the next day. If he did come to her, what was in store for him, he could lose his job or his life. He had better do as she wished so he took her outstretched hands.

"That's better, now we can talk about you and forget about Barbara for tonight, can't we?" She said, smiling up at him.

Mark looked down and saw her wetting her lips with her tongue.

"Kneel down in front of me Mark."

"Mrs Williams I have to be on guard duty in twenty minutes, I can't leave Jack on his own." He said.

But his words went unanswered as she looked into his eyes and completely dismissed his plea that he had to be elsewhere.

She gave his hands an extra pat to insisted that he comply with what she desired. Mark began to realise that he would have to do as she bid. The consequences of disobeying her were far greater than doing what she wanted. Not that he fully understood why he was there in the first place.

As he started too descend to his knees she moved her feet so that his knees could be placed on the floor between her feet. She released his hands, only once she had placed them just above her knees. She moved her hands up his arms and neck, until they both held his face.

Mark didn't know what to do, to look at her face, look at her breasts, or to lower his face even further, to the floor. Mrs Williams took this decision from him by turning his face up towards hers.

He looked into her blue eyes and felt secure. Not the motherly security he felt when he looked into his mothers eyes but the security of being close to a woman who wanted him close to her. Her damp lips started to come closer to his and he felt his head being drawn closed to these lips until both set came into contact.

When he had kissed Barbara, the other night, he had stayed still and let her do the kissing but tonight he felt that he should also kiss back and did so. He felt very uncomfortable between his legs. When he had knelt down he had his thighs together and that was now causing him discomfort. Mark raised himself up slightly and then parted his knees, at the same time moving her feet further apart.

One of her hands reached around his head and kept his lips in contact with hers. He could feel her slightly parting her lips and his with them. There was warmth between them, as their breaths were crossing the gap and intermingling. He then felt something running around his slightly opened mouth.

It took him a few moments to realise that it was her tongue. Their mouths opened more, as her tongue moved further into his mouth and started to interweave with his.

He was really finding it difficult to concentrate with the uncomfortable feeling between his thighs. He took his hand from her knee and adjusted himself so he wasn't distracted.

"I would have done that for you." She said, as she removed her tongue from between his lips and her face slightly away from his.

"I'm fine, thank you." He answered.

"I'm sure you are."

She took his hand from her knee and placed it onto the flesh of her breast, which was now showing from the gap left in her blouse, as she had undone a few more buttons, revealing nearly everything. At the same time she reached down and took his other hand and placed it on her breast.

"Are Barbara's like mine?" She asked.

"It is difficult to say." Mark replied, "She had no clothes on and it was virtually dark."

"Then why don't you take my clothes off?" It seemed to be an order.

With that Mark ran his hands up on to her shoulders and then outwards so that he gathered up the neck line of her blouse and brought it down over her arms. After a short while more and more of her breasts came into view. He found that he couldn't look away. Within a few moments her breasts were in full view.

"If you like what you see, why not take them in your hands."

Mark looked into her eyes and smiled. He felt like when his grandfather had given him his pair of pistols. He wanted to feel their every part, get the feel of them and appraise their balance. These were different but still they were new and he couldn't hold himself back from wanting to know all about them, their feel, their size and how warm and comforting they were.

He noticed that like, with Barbara, as he moved his hands over her breasts, the nipples appeared to harden and this interested Mark. He looked into her eyes.

"As a child you would have taken them into your mouth to get your mother milk." Mrs Williams said. "All the men I have known still like to take them into their mouths. Why didn't you Mark?"

It was not something Barbara had asked him to do but this was a more experienced woman. Mark lent forward and took her left breast into his mouth and this made him feel very happy. The only problem was that he didn't know what to do next. He took his mouth away after a moment.

He looked into her face, feeling very inept. She realised that he lacked experience so she would wait for another time, then his education would really begin.

She stood up, letting his hands slip down her body. Her skirt fell down, with a little encouragement from herself and landed at Mark's feet. All she had on now were lace trimmed pants.

"Take my pants off for me, please Mark." She said.

He placed his hands on her waist, taking hold of her pants and started to draw them down, over her tummy and releasing the sight of her hidden area. He didn't stop there; he continued to take them down to the floor. Once she realised that he had achieved his task she stepped out of her pants and sat back down onto the end of her bed.

"Stand up Mark. Now it's my turn to undress you."

Mark appeared reluctant to obey. She knew that Barbara had undressed him, so couldn't see why he might object to do this now. After all if he was to make love to her he would need to at least have taken off his trousers.

"Mark your not leaving my bed room until you've not only shown me your naked body but made love to me. Do I make my self clear?" This time she was being very assertive.

"But this is very wrong Mrs Williams, your married and to my boss. If he hears of this he'll be very angry with both of us." He pleaded.

"Firstly, if you do as I ask, no one need ever know what has happened here tonight. If you refuse me, I'll tell Mr Williams that you pushed your way into this room, after I had entertained you for dinner, climbed into my bed and forced yourself on me. Who do you think he'll believe?"

Mark realised he had no choice. If only Barbara hadn't told Mrs Damson about them in the barn, he would not be in this predicament. With that he stood up, in front of her. He took of his blouse and untied the belt around his trousers and let them fall to his feet. He was not wearing any pants so he came into full view.

Mrs Williams took a good long look, put her hand out and held him. She looked into his eyes and gave him a sensuous smile.

"Now that wasn't to bad, was it?" She mused.

Mark smiled back. No it wasn't and easier than he thought it would be. She was now being very gentle with him or was she playing with him, he didn't know.

She noticed that he had scratch marks across his chest.

"Barbara seems to have branded you well Mark." She observed.

"Yes she did."

"I'll be far gentler with you, if you can be gentle with me?"

Mark was looking down at her. He knew that he would never be able to look at a lady in the same way again. Her breasts were standing out from her body, tipped by the pert nipples. Lower he could see her tummy rolling out and, although he couldn't see it now, he knew that below that, was her special area, the one he was hoping to be allowed to probe.

"Your shoes are still on Mark."

This brought him back to the task at hand, undressing himself.

"Sorry, I'll take them off now." He spluttered.

He took a pace backwards but forgot that his trousers were around his ankles. He fell onto his backside, much to the amusement of Mrs Williams.

"I haven't had a man falling at my feet for many years. I've never had a naked man falling at my feet." She said, with big grin.

Mark jumped up and quickly took off his shoes and released himself from his trousers.

While he was doing this she got up and went around to the side of the bed. She knelt on the bed and sat back onto her haunches and looked around for Mark. He was now standing at the end of the bed, naked.

"Come around the other side of the bed and join me."

Mark moved around the bed and climbed on to it and sat in the same fashion, directly opposite her.

She smiled and rose up slightly and moved her knees apart. Mark found that his eyes had moved down to the gap that had opened up. His thoughts were broken into when Mrs Williams took his face into her hands and return his gaze back to her eyes.

"That is not for looking at tonight Mark. That requires your special attention." She said, as she moved her hand down across his chest, lingeringly over his tummy and took hold of him again.

With her free hand, she placed Marks other hand between her legs. She placed her fingers over his, while still holding his gaze with her eyes.

Mark had no idea what she expected of him. This hand began to feel the warmth of her body. She started to move her body against his hand and then back away, only to repeat this time and time again.

He noticed that she was closing her eyes and her mouth started to hang open. A smile of apparent satisfaction spread across her face. Mark lent forward and kissed her lower lip and felt a stirring down below. Was it the reaction to the tenderness he felt with that kiss or was it the way her hand was caressing him? He didn't know and for that matter, right now, he didn't care. He was just happy for the moment.

Mrs Williams really wanted Mark now. So she gradually moved her body in such a way that she would end with her back on the bed while at the same time leaving his hand still in contact with her. Mark realised what she was doing and moved his body so as to ease her movement and so that by the time she was laying back, he was kneeling between her legs, with his hand still where she placed it.

She now reached up behind her head and took a grip of the top of the headboard with both of her hands. Using this as a brace she continued to push her body against his hand. Faster and faster she moved until she gave one final push against his hand and remained hard against it.

"Oh Mark, you are a good boy."

She released one of her hands and held it out towards Mark.

"Mark, come closer. You know what I want, what you did with Barbara. I need you to do that for me."

Mark took his hands away from her and placed them on the bedding, beside her chest. He eased his body further up, between her, until the two of them came into union with each other. She smiled and he saw her eyes sparkle.

Their bodies moved together, slowly at the start and gradually the pace increased. Both of them were breathing more shallowly as the pace increased. They were in their own particular worlds but one thing they had in common was that they were both really enjoying each others bodies.

He opened his eyes and looked down. Her eyes were wide open and likewise her mouth. Her body seemed to shake, below him and it rose up, pushing him away from the bed. She let out a slight sigh then her movements stopped and her body collapsed down onto the bed, leaving him disconnected and well above her.

Mark stayed where he was, he didn't know what had just occurred. Had he done something wrong, was she in pain, what had happened?

"Are you all right Mrs Williams?"

A smile came to her face, her eyes focused on Marks and she licked her lips. Her hands went up his arms and around his head. She pulled him down towards her.

"Oh Mark I'm just as right as I've ever been."

Their lips meet and they kept contact for, what seemed to Mark to be a very long time. In fact it was only about a minute. At the end of the kiss she pushed Mark away from her and off her body.

Mark was quite happy to, now, lay beside Mrs Williams. He was very happy with how he felt and what he had experienced tonight. There had been a distinct difference between what had happened in the barn with Barbara and what had happened here. With Barbara he didn't know what was going to happen, what was expected of him, or how he would feel. Tonight, although at first he didn't understand what was happening, once he was naked he was much more aware of what she expected from him. He just hoped he hadn't disappointed her.

After a minute or two Mrs Williams rolled towards Mark and laid her head on his shoulder. Took his arm over her head so that she could move closer to him and placed her hand on his waist.

"Thank you Mark, you were very good. I only whished that I'd understood this some weeks ago, when Mr Williams last went away. If so I would've invited you to dine with me a lot earlier and may be you wouldn't have needed Barbara."

"If it hadn't been for, Barbara you and I wouldn't be laying here now." He replied. He didn't want her to belittle Barbara's roll in how they both came to be here right now.

Her hand started to move across his chest and down over his tummy when Mark heard a sound like a pistol shot. He sat straight up in the bed, discarding Mrs Williams.

"Did you hear that?" he asked.

"What, I wasn't listening to anything but the beat of your heart." she said.

CHAPTER 20
The taking of the Customs House

Tonight George was going to get his consignment back from the Customs House. He had planned it well and with the use of one of the fishing boat from Seaford he was going to get it all back and anything else he could find in the Customs House.

He was taking forty men with him. Some were to assault the Customs House. Some were to guard the area, to ensure that no one tried to prevent their activities. The rest were to help in moving the goods.

The fishing boat was the main part of the plan, provided it arrived on time. This would ensure he could get everything back to Aldfriston with less chance of it being intercepted by the Riding Officers or Dragoons. His brother, Alfred, worked on his fishing boat. He had paid the Captain two sovereigns to go along with his brother's plan. If everything went well, the Captain would also get to keep some of the Brandy and Geneva they brought back.

The plan was to set sail so that it arrived outside the Customs House at nine o'clock that evening. Some of the men travelling with George wouldn't only be helping to load the boat but a few would be travelling back with the fishing boat, to Aldfriston.

A few of the men had left the village earlier. They were ones who were to take their horses over the River Ouse, into Newhaven, to be in a position to take on the Dragoons or Riding Officers. Their journey took them further up the River Ouse, to Stock Ferry. Here they would be able to take their horses over the river, without having to go all the way into Lewes to cross over the bridge.

George and twenty of his men had ridden over the hills to reach Horfe ferry at Newhaven, by eight thirty in the evening. They took the horses into the field, behind the ferryman's barn. Tied them to the fence rails and left John and the youngest member of the party, to look after them.

He was instructed to have George's horse at the ready, in case he needed to escape, if being chased by Riding Officers or Dragoons.

"Remember John, no one takes these horses and you're to have them all ready for us when we return." He instructed.

With all his men safely dismounted and ready for the nights work, George led them towards the Ferryman's house. He took out his pistol and, using its butt, banged on the door.

"Ferryman I need your services." George called out.

The door was opened by Barbara who informed George that her father was not here and that the ferry didn't run at night. This didn't please George one little bit. He turned around the pistol and pointed the barrel at Barbara.

"I don't care what time it is. If your father's not here then you can row me and my men over the river. Now!" He ordered.

Barbara turned to go back into the house, only to find George reach out and grab her by the arm.

"I said that I wanted you to row me over right now." He shouted.

"I was just getting my coat." Barbara said, brushing his hand away.

With that she went into the house, found her coat and headed back past George and, while putting the coat on, walked over to the ferry.

George didn't trust her, so kept his pistol in his hand and followed Barbara to the quay side. She stopped and looked over the edge and walked a few feet then turned around to face George.

"The ferry's here." She said.

"Then after you my dear." Came the reply, but at the same time he motioned two of his men to go down to the ferry before Barbara. He wanted to ensure that she didn't slip the rope and sail off without them.

He watched as Barbara went down into the boat and his two men were in place, he then descended the ladder and took a seat facing Barbara.

George was not a patient man and barked orders for his men to hurry and get into the ferry boat. Once all his men had embarked he gave the order for her to row them over to the other side of the river.

If everything went as planned there would be no one guarding the Customs House. He had left instructions that Jack was to be lured away from the Customs House for a drink or two, so that the coast would be clear for him and his men to do their deed without interference.

While Barbara was rowing George over the river, Mark was lying on Mrs William's bed, away from his duties at the Customs House. As it turned out, this very act saved his life, but Barbara wasn't to know that, at the time.

The current was quite strong. This pulled the ferry further up river than had been intended. Having so many people in the ferry made it much harder work. Had they been fare paying people, Barbara would have asked some to remain on the quay while she took the others over and would return to take them. In the long run this would have got them all over the river much quicker than was possible now.

George was getting very inpatient at the progress they were making. He could see that the fishing boat was entering the harbour and would be outside the Customs House before he and his men arrived.

"Row harder or by gum I'll shoot you girl." He ordered.

"Well if you can do better then you can row." Barbara snapped.

With that she let go of the oars, stood up and dived into the water, letting the current carry her upstream, away from the ferry.

George was caught completely by surprise. He had never expected her to jump overboard and leave them without control of the ferry.

"You two." He said, addressing the two men, one each side of him.

"Take the oars and get us over to the other side."

He was in luck. By chance these two men were from Denton and were Wendy's brothers. They were well acquainted with rowing and of the river currents. Had they just been two of George's men, from Aldfriston, things would have been much different.

It was half an hour since they left the far side of the river and only now that they reached their destination. Once they had tied the ferry onto one of the shackles set into the quay side, they all clambered up the ladder and set off for the Customs House.

"Well done you two. On the way back I want you both to row us back over. Then I'll teach her a lesson she'll not forget." George said.

By this time Barbara had reached the river bank, on the opposite side to that of George and his men. She knew she would have to get home as quickly as she could to get into dry clothes. Her mind was racing. Mark was due to be on duty, at the Customs House tonight. There was no way she could get a warning message to him.

On reaching her home, she raced up the stairs and into her room. Quickly she took off her wringing wet clothes. She had shed her coat in the river. Once dressed, she headed back to the kitchen.

Her mother and father were over the river but she knew that her mother kept a second coat by the door. Barbara was sure that she wouldn't mind her borrowing it. She grabbed it and left the house.

If, what she overheard on the ferry was right, then George Styles and his men were going to attach the Customs House to get some goods. She also knew that with Mark over the other side of the river, his fine horse was in her father's barn.

Barbara started to run to the barn but as she got halfway she thought she could hear some horses in the small field behind the barn. This is where her father let customer's graze their horses. There were not supposed to be any in that field tonight. She heard talking from the field.

What was she to do? If she stayed in the house, when George Styles returned, he may well kill her. She had to flee and get help for Mark. The only person she knew and trusted was Geoff Climpson.

She entered the barn and headed to where Mark's horse was stalled. Having helped Mark clean her and get her ready to ride, so she didn't think that his horse would mind her doing the same tonight. She had ridden her one day. She was a wonderful horse, strong but obedient. Just the type of horse she needed tonight, if she was to flee from George's men.

Quietly she fitted the horses tack and threw over the saddle cloth. She then felt around and found the saddle. It was heavier than she expected but managed to get it off its pegs and carry it over to the horse. With a lot of effort she heaved it onto the horse's back then fastened the girths, tightly. The one thing she didn't need was to have the saddle slip, as she rode away from the barn, only to land at the feet of George's men.

Having got everything in place and as tight as she could, she lead the horse to the barn door. She closed the barn doors and then jumped onto the horses back.

With a sharp slap of the reins, on the horse's neck she urged her forward, swung around the corner of the barn and headed, at a gallop, towards the main track from Seaford to Beddingham.

John and the young man with him were just standing together talking about what they would do with the money they were earning tonight, when they were disturbed by the sound of a galloping horse.

At first they had no idea what was happening or where it came from. Being dark they lost sight of it in a matter of moments.

Once they had gathered themselves together they could now hear the sound of the horse's hooves heading away from them, towards the Downs.

They looked at each other, what were they to do?

"We saw nothing, do you understand." John said.

"But..." spluttered his junior.

"We saw nothing. If George finds out we didn't stop whoever it was, we'll be in big trouble. So we saw nothing, understand?"

The young man understood. It was in both their interests to say they saw no one.

By now George and his men had met up with the party that had crossed at Stock Ferry, to get here. The men on the fishing boat had tied it up against the quayside. The men, who travelled on the boat, were standing on the quayside awaiting their orders.

"Has Jack been taken care of?" George asked.

"Yes, I got his brother to invite him for a meal and then take him for an ale or two. The innkeeper will keep him supplied with enough drink. He won't be coming back tonight." Gordon said.

"Remember to leave a pair of half-ankers of brandy outside the backdoor of the inn when we leave." George ordered.

"Let's get into the Customs House and get our goods back."

The men stormed the front door of the Customs House but found the door locked. Some of them banged on the door but, as there was no one there, they were not likely to have it opened for them.

"Get around the back and see if there's a way in."

Two of the men went around the right hand side and three others took the left hand side. It was not long before they had found a small door at the back. Both the door and the lock were not very strong. The men heaved and very soon it gave way, letting them enter the Customs House.

They raced through the dark building, some falling every few steps, others picking their way more carefully until they reached the main doors.

The door was secured by a large pole across the two doors, held in place by big pieces of iron, shaped to hold the pole in place.

Once the pole was lifted and the doors opened, George and the rest of the men were able to enter.

The first thing George ordered was to find lanterns so that they could see what they were doing. In a few minutes there was sufficient light, in this large room, for them to see all the goods they had come for.

"Right, get to it. I want this place empty." George shouted.

George realised that this was the most dangerous time, when most of his men were moving the goods onto the fishing boat. Everyone here was looking at what was going on and not checking that no one came near the Customs House. He moved away from all the feverish work and moved out towards the men guarding the area, around the Customs House.

What Gordon hadn't taken into account was that, although Jack liked his sister's cooking, he couldn't stand being in the company of his brother-in-law for very long.

After just one pint of Thomas's fine ale, Jack had excused himself to go out side and relieve him self. In fact he just wanted to get back to his room in the Customs House. He would have young Mark to talk to, a much better person to spend the evening with than his brother in –law.

Jack's mind was on getting home. He didn't hear or take any notice of the sounds around him, like the muffled sounds of horses or that of men coughing. He weaved himself through the buildings until he reached the boats that had been brought up onto the quayside.

As the Customs House came into Jacks view, and he passed the last of the big boats on the quay, he could see men moving between the Customs House and the quayside. The lights in the main room were not only lighting up the room but also the area outside the building. These men were in clear view of Jack.

"Hey, what are you doing? In the name of King George I tell you to stop that and put everything back." Jack called, as he started to walk much quicker.

They were the last words Jack ever said, He hadn't seen George Styles heading towards where he was.

George was already holding a pistol, in case of trouble. He raised the pistol and fired at Jack. The shot hit Jack in the forehead and sent him tumbling to the ground.

CHAPTER 21
What have I done?

"It was a shot from the Customs House. Oh my god what have I done?" Mark said, as he sprung up from Mrs William's bed.

"I must go and help Jack." He said, as he headed for the door.

"Mark, be careful." She said, with a certain amount of feeling.

"Will I see you at breakfast?" She enquired.

He turned and looked at her.

"Hopefully I'll see you at breakfast." He replied, then ran from her room, clutching his clothes and shoes.

Along the corridor he ran, up the small staircase and into his bedroom. Until he had thrown his finer clothes onto his bed he hadn't realised he had run through the house, naked. He believed that, other than himself and Mrs Williams, they were the only people left in the house. He hoped that Mrs Damson had, by now, gone to her home.

What he didn't see, in his rush to get to his room, was that Mrs Damson had just reached the top of the stairs, on her way to inform Mrs Williams that she was leaving for her home.

The sight of Mark's naked body, be it just his back, running down the corridor, towards the end staircase, brought a smile to her face. Well Mrs Williams has had her second desert tonight. She turned around and walked back down the stairs. Mrs Williams wouldn't be interested in whether or not she had left.

By the time Mrs Damson had reached the kitchen, Mark was scrambling into his work clothes, tied his belt and, after checking that his pistols were loaded and ready. He slid them into his belt, took up his cutlass and slid it into the place in his belt that had been made to hold it.

Mark thrust his feet into his boots, took up his coat and hat then ran from his room. He continued to run down the staircases and out of the house. His promise to check that the house was secure had gone out of his mind. He intended getting to the Customs House quickly.

He started to run in the most direct route but saw that his way was blocked by men. Some on foot and others on horse back. They were not together but were all looking towards the area of the Customs House.

Mark quickly changed direction and made for the boats drawn up on the quayside. He had walked through them many times, so was confident that he could navigate himself through them and evade these men, until he got nearer to the Customs House.

When he reached the last of the boats, that had hidden him from these men, he could see men scurrying between the main door of the building and the quayside. A man was walking from the Customs House, carrying a lantern. Mark drew back into the shadows of the boats but not too far as he needed to see and hear what was going on.

The man with the Lantern was George Styles. After shooting Jack he had gone back and collected a lantern so that he could check exactly who it was he had shot.

"Who the hell let Jack back here? He should be at the White Hart?"

"Ned, find out how he slipped the guards. This could ruin everything."

"Why did you shoot him George?" Ned asked. "We could have tied him up and left him in the cellar of the Customs House."

Now was not the time to be asking such a question of George, as Ned soon found out. George levelled his pistol at Ned's face.

"If your men had done their bloody job, this wouldn't have happened. If anyone's to take the blame, it's you." He snapped, as he pulled the trigger.

Luckily for Ned this was the pistol George had discharged into Jack and hadn't had time to reload. Ned quickly scurried away and out of George's long reach.

While this was going on, Mark had heard everything that was said. Jack was dead, someone had been meant to keep him away from the Customs House. It appeared that George Styles had only expected Jack to be guarding the consignment. He hadn't been aware that Mark would be there too.

A cold shiver came over Mark. If he hadn't been in Mrs William's bed, it could very well be his body lying on the quayside, not Jack's.

Mark could see there was nothing he could do, by himself. Trying to make his way back to the Comptrollers house could be dangerous. He would be going back passed men looking in his direction, thus more likely to see who he was and apprehend him. He would stay where he was and observe what was happening and, where possible, who was doing what.

Barbara had found that Mark's horse was a wonderful ride. After the initial gallop away from the ferryman's barn, she had brought her down to a canter. Her gait was such that she just ate up the miles. It was not long before she found herself passing through Beddingham and joining the road to Lewes.

Once she was in Lewes she went directly to Geoff Climpson's cottage, tied up Mark's horse and hammered on his door.

It took a few minutes before Geoff came to the door.

"What do you want?" He called, from behind the door.

"Mr Climpson, its Barbara, the ferryman's daughter. There's trouble in Newhaven." She shouted back.

Geoff threw open the door and invited her in.

"What's this all about?" He asked.

"George Styles and a lot of men are in Newhaven. He made me row a lot of them over the river, but I jumped overboard halfway over."

Before Geoff could interrupt she continued.

"I gathered, from what George was saying was that they were going to the Customs House to get their goods back. I could see a fishing boat tying up at the quayside near the Customs House and men getting off and heading towards the Customs House." She now paused.

Geoff thought for a few moments. It was then that he realised that the horse she had ridden was Mark's fine mare. There was no way she would have taken that if it hadn't been urgent. Her story was more than likely to be true.

"If what you said is true, then you'd better not go back to Newhaven tonight Barbara." Geoff said.

"Mary, I've to go out. Will you look after Barbara and find her a bed for the night. She'll explain everything."

With instructions shouted to his wife, Geoff grabbed up his pistols, cutlass, coat and hat. Quickly put on his boots and left his cottage.

He knew he would have to travel as fast as he could. For that reason he didn't take Mark's mare as it had already travelled a distance and at some speed. She wouldn't be reliable for the journey back.

He ran to the stables, where he kept his horse. He quickly fitted the tack and the saddle. After ensured that everything was not going to slip he jumped into the saddle and urged him forward.

Geoff couldn't afford to take the same route as Barbara as it would bring him onto the wrong side of the River Ouse, when he arrived at Newhaven. He would head out so that he came in through Southease and Piddinghoe and he would arrive in Newhaven, on the right side of the river.

He was in luck, as he rounded a bend, having passed through Southease, he found himself riding into a Dragoon patrol, heading back to Lewes and their temporary barracks.

"Corporal, I'm Geoff Climpson a Riding Officer, I need your help. The Customs House in Newhaven is being attacked and goods taken."

"We came from there about an hour ago, there was no trouble then." The Corporal replied.

"That may be but someone has ridden hard to tell me and it's a person I trust." Geoff said.

"Corporal, lives are at stake, I need you to help me and King George"

The Corporal realised that he would have to help and the troop would have to miss out their beds. He ordered his men to turn around and follow the Riding Officer back to Newhaven.

George was not a happy man. He was snapping out orders and driving the men who were emptying the Customs House, of his goods, and loading them onto the boat.

Within half an hour, everything was loaded into the fishing boat. He had assigned four of his trusted men to accompany his brother and the cargo back to Aldfriston. He trusted his brother but the Captain of the boat was another matter. He may have to be dealt with later, to ensure he doesn't talk to the authorities. The reward that would be offered, after what they had done tonight, would be very large, possibly up to two thousand pounds, enough to bring out the brave, but not the stupid.

The fishing boat left the quay side and headed out of the harbour and back to the sea. It would then set sail for the Cuckmere river mouth. The Captain had said that he didn't expect to be back in Aldfriston until about 7 o'clock, the next morning.

George gathered all the men together, outside the Customs House.

"Right you lot, other than the loaders, the rest of you'll only get half the money promised you. You have failed me tonight. You have risked all of our lives by being sloppy." He paused, no one said a thing.

"Ned, pay off the loaders, the rest of you will get paid once the cargo is unloaded and hidden away. Be at Crow Lane at 6 o'clock tomorrow morning." George ordered.

No one was going to disobey, they would all be there. No one was going to question the money they would now be getting. They understood what had happened and that necks could well be stretched.

"Ned you take your men, gather the horses and get off back home. Take care there may be riders out there. Remember the Dragoons we saw earlier." George said.

George and about fifteen men walked back to the ferry, arriving at the same time as the ferryman and his wife.

George took his pistol, still empty from earlier, pointed it at the ferryman.

"You! Take me and my men back over the river." He ordered.

John looked at his wife and quickly moved to stand between her and George. What was going on and why was the ferry over this side of the river? Barbara was going to come over, in ten minutes time and collect him and her mother.

"I don't understand. Why's my ferry over here?" He asked

"Because that traitorous bitch of yours left us high and dry in the middle of the river, that's why. You're lucky to have the boat at all, if it was not for my men it would have been lost." George reported.

"When I get over the other side I want you to bring that bitch out to me, do I make myself clear?"

John could understand why he was angry, she had a wilful way about her but he had to smile to himself about what she had done.

George trusted John no more than he had his daughter so sent three of his men down into the ferry first. Then he let John get into the ferry but not his wife.

He turned to her, "You can wait here until your husband has got us safely over to the other side and brought me that bitch of a daughter of yours. Then he can come and collect you."

"Do you understand, ferryman, no daughter, no wife."

George then descended the ladder and was the last of his men to get aboard. John wasn't at all happy leaving his wife back on the quay but she was safer over there than coming with him. If Barbara was not there he guessed that George may well take out his anger on whoever is close by and he would prefer it to be him than his wife.

It took John about ten minutes to row across the river and tie up at the other side. Half of the men climbed the ladder and waited on the quay side for George. George told John to climb up next and followed him up the ladder.

"Now go and find that bitch of yours." He ordered, telling two of his men to go with John, so that they ensured that he didn't lie about not finding her.

While George was giving John his orders, the rest of his men got up to the quay side and started to head for their horses.

"Tell the lad to bring him my horse around here." He shouted after them. While he waited for Barbara to appear.

He waited for five minutes but she didn't appear. Just as he was about to stride into the ferryman's house, his men came out.

"She's not here." One of them said.

"Where the hell is she then?" He snapped.

"We don't know but there was a pile of wet clothes in her room, but she's nowhere to be found."

"Right you two wait here, when she returns, you bring her with you, back to Aldfriston. I'll deal with her there." George ordered.

John had listened to what was being said and he was frightened for Barbara. With the two men outside he wouldn't be able to go back over the river for his wife either.

At about this time, Ned and his men were heading towards Piddinghoe when one of the men reported sounds of fast moving men on horses, heading towards them.

They were in luck. Just ahead of them was a track leading off to their left, which ran diagonally away from the road they were on. Unless they were very unlucky these unseen riders would not see them, as they would have to look behind themselves to see him and his men.

They quickly galloped onto this track and a short way up Ned called a halt, so that they made little noise, to attract the attention of the other riders.

In a couple of minutes a group of riders went passed the lane, at a gallop. None of them were looking around, they appeared to be riding with a purpose and if Ned was right, they were after George and all the men that attacked the Customs House.

After a few minutes, Ned gave the order for his men to turn around, get back onto the road and make a hasty return to Aldfriston.

From the time Barbara had arrived at his cottage and Geoff rode into Newhaven was about an hour. How long it had been since Barbara jumped out of the ferry, he didn't know, most likely a couple of hours. He couldn't be sure.

Now he had a troop of Dragoons with him, he felt safer, in taking on George Styles and his men.

CHAPTER 22
Give me your Report

Geoff Climpson and the Dragoons rode into Newhaven and headed for the Customs House. They were all warned to have their pistols at the ready, in case some of the smugglers were still about.

On arriving at the Customs House they dismounted. The Corporal assigned four of his men to stay outside and make sure that they weren't disturbed and a fifth he assigned to look after all the horses.

Geoff led the way into the Customs House, as the smugglers had left in a hurry one of the lanterns was still alight. He looked around and saw that all the contraband, which Graham had captured, was gone.

Where were Jack and Mark? They were supposed to be on guard tonight. He had to find them to get a report on what had gone on tonight.

As he turned around and started for the main door, Mark walked in, tears running down his face.

"They killed Jack." Was all he could say.

"They killed Jack." He repeated.

Geoff walked up to the young man, took him to his chest and held him tight. He so much wanted to question him as to where he was and what had happened but felt that this was not the time.

One of the Dragoons came running into the Customs House.

"There's a body, over there." Pointing towards where the boats were pulled up on to the quay.

Geoff let go of Mark and followed the Dragoon out of the building and over to where the body of Jack lay. He was followed by Mark and the other Dragoons. They gathered around the limp body of Jack.

The Corporal called for the lantern, so that they could see, not only who it was but what had happened to him.

The lantern soon arrived and enabled Geoff to see that it was Jack. He appeared to have been shot in the forehead, at a fairly close range.

"Let's get Jack back into the Customs House." He ordered.

This was picked up by the Corporal who detailed off some of his men to carry Jack's body.

"Mark, you come with me. We'll go into the Comptrollers office and have a talk. I need to know what has happened here tonight. Who was involved and, most importantly, who killed Jack."

Geoff asked the Corporal to get his men to look around and see if they could find anything and see if anyone was still around. When he had done this, come and report to him in the Comptrollers office.

Mark left Geoff to give his orders and started up the stairs to Mr William's office. He had to get a story ready. Particularly why he hadn't been on duty and why he hadn't stopped Jack from being killed.

How was he going to hide the fact that he was in Mrs William's be?

By the time Mark had reached the office Geoff had caught up with him, opened the door and led the way in. Geoff went around the large desk and sat in the leather backed chair. He beckoned Mark to sit in the smaller, oak chair.

"Give me your report young Mark."

Geoff was looking directly into Mark's eyes. Mark felt very uneasy, like when his father had questioned him about a misdemeanour.

"Sir, I had a good dinner with Mrs Williams and returned to my room. As I had half an hour to go before I was due on duty, I laid on my bed and fell asleep." He reported.

"I was suddenly woken up by the sound of a shot. I didn't know what had happened for a few moments. I then remembered that I should have been at the Customs House, guarding it with Jack. I sprung to my feet and gathered up my weapons, coat and hat, then ran out and headed here."

While he was saying this, Geoff was writing it all down. Once he had finished writing he looked up.

"And when you arrived here, what did you see?" He asked.

"I had seen some men on the quayside, so I went though the boats, so they couldn't see me. I was about to break cover when I saw that there were men coming and going, from the Customs House main door. There were three men standing about 10 yards from me, gathered around a body." Mark reported.

"Who were these men?"

"I could see one, holding a pistol in his right hand. It was George Styles. I heard the voice of another and that was a man I only know as Ned." Mark said.

"That must've been Ned Turner." Put in Geoff.

"Who was the third man?"

"I don't know. I could see a little of his face but can't give you a name. I believe I've seen him before, when patrolling with Graham, but I can't remember were." Mark replied.

"What happened then?"

"I thought that I would be of more use if I kept where I was, observed what was going on and who were involved." Mark said. Then continued his report.

"George got very heated. He pointed his pistol and Ned and blamed him for this. It was his men who left Jack through their cordon. He pulled the trigger but, luckily for Ned, it was the same pistol that George had used to shoot Jack. Ned left to find out how Jack got through and George returned to the Customs House. He shouted at the men to work harder."

"How long before they had finished and left?" Geoff asked.

"It took them half and hour to finish loading the fishing boat and then some of his men joined the boat, the rest went with George, to the ferry."

Mark waited for Geoff to finish writing. It took some minutes to write it all out. Geoff looked up straight into Mark's eyes.

"Now again, why were you not at the Customs House?"

"As I said, I had fallen asleep, after having dinner with Mrs Williams."

"I don't believe you young man." Geoff said. "I may not have known you very long but I do know that you're not the kind of person to neglect their duty."

Geoff looked at him for some minutes but there was no reaction from young Mark. He was right, there was something Mark wasn't telling him.

He would have to ask Graham to question him. In the mean time there was nothing to be gained sitting here. He would lock up the Customs House and wait until Mr Williams got back.

"OK young man, you can get off home now. I'll lock up and we'll see what Mr Williams has to say tomorrow."

Mark wasn't happy having to lie to Mr Climpson but there was no way he could tell him what he had been doing, that kept him away from his duty. If he did, he would be sent back to his father and Mrs Williams would be thrown out of her home.

Mark was paying a big price for what had happened in the ferryman's barn, the other night. It was a revelation, a step towards manhood. The only trouble was that such steps can have their repercussions.

It took Mark a long time to get to sleep this night. Many things were going around his head but each time he came back how he felt while making love to Mrs Williams. With Barbara it had been a quick encounter, over nearly before it started. Although he had felt many areas of Barbara's body, with Mrs Williams he hadn't only felt but also seen her completely naked, in the candle light of her bedroom.

Mark eventually drifted off to sleep but was rudely awakened at about seven o'clock, by Mrs Damson banging on his bedroom door.

"You'd better be quick if you want breakfast young Sir."

"Be there soon." He called.

He got dressed and started down the stairs, towards Mrs Damson's kitchen. As he was coming up to Mrs William's bedroom door, it opened and Mrs Williams stepped out.

"Good morning Mark, I hope you had a good night's sleep?"

Mark reached out and took her arm.

"Mrs Williams, no matter what they ask. Last night I had dinner with you and then went to my room." He insisted.

"I don't understand Mark." She said, as she pulled her arm free.

"Jack was killed, last night, while I was in your bed. I should have been with him at the Customs House." Mark snapped.

"I don't understand, Mark, who will be asking?"

"Well Geoff Climpson for one and I expect Mr Williams for another."

Her face lost its colour. If Mr Williams found out about her and Mark her comfortable life would be over. How had she been so silly to risk all this for a bit of fun, with this handsome young man. Her mind went to last night and how much she had enjoyed herself. More than she had done with Mr Williams for very many years. On reflection it wouldn't have been worth all that pleasure, to lose everything she had.

She turned around and retreated into her bedroom but before she closed the door she asked that Mrs Damson bring her up a tray of food for her breakfast.

When Mark arrived in the kitchen he asked if Mrs Damson would take some food up to Mrs Williams.

While she gathered the food together, for Mrs William's tray, she enquired what had gone on at the Customs House, last night. Mark gave her an edited account and told her that Jack had been killed.

Mrs Damson arrived at Mrs William's bedroom door with the tray of food. She knocked on the door and heard a muffled call for her to enter.

"Oh, Margaret, I'm in trouble. If Mr Williams finds out about last night I'll be in so much trouble." Mrs Williams said.

"He'll not hear it from me Madam." She replied and smiled.

"Was he worth it?" She asked

"Last night I thought so, but with this killing I'm not really sure."

Mrs. Damson returned to the kitchen and found Mark still sitting at the table. He had finished his breakfast but appeared to be deep in thought.

"A penny for your thoughts, Master Mark." She said, in attempt to bring him back to today.

"Oh Mrs Damson, what I have done? I was so silly last night. I should have gone back to my room after dinner. Had I done so I would have been there for Jack." He said, looking into her eyes.

"From what I've been hearing, if you'd been there, with Jack, you would also be dead, along side him. How would that benefit anyone?" she said, trying to heal his sorrow over Jack.

"But..." he started.

"There is no 'but' young man. You would be dead and that is an end to it." Mrs Damson said angrily.

With that she turned away and walked out of the kitchen, into the fresh air. She was as much involved in this as anyone. If only she hadn't told Mrs Williams about Mark and Barbara. If she hadn't encouraged Mrs Williams with her plan, to have her fun, with Mark.

It then struck her that when Mr Williams returns from London, all hell would break loose. Questions would be asked. What was she to say? If she kept it to just what she saw, Mark and Mrs Williams would be in trouble. If she left out all she saw or guessed, in connection to Mark and Mrs William's bedroom, she might well keep her job. Just keep to what she saw when she served Dinner would be her best plan.

It came to her that Mark was an honest young man. If he told the truth, then they would all be in enormous trouble. Thinking again, yes he was honest but he was also an honourable person. As such he would say nothing about being in Mrs William's bedroom.

Barbara had a restless night. Mrs Climpson had looked after her well enough but the bed was not hers, the sounds around were also not familiar. She woke at daybreak and listened to the morning chorus. She stayed in the bed until she heard movement in the house and then got up and dressed in last nights clothes.

"Good morning Mr Climpson." Barbara greeted, as she entered the scullery.

"Good morning Barbara, did you sleep well?" He asked.

"Not really. I had so much on my mind."

"Mark is alright, he didn't get involved but was able to watch what was going on and made a full report to me afterwards. He gave me the names of some of those involved, to add to what you had already told me."

This pleased Barbara. Mark had been on her mind, he had told her earlier that he was on duty in the Customs House last night.

She suddenly remembered that she had Marks's horse tied up outside the Mr Climpson's cottage.

"I must get back to Newhaven, I have Mark's horse." She said, as she got up and headed for the door.

"Come back young lady and have breakfast. Then you can ride back to Newhaven. I'll come with you, to make sure your safe." He ordered.

"I'll be safe. At this time there'll be few people around." She protested.

"George Styles can be a very nasty man. He burned down the Seaford Magistrates home, just as a lesson to him. Hopefully in a few days time he'll have a laugh about you jumping overboard. Something he may well have done himself, in your place. But until then you'll need to keep your head down." Geoff explained to her.

Barbara realised he was right. It would be safer if he accompanied her back home. He could explain to her parents where she'd been last night.

Once the two of them had finished their breakfast they put on their coats and boots. Geoff said goodbye to his wife and Barbara thanked her for giving her a bed overnight. It took them an hour to ride back to the Ferryman's house.

Geoff would like to have ridden there on the other side of the river but he needed to make sure that Barbara arrived home safely. When they arrived, there was no sign of the two men George Styles had left outside, to await her return.

Barbara took both of the horses into the barn and tended to them. Rubbed them down and made sure that they both had food and water. In the mean time Geoff had found her father and explained what she had done and where she had been, overnight.

Barbara walked into the kitchen and found her mother and father seated at the table, talking to Geoff. Her mother got up and ran to her and took her into her arms.

"You silly, silly girl, what were you thinking of. You could have been killed by the river or Mr Styles." She said, holding her very tightly.

"I'm sorry mum but I was trying to stop them going over there, Mark..."

"I know love. He is strong, he could look after himself. I only have one child and you are important to both of us." She interrupted.

Geoff stood up, nodded to Mr Ferris and picked up his hat a left the house. Mr Ferris followed him and they walked side by side to the quay.

The ferry was tied up where he had left it after he had rowed over to collect his wife, earlier this morning. Mrs Ferris had returned to stay the night with their friends. She got up early, hoping that all was well and that John would see her and come over to take her home.

As they crossed the river Geoff looked at Mr Ferris.

"Keep Barbara close for the next few days. George Styles may well come back to take out some of his anger on her."

There was no need for him to answer, he knew the danger she was in. He would ensure that she kept her head down.

Geoff walked to the Comptrollers house and enquired when Mr Williams was due to return. He was told that they expected him back later this afternoon.

Geoff went on to the Customs House and let himself in and went up to the office. He found some paper and an envelope. He started to write a couple of letters. The first one was to Mr Downer, Mark's father. He told him the brief outline of what had happened and that he thought it would be good for Mark if he came here as quickly as possible, before Mr Williams went off half cocked.

The second letter was for Graham, again outlining what had happened and that he needed him to come to Newhaven as quickly as he could.

He had just finished the second letter and sealed it when Mark walked into the office.

"Is there anything I can do, Mr Climpson?" Mark asked.

"Yes, you can ride over to Seaford and give this letter to Graham. Don't wait for a reply or anything else, just come directly back here. Do I make myself clear?" Geoff ordered.

"Yes Sir." Mark said, taking the letter and walked out of the office.

Geoff looked at the clock on the office wall, it was half past eight. If he was quick, he could catch the stage coach that went to Chichester, leaving Newhaven at nine o'clock. His letter to Mr Downer would be in his hands before nightfall. If he was the man he thought him to be, Mr Downer would ride over to here, first thing tomorrow.

When Graham received Geoff's note he sat at Mrs Jefferies kitchen table and read it through a couple of times. He couldn't understand what had been going on and in particular why Geoff doubted what Mark had reported.

At first he was going to ride over to Newhaven and speak to Mark but then he decided not to. Geoff had said that there would be a meeting, in the Comptroller's office at seven o'clock tomorrow morning, Graham was to be there.

CHAPTER 23
The trial

Mr. Downer received Geoff's letter earlier than expected and set off immediately, to be by his son's side. When he arrived in Newhaven he headed immediately to Mr William's house and sent for Geoff.

Mr. Williams arrived home not long after Mr Downer's arrival and found himself confronted with a situation he couldn't have envisaged and one that would undo all the hard work he had done in London.

When Geoff arrived, Mr Downer asked him to present his report to both Mr Williams and himself. Geoff gave them the facts that he had discovered, mainly from Mark, but also what Barbara had told him. He also stated that he didn't believe all Mark had told him.

After talking to Mr. Williams, Mr Downer decided not to go and see his son but would wait until tomorrow. Mrs. Damson took him up to the guest's room and offered to bring him a meal, which he accepted.

From the shouting that went around the house, after Mr. Williams arrived back home, Mark had decided to keep very much out of his way. He didn't know his father had arrived otherwise he would have gone to see him and asked his advice. As it was he thought that he would escape Mr Williams, in the morning, by going off to Seaford before he was about.

Before Mark went to his room, after dinner, Mrs Damson gave him a message, from Mr Williams. Mark was to report to his office tomorrow morning. Mr Williams rarely got to his office before ten o'clock in the morning so Mark could have a late breakfast. He would have a lay in until nine thirty.

These plans were scuppered and, as he stood outside Mr William's office, in the Customs House, his mind drifted back to earlier that morning when he had been told he was to report earlier than he had expected.

It was about six o'clock, just as he was stirring from his sleep, when there was a knock on his door,

"Come in." He called.

The door opened and in walked Mrs. Williams, dressed in what looked like a night dress.

"Mark you mustn't tell my husband about what you were doing on Tuesday night. If you do he'll destroy me." She pleaded.

He noticed a tear running from her eye and realised she was very afraid.

"Don't worry Mrs. Williams. What went on between us is our business and no one else's. I don't expect you to tell Barbara either."

"No, her job is safe for as long as she needs it." She said hurriedly.

"I'm staying out of your husband's way for as long as I can. Last night he sent a message I was to report to his office this morning. As he won't be there until about ten o'clock, I'll stay here until then."

"Oh I forgot to say, he wants to see you in his office at 8 o'clock this morning and you're not to be late." Mark was not sure why she hadn't said this when she came in.

"Thank you I really needed to know that." Mark said, more to himself than as a reply to Mrs. Williams.

Mark got off his bed and stood there in his nightshirt.

183

They stood there looking at each other for a moment and then Mark took up the hem of his nightshirt and raised it above his head and discarded it on his bed. He didn't feel embarrassed to be naked in front of Mrs. Williams.

Sex was not on his mind at that moment. As he looked at her, she smiled. He saw what he construed as a certain amount of desire in her eyes. She untied the string that held the top of her nightdress together and slipped the top of the nightdress off her shoulders, letting it fall to the floor. Now they stood facing each other, naked. She stepped forward and stood with her toes touching his and her lips just inches from his.

Mark knew what was happening was foolish but so was the other night and he had enjoyed that. He put his hands onto her waist and pulled her closer to him and at the same time their lips met for a lingering kiss. Without realizing what they were doing they had manoeuvred themselves so that they were now standing alongside Mark's bed.

Mrs. Williams looked at him and release her self from his hold, climbed onto his bed and lay back, inviting him to join her.

Mark didn't need the invitation. As soon as she was lying on the bed he joined her, placing his knees between her legs. She reached up to his chest and ran her hands around to his back, pulling him into her

This was not like the other night, where they both enjoyed and explored each other's body, this was animal passion. Each one of them was trying to get their own gratification, from the others body.

The only thing to spoil this was the fact that Mark's bed was a little to close to the wall and as the passions rose, so the bed started to bounce off the wall, banging in time to their movements. At first they hadn't realised what was happening but there was a sudden look of fear from Mrs. Williams's eyes. She heard the sound and knew this could be heard all over the house.

"Stop this, oh stop this." She called.

Mark thought that she wanted him to stop making love to her and was about to move away from her. She realised what he was about to do, "No stop the bed hitting the wall." She ordered.

He looked around and there, on the chair by his bed was his coat. He reached over, grabbed it and hung it over the head of the bed with as much material as he could get between the bed and the wall. She smiled up at him and together they soon returned to the rhythm they were enjoying.

Mrs. Williams ran her hands up over his back, pushing her finger nails into his young skin.

As her hands passed down his back he increased the speed of his movements and as her hands gradually moved back up to his shoulders, so the speed decreased. After a few forays up and down his back she settled for the faster movements of her young lover.

She couldn't spend long with Mark. The sooner she could return to her bedroom, the least chance she had of being caught by her husband.

The bed was still creaking and the faster he went the more noise was coming from it. He so much wanted to decrease the noise of the bed but the way her hands were moving over his back he found that his body was involuntarily moving in response to where her hand were. Mark didn't seem to care about the noise anymore.

He opened his eyes and looked down into hers. She smiled and then closed hers as she moved her hands down to she take a firm grip of his buttocks. Her body rose up from the bed, in one almighty push towards him. At the same time Mark felt the same feeling rush through him, which he had during his first encounter with Barbara.

"Oh Mark, Oh Mark." She said.

She released his buttocks and ran her hands up to his chest, then to his face, cupping his face in her hands.

"Oh Mark, that was wonderful."

But instead of holding him to her she pushed him away.

"I must get back to my room now." She said, swinging her feet to the floor.

Mark was stunned by this. He had expected her to stay for a while but she was giving him the brush off, dismissing him like a servant. By the time he had taken this in she was slipping herself into her nightdress and heading out of his room. As she left she turned and with a loud voice she called back to him

"And don't be late at the Customs House, eight o'clock remember." With that she closed the door and went off down the stairs to her room.

Mark flopped back onto his bed, face down. There was no need for him to rise yet. If he was not going to escape the inquisition by Mr. Williams, he may as well stay here for a while and get up at seven. The cook will have served the breakfast for the Mr and Mrs Williams, by then, so he could slip into the kitchen and eat with her. This way he could keep out to the way of both Mr. and Mrs. Williams, for totally differing reasons.

He couldn't remember how long he had been lying there, or if he had drifted back to sleep. All he remembered was that out of nowhere came a gentle hand resting on his buttock and gently massaging it. At first he didn't believe it, he thought it was his mind playing tricks with him and re-enacting the feelings he got when Mrs. Williams first put her hands there, earlier.

He put his hand around to brush off whatever was there but discovered that there a hand there. Had Mrs. Williams returned for more? He would have expected to have heard her coming up the stairs. He raised his head from the blanket and looked around. To his surprise and pleasure he found himself looking into the eyes of Barbara.

"I thought you'd like a mug of tea Mister Mark." She said, showing him the mug in her hand.

"Do you always sleep with nothing on?" She asked.

Did he tell the truth or fib a little. If he didn't want a mug of hot tea all over him, he'd better lie a little, after all he was in enough trouble already today.

"No I was a bit hot so I ended up taking off my night shirt and lying on the bed." It hadn't been a particularly cold night but Barbara didn't think it was hot enough for this.

As he turned over it didn't occur to him that she wouldn't be dressed but as he looked up, he saw that, like Mrs. Williams earlier, she was naked.

He looked around and saw her clothes in a pile by his bedroom door. He was grateful that she'd closed the door so no one saw them together.

Barbara ran her hand up his leg and onto his stomach.

She circled his tummy button with her fingers and headed back down to his legs. Mark felt that this was not right. Even though his body was saying different, he wanted to stop. He reached down and took her hand.

"Not here and not today." He said.

"You can't waste such as that Mister Mark, it would be criminal. I know what a law abiding young man you are." She said, in a teasing voice.

She smiled down at him and, before he could stop her, she was onto the bed and sat astride him. With only one hand free he had totally misjudged her desires and his ability to resist her.

He released her hand and placed both his hands onto her breasts. They were not as big as those of Mrs. Williams but firm and her nipples fitted neatly into the centre of the palms of his hands. Barbara lifted up her hips and moved forward and above him, feeling him against her she slowly lowered herself down so that her body devoured him.

Mrs. William's may have been an awakening for him but Barbara was here to get the most from him. She moved at an ever increasing speed. Mark looked up at her face and saw that her mouth was open. She appeared to be gasping in air to drive her on to greater and greater heights.

He could feel that the explosion he had let go, so early in the barn the other day, was about to happen again and there was no way he could stop it. He had been trying to hold on but his body could only take so much of this.

She looked down at him but didn't smile. Her face was impassive to what he had done, she was still working for what she wanted and before long produced a massive shudder up along her body.

Barbara now looked down at Mark,

"Your tea should be ready to drink now Mister Mark." She teased.

She bent forward and kissed him passionately, still not removing herself from him. Mark found his hands following the contours of her body until they reached her hips, there they stopped and he pressed her closer to him.

"I have my chores to do Mister Mark."

With that she raised herself up so that she was kneeling astride him. She then rose and stood above him, looking down and into his eyes.

"When I've finished my chores and you yours, I'll be at the barn."

With that she stepped over him and down onto the floor, walked over to her clothes and dressed, with her back still to him. Without turning around or saying anything more she left his room as soon as she was dressed.

Mark was very confused, up until this week he hadn't been able to even hold or kiss a girl. Now, here he was with a girl his age and an older woman, near the age of his own mother, climbing into his bed and making love to him.

Everything he had heard and stories told by older men, it was the man who went after the woman for their own wanting. No thought was ever paid to the desires of the woman. The man was the dominant creature and so had a woman for his gratification either from marriage, finding a woman of easy virtue or, as he had heard, paying a woman.

From his confused mind, he could only assimilate himself as a man of easy virtues being prayed on by woman who were not being satisfied by their current partners. Yes he did believe Barbara had a steady boyfriend, what he didn't know was that he was married and Barbara was his mistress.

Mark stood up and reached out for his pocket watch, it was nearly seven o'clock. It was time for him to go to the kitchen and have his breakfast.

He poured some water from the jug, into the bowl on the small table and washed his face and arms. Mark reached out and took the cloth to dry him self before getting dressed. It wasn't long before he was ready to go downstairs. He had chosen a pair of soft-shoes, as he didn't want his movements to be heard around the house.

"Good morning Mister Mark." Mrs. Damson said, as he entered the kitchen,

"Not eating with the Master today?"

"No I don't think he's in a very good mood, so I'll keep out of his way."

She wanted to ask him if he had a good night when Mr. Williams was away but decided that could wait.

"Did Barbara bring you up that mug of tea earlier?" she asked

This brought a real flush to his face and he knew it. There was no way he could hide this.

"Yes thank you it was very welcome."

"And Barbara?"

How did he answer this without letting her know what had gone on? Although his flushed face told most of the story.

"She left it and went about her duties, I believe."

"Yes I know, she told me you were satisfied with it ... and the tea." She smiled and turned away from him.

Does everyone know his business in this house? If all the women are telling each other about him, he was sure that Mr. Williams was going to find out and if so, he would be in very big trouble. As he ate his breakfast of meat and eggs he thought it through.

This was women's talk, a secret they were keeping to themselves and if he was right, the only one who knew exactly what was going on was Mrs. Damson. She had the ear of both Mrs. Williams and Barbara. There is no way Barbara would be talking of such things to Mrs. Williams.

Mrs. Damson came over to the kitchen table with two mugs of tea, one for Mark and the other for herself. Mark knew he would have to tackle her about what she knew and more importantly who she was talking to.

"This is none of my doing you know Mrs. Damson I'm the victim, not the villain." He said.

She looked into his eyes, "I know that Mark, if you were, then I would be very upset with you and you wouldn't be allowed into my kitchen."

"What can I do, I feel trapped?" He asked.

"Have you told the two women about the other?"

"Of course not. I know Mrs. Williams knows about Barbara, she used that to get me into her bed."

He decided not to tell her about this morning.

"If Barbara knew about Mrs. Williams I believe she would tell Mr. Williams to get both of us into trouble."

Mrs. Damson thought for a moment.

"You're right, Barbara can't know about you and Mrs. Williams, if she did I may well be out of a job as well."

She continued, after a pause, "I'll ensure that she doesn't find out from in the house and you'll have to ensure that you say nothing, not even to Mr Johnson."

"Thank you Mrs. Damson."

All this seemed a long time ago now, but it was less than half an hour since he left the kitchen, to dress for this meeting with Mr. Williams. One thing he remembered was to go fully dressed, that meant taking along his matching pair of flintlock pistols and cutlass.

As he heard the clock, in the office, strike eight o'clock it brought Mark to the reason for being stood outside Mr. William's office.

He knocked on the door and waited for a call for him to enter. There was no way, with the mood Mr. Williams was in, that Mark would enter the office without a specific invitation.

There was no call from inside the office, so he would knock again. Just as he raised his hand to knock on the door it opened and there before him stood Mr. Johnson.

"Come in Mark."

Mark entered the office to see that the desk had been moved. Mr Williams desk was now immediately in front of him. Behind the desk was not only the Comptroller but Mr. Climpson, the senior Riding Officer and the Comptroller of Customs in Chichester – Mark's father.

"Stand in front of the desk Mark." Mr. Johnson said.

He heard the door closing and Mr. Johnson moving, unseen to Mark, to take his seat by the wall.

Mark came to a stop, two paces in front of the desk and waited for Mr. Williams to speak. It seemed like forever before Mr. Williams said anything. He was looking down at some papers on the table. Mr. Climpson was looking very sternly at Mark and his father was scowling at him.

If this was meant to make him feel uncomfortable it was very successful, he wanted to just turn and run but he knew that would solve nothing.

Eventually Mr. Williams looked up into Marks eyes.

"Well what have you to report about the other night?"

How was Mark to begin, he couldn't say what kept him at the house and he had no idea how he would explain why he arrived so late, to guard the Customs House.

"I was late taking up my post at the Customs House, Sir," Mark said, offering no other explanation than that.

"We know that young Sir. Why?" Mr. Climpson asked.

"I fell asleep after the evening meal and was woken when I heard a pistol shot." Mark replied.

The three men huddled together and talked in whispers. Mark couldn't make out what was being said. After a few moments his father turned and faced him. The others also looked up.

"I don't believe you young man. You were brought up that your duty was the most important thing. You wouldn't have gone to bed when you should have gone to your duty."

This was not just his father talking. The other two were also nodding their heads to this. Mark could guess that Mr. Johnson was doing the same.

His father was right he would never have deserted his duty unless there was a good reason. The one he had given was so out of character that it showed up to be the lie it really was.

"Was it a woman who kept you?" Mr. Climpson asked.

This was a shock to Mark, he had only told Bob Climpson about Barbara the other night and here he was using it against him. Perhaps he was trying to help him out or did he know about Mrs. William's? Had she done this with a previous guest to the house and he suspected this is what had happened.

"I don't understand what you mean Mr. Climpson." Mark said, looking straight into his eyes, hoping he wouldn't press this avenue of questioning.

"You told me the other day that you had just discovered the pleasures of a woman's body. Were you looking for this again?" Mr. Climpson replied.

Before he could reply Mr. Williams cut in

"I'm not interested in why you were late, right now, that can wait."

A weight seemed to lift from Mark, Mr. Williams continued,

"When you did arrive what did you see, who was there and what did you do about it?"

From behind him came a prompt.

"Report like I told you, miss nothing Mark." Mr. Johnson said.

This brought a scowl from Mr. Williams towards Mr. Johnson. He had been told not to interfere, unless invited to do so, by those at the desk.

"I headed from your house, Sir, down to the quay. I saw some men, down towards the Customs House so I decided to walk through the boats, on the quayside. This way I would get closer to the Customs House, unseen." He might regret that statement later but he was telling the truth.

"On reaching the last of the boats, I could see the Customs House, a band of men gathered around the main door, it appeared to have been opened."

"Did you recognise anyone?" Mr. Climpson asked.

"Not at that time, it was quite dark, although there was light coming from inside the Customs House. I presumed that they had lit the lamps to see what they were doing."

He paused for a moment, looking from one to the other to see if there was any sign of encouragement coming back but he saw none.

"I was just about to advance when I heard a sound coming from around the boat I was stood by." He paused but got no questions, they were waiting for his report.

"As I looked around the corner I saw two men standing over a body, that I later discovered was Jack."

Again he looked for encouragement and still found none.

Mark was finding this very difficult indeed and with no help, he could see that they were looking to blame him for both the loss of Jack and the consignment.

"As they turned to walk back to the Customs House, one of the men spoke and I recognised his voice, it was George Styles from Aldfriston."

This brought some reaction from his inquisitors; they looked at each other and towards Mr. Johnson but said nothing.

"In his hand was a pistol, the other man was not carrying a weapon."

"Did you hear what was said?" His father asked.

"He said if he found out who had let him get this close to the Customs House he would do to that man what he had done to Jack." Mark said.

This did bring a reaction from Mr. Williams and the others, more or less in unison they all asked

"Are you sure?"

"Yes, I relive his words all the time." Mark said, not looking for sympathy but hoping he would receive less harsh treatment.

After a few moments of letting that sink in, Mark realised that he still had some explaining to do.

"Although I had my pistols with me I believed that if I intervened I wouldn't be able to arrest Mr. Styles or his companion. Had I done so, the gang would have pursued me; taken him back and most likely have killed me, as well."

Not even his father said he had done right. From the looks they gave him, he should have tried something. The main purpose of the enquiry had been achieved. They had discovered who had killed Jack and who was responsible for the attack on the Customs House.

The atmosphere in the room seemed to become less formal and more relaxed now, that was until his father asked

"So what were you doing to keep you from your duty?"

This was like a sword entering his stomach, just as he thought that that part of the night was behind him, it came rushing back.

"I was with Barbara, the ferryman's daughter." He said, smiling all over his face.

He knew that Mr. Climpson knew that he had been with her the other night. Mr Climpson had brought it up earlier, so it would follow that Mark had been with her. She wouldn't mind telling a lie for him, if asked.

The room became very cold again. All the men at the desk suddenly looked up at him, with cold eyes.

"Are you sure?" Mr. Williams asked.

"Yes Sir." Mark replied.

The three men looked at each other and then back at Mark.

"Wait outside, we need to discuss this." Mr. Williams said.

He stood there for a moment not understanding what was going on. Why had they looked at him that way? Why were they dismissing him? From behind him he felt a hand on his shoulder and Mr. Johnson pulling him around.

"You'll have to go outside for a few moments Mark." Mr. Johnson said, with a most serious tone to his voice.

Mark turned around and followed him to the door. Mr. Johnson opened it for him and closed it after he had gone through.

He stood there wondering what he had said. He knew it was a lie but Barbara would back him up so there was no problem there. What had he said that caused such a change in their attitudes towards him?

Mark walked up and down the corridor, waiting to be recalled. He knew, he would be summonsed back for more questions.

It seemed like hours but in fact it was just five minutes before the door opened and Mr. Johnson's head peered out, looking around to find Mark.

Mark was at the far end, looking out of the window and over the buildings that surrounded the Customs House.

"They will see you now Mark." He called.

His daydreams could wait for another day. It was time to return to Mr William's office. Mr. Johnson closed the door behind him and Mark again stood in front of the desk, with the three men seated behind it.

"We know you've lied to us about Barbara. Unless you tell us the truth we will not be able to use what you said about George Styles. That will mean the death of Jack will go un-avenged." Mr. Williams said.

"But I was with Barbara, you can ask her."

There was no looking around this time, just straight-faced men looking directly at him.

"We talked to her earlier and she was able to tell us many things about where she was and what she was doing but you featured nowhere in what she said." Stated his father.

Mark had to think quickly now.

"Of course she wouldn't tell you about me being with her. She wouldn't want to get me into trouble."

He looked from face to face but they didn't appear to believe him.

"If I asked her, she would tell you the truth." Mark said.

Now the three men looked at each other and then back to him.

"Mark you are lying and trying to bring this young girl into your web of lies. We want the truth and we want it now or you are finished with the Customs Service." Mr. Williams said.

Mark looked at his father and he nodded in agreement with what had been said. His father had so desperately wanted him to advance in the Customs Service and there he was saying that he would be finished if he didn't tell the truth.

What could he do, tell the truth that no one would believe, especially Mr. Williams, or insist he was telling the truth and be finished with the job he was beginning to really enjoy.

"Sir I was in bed resting when I heard the shot. That's the truth." Mark said, with a stern face.

He was telling part of the truth, he wasn't saying who he was in bed with.

"And the woman you were with?" Came a question from behind him.

Oh no, he couldn't face Mr. Johnson and lie. He couldn't face the others while answering the question either.

Mark turned around to face his inquisitor, with all the effort he could muster he looked into his eyes and tried to plead with him to withdraw the question but there was no response.

"I was resting." He said, in a near scream. "Does no one believe me?" He said, as he turned around to face the men at the table.

They looked at each other and Mr. Williams turned back and said "No."

He realised that if he now gave over Mrs. Williams as his lover, it would be thought of as just revenge and he knew there was no way she would back him. She would lie to protect herself and her reputation.

"That is the truth, you always told me that no harm would come to me if I told the truth, father. Well that appears to be a lie now doesn't it?" Mark said.

He realised that he had lost and was about to be thrown out of the Customs Service. In a one last desperate effort he turned back to his father.

"Father, can I talk to you outside please. I need to ask your advice."

"What you've to say to me can be said in front of these gentlemen Mark."

"No it can't." Mark screamed.

There was no reaction from his father so he knew all was lost.

"You can keep your job, I quit." Mark said, turned to head for the door.

"Not so fast young man." Mr. Climpson said.

"You are in the Kings service and can only be dismissed by his officers."

"Well you are about to do that anyway. So get on with it and I'll leave." Mark said, turning to face Mr. Climpson.

"I'm not happy about your answers young man." Mr. Williams said.

"As such I'll have you arrested and put into jail until you can give me the right answers."

Mark looked at him then to his father, but got no help there. Before he could say anything Mr. Williams ordered,

"Arrest him and take him to the local jail Mr. Johnson."

This really shocked Mark. This morning he was making love to two beautiful women, both the reason for his current situation and he was now about to go to jail.

Like earlier Mr. Johnson put his hand onto Marks shoulder but this time the grip was much firmer. He was arresting Mark, he was now his prisoner. Mark had seen him do this before, with smugglers, so knew that he wouldn't be able to loosen that grip, as it was well practiced.

No one expected what was to happen next, especially Graham. Mark was a young man brought up to respect his elders and all that they had seen so far today, had showed that he had done that. They couldn't understand why he was lying to them. Here was a young sixteen-year-old, under training to be a Customs Officer and what he did next would ensure that this training was never completed.

Mark didn't turn around as soon as Graham's hand clamped itself on to his shoulder. Instead Mark looked at the three men sat in front of him with disbelief. There was no way he was going to jail. He was not going to tell them what they wanted to know.

Graham couldn't see what Mark was doing but as he looked over to the men at the desk, he saw an instant sign of amazement come over their faces. Geoff started to rise from his seat but suddenly stopped.

This split second of hesitation was all that Mark needed to get away from Graham's grip. While he was trying to understand what was happening, he had relaxed his grip on Marks shoulder. Mark stepped away from Graham and half faced him, whilst still keeping an eye on those at the table.

In his hands he now held his brace of pistols. With his left arm free, he had been able to retrieve his second pistol from under his coat. It was the production of his first pistol that had caught the others off guard and consequently Graham.

"Get over there by the desk Mr. Johnson." Mark ordered.

Graham didn't know what to do? He had seen Mark fire his pistols and knew that he was a good shot. At this range he wouldn't miss his target.

"Now!" Mark shouted.

Raising his right hand pistol and aiming it directly at Graham's temple. Graham could see that now was not the time to try and talk him out of this action, so he started to move off towards the rear of the desk.

"Before you go, drop your pistols and cutlass on the floor." Mark ordered.

Geoff thought that Mark was engrossed only with Graham, so made a move to get his pistol into his hand. He moved his hand under the table and took hold of the butt of his pistol.

"If your hand comes back holding your pistol, I'll kill you Mr. Climpson." Mark said.

With that said he raised his left hand pistol and pointing it directly at Geoff, without even apparently looking his way.

This brought a cold shiver over Geoff. Never before had he come across a person so adapt with their pistols. Graham had told him, but he just thought it was him boasting about his ward.

Geoff quickly released his hand from the butt of his pistol and slowly brought it back onto the desk top, showing Mark that his hand was empty.

Graham placed his pistols and cutlass on the floor and stood up.

"Now go and get the weapons from the other gentlemen, remember I'll kill anyone who doesn't obey."

Graham did as he was told and gathered up all the weapons, five pistols and three swords, of various kinds. None, not even his father's pistols, were a match for Mark's.

"Now go and sit behind the desk, Mr. Johnson." Mark said.

With all the weapons together on the floor and Graham also sat behind the desk, Mr. Williams could hold himself back no longer.

"Pput up your pistols this instant." He stood up and barked his order.

"Sir, sit back down. I don't have to take orders from you anymore. I've told you the truth about what I was doing when Jack was shot. I told you who did it and still you don't believe me, well that's your problem. You are not putting me in jail just because you want to know everything I did that evening." Mark retorted.

"If I told you the truth you wouldn't believe me and you, Father, I could have told you but you wouldn't listen to me, so now I'm leaving you all." Mark turned his eyes from his father's to Graham,

"Mr. Johnson you have taught me a lot and been very kind to me. For that I am grateful and sorry for letting you down in this way. When I can, I'll tell you what happened and you'll understand."

All the time he kept his pistols pointing at the four men, the left hand one at Geoff Climpson and Graham Johnson and the right hand one moving between Mr. Williams and his father.

Mark backed towards the door and put away his left-hand pistol. With them all unarmed and on the other side of the desk, he didn't feel in too much danger of attack.

He put his hand behind his back and felt for the door catch, he undid the catch and, stepping forward, opening the door.

"Don't follow me. You know I'm a good shot and I'll shoot anyone of you who tries to capture me." With that he backed out and shut the door.

Mark ran down the corridor and down the small flight of stairs to the main door. Here he didn't stop other than to pick up his hat, which he had put on the small table when he arrived. He opened the door and picking up the keys that were hung just inside, on a post. He left the Customs House for the last time and closed the door behind him. He had done this many times before; He put the key in the lock and locked the door.

The previous day the door to the Customs House had a new lock fitted. It was the finest in the area.

He walked hurriedly away from the Customs House. Mark didn't want to invoke any interest in his movements but as he was a pleasant person who talked to everyone. Everywhere he went he was observed and reported on. Up to now he hadn't minded that but now was different, he needed to be able to move around without being noticed or he would soon be in the town jail.

CHAPTER 24
I didn't tell your husband about us

Mark entered the home of Mr. Williams, by the front door, he saw no need to go round the back. He wasn't going to be there long and he didn't believe his four inquisitors would be out of the Customs House for some time.

He ran up the stairs, along the corridor and up the further set of stairs leading to his bedroom. Barbara was sweeping up the floor but turned around as he entered.

"What are you doing back this soon?" She asked. "I haven't finished my chores yet."

Mark was still angry and in no mind for her flippancy.

"What did you tell them about us?" He screamed.

"What did you tell Mr. Williams about Tuesday night?" He demanded.

This took her aback. She didn't know what was going on.

"Mark, I told them what happened when the smugglers made me row them over the river. Half way over I jumped out and swam back home, changed out of my wet clothes, took your horse and rode over to Lewes to fetch Mr Climpson. That's all I told them."

"And what about me, what did you tell them about me?"

"I said nothing about you; we never saw each other on Tuesday night."

Mark realised he was taking out his anger on her. It wasn't her fault but his and his gullibility that led him to go to bed with his boss's wife.

"I'm sorry, Barbara." He said, as he took her in his arms and squeezed her tightly to him.

"I'm in very big trouble. I nearly shot Mr. Johnson and locked Mr. Williams, my father, Graham and Geoff Climpson in the Customs House."

Barbara pushed herself away from him,

"You had better get out of here straight away Mark. When they get free this is the first place they'll come looking."

"But where will I go, I can't go home and I can't stay here?"

"Where ever you go today I don't know but be back at my father's barn tonight, after dark and I'll help you." She said.

"Now gather up what you can carry and I'll go and get the ferry ready. You've got to get to your horse before they get free."

"Thanks, but you'll get into real trouble if they find out you've helped me."

Barbara took hold of him and kissed him fully on the lips,

"Now get going, I'll see you by the quay." She said. She rushed out of the room, down the stairs and out of the house.

Mark didn't need to be told twice. He gathered up his belongings and thrust them into the bag his mother had given him when he left home. He looked around and remembered that he needed to get his powder and shot from Mr. William's storeroom.

He ran down the stairs and back along the corridor. As he reached the top of the main staircase he meet Mrs. Williams coming out of the sitting room.

"Mark, what is all this noise? All the running about?"

He didn't stop, he just flew down the staircase and away.

"I can't explain Mrs. Williams. I didn't tell your husband about us and because of that I'm now on the run from him and his men. If they catch me I'll be arrested and thrown into goal." With that he fled down the stairs and turned to the kitchen.

Mrs. Damson was standing by the fire, boiling some water, as Mark burse into the kitchen.

"Do you want a mug of tea, Mister Mark?" she asked, on turning to see who had entered her kitchen.

"No thanks, Mrs. Damson, I don't have the time." He said as he went through to door leading to the storeroom.

Mrs. Damson thought this was unusual and followed him.

"What's up Mister Mark?"

"I can't explain Mrs. Damson, but I have to leave and I'm in a hurry."

The least she knew the least she would have to tell, so she left the storeroom and returned to her kitchen.

Being left alone, Mark went over to the cupboard that held the weapons, shot and powder. He took a barrel of powder and a bag of shot for his pistols.

Mark looked around the storeroom and saw an empty flour sack in the corner. He picked it up and placed the barrel of powder and the shot into sack, swung the sack over his shoulder, picked up his bag and walked back into the kitchen.

It took Mark five minutes to get to the ferry and, true to her word Barbara was there with her father's ferry. He passed down his bag. With the powder and shot still in the sack, over his shoulder, he climbed down into the boat.

"Quickly Barbara, I must get away before anyone sees me with you or you'll be in trouble as well."

"Don't you worry about me Mister Mark, I'll say you held a pistol and made me." She said, with a smile.

"Cast off at the bow will you." She asked.

He did as he was bid and pushed the boat away from the quayside into the main stream of the river. Barbara was soon into her rowing and before long they were over the river, tying up and away from the possible pursuing customs men.

Mark threw his bag up onto the quayside, picked up the sack and started to climb up away from the boat.

"I will see you tonight Mister Mark, won't I?" she asked.

On reaching the top he put the bag onto the quay and climbed back down again. He moved over to her and held her in his arms. Mark didn't want to leave but he knew he must. He released her and pulled back a little.

"Thank you for today, I'll be back to see you later in the week. I don't want to get you into more of a mess than you are in now."

"But you promised tonight." She pleaded.

"I know but I can't. I'll try to come back either tomorrow or the next night, I promise." He said.

With that he climbed back up the ladder, picked up his things and headed off to the barn, to collect his horse.

As she rowed back across the river Barbara could see into the barn, she longed to see him again, before he rode off and possibly out of her life.

When she had finished tying up the ferry she turned around but still there was no sign of him, so she climbed the ladder to the quayside.

Before she headed back to the William's House she took one last look over to the barn and there he was, sitting astride his magnificent horse. He appeared to be waiting for her to turn around, so she waved over to him.

As he turned his horse around and headed off she could feel a tear rolling down her cheek. What a silly girl you are, no man is worth that, she said to herself but her heart thought differently and the tears flowed until she was nearly back at the house and her chores.

CHAPTER 25
If only I'd put him over my knee.

As Mark closed the office door behind him, both Geoff and Graham jumped to their feet. Graham was first up and moved quickly over to the pile of weapons on the office floor. Geoff was just behind him, they gathered up their own pistols and cutlasses.

"We'll go after him Mr. Williams, don't you mind, we'll bring him back." Geoff said, as he straightened up and took a pace to the door.

"I wouldn't go through there Geoff." Graham said, "He's a good shot."

"Yes he is at that." Mr. Downer said, "May be I should've spent more time with him over my knee than teaching him how to shoot."

"We can't chase him down like a dog." Graham said, "He's made a fool out of himself, that's all. If we chase him we'll either have to kill him or worse, he'll kill one or both of us."

This stopped Geoff. "He wouldn't kill us, we're his friends."

"Yes he will." Mr. Downer confirmed. "If he's cornered and thinks we don't believe what he told us, he won't be taken in."

"Go and bring him back." Mr. Williams demanded, "I want that young rascal in front of me, unarmed and telling me what I want to know."

"Hunt him down like a rabid dog." Mr. Williams was in a fury now. If he got hold of him he would run him through with his sword.

"No." Mr. Downer ordered. "Stop where you are."

The one thing he had over Mr. Williams was that he had commanded men in battle and knew how to gain their respect.

"No one goes anywhere until we know what it is we want to achieve out of this?" He said, now looking at Mr. Williams.

"I'm in charge of this area Mr. Downer. I only asked you here out of courtesy, as your son was involved in what went on." He snapped.

"You may have asked me for that reason but I'm the senior officer here and I'll take over this investigation." He said firmly.

"I could ask my cousin, at the Customs House in London, I'm sure he'd confirm my authority, in this matter."

This may not have been true but where family and friends dictated ones position in an organization such as this, more than anyone's ability, Mr. Williams knew that he had neither in the Customs House in London so he would have to yield to Mr. Downer.

Geoff and Graham looked at each other and realised that there had just been a change in command. Neither of them wanted to kill Mark nor did they want to give him the excuse to kill them.

"I agree. We need to talk about this before we go any further." said Graham.

Geoff thrust his pistol into his belt and his sword into its scabbard and picked up the weapons belonging to Mr. Williams and Mr. Downer.

Graham put his pistols into his belt and went over to collect the chair he had been sitting on and move it to the office desk, across from Mr. Williams. He sat down and waited for Geoff to return the weapons to the two Comptrollers of Customs before he, himself, sat back at the desk.

"Right gentlemen, what are we going to do now? We have a man on the run, a dead guard and all our captured contraband gone." Mr. Downer said. He looked around at the three local Customs Officers.

There was silence for several minutes whilst they all took in what had happened this morning and thought out what should be done.

"Do we believe what Mark said about who killed Jack and was responsible for the raid on the Customs House?" Graham asked.

"It wouldn't be passed George Styles to do any of this." Geoff said, "and yes I do believe Mark."

"I don't believe he lied, but he didn't tell the truth about where he was earlier." His father said.

"I agree." Graham said.

"Barbara had already told us that it was George Styles that made her row his men over the river and to be ready to take some back over later on." Graham said.

"Does it matter where Mark was before Jack was shot?" Geoff asked.

"It most certainly does." Mr. Williams snapped.

"He should have been down here, helping Jack guard the contraband. If he'd have been here, then Jack may still be alive." he insisted.

"And we would be asking who had killed them both." Graham said.

Not meaning to speak against his boss but rather bringing out the other truth, in that George Styles would have killed anyone in his way that night.

"Right it would appear that Jack was killed by George Styles, agreed?" Mr. Downer asked.

There was a murmur of agreement to this statement.

"Do we also agree that it was his gang that broke into the Customs House and stole the contents of the building?" He asked.

Again there was full agreement to this.

"Was Mark Downer involved in this in any way? Did he help the smugglers in any way? Did he deliberately stay away from his duty, in the Customs House, so that it could be entered?" He asked.

There was no immediate answer from any of the men to those questions, so he decided to ask each one for their verdict.

"Mr. Johnson, you know my son best among the group of you, what do you think?"

Graham thought for a little longer before replying.

"He wouldn't intentionally help the smugglers. He wouldn't stay away from his duty. He was always waiting for me when we were going on patrol. Whether we met here, at my cottage or some fork in the road, he was always there. No he didn't stay away intentionally and in no way help the smugglers."

Turning to Geoff. "Mr. Climpson?" Mr. Dawson prompted.

"I saw Mark yesterday, after Jack had been killed and he was devastated. He vowed that he would get George Styles for what he had done." Geoff said.

"Was he talking about the taking of the contraband or because he would not get his bounty?" Mr. Williams asked, spitefully.

"No Sir, he was talking about what he did to Jack." Geoff said.

"He didn't take part in this but I don't know why he wasn't here? He wouldn't answer that question, when I asked him." He concluded.

Now Mr. Downer turned to Mr. Williams.

"Well Sampson, do you think one of your young officers permitted the murder of one of your staff?"

This question left Mr. Williams no space to manoeuvre, if he said he did he would be going against all the other men in the room and if he said he didn't then he couldn't have him arrested.

He looked around the room at the men around his desk before he answered. Hoping that one of them may show a sign that they would support him saying that Mark was guilty, but there was none.

"NO" he said, "No he wouldn't have done that, but he hasn't told us the truth about what he did that night."

Everyone at the desk agreed with that but no one thought it changed the fact of who the real criminals were.

Mr. Downer was pleased at this outcome. He knew that there was no way his son had done what Mr. Williams was accusing him of but he had to get those present to agree so that Mr. Williams couldn't change his mind.

"How are we going to get hold of Mark?" His father asked.

"I'll find him." Graham said. "It may take some time. In the short time he's been with me he's got to know the hills well and if he feels he's on the run he may well meet up with the criminal elements and stay hidden for some time."

"If it takes money to find out where he is, you can count on me reimbursing you." Mr. Downer said.

"Thank you Sir. I may need some if I can't find him in the first week or so." Graham said.

"I'll ask around as well. If he comes into Lewes, I'll hear about it and get hold of him." Geoff said.

"Right Sampson, send out an arrest warrant for George Styles for the murder of Jack and the raid on the Customs House. Offer Five Hundred Pounds for his capture." Mr. Dawson ordered.

"We haven't got Five Hundred pounds." Mr. Williams said.

"We'll have it when I've reported the facts to Customs House in London."

"I'll spread the word along the coast and to the Dragoons." Graham said, "They'll want George Styles out of the way, like the rest of us."

As a sign that the meeting was over, Mr. Downer stood up,

"Right gentlemen, I must go and tell his mother what's happened. Sampson, keep me informed."

With that he strode to the door and left without a backward glance. He didn't fancy having to tell Mark's mother that Mark was on the run.

"I'll be about my duties Mr. Williams." Graham said. "I've a lot of riding to do today, if I'm to catch up with young Mark."

"Ok Mr. Johnson but remember, Mark is not to be harmed, he must realise he has nothing to fear in coming and talking to me." This was said by Mr. Williams, more out of fear of Mark's father than how he actually felt.

"Geoff, are you coming?" Graham asked,

"Yes, I must get back to Lewes or the rascals up the river will be up to something or other."

Geoff rose and along side Graham left the office. Leaving Mr. Williams on his own, to contemplate what to do next.

How was he to report the incident to London, without letting them see it was his fault? It was then that he remembered that he was in London when all this happened. Geoff Climpson was in charge, he would put all the blame on him.

CHAPTER 26
I'll give you ten sovereigns

Mark didn't look back as he rode away from the ferryman's barn. He didn't see Barbara's wave or the tears in her eyes. He needed to get away from Newhaven as fast as he could.

His horse was strong and fast so Mark was confident in being able to outride anyone pursuing him but, he would need to conserve his horse's energy, just in case he needed to outrun his pursuers.

He started off heading for Lewes, from where he would go to London and disappear in the big city. Once there he wouldn't be found or arrested.

As he thought about a place to stay and how he would feed himself he realised he had no money. In fact since he left home he had never had any money of his own. His father had paid Mr. Williams for his board and lodgings and Mr. Williams had kept his meagre wages back to pay for the stabling and feeding of his horse. He hadn't needed any money until now, how would he survive.

He pulled up just below Denton and looked around. No one appeared to be following him. He could see no one in the fields or on the roads.

It was as he looked around that he saw a group of gorse bushes on the hillside. This reminded him that Graham and he had hidden three pairs of half-ankers of brandy and Genever in the gorse bushes on Seaford Head. Had Graham gone back and retrieved them? He doubted it. It had been their intention to get them, over the weekend, as a present for Mrs. Jefferies.

If Graham hadn't retrieved them, then Mark could and sell them to raise money to support him self. It would take him about half an hour to reach Seaford Head but he would need to go carefully and take a route around the town, also bypassing some of the villages in the area.

Turning his horse around and headed off towards Seaford. As he past through Tide Mill he saw no one and was pleased about that. The more time it took his pursuers to find where he had gone, the further away he would be.

He turned up the track, leading to Bishopstone and passed by many fields, laid out to the right of the track. There were no workers in the fields, so he urged his horse on at a fast trot to get around these obstacles quickly.

As he reached the third field, he realised that he would have to pass five cottages before he could get by the village. If the men were not in the fields, then they were likely to be in or around their cottages.

The fields were surrounded by three feet high flint walls. High enough to keep sheep penned in but not keep a horse out. Mark looked around and saw a part of the wall that was lower than the rest and headed his horse towards it. The horse realised what was expected of her and prepared itself to hit the right stride to jump the wall in safety.

Over they flew and down into the field, scattering a few sheep as they went. He headed the horse down the slope of the field and into the valley that held the course of a stream, which wended its way down to the sea.

Before he reached the far side of the field Mark looked back to see if he was seen but he could see no one. In fact the hill had taken him out of sight of all the cottages. He felt safe.

He didn't go fully down into the valley but continue along the field and cross the wall into the last of the fields. It took only a few moments before he had crossed the last of the fields and reached the track out of the village.

His very instinct was to continue to head towards Seaford but he realised that he couldn't ride through Blatchington without being seen. He would need to head out onto the Downs and back to Seaford Head the long way around.

By turning back towards Bishopstone and then heading out onto the Downs no one would take notice of him or what he was doing. Mark was known in the area. Anyone seeing him on patrol, over the Downs, was not a sight that registered much with the villagers now. He was no longer a foreigner. Mark turned and headed out onto the Downs at a gallop. Before long he would be totally out of sight of the village and could head back in the general direction of Seaford.

By taking this longer route Mark had been able to bypass Blatchington, Seaford and Sutton but didn't let him off completely. There was still Chinting Farm to negotiate. He could go on down to Excet Bridge and along the river down to the haven and then head on up onto Seaford Head. He dismissed this as he had already taken time out in getting to the half-ankers and he didn't want to waist any more time.

As he rode up to the Farm he noticed that the farmer was riding towards him. He hoped Mr Harris wouldn't stop to talk today, sometime he did and sometimes he would just pass him by, as if he didn't exist.

"Good day Mr. Harris." Mark said, as their horses neared each other.

"Good day to you, Customs Officer." Mr. Harris replied.

Mark noticed that he wasn't slowing his horse so Mark did likewise and just rode on past.

Everything about him wanted to look back and see if Mr. Harris was watching him but he know that to do so would make him look suspicious and he just wanted Mr Harris to forget he had seen Mark.

As he passed by the farmhouse, he looked in and saw Mrs. Harris working in the kitchen. She looked around at the sound of his horse passing by. May be she thought her husband was returning, having forgotten something for his business trip to the Duke's Head in Seaford.

Noticing that it was Mark, she waved out to him and beckoned him to visit for a while, but Mark was in a hurry so waved back to decline the kind offer.

Before she could come to the door Mark had left the vicinity of the Farm. Again he didn't look back.

On reaching the Head, Mark rode towards the series of gorse bushes running over the Head. It was now that Mark realised that he should have taken a bit more notice of where they had hidden the half-ankers.

He rode up and down two or three times but still he was not sure which ones they were in. He decided that he couldn't waste any more time. He would have to take his best guess and if he was wrong, then go on to the next and so on until he found them. He couldn't leave without them.

Mark dismounted and left his horse with its reins dangling on the ground. It was well trained and wouldn't move off, away from him. This left him free to carry out his search. After walking over to the first set of bushes, he started to push his way forward, through to the centre.

The thorns on the bushes were very hard and pierced his clothes, all the way up to his thighs. This was a more painful experience than he had expected. After all, when Graham had taken them into the gorse bushes, he hadn't said he'd been hurt.

He pulled the branches apart and looked deep into the bushes but could see no half-ankers in these bushes. He turned around and found that his horse had moved off, about fifty yards further along the Head.

Mark was about to call her back when he noticed that his horse was looking into the bushes in front of her and nodding towards them. Mark may not have remembered where they had hidden the brandy but his horse had.

Once he had got himself out of his current predicament he walked to where his horse was standing. But before he went into these bushes, he went over and patted his horse's head and thanked her for pointing out where he should be. This set of bushes was the fourth on Mark's list, by the time he had got to them his clothes would have been in ribbons.

Mark realised, as soon as he started to move the branches apart, that this was the right place. They were easy to part and many of the thorns had been broken off by Graham, so the whole journey in was much less painful than his last.

Once he had reached the spot, he thought that Graham had stood the other day, he looked down and there were the three pairs of half-ankers. Being roped together it made Mark's job so much easier. He picked up a pair at a time and carried them out onto the grass and returned for the others.

Being tied together, in pairs, it was easy for Mark to carry them over his horses back. The two of brandy, he placed across the front of his saddle and the one of gin, at the rear.

All he had to hope was that he wasn't spotted by a Riding Officers, from another area.

Having secured his load and remounted his horse he headed away from Seaford and down to Cuckmere Haven, from where he would ride upstream to Excet Bridge. Both he and his horse had ridden this route many times, whilst on patrol with Graham, so they knew where any dangers may lurk and also how best to go unobserved.

Mark kept a good lookout for any other travellers. He wanted to keep out of view of anyone. Being known here abouts, he was sure that he could pass himself off as transporting captured contraband.

By now word would have been passed around for All Customs Officers and word would be sent to the Dragoons to keep an eye out for Mark and he was to be arrested on sight.

On reaching the bridge, Mark rode over and headed towards South Bourn. He needed to get out of this area, patrolled by his colleagues. The bridge was the unofficial boarder between the Newhaven and South Bourn Riding Officers areas.

The most important thing, on his mind, was to exchange these half-ankers for money.

He had heard that in the village of Jevington, the innkeeper might not be averse to purchasing some contraband. For that matter any innkeeper in the Downs area would buy such goods, at the right price.

Not being familiar with the lanes and tracks on this part of the South Downs he remembered that Graham had said that the quickest way to the village was via West Dean. Just follows the track into the hills and you would enter the valley. Head down the valley and you'll come to the village.

He was a little nervous as he rode into West Dean. He had bypassed Excet hamlet without any encounters with its inhabitants but West Dean would be another matter. It was a little larger than Excet but it could hardly be classed as a village, although it did have a substantial church at its centre.

As he rode past the church, he noticed that there were people coming out of the church. He pulled his hat down over his face and hoped that they wouldn't see the half-ankers he was carrying. If they did they may think that he was either a traveller or a smuggler and so give him a wide berth.

The vicar looked up as he saw the young man riding by. "Who is that?" He asked the people around the church door. They looked over at the rider.

"That's the young Riding Officer from out at Seaford." Fred Paul answered.

"I wonder what he's doing over here and it looks like he has some contraband with him."

The vicar looked after him, "I hope he knows what he's doing. He's riding into trouble if he's heading for Jevington. Jiggs will have him and take those half-ankers away from him." He said.

Those gathered by the door agreed with those sentiments. Only people known to the villagers would ever ride into the village in such a way. Foreigners were definitely not welcome in Jevington.

Jevington Jiggs was the name by which the leader of the Free Traders, working from the village, was known. His actual name was known only too a few members of the village. No foreigner would learn of it and for this reason he had been able to evade capture for many years.

Mark rode on aware that his presence had been noticed. No doubt questions were being asked about his identity and the reason for moving through their village.

Being in parts of the hills he had never been before, he felt venerable. He was in no mood to be taken unaware, in a strange area, so he ensured that his pistols were not only loaded but ready for use. He checked that the pistol he had thrust into the left-hand side of his belt was not caught up with any of his clothes. If he wanted to get at it he wanted it into his hand quickly and for him to be able to aim it at anyone proving a danger to him.

Mark's horse was well trained and so, even if they were surprised, he doubted that she would spook. This would give him the edge in drawing his pistol and confronting whoever tried to intercept him.

After about a quarter of a mile the track turned to the left and appeared to be heading north along the valley. He had only gone about one hundred yards when he came across a large house buried deep in the fall of the hills surrounding it. It appeared to be strongly built, standing in good grounds with a barn and stables opposite.

He pulled up his horse and looked around to see if there was anyone about but could see no one.

It had been a long and tiring morning and he felt quite hungry.

He couldn't remember such an eventful day, in his young life. Here he saw a chance to hide up for a while and rest. With his boyhood looks he was sure that he could persuade the owner or his wife to give him a meal before he continued on his journey.

As he was about to turn off the track, towards the house, the ankle he was holding on his saddle moved and reminded him of what he was doing. He couldn't go down there with the three pairs of half-ankers of spirits on his person. He looked around and saw a bush by the side of the track. There would be room to put the half-ankers behind the bush and they would not be observed by passers by. It took him only a few moments to dismount, hide away his goods, before remounting and riding down to the house.

When he arrived at the house he still couldn't see anyone about, so he tied up his horse by the barn and walked over to the main house, up the three steps to the door and knocked. There was no answer to his knock or second.

He looked around and thought it would be best if he walked around the house. It didn't take him long before he reached the rear and found the door leading to the kitchen, again he knocked and again there was no reply.

There was no point in leaving without having something to eat, so he tried the door and found it was open. Mark walked in and there on the kitchen fire was a kettle of hot water and stood on the table, in the centre of the kitchen was a plate of biscuits.

It took him only a few minutes of searching in the various cupboards and larder, before he had found the ale and a tankard. After helping himself to the ale, he settled down on a kitchen chair to drink his ale and eat the biscuits.

After fifteen minutes, he had emptied the plate and drunk his ale. He hadn't realised just how tired he really was. The next thing he knew was the sound of someone screaming.

Mark shook his head, reached for his pistol and stood up. He looked around for the source of the sound, which had awoken him. There, stood in the doorway to the main part of the house, was a young girl, about ten to twelve years old.

He quickly put away his pistol, realising that the girl posed him no real threat. He didn't want to frighten her any more than she was already. As he took a step towards her he saw the shape of an older woman appear behind the girl. He looked up from the girls face to that of the woman behind her.

"What are you doing in my kitchen?" demanded Miss Badger, the housekeeper. She pushed the girl to one side and away from the intruder.

"Sorry madam, I did knock but there was no answer." He said.

"I asked. Why are you in my kitchen?"

"I have travelled a long way and needed somewhere to rest." He said, trying to put on his best boyish charms.

"There was no answer so I took the liberty to come in and appeared to have fallen asleep." He said.

She looked around her kitchen, "Not before you cleared up the plate of biscuits I see." She said.

"Sorry but I was very hungry."

She looked at his boyish face and realised that he was too young to be telling lies. She was a formidable woman whom no one took advantage of.

207

"All right young Sir. Now you have rested and cleared me out of biscuits you can be on your way." She said.

Mark looked at her, would she be telling on him or was he safe,

"Madam, I'm a stranger in these parts. Do you know of a safe place I can stay tonight?"

If she said no, he would be on his way. If not then he felt safe in her care.

"Can you use those pistols you carry young Sir?" she asked, looking at his fine pair of Heylin brass flintlock pistols.

"Yes Madam, I'm a good shot with these and can handle my sword with any man." He said, puffing out his chest with adolescent pride.

"In that case I'll put you up here. The master and mistress are away for a few days, so I could do with someone to guard my daughter and myself from any ruffians that may pass by." She said, with the first sign of a smile coming from around her lips.

"That's kind of you Madam, I'll guard you well."

Good he had somewhere to hide up for a few days. There was no way that Graham would think of looking here. He had never mentioned the existence of this house, when they had been talking about this track.

"Madam, I do have an errand to do for my father before this night is out." She looked at him with a questioning look,

"What's this errand and where have you got to travel, for your father?" she enquired.

"He sent me to see a John Pettit, in the village of Jevington, which I understand is in this valley." He said, with true innocence.

John Pettit was the village innkeeper and it was to him that Mark hoped to sell his Brandy and Genever.

"Aye the village is in the valley, about two miles along the valley floor." Miss Badger said.

"John is the innkeeper of the Eight Bells. You'll have no trouble finding him."

"Thank you Madam, if it's alright with you I'll leave now to complete my father's errand. I'll return before it gets dark. Then I can stable my horse and ensure that the house is secure."

Miss Badger was reassured with what she had heard from this young man. He may look young but was apparently well versed in guarding and looking after ladies.

From behind the housekeepers dress, peered the face of the young girl who had woken him earlier.

"I'm sorry if I frightened you earlier." Mark said.

"My name is Mark." He said with a smile, trying to reassure her that she had nothing to fear from him.

"Come out and say hello to Mark, Carol," Miss Badger said.

"Mark this is my daughter Carol. She doesn't see many people around here and visitors are rare."

"That's all right, I understand. By the time I leave I hope we'll be friends."

Making friends with her daughter would take more than one night. It looked like Miss Badger might have this visitor for a while. She would have to ask him to leave, before the master returned, next week.

"If you want to be back before its dark you had better leave soon Master Mark." Miss Badger said, as she moved across the kitchen to place her bag of shopping on the small table by the kitchen window.

Mark looked at Carol, smiled and headed for the door. He picked up his hat as he passed the table he placed it on when he arrived.

"See you later Madam."

He would guess that the woman would stay in the kitchen but young Carol would run through the house to watch him collect his horse and ride away. This is exactly what he saw. There in the window, to the left of the main door was Carol's face watching after him.

As he reached the track, he looked back towards the house but couldn't see the window where Carol had been watching him. This pleased him, as he was concerned that she would see him collect his goods from behind the bush and tell her mother or ask him about it later, in her presence.

Having secured his load he set off, firstly at a walk and then as he felt more secure with his load, he urged the horse up to a trot.

It took him half an hour to reach the outskirts of the village. He had passed a farm, about a half a mile outside the village but there was no farm house there, just a large barn and stables.

The first house he came across was situated on a bank to the right of the road. Like many houses in these hills, it was constructed mainly of flint.

Just passed this house was a track on his right that lead up onto the hills leading over to South Bourn. Also at this junction was a well for the villagers to collect their drinking water. A small wall surrounded the well. A bucket and rope were stood against the wall, ready for use.

There were now many more houses on each side of the road, to his right was a building that had a sign showing that it was the house for the poor of the village. Opposite this building were farm workers cottages, again made of flint. This was quite a substantial village, for this time, especially in these hills where traditionally the local countryside couldn't sustain many people.

As he rode along he could look to his right and up another track where there were many cottages, along its length. To his left was another track that appeared to lead up to the village church of St Andrews. He could see no sign of the Inn so he continued on along the road.

CHAPTER 27
I am John Pettit

Once Mark had ridden passed the vicarage, he continued up the small hill, into the upper part of the village. Here he found more flint houses and several large, flint built, barns. The most important discovery was at the end of a high flint wall. It was the Eight Bells Inn. Now he would have to be on his guard.

He couldn't take the half-ankers into the Inn but he also couldn't risk leaving them outside either or they may be seen by any passing Dragoons or Riding Officers. What was he to do?

Mark passed the Inn and, on the far side, he could see an opening, beside what looked like a small stable block. If he went down to the stable, he might be able to find somewhere to hide his booty.

He dismounted and walked his horse through the gap, to the far side of the stable. At first he could see nowhere to tether his horse but he could conceal the half-ankers there for a short while. After placing the pairs of half-ankers down by the wall of the stable, he took his horse to the side of the stable and found a hook to tether his horse to.

As he turned around and started to head back towards the Inn, the rear door opened and a man appeared, holding a coaching blunderbuss, pointed in Marks direction. At this range, if the man decided to shoot, it may not kill him but Mark was not prepared to take any chances.

"What are you doing by my stables young Sir?" The man asked.

"I was just securing my horse before I came into the Inn for an ale Sir." Mark replied, with a smile, hoping that this would disarm this man's intent on doing him harm.

Mark guessed that if need be he could get one or both of his pistols into his hands and fired at this man. Mark was not a killer at heart. He wanted to cause little trouble, at the moment. If he could pass by this village without being notices by too many people, word of his whereabouts wouldn't back get to Mr. Climpson or Mr. Johnson, who were likely to be searching for him now.

The man stepped out of the kitchen and headed towards Mark. He was about the same height as Mr. Johnson but much thinner, he had a thin face and piercing eyes.

Mark thought that he was not a man to be trusted but he was not sure where he fitted in here. Inn Keepers are traditionally large men with round faces and even rounder wives.

"What is it you placed behind the stable young Sir?" He asked.

Mark realised that he must have been watching him since he arrived, so most likely saw the half-ankers he was carrying.

"I have something to sell and thought that the Inn Keeper may be the person who would buy what I have." Mark answered.

"What is it you have to sell?" He asked.

"I will discuss that with the Inn Keeper, John Pettit." Mark replied, in a firm business like voice, intimating that he would not do business with just anyone.

The man looked at him and brought the drooping barrel of his blunderbuss up towards Marks face.

"I'm John Pettit, what business do you have for me?"

"Then Sir, I have something that may be of interest to you." He said.

Mark turned away from John and walked around the rear of his horse, towards the back of the stables. John began to follow him and as he passed the rear of Mark's horse, he found that this young man was not as innocent as John had first thought.

As Mark passed by his horse he took a quick side step and turned to greet John as he rounded the horse's haunches. As he turned he drew his pistol and lifted it to be level with John's face, when he came into view.

John wasn't sure what was happening until he passed the haunches of Mark's horse. He looked towards where Mark had gone and found that he was facing the barrel of a pistol and heard the hammer being cocked. He had no opportunity to bring up the barrel of his own gun. To do so would have most probably cost him his life.

"Put your gun on the ground, Sir." Mark ordered.

John hesitated, was this young man going to kill him, rob him or arrest him, was a fight worth the risk or not?

"NOW" Mark said, impatiently.

This time John decided to obey, he bent forward and placed his blunderbuss on the ground and stood up, waiting for the next instruction.

"Sir, after you." Mark said, indicating with his pistol that John was to continue around the end of the stable block.

Mark followed but he was ready for John to try the same trick on him. As John turned the corner he quickly turned and moved towards the wall of the stable ready to disarm Mark as he came around the corner.

Mark hadn't followed John that closely. As they neared the corner he had stepped away from the corner and was some three yards further from the corner than John.

As John faced Mark he realised what he had done, this young man was no fool, he was standing out of reach, with his pistol still levelled at Johns body, 'Good try,' thought John.

"Mr. Pettit I'm here to do business not to fight. Killing you would do neither of us any good." Mark said, with a smile.

John took a deep breath, "OK, no more antics." Then he took a less aggressive stance.

With that, Mark lowered his pistol and, as he believed John meant what he had said he put it back into his belt.

"I've these three pairs of half-ankers of spirits to sell, one is Genever and the others are Brandy." Mark said, indicating the half-ankers standing by the wall. John looked at them and recognised them as being smuggled goods.

"I can't take them young Sir. They are Free Traders goods." John said, with all innocence.

"No Sir they are mine to sell." Mark insisted.

"They may be yours now, but they haven't had the duty paid on them, so I can't buy them." He replied.

Mark knew he would have to push him here. He needed to let him know that he was aware of his activities without letting on that, until today, he had been a Riding Officer.

"Mr. Pettit if I looked around your Inn or that of any Inn for twenty miles, I would find such items as these." Mark looked directly into John's eyes to see what reaction that statement brought.

"I have heard tell that more Genever comes through this valley than all the genever landed at all the legal ports in this country."

He let that sink in for a moment, "And the word is that the innkeeper in this village knows the man running the Free Traders and takes his cut."

John thought for a moment, was this a clever young man trying to bluff his way into a sale. Did he actually know what he was saying? If so how did he get his information?

Only a few people outside the village knew the extent of the Free Traders operation in this valley. Some were the buyers and the others were the Riding Officers but they had never been able to prove anything and had only captured a very small amount of the goods that did pass this way.

"You have a vivid mind young Sir." John said.

"No Sir, I tell the truth. Crowlink Genever is renowned throughout the country as the best you can buy. It doesn't go through the Cuckmere valley and it doesn't go through South Bourn, so that leaves this valley. The tracks over these hills are a maze. You know I'm right Sir, so can we get down to business and I'll leave here and tell no one."

There was no point in prolonging this any more, if he sent him on his way this young man could cause him much trouble. He had better buy these half-ankers and send him on his way.

"I'll give you ten sovereigns for the lot."

"Twenty." Mark insisted.

"You said you wanted to talk business not charity, Twelve." John said.

"Twenty Sir and you'll see me no more." Mark said.

"No, just fifteen and that's my final word." John said.

Fifteen sovereigns were three more than Mark had expected to get.

"You have a deal Sir." He said, holding out his hand to seal the deal.

There appeared to be respect for each other in the way they shook hands. Mark suggested that John went and collected the money while he brought the pairs of half-ankers over to the back door.

All John's instincts told him to double cross this young man but his brain said he should be careful. He appeared to have some information about John and if it became common knowledge his business would become difficult to run. To attempt to kill him seemed to be futile, from how he had handled himself earlier.

'No let him go' thought John. After all he could afford the money and the half-ankers were worth more than that anyway. By the time he had brought them down from full proof, he would more then double his money anyway.

John went back to the kitchen door, picking up his blunderbuss on the way. As he entered his wife was standing by the table with a tankard of ale in her hand.

"Is everything alright?" She asked.

"Yes, just business."

"I saw him take you around the corner of the stable with a pistol held at you."

"He is a young man who is very cautious. He doesn't trust me!" John said, with a smile on his face.

"Not such a fool then." Susan said, as she turned away and headed out of the kitchen, into the barroom.

Susan didn't know all of John's doings but she knew that he was no angel. He was mixed up with the Free Traders, friend of the Riding Officers and the Dragoons. He appeared to be in both camps, which in her mind was a very dangerous place to be. Neither would trust you and more than likely blame you for any trouble that happens.

John followed her through to the barroom and placed the blunderbuss under the bar. He went to the end of the bar and knelt down, lifted a floorboard to reveal a metal box below. He opened the lid and took out a small leather pouch, filled it with fifteen sovereigns, closed the pouch and the lid of the box. After replacing the floorboard he retraced his steps to the kitchen and headed out towards the stable.

Mark had taken the time, after moving the half-ankers, to look around the area to find his way out of here. If John was to double cross him, then he would most likely do it as he rode away from the stable.

Behind the stable block was a large field, with sheep and a few cows grazing. On the far side of this field he was sure that he could find an opening in the hedgerow. That would take him onto one of the many tracks that crisscrossed the Downs and take him away from this village.

Having decided his route out of here he needed to prepare himself and his horse to depart. He went back around the stable, unhitched his horse and took it around the corner, then remounted her.

When John walked towards the stables, he couldn't see Mark or his horse. He looked around, towards the road to see if he had begun to head out and away from the Inn.

"You have the money?" The voice came from behind him.

John turned around to find Mark on his horse, at the end of the stable. The whole of the horse was not in view, the haunches were still out of view, behind the stable. It was obvious to John, that Mark was ready to depart once he had his money.

"I've your money young Sir, will I be seeing you again?" John enquired.

"I think not Sir." Mark said, as he held out his hand to receive his money.

John noticed that his other hand wasn't holding the horse's rein's, it could only be that way if it was holding a pistol. This young man was well versed in taking care of himself. He could do with someone like him.

"Throw it over Sir. Otherwise my horse may spook and kick out."

John knew it wasn't the reason but he decided to go along with him. He threw the purse up to Mark, who caught it with ease, without apparently taking his eyes away from John.

Mark didn't insult him by opening the purse. Placing it into his coat pocket he took hold of the reins with one hand and raised his hat, to John, with the other. He wasn't holding a pistol at all, John realised. At the same time Mark pushed his heels into the girth of his horse, to urge her forward.

John hadn't taken much notice of the young man's horse until now. As it burst away from the stable, he saw the full magnitude of the beast.

It was a full fifteen hands, black with an intelligent head, strong muscular legs and hindquarters. An expensive animal.

He didn't have long to observe it as the horse and rider were galloping across the field, before him. Within a few moments they had reached the far side of the field.

CHAPTER 28
I have a room at the top of the house

It wasn't long before Mark reached the far side of the field. It was only then that he noticed the gap in the bushes which appeared to be a path going into the hedgerow, so he urged his horse to enter at the gap.

As soon as he had entered the undergrowth the path turned around and headed back to the left for twenty yards, it turned right and right again so that they were travelling back in the direction they had just come from but much further into the hedge.

After thirty yards the path turned to the left, again, and within a couple of paces they exited out of the hedgerow onto a track. Mark looked around to see if anyone was coming along the track or if any were working in the fields around but he couldn't see anyone.

It was time for him to get back to the house where he had been offered sanctuary. There was no point in him staying out in the open. He was sure that Mr. Williams would have offered a large reward for his arrest. Mark had few friends around this part of Sussex.

Mark was not familiar with this area but he knew that he needed to head south, towards the coast. So he rode in that direction, taking him as quickly as he could away from Jevington and, in particular, John Pettit.

After ten minutes he was on top of the hill and could see for miles. Down to his left was Jevington and in the field over his left shoulder was the village church. High to his left he could see over to Beachy Head and the hills overlooking South Bourn.

There were rolling hills, to his right, leading over towards Seaford and Newhaven. Once he had travelled another three hundred yards he could see the mouth of the River Cuckmere, as it wound its way down to the sea. It felt good to be alive riding along the hilltop.

You should never be relaxed when you're on the run from the Law. As he smiled to himself he caught a glint of light coming from the hill to his left. He examined the area to see what had caused this. What he saw was not to his liking. There, on the other side of the valley, was a troop of dragoons and they appeared to have spotted him.

Mark took out his telescope and quickly looked at the soldiers, were they coming after him or returning to their patrol. At first they appeared to be riding in parallel with him but that was just until they reached a track down into the valley. Here they turned and headed down the track at a gallop and apparently in pursuit of him.

The trouble was that the house, Mark was heading for, was the other side of the intersection between him and the dragoons. Even with the fine horse under him, he couldn't reach the intersection, before the Dragoons

If he continued in this direction there was a good chance he would also lead them to the house. He had to think quickly, find a way of taking them away from the house. Later he could double back and get himself hidden away without raising suspicions.

There was no way that the dragoons could come directly up onto the part of the hill he was on.

They would either have to head for Friston Place and catch up with him at West Dean or they would have to head towards Jevington and ride up Pentlands track, onto the hill.

Mark thought for a moment and decided that he would draw them away from Friston. He turned his horse around and, ensuring that the Dragoons were watching him, he headed back along the track towards the back of the village and possibly on to Folkington. It was important that the Dragoons saw which way he was going so he came off the track so that he could see the Dragoons, ensuring they could also see him.

After he had travelled four hundred yards, more at a trot then a gallop, he saw that the Dragoons were turning towards Jevington.

'Good' he thought 'now I had better ensure that they continue to follow me for a while.' He manoeuvred his horse towards the top of the hill again and on to the track. All the time he kept his eyes on the patrol.

After the Dragoons reached Oxendean farm they came off the road and headed across the fields towards the top of Pentlands track, cutting off a big corner of their journey. Now that Mark was sure they were after him. He thought it was time for him to make tracks and get as far away from them as he could, preferably before they reached the top of the hill.

He headed towards the hilltop above Wilmington. He urged his horse on to a gallop now. It may take his pursuers a few moments to find his tracks and set off after him but when they did, he wanted to be both visible and as far away as possible. This time he didn't bother to look back to see if he was being pursued, he could leave that until he was up on the ridge of the hill.

After ten minutes Mark reached the top of the ridge and although still urging his horse forward he allowed her to come out of the fast gallop he had insisted on. Mark could now look back over his shoulder to see if and where the Dragoons were.

It took him a few moments to locate them, as they had been travelling through a small wooded area but there they were, in full flight, headed in his direction. As they had been in full pursuit for quite a time now Mark guessed that some of their horses would begin to tire.

The Dragoons would have to choose to either call of the pursuit or to split up. The faster, fitter horses following him and the others looking out for him to detour off and they would then be in a position to cut him off. He could well find himself caught between the two groups.

Mark looked around and found that the track dipped, some hundred yards ahead and as he reached the start of the dip he saw a track leading to his left and down into a discreet valley. This may well be his only chance to give them the slip to get back to the manor house and sanctuary.

On reaching the junction, he slowed his horse and turned onto this new track then urged his horse back into a gallop. He now needed to be out of sight of this junction, well before the Dragoons reached it. He was hoping that they would continue on to the top of the hill, overlooking Wilmington, before realizing that he had given them the slip.

He reached a fork in the track and decided to take the one to the left. This gave him the best chance of being out of view of his pursuers. There was a bend, about a hundred yards away and some bushes that would hide him.

The Dragoons were starting to find the pace being set by their quarry was too much for them. To stay together they would have to slow down and the leader realised that none of their horses were a match for that ahead of them.

With this in mind he called for his troop to come down to a trot, they would track him for another half an hour. If they hadn't found him by then they would make tracks and head back to their barracks in South Bourn.

By the time the Dragoons reached the place where Mark had turned off, they weren't in much heart to pursue him anyway. Any reward may not have been very good anyway. This man was outpacing them and appeared to know the terrain well. The chances of them finding him would be slim.

They continued on to the top of the hill but could see no sign of Mark. Three of the dragoons used their telescopes to scour the valley below them but to no avail.

"Let's go down to the Inn and ask if anyone has seen him." One of the dragoons suggested.

"Good idea, It's your turn to get us a drink anyway." The Corporal said. This brought a murmur of agreement from the rest of the troop.

As Mark rode up to the house, Carol came running around the corner.

"You've been a long time going to Jevington Sir." She said, in the innocence of a child, not knowing she shouldn't be asking such questions.

"The business took longer than I expected." Mark replied.

Mark dismounted and walked his horse over to the barn and opened the large door. There were some stalls for his horse, hay to feed her with and a bucket of water.

He took off the saddle and placing it over a rail. It took him half an hour to rub his horse down, feed and water her. He left the on bridle but took off the reins. Mark took her to an empty stall so she could rest.

Before leaving the barn Mark looked around to see what exits there were from the barn. It may not always be possible for him to leave by the main door so he looked for others. There were two other doors, one at the far end of the barn and another at the back. He would have to walk his horse out of either of these doors but they did offer him escape routes.

Carol had been sat watching him tend to his horse and looking around the barn. She didn't understand why he was looking around the barn with such interest but didn't question him further.

"Shall we go and find your mother?" Mark asked, as he headed back to the main door.

"She'll have some ale for you by now and there are some fresh biscuits. She cooked them after you'd eaten all the others." Carol said, with a smile.

As they left the barn, Mark looked around and listened to find out if anyone was around. If the Dragoons had been able to follow his tracks, they could be in the vicinity by now. He heard nothing except the sound of the birds in the trees and the rustle of the branches in the wind.

Carol ran on in front of Mark, to alert her mother that he was coming and to get his tankard of ale ready for him. Carol hadn't had a brother and saw Mark very much as if he was her long lost big brother.

By the time Mark at reached the kitchen Miss Badger had indeed poured out the ale and was standing by the table with it in her hands.

"Come in young Sir." Miss Badger said, as Mark halted by the doorway.
"Thank you Madam."
He entered and took the seat at the table.
"Did you get your business done in Jevington?" She asked.
"Yes, it took a little longer than I expected but it was successful."
"Did John try to rob you?" She enquired.
"We came to an agreement. He wouldn't rob me and I wouldn't harm him." Mark said, with a smile on his face.

Miss Badger looked deep into Mark's eyes. She knew of John's reputation and found it hard to believe that this young man could get the better of him. As she looked she saw steel in his eyes, there was a sudden realisation that this young man may have the face of an angel but he was hard. She could see how he would have been able to convince John that any threat he may have made against him, would be met with force.

"I've got a room at the top of the house for you Mark. You'll not be disturbed there."

"Thank you. I think I should retire now if you don't mind? I've had a long day and do need to rest."

"Carol you get our plates ready while I show our visitor up to his room."

"I could take him up for you." Carol pleaded, to no avail.

"This way Mark." Miss Badger said

She turned towards the door, leading into the main part of the house. Mark rose and taking up his tankard and a handful of biscuits, he followed.

Miss Badger took him down a corridor and away from the front of the house. This lead to a staircase used only by the servants of the house. She ascended the spiral stairs for two floors, with Mark close behind her.

At the top she opened a door that lead into a narrow corridor, in the rafters of the house. Once she reached the end of this corridor she stopped outside a door, opened it and stood to one side to allow Mark into the room.

It was a small room with just a bed, a horsehair mattress, some blankets and nothing much else.

"I hope this'll do for you Mark, It's the only room that has a tree outside the window." She said, with a knowing smile.

"The room is fine. Thank you." Mark said.

"No one will disturb you here, I'll see to that Mark."

Mark put his hand into his coat pocket and drew out his purse, opened it and handed Miss Badger a sovereign.

"I hope this will pay for your kindness Miss Badger?"

She looked at what she had been handed and looked back into his eyes.

"Thank you. I'll need this room empty in three days. My master returns then and he'll not take kindly to me entertaining, while he's been away."

With that she left and closed the door. He could hear her walking along the corridor and back to her duties. It had been a long and tiring day and he needed to recharge his batteries, ready for whatever lay ahead tomorrow.

Mark turned to the bed, laid down on it and was out like a light.

CHAPTER 29
There's not a sign of him anywhere

Graham Johnson had ridden hard that day. Trying to catch up with Mark was proving to be a difficult task. It became obvious, after the first hour that this young man had been listening to what he was being taught and had apparently learned far more than Graham had realised. He knew his charge was bright and took in everything he had to tell him, what he had forgotten, until know, was just how much information he had passed over.

Mark's horse was far better than Graham's. It was larger, stronger and better bred. What Graham had hoped was that with his local knowledge, he would be able to eradicate these advantages and catch up with him.

When he eventually crossed the river, at the start of his pursuit, he found his horse, saddled him and rode out. Scanning the countryside for the sight of a lone horseman but saw none. He outwardly cursed the ferryman's daughter. He believed she had deliberately slowed his progress when she brought the ferry over the river to collect him. She had gone downstream and made out it was difficult to get to the landing point.

Only after Graham had raised his pistol towards her had she brought the ferryboat into the landing point and taken him on board. The journey back to the far side of the river was much longer than normal. She pleaded that she was tired from last nights work but Graham would have none of that. So he had taken the oars and rowed the last half distance himself.

She must have delayed him half an hour, plenty of time for Mark to have got into the hills and beyond before Graham was ready to pursue him.

Graham rode over to the track leading along the bottom of the hills. Should he turn right to Seaford or left towards Lewes? Where would Mark head? Only Mrs. Jefferies was in Seaford. She may give him a meal but she wouldn't hide him from the law and especially not from Graham.

If Mark had gone to Lewes, he could well disappear up into the countryside and the Customs service would have no chance of arresting him.

Geoff Climpson was already headed out to Lewes, which was his area of responsibility, so if Mark headed in that direction Geoff may not catch up with him but he would hear of his passing and notify Graham.

Graham decided that it would be best to head home and talk to Mrs. Jefferies. If he told her what had happened and why he had to find him, before anyone else did. She would tell him anything she knew.

He turned his horse and set off, at a trot, to Seaford. He didn't want to tire his horse, this early in the day. He expected to be in the saddle for most of the day, in pursuit of Mark. If he caught up with him, he would need all his horse's strength, especially if Mark decided to flee.

Graham asked three men, along the way, if they had seen Mark or any lone rider that morning. They had all answered they hadn't. He was not sure if it was just their habit of not answering a Riding Officer's questions, in fear of being thought of as an informer or that they hadn't actually seen anything.

As Mark was known to work with Graham he couldn't see why they wouldn't tell him of Mark's passing. After all he hadn't told them why he was looking for him.

Instead of heading directly to Mrs. Jefferies cottage, he went over to the farrier's barn to see if he could tell him anything. Even if he hadn't seen Mark, he could have heard from his customers of Mark's passing.

Graham didn't trust the farrier too much. He was well aware he was in league with the smugglers but as he hadn't bothered him too much, he believed he could find out what he needed to know.

"Good morning John." Graham said, as he rode up to the barn.

John was working on a customer's horse, checking out its rear hoofs. He looked up and saw that it was Graham. He would have to be careful what he said to him. This horse belonged to one of the Aldfriston Free Traders. They and wasn't pleased with Graham, his dragoons or anyone on their side.

Fred Cannon, whose horse this was, was at that very moment about to leave the sanctuary of the barn when he heard Graham riding up. He had remained hidden, so he could listen in to what Graham was saying.

"I've lost touch with young Mark, have you seen him John?" He asked, hoping that this would get the information he needed.

"No I haven't seen him today." John replied.

"If you hear of him today, from any of your contacts, there's a florin in it for you, if you send me word." Graham said.

He knew that this would bring about some active enquiries. John would pay for the information, far less than the florin that Graham was offering and turn a quick profit.

It may be possible that the man hiding in the barn knew of Mark's whereabouts. If so, he would get what he wanted sooner than later.

"I'll be up at Mrs. Jefferies cottage if you do hear of anything." He said, as he turned his horse away from the barn and rode away.

John breathed a sigh of relief. Fred was also pleased that he hadn't stayed longer. Fred walked out of the barn and up to John.

"What's all that about?" Fred enquired.

"Graham must really want to find young Mark to be offering money."

"Aye" John replied.

"I'd better tell George about this. He'll want to know if a Riding Officer is in trouble. Mind you he's not that happy with them at the moment."

"Be careful what you tell him Fred. This may be a trap. Graham is a crafty bugger and I wouldn't put it past him to set a trap for all of us."

Fred thought for a moment. "Aye, I'll just tell him he is looking for Mark. I won't mention the florin."

With that and the fact that John had finished clearing away the stone from his horse's hoof, Fred paid John, mounted his horse and rode off towards the Windmill at Sutton.

John went about his business, giving no more thought to Mark's whereabouts, except if he should hear anything that day.

By this time Graham had reached Mrs. Jefferies cottage. He rode around the back, dismounted and tied his horse up at the post, put there for just such a purpose. When he entered the kitchen, Mrs. Jefferies was sitting at the table drinking a tankard of ale.

"Would you like an ale?" She enquired.

"Aye, please Mrs. Jefferies."

Gladice rose and went over to the larder and poured him a tankard of ale. She noticed Graham was very quiet, this was unusual? He was generally quite talkative whenever he returned to the cottage. Telling her what had happened that day, all that he could that is. She couldn't remember, except when her husband was reported missing, when he had acted like this.

Having handed him his ale and sat back down again. She picked up her own tankard of ale and waited for Graham to say something but nothing came. She would have to ask and hope that her thoughts were not right.

"You have trouble, don't you Graham?"

"Is it young Mark?"

She could think of no one else who would cause Graham this amount of torment.

Graham looked up and saw that he would have to tell her all about it. He needed to talk to someone about this and there was no one closer to him than Mrs. Jefferies.

It took him half an hour to tell her everything he knew about what had gone on the previous night and what had happened that morning. They both sat in silence for some five minutes.

"We must find him before anyone else or he could get killed." She said.

"That's all very well, but how do we do it without having to fight him? He can be a fiery young man, when he feels threatened." Graham said.

"I'll ask around the town. I still have many friends about. If they know that I want him, they'll not ask why, neither will they want a reward."

With that she got up, went over to the door, took her coat off its hook and then her hat. Putting these on, she left without another word. She was heading for the town and the acquaintances in the Free Trading fraternity. If anyone could find him, it would be them.

Graham sat there for a few more minutes and then decided that he'd better start searching, himself. He left the cottage and remounted his horse. The first thing he would do was to go up to the Head and retrieve the Brandy and Genever.

One thing he had realised was that Mark had no money. Graham thought he may be carried a few shillings but that wouldn't last him. Especially when it was known that he was on the run from the law. He had puzzled how Mark would get money. He was not the type to steal or rob so what would he do?

That's when it came to him, if he got hold of the half-ankers they had hidden in the gorse, on the Head, he could sell them. He would then be able to go anywhere he wanted.

In normal 'Free Trade' they would fetch about twenty sovereigns. If Mark got only half, he would be set up for some time.

As he rode up to the Head he found himself urging his horse to go faster and faster. Something deep down told him that he was already to late but the thought of catching up with Mark, with the half-ankers, drove him on.

Graham reached the gorse bushes where he remembered hiding the half-ankers, the other night. Unlike Mark, Graham knew the Head very well and the bushes were familiar to him, so there was no need to go around searching each bush.

After dismounting, he let the reins fall to the ground and walked over to the bush. He pushed himself into the centre, keeping his hands up so as not to get them torn to pieces by the thorns. When he reached the centre he used his gloved hands to push aside the branches, so he could find the half-ankers.

He had guessed right, Mark had already been there. All three pairs of half-ankers were missing. Now Mark would be able to sell them and obtain the money he would need to leave the area. He may hide out, pay for lodgings and in a while come back to see Graham to clear his name.

Graham retraced his steps and remounted his horse. Where to now? He didn't believe that Mark would head into Seaford, not if he wanted to go about unnoticed. Everyone in the town knew him and would tell Graham about seeing him.

The local innkeeper of the Duke's Head, Mrs. Midhurst, wouldn't purchase them from him, not that she was averse to making such purchases. She would know that if Mark was selling them, he was either trying to trap her or was in trouble. She didn't need the type of trouble that Graham would bring her, if he found out.

The next place he could head for would be Aldfriston, with its two inns, but this was George Style's stronghold and he wouldn't be pleased to find a Riding Officer trying to sell contraband in his area. No he must have gone further afield, but where? Mark was not from around here so he didn't know the area that well.

After sitting on his horse for some time, staring out to sea, Graham started off. He would have to tour all the local villages, along the Cuckmere and around under the hills to West Firle and back along the Ouse valley, to Newhaven. If he hadn't heard anything by then he didn't believe that Mark would still be in this area but headed out towards London or some such.

He set off down to Excet and West Dean. If Mark had headed this way then someone should have seen him or heard of him, in one of these two hamlets.

There were few people around and the two he did find were not very cooperative. After the capture of the contraband from George Styles gang, no one was going to help any Riding Officer. Many of them had lost a nights money and they couldn't forgive anyone for doing that. This money made the difference between there being food on the table or none.

Graham rode on to Charleston, Littleington, Lullington, Milton Street and Wilmington. In each of these villages there was a wall of silence, even if they knew anything, even about this other Riding Officer, they were not telling Graham.

By the time he reached the inn at Wilmington he was ready for a meal and a tankard of ale. He ordered these and sat down in the corner of the room, drinking his ale and waiting for his food.

"Good morrow Luke."

"Hello Simon."

Simon went over to the bar and sat on a chair by the fire, with his back to Graham. He hadn't noticed that anyone else was in the room, so was ready to give out all the local news he had, to Luke.

"Did you hear that that young Riding Officer, from Newhaven, has gone on the run? They say there's a hundred sovereigns reward for his arrest."

The sound of the size of the reward pricked up the ears of the innkeeper, he forgot completely about Graham's presence.

"Why is there such a reward? What's he done?" Luke asked.

Simon hadn't heard about this but it didn't stop him making up a tale.

"I hear that he let George and his gang into the Customs House in Newhaven, so that George could get his goods back." Simon said.

Just what Mr. Williams had been accusing Mark of, thought Graham, but this would have been far from the truth, Mark would not have done that?

Luke turned towards Graham,

"Is that true Mr. Johnson, has Mister Mark's in league with George?"

Simon now turned around and saw that they were not alone in the room and finding that Mr. Johnson was the other person; he began to splutter out a form of apology.

"No it's not true. Yes we want to talk to Mister Mark and there is a reward for him but it's only a florin, not a hundred sovereigns. He's not involved with George Styles." Graham said, sternly.

"If anyone can tell me of his whereabouts, they will get my personal gratitude."

This was a veiled message that he would be turning a blind eye at anything they were up to. This could be worth far more than the florin the Riding Officer had offered.

Simon and Luke looked at each other with knowing looks. They understood what Graham meant.

"We'll let you know if we hear of anything, Mr. Johnson." Luke said.

Graham's meal arrived, delivered by Helen, Luke's wife.

"This looks good Helen. I feel I deserve this today."

"Thank you Mr. Johnson, I hope you enjoy it?" Helen said. With that she turned around and headed back to her kitchen.

Once Graham had finished his meal and a further tankard of ale, he bade farewell to Luke and Simon and left to continue with his search.

It would be foolish to go into Aldfriston this close to both his capture of George's contraband and George's attack on the Customs House. In a week or two it would be safe and only then, if he was accompanied by a Dragoon or two as his escort.

With that decided, he headed to Chilver Bridge, across the River Cuckmere and on to Berwick village. Firstly Graham went to the Constables cottage. He was more likely to get an answer to his questions from him than from any in the village. The Constable was in the pay of Lord Grade and not of the Free Traders. Even so, Graham had to be careful of what he said. This man lived in among many people who helped out the smugglers, either working with them or in hiding their goods.

Graham spent half an hour with the constable. Drinking ale with him and talking about the goings on of the last few days. He learned nothing he didn't already know from the constable, but his wife did let slip the fact that Mark had been to Mrs. William's bedchamber, that night, whist her husband was in London.

Graham tried not to act surprised at this piece of information but he was. He never suspected Mark would do such a thing. This young man had been brought up well and trained to look up to his elders and betters. A roll in the hay with Barbara was one thing, but with Mrs. Williams? This put a different perspective on the whole situation.

He didn't probe to deeply as to how the constable's wife came by this information. By the end of his visit he had established that she was Mrs. Damson sister and they had meet up the previous day, at Lewes market. That is when she was told about the goings on in the household.

After departing from Berwick, Graham headed for West Firle, not to get information but to have a drink and think about what he had just learned. It took him a quarter of an hour to reach the Beanstalk Inn. This was not an Inn he frequented to often but he needed somewhere where he could sit and think, without the distractions of the innkeeper or others.

The Beanstalk was not a very welcoming Inn. It was used more by traveller's who had little knowledge of the area. Anyone who had stayed there once was not likely to call again. It was not clean, the food was of poor quality and you were likely to have a bad stomach, the following day, unless you were lucky.

The innkeeper was a very nasty man. He gave the impression of being helpful but the only thing he intended to do was help him self to as much of the traveller's money as he could. He would weigh up their worth as they walked in the door and charge them accordingly.

For the right price he would avail one of his daughters or, if one was not available that week, his wife, to spend an hour or so in the visitor's room. He would stoop lower than a grass snakes belly to remove the travellers money.

As Graham entered the inn the innkeeper's face lit up and his welcome was most sincere, that was until Graham took off his three cornered hat and revealed his face. This recognition wiped the smile off the innkeeper's face, instantly.

"How can I help you Mr. Customs Officer?" he asked. Graham knew that he was aware of his name so took this as an intentional insult.

"I'll have a clean glass of your best brandy." He said. Making it clear that he was not going to accept the service he handed out to his passing visitors.

Graham took up a seat in the corner of the room, with his back to the wall, facing towards the bar and main entrance door. He wanted to be sure that while he sat thinking, he wouldn't need to worry about looking after his back. Anyone advancing towards him, would be seen well before they arrived at his table.

The innkeeper arrived with his glass of brandy and put it down in front of Graham.

"Wait a moment." Graham commanded.

He picked up the glass and took a sip of the brandy, to see if he was getting the good one or the one he served up for the travellers. Having tasted it he was pleased with its quality, the type that George imported if he didn't miss his guess.

Graham drew his pistol and after pointing it at the innkeeper's face he lowered it onto the table in front of his right hand.

"I don't want to be disturbed, do you understand?" He said, looking him straight in the eyes.

"You'll not be disturbed Sir." The innkeeper said, as he turned, scurried back behind the bar and went about his business.

What had the Berwick Constable's wife meant by her statement that 'Mark had been to Mrs. William's bedchamber whist her husband was in London'? This had bothered him all the way from Berwick. Was this just the cook telling tales to her sister, to enhance her standing with her or was she telling the truth. The only person she felt she could share such a secret with was her sister?

If what she had said was true, then what had Mark been doing there? Was it just for a chat or, after finding out how satisfying a woman's body could be, with Barbara, had he gone looking for an older woman?

Mark was brought up better than that. Had he gone back to Barbara, on that evening, he could understand that but this was not within his comprehension.

Mrs. Williams was a fine woman, no one could deny that. She always gave the impression that Mr. Williams was the man she loved and although they had no children, there had never been any rumours of her taking up with another man.

Mr. Williams had been away on occasions both before and since Mark had been living in their house. So what was the truth?

As he stopped to take a sip at his brandy, the door of the inn opened and a young man and his wife entered the barroom.

The young man looked around, after seeing the grinning innkeeper advancing towards him. His eyes met those of Graham's and stayed there for a short time. Graham saw that these two young people were not the type to be ripped off by such a fiend as this innkeeper. He picked up his pistol and growled at the young man.

It took only a second for the young man to take hold of his wife's arm and leave the inn far quicker than they entered. The innkeeper virtually ran after them, to stop them leaving, but they were much nearer the door than he and so were outside before he could stop them.

He came back into the Inn and looked over to Graham.

"They wanted a room and I need their business." He snapped.

"And I told you that I wasn't to be disturbed." Graham said. Raising his pistol towards the innkeeper again, only this time he cocked it ready to fire.

That was all he needed, the innkeeper was not going to argue with Graham in such a mood. You don't survive long in this trade if you can't recognise when your customer is a danger to you and your life.

After taking a further sip of his drink, Graham returned to his thoughts. Okay so he went to her room, was it to talk or had Mark other intentions. Then he remembered that the constable's wife had intimated that Mark had gone to Mrs. William's room at her request. If this was so, then it was her who made the advance.

If Mark had gone to bed with her before he heard the shot that killed Jack, then that could explain everything. In particular why he had tried to talk his way around what he was really doing that night.

There was no way of Mark knowing what Barbara had been doing that night. So to try to implicate her was very much his undoing.

Because of Marks upbringing, as a young gentleman, he couldn't tell Mr. Williams or even his father, what he had really been doing and who he had been with.

Everything was becoming clearer to Graham. All he needed to do now was to confirm this with Mrs. Williams. Then he could clear Mark's name and send word that he was clear to come back, without fear of repercussions.

Graham finished his brandy and bade farewell to the innkeeper. He was not sure if he was feeling dirty due to his thoughts about Mrs. Williams and Mark or the fact that he had actually stopped off at the Beanstalk Inn.

All Graham wanted to do now was to get back to Newhaven, as quickly as he could. Normally he would have called in at the Ram and the Polecat Inns when he travelled in this direction but he didn't have time for that today.

Both innkeepers were rascals and took contraband goods but they were also a mind of information, on the comings and goings in the area. He never pushed them for information on the Free Traders but listened carefully to what they said. From what he knew about others in the area, he was able to build up a good idea of what was going on.

Today he just rode on by and out of the West Firle. There was a choice of either going up over the Beacon or around the hills via Beddingham to get to Newhaven. He decided that to take his horse over the Beacon would be unfair on him, so rode on a level road around the hills to Newhaven. Then he could cross over on the ferry, to get to the Comptrollers house.

It took Graham half an hour to reach the ferry and then he had to wait ten minutes before the ferry was brought across. It was Mr. Ferris himself who was rowing the ferryboat today.

"Good day Mr. Johnson."

"Good day to you." He replied.

Graham climbed down into the ferryboat and sat facing the ferryman.

"Is Barbara around today?" Graham asked.

He didn't want to explain to her father why he was asking about her, so hoped that he would not be asked.

"She's not to well today and hasn't left her room since she brought you over, earlier today."

"I don't know what is up but she was crying when she came into the house. Is there something going on that I need to know about?" he asked.

Graham was not sure how to answer him.

"I think it's all to do with the raid on the Customs House last night. Mark has a lot on his mind and he may have said something to her, that's not in character with him."

To some extent that was true. Mark did have a lot on his mind with a warrant for his arrest.

"Could the fact that there is a One Hundred Pounds reward for his arrest have anything to do with it?" John asked.

"Don't believe everything you hear. That warrant will be removed later today, once I have presented some evidence I have received this afternoon." Graham said, with a smile on his face.

"Can I tell Barbara that? I'm sure that she'll be relieved and come back to work then. She has a soft spot for Mister Mark and I'm sure if she knows he's not in trouble she'll be better."

"No don't say anything yet. I still have to get one more piece of evidence before I can clear Mark."

By this time they had reached the town side of the river and Graham needed to get on his way to clear Mark's Name.

CHAPTER 30
Was it you?

Graham left the ferryman and walked along the quayside and headed towards the Comptroller's house. He needed to get inside without Mr. Williams seeing him, so he took a looping route that brought him to the rear door. He didn't bother to knock at the door as he could see through a hole in the door that the Mrs. Damson was there. It was her that he needed to see.

Hearing the door open Mrs. Damson turned around to see who was entering her domain without an invitation. She was just about to raise a shout when she realised who it was.

"Mr. Johnson, please knock when you enter my kitchen." She said sternly, trying to get some form of authority into her voice.

"I'm sorry Margaret but I need to ask you a few questions, without us being over heard or people knowing I'm here." He said.

This puzzled Mrs. Damson. What questions or answers she could give that would interest Mr. Johnson? She had never been involved in the smuggling trade so she couldn't help him there. Her mind was working hard but nothing came to mind as to why he wanted to talk to her.

"Would you like a tankard of ale Mr. Johnson, while you ask your questions?"

"Aye, that would be nice; it'll wash the dust from my thoughts."

While she found the ale, Graham took off his hat and coat and hung them by the door. He sat at the table, in the middle of the room, ensuring that he could see both the back door and the doorway leading to the main part of the house. He didn't want someone walking in whilst he questioned Margaret.

Having brought Graham his ale Mrs. Damson sat opposite him.

"Well how can I be of assistance to you then Mister Riding Officer?" She asked, with a smile.

Graham decided it was not a time for pleasantries. He needed to get to the truth as quickly as possible. So he went straight for the jugular.

"Is it true that Mister Mark slept with Mrs. Williams the other night, the night of the raid on the Customs House?"

The shock on her face was evident. Not the sign that she didn't know what he was talking about but the fact that he had asked about that secret.

"You told your sister about it, at Lewes market." Graham said, so that she could understand how he knew what had happened.

Mrs. Damson started to cry. She had let her mistress down, in telling her sister. She wouldn't be trusted again and would most likely lose her job. If she denied telling her sister, then it would mean that Mr. Johnson would have to tackle her sister again and it was all her fault.

"Look Mrs. Damson, I'm not blaming you. All I want is to find out is the truth. I won't be telling anyone about it, but I must find out the truth so that I can clear Master Mark or he will surely be killed.

After a few moments the crying stopped and she turned her face to look Graham in the eyes.

"You promise that Mrs. Williams won't find out about how you know this?"

"She'll hear nothing of it from me." He assured her.

"It's true. Mark did go to her bedroom, after they had dined together that night. I don't know what they did but when I took up Mrs. William's supper she was very pleased with herself and remarked that Mark was now a real man." She stopped and took a sip of her ale.

"Why did she say that?" Graham asked.

"Well I'd been talking to Barbara and she told me that she had made a man out of Mark, in the barn behind her father's house." She thought for a moment and continued.

"She said that it was his first time but if she had her way, it wouldn't be the last." This brought a smile back to her face.

"Barbara is quite a girl. She has made quite a few men and boys happy in the last year, since she found out how."

Graham looked into her face and said nothing. He wanted her to continue and found that by saying nothing generally brought about further revelations and that was true this time.

"With Mr. Williams away in London, Mrs. Williams was feeling at a loss and while I was giving her lunch she asked me to stop and sit with her."

"I don't know what brought it up but I let slip what Barbara had told me about her encounter with Mark, in the barn, the previous night. She took a distinct interest in this and said that he wasn't a man just because he had sex with a slip of a girl. She said that he needed a woman to make him a man."

Mrs. Damson said that they both had a laugh about this and then changed the subject to more domestic matters.

Later that day Mrs. Williams had asked for some water so that she could have an all over wash. She added that she must prepare herself for this evening.

Graham continued to listen and nod at the right time, hoping for all the evidence he was after.

"It was when I was preparing the dining room to serve Mrs. Williams and Mister Mark their dinner, that I realised the truth of what she had said earlier. As I crossed over the entrance hall towards the dining room, I looked up and there was Mrs. Williams coming down the stairs on Mister Marks arm."

"I though, that wasn't the way for a lady to behave, when her husband is away. Then I remembered what she had said and I realised that she was intending to take him to her bed."

She suddenly stopped here. Not sure if she had said too much or too little, who was she protecting herself, Mrs. Williams or Mister Mark?

"Do you think Mark was leading the way or was he just following?" Graham asked, when he realised the Mrs. Damson had come to a stop,

"He was being led, like a lamb to the slaughter, only a far more pleasurable experience I'd expect." She replied.

Graham had all the information he needed from Mrs. Damson. It was now time to confront Mrs. Williams. Only by her confirming what he already knew, could he get Mark's named cleared from the accusations against him.

"Where is Mrs. Williams now?" He asked, as he finished his tankard.

"She went into the sitting room earlier. I don't think she'll have left there for her bedroom, just yet."

"Is Mr. Williams in the house?"

This was an important question. He didn't want to put Mrs. Williams in such a situation where her husband might walk in while she answered Graham's questions.

"I believe he went to the White Heart Inn to have some of Thomas Kemp's famous ale. He won't be back before dinner, if I know him." Mrs. Damson said.

Graham stood up and asked Mrs. Damson to take him up to see Mrs. Williams. She wasn't too happy with this but she could see that Graham was very determined to clear Mister Mark's name. If she didn't take him, he would go up there himself.

Mrs. Damson rose and led the way through to the sitting room door.

"Please wait here Mr. Johnson. I'll see if Mrs. Williams will receive you."

She knocked on the door and upon receiving a reply she walked into the sitting room. There, sat on a chair, at the far side of the fireplace, was Mrs. Williams. Her face was white and her eyes looked as if she had been crying.

"What do you want Mrs. Damson, I said I wasn't to be disturbed today." She said, as Mrs. Damson approached her.

Mrs. Damson stopped before the fireplace and gave a small curtsey.

"Mr. Johnson has requested that you receive him. He says it's a matter of the greatest urgency. He has some information that will clear Mister Mark."

Mrs. Williams didn't answer for a moment. She was thinking what to tell him, if she refused he may confront her husband with this information. If it concerned her, then she could find herself in a lot of trouble.

"You may ask Mr. Johnson to enter." She said.

Mrs. Damson gave a little curtsey again and returned to the sitting room door, opened it for Graham to enter.

"Mrs. Williams will receive you Mr. Johnson."

Having done her duty she returned to her kitchen.

On arriving at the fireplace Graham bowed slightly towards Mrs. Williams, to show her respect for her position. He most certainly didn't respect her, if what he had learned that day was true.

"Thank you for receiving me Mrs. Williams."

"Take a seat Mr. Johnson." She said, indicating a seat on the far side of the fireplace. Graham looked around and sat down.

"What can I do for you Mr. Johnson? Mrs. Damson said you have some information that may clear Mark's name."

"I must be very blunt with you madam, I received some disturbing information that will clear Mark of the accusations being laid against him."

Graham was determined to get out what he had to say before the enormity of what he was saying stopped him.

"And what's this information you want to share with me, rather than my husband?" she asked, looking him directly into his eyes.

It was now that Graham could see that here, before him, were the eyes of a beautiful woman, sexy eyes. She had the type of body that could easily turn a young man from his duty.

"Is it true that you took young Mark to your bed chamber, on the night of the attack on the Customs House? The night your husband was in London." Graham asked, with a slight shake in his voice.

There was no reply to his question. She just sat there and looked him straight in the eyes without a flicker of recognition of what she had been asked.

"Mrs. Williams, if I wanted to cause trouble I would've gone over to the White Heart Inn and spoken to Mr. Williams."

Still there was no reaction.

"Madam" Graham said with a sharp voice.

"I must have an answer. Mark is likely to be arrested or worse, killed. I don't care about what you and Mark did in your bed chamber but I do need the truth." He snapped.

As he looked back into her eyes he saw tears start to run from her eye and down her soft cheeks. It was now that Graham realised that what he had been told was true. It was just that she couldn't find it in herself to admit it to anyone, not even herself.

That hour and a half of fun and pleasure was behind this young man's downfall and she didn't know how to get him out of it. To admit to her husband what had happened would end their marriage and ruin her husband's career. He would be held responsible for her actions and consequently for the loss of the contraband held in the Customs House.

"Mrs. Williams please, nod your head if what I have said is correct." He pleaded with her for some response. Still nothing happened.

"I won't be telling anyone about what I've found out or what you tell me but I must have an answer." He was becoming very insistent now, but still she wouldn't answer him.

Graham sat back in his chair and waited, he hoped that she would come to realise that his only interest was to clear Mark's name, not to get her into trouble.

She sat there motionless, staring into the unlit fireplace, with tears trickling down her face. Her hands were on the arms of the chair and her hands gripping the rest, with such force that her knuckles were shining white.

Five minutes had passed and still she sat immobile. Not a muscle was moving, other than her chests rising and falling as she breathed. Graham found himself transfixed with this sight but when his thoughts reached the point of where he was thinking what he would like to do with them, he remembered why he was here.

He quickly stood, hoping to jolt her into some reaction but none was evident.

"Mrs. Williams I believe that you took Mark to your room the other night and as a result of his good manners he has got himself into so much trouble that you can't imagine."

Still there was not response so he bade her fair well and strode to the door. Here he stopped and turned back to face her, in one last attempt to discover the truth.

"I must now go over to the White Heart Inn and lay before Mr. Williams all I've discovered this day. No doubt he'll be wanting some answers, when he returns?" Graham said. He turned back to the doorway and put his hand on the handle.

"Stop" Mrs. Williams shouted. "Stop, you can't do that to me."

Graham let go of the door handle and retraced his steps to the chair opposite Mrs. Williams, here he sat down and faced her again.

"Mrs. Williams, I've no intention of telling your husband of your part in this, unless I have to. I do need to know the truth so that I can give Mr. Williams as much of the truth as possible. I have to ensure that he'll realise that Mark is innocent of what he's been accused of." He said, with a soothing voice, hoping to reassure her.

Mrs. Williams looked him in the eyes again. This time she wiped away her tears and asked what he needed to know. Graham wanted to know what went on that night and if Mark had deliberately disregarded his duty.

It took her ten minutes to tell him about the whole evening and how much she had led Mark on, without going into the full details. She told how she had taken him to her bed and that once he had heard the shot; Mark had quickly dressed and left for the Customs House.

Graham sat back for a moment, starring into the fireplace. Then he stood up and left the room without further words with Mrs. Williams and without looking back. He could understand that one person can have desires for another and that sometimes the fact that one or both are married makes no difference. What he couldn't see was how a wealthy woman, in her thirties, could have such feelings for a person young enough to be her son.

Mrs. Damson was standing at the foot of the main staircase, waiting for him to return from the sitting room.

"Have you the information you needed to clear Master Mark?" she asked, as Mr. Johnson flowed passed her, towards the door.

He said nothing. The fact that it was Mrs. Damson who had led him to find out what may well clear Mark, didn't dispose him to answer her.

He felt so much anger at this moment that if he had said anything he may well have ended up running Mrs. Damson through with his cutlass, had she uttered another word.

He walked virtually through the door. He didn't appear to have opened it. It just parted as he reached it. He made no attempt to close it behind him. He was a man with a purpose this night.

Mrs. Damson went over to the door and closed it, turned around and looked up the staircase. There, stood at the top, was Mrs. Williams starring down in to the entrance hall.

"Mr. Johnson has left, Madam." Mrs. Damson said.

Mrs. Williams smiled, an inane smile, and turned towards her bedroom.

"Madam, would you like supper in your bedroom tonight?" Mrs. Damson asked.

"Nothing tonight." She replied.

CHAPTER 31
The Warrant stays

Mr. Johnson needed to clear up this whole matter tonight. He couldn't go back to Mrs. Jefferies and tell her that he hadn't done everything he could to clear Mark. His initial thought was to head straight for the White Heart Inn and confront Mr. Williams. Then he realised that he needed to gather his thoughts before he saw him. Otherwise he could well say things he shouldn't. So instead he headed for the New Inn to get an ale and a space to think. He just hoped that it was a quite night at this Inn.

Mr. Williams, on the other hand, was just starting his fourth tankard of Thomas Kemp's best ale and telling the tales of his visit to London, the women he had taken to his bed and the ale he drunk.

There was no chance that word would get back to his wife and if it did he didn't bother too much, she was his property and was dependant for her money and status, in this area, by remaining married to him.

When Graham arrived at the New Inn he ordered a tankard of ale and sat by the fire to think about what he should do. Within fifteen minutes he had got his thoughts together. The best place to tackle Mr. Williams would be in the White Heart Inn. He would be among drinking friends and, although he may well want to show that he was in charge, it would be easier for Graham to get around the fact that Mark was in his wife's bed.

By the time Mr. Williams was half way through his next tankard he saw Mr. Johnson entering the Inn and walking towards his table. He had another drinking partner, someone else he could tell of his adventures in the big city.

"Sit down next to me Mr. Johnson." He said with a drunken slur.

"Give my man a chair" he ordered Mr. Kemp, "and a tankard of your ale."

Both the chair and the tankard arrived together. Graham thanked Thomas and sat down next to Mr. Williams.

"What have you been up to today? Did you catch that young rascal?" He enquired.

"No, I searched the villages and hills, all around my area and Mr. Climpson was searching his area around Lewes. We have found nothing." Graham reported.

"Then we'll have to offer a reward. That should bring him back to us, if both my best men are so incompetent." He said, raising a laugh from those he had been drinking with for the last hour.

He was a cruel man, with no idea about loyalty to his men.

This made Graham really mad and brought him to a state where he was about to be just as cruel, by telling all those present that Mark had been to bed with Mr. William's wife, while he was away in London. He stopped him self. There was no point in upsetting Mr. Williams, when his objective was to get him to lift the warrant for Mark's arrest.

"I don't think that is necessary, Sir." Graham said.

This brought about a change in Mr. Williams. He hadn't been use to being rebuked by his subordinates, especially before his friends.

Graham noticed the change in his boss's attitude and quickly went on to explain why.

"In my travels I discovered the truth about Marks whereabouts on the night in question. I can assure you that he was no way involved in the capture of the goods from the Customs House." He said, looking directly at Mr. Williams.

There was a silence for a moment as Mr. William's took in what Graham had said. Not that he had actually said very much. Graham had been relying on the fact that he was an experienced Riding Officer and Mr. Williams should take his word on what he had found out.

"Explain yourself Mr. Johnson. How can you be so sure that Mark was not involved? If you can't convince me the warrant stays."

"I was told, on my travels, about a married woman from this town who had taken Mark to her bed, that night."

"Who was this woman?" The local tailor asked.

"I'm not at liberty to say." Graham replied.

"To give up her name wouldn't solve the problem and could well cause more. I've promised her that I wouldn't divulge her identity." Graham said with some authority.

"If you want me to call off the search for Mark, you'll have to provide me with more that that." Mr. Williams said.

"To give her name wouldn't be of any interest to you Sir." Graham said.

"You must take my word. I have spoken to her and she has confirmed that Mark was with her. She had stopped him from carrying out his duties."

This brought about gasps from those at the table. Not only did he say that a married woman was responsible, but he had already spoken to her.

"You must name her." The tailor snapped.

He appeared to be interested to find out if it was his wife or that of another at the table. The tailor's wife had been known to befriend some of the local men, when her husband was away but he hadn't been away that night.

"Mr. Johnson, I must know who this woman is. Then I can put the details in my report." Mr. Williams said.

"I'm sorry Sir but I gave my word. Without it I wouldn't have discovered the truth of why Mark was not at his post." He insisted.

"That young man lied to you, me and his father, when we asked him to explain why he was not at his post. I can't let this matter drop without knowing the lady's name, for my report." Mr. Williams insisted.

"Sir, you know how much I think of Mark and the fact that I would want to prove his innocence to the charges you brought against him. As he is not here and the fact that I have always been straight with you, over the last few years, as I have been here, you must take my word what I said is the truth."

"Name her." The innkeeper said.

"Name the woman." Came a volley of voices, from around the table.

"No" Graham said.

"I will not name her. All I will say is that she holds a good position in this town." He said, turning his face to look at every man around the table.

"And her husband wasn't in the house at the time."

This brought about some murmuring from those gathered at the table.

"And where were each of you? Were you at home that evening?" Graham asked, knowing that they weren't.

They all looked at each other and then back at Graham. Each of them realised that they had all been in this very place that evening. With the exception of Mr. Williams who was in London. All of them had been here when the sound of the shot came from to direction of the Customs House. Not one of them was at home with their families or their wives.

Realising that he had the upper hand now, Graham decided to go for the kill and get Mr. Williams to withdraw the warrant.

"Do you want me to name the woman?" He said, looking around.

"I don't think that's necessary Mr. Johnson." Mr. Williams said. "I think we can all trust in your discretion not to give out this woman's identity and that what you have said is the truth."

"Thank you Sir." Graham said.

"You will cancel the warrant on Mark and give me a chance to get him to come and tell you his side of the incident, without naming the lady in question." He enquired.

He had Mr. Williams in a corner. There was no choice other than to agree to Graham's demands. To say otherwise would take away the sense of authority he had just established, among those gathered around the table.

Mr Williams agreed to Grahams demands and told him to send word out, in the morning, that Mark was not to be arrested.

Graham didn't want to stay any longer than necessary so he drank up his ale and excused him self from the table. To stay longer would put him in an impossible position. Each of those present would try to elicit the name of the woman or at least try to establish that it wasn't their wives who were involved.

He walked towards the ferry, once he left the Inn. If anyone watched him go they would believe that he was heading that way and home. Had he gone in any other direction, they would have thought he was going to see the unfaithful woman and they would try to shorten the list of suspected wives.

Once out of sight of the Inn he turned away from the ferry and head for the Comptrollers house. He wanted to give a message to Mrs. Williams that her secret was safe.

As he approached the house he saw there was a light in one of the upstairs windows, Mrs. William's bedchamber. He couldn't disturb her tonight so decided to head on back to the ferry and home to Mrs. Jefferies. Mrs. Williams could wait until tomorrow. It wouldn't hurt her to suffer a little, after the trouble she had caused Mark.

As he came near to the quay and the ferry crossing point, he saw the ferry heading in his direction with three men on board, two he recognized as men from the town but the other was not known to him but he appeared to be in close conversation with the others.

The men from the town were John Swan and his brother David. They both worked in their father's boat yard, just up stream from the ferry crossing.

Graham kept himself back in the shadows, he didn't want to be noticed and if possible, he would be able to listen into their conversation and may be able to find out some useful information.

As the three men climbed up onto the quayside John and David stated to head towards the boat yard, apparently excepting the third man to follow them.

This man had, in fact, stopped and thanked the person who had rowed them over the river. Graham recognised not the voice but the country of origin of this stranger. He had a very thick French accent.

What was a Frenchman doing here and especially out this late at night?

He had never seen John or David out this late, unless it was on their way back from one of the town's Inns.

John turned around, when he realised that the other member of their party was not with them.

"Phillip, hurry up, we don't want to be seen by the Dragoons or they'll ask too many questions about you."

Reluctantly Phillip left the quayside and ran to catch up with them.

Before they had disappeared Graham had to break cover and get to the ferry, preferably without those last passengers knowing who he was.

As he reached the edge he could see that the ferryman was still tied to the rungs of the ladder, so rather than call out he descended the ladder into the ferry. When he stepped onto the boat he turned around and instead of finding the ferryman he was confronted by Barbara.

"Good evening Mr. Johnson, I presume you want to cross the river?" She said, but not with her usual tone, tonight she appeared to be despondent.

"Yes please Barbara." He said, as he sat down.

She asked him to reach up and untie the boat and then she pushed it away from the quay and started the boat across the river.

"If you see Mark, will you let him know that the warrant has been lifted and that he should come and see me." Graham said.

Barbara looked up with surprise. That wasn't the news she expected to hear.

"What do you mean, is he innocent?" She asked.

"I don't know that but he's not wanted for any crime, only bad judgment, as far as I know."

Barbara rowed in silence for the rest of the journey across the river. She wanted to believe Mr. Johnson but was afraid to hope that Mark was in the clear.

Before climbing up the ladder and after he had paid Barbara for the crossing, Graham told her that he had been able to clear Mark of the most damming of the charges against him. He may still lose his job, if he's not completely honest with Mr Williams, when next he sees him.

Barbara assured Graham that if she saw him she would pass on the message and persuade Mark to come and see him before he talked to Mr. Williams.

Graham thanked her and left the boat, climbed the ladder and walked over to the barn to collect his horse, for his journey home.

Chapter 32
The last time I saw George

Wednesday was a busy day for George and his lieutenants. Having retaken their goods from the Customs House in Newhaven, they needed to get them ferreted away so there was no evidence of it around, if the Riding Officers or Dragoons came calling.

He also had to get messages to his customers, those whose goods were captured. He needed to tell them where and when they could collect their stock.

Once all this was sorted out and he had received confirmation that everything was safely hidden and his customers had accepted the new arrangements, George went to the Star Inn. Here he met up with Henry and Norman, to discuss tonight's escapade.

It had already been agreed that, because of his injuries, Norman wouldn't accompany George to Jevington but Henry would go in his stead.

"Well is this a trap or what?" George asked.

"I don't think Jethro is up to planning a trap for you, even if he was put up to it. He didn't look that he was trying to hide anything." Norman said.

"Right, this is what we'll do. We will ride in from West Dean and cross over into Jevington valley. It may take longer but we'll not be expected from that direction so if it is a trap, we should spot their preparations."

"What about when we get there?" Henry asked.

"You go in first and check it out. I'll hold the horses. If it looks allright you come back out and hold the horses while I go in." George said.

"What if someone wants to enter the Inn?"

"Stop them." George ordered.

"Norman, if this is a trap; I need you to punish this Jethro?"

"He's a dead man!" Norman confirmed.

The three of them finished their tankards and left the Inn. Norman headed for his home to rest while George and Henry went to the Blacksmiths stables to collect their horses.

The two of them were very familiar with the Cuckmere valley, its tracks and paths but they would be in unfamiliar grounds once they entered Jevington valley. A formidable Free Trader's gang worked out of this valley controlled by 'Jevington Jiggs'. They would have to be on their guard tonight.

It was an uneventful journey. They arrived at the Eight Bells Inn just after six o'clock. At the side of the inn was a space where customers could tether their horses. There were already two horses tethered, so it looked as if Jethro and the Frenchman had already arrived.

George was not going to tether their horses until he was sure that it was safe to do so. He needed them ready if they needed to make a speedy departure.

Henry dismounted and walked down the three steps and into the bar. He had placed his right hand on the stock of his flintlock pistol, tucked into his belt. He needed to be prepared if it was needed but from what he could see there was nothing to worry about.

Behind the bar stood the Innkeeper, across the room, sat at a table was a buxom young lady. Behind her, at a table near the fireplace, were two men. Henry recognised the first one, this was Jethro. The other was dressed like a sailor, so this must be the man who asked for this meeting.

Satisfied that it was safe, Henry went back through the door and reported to George. Henry remounted his horse and took hold of the reins of George's horse. In the meantime George had entered the Inn. Henry moved the horses so that they could block anyone from following George.

The Innkeeper was about to greet George when Joan got up from her table and rushed across the barroom and flung her arms around George.

"Oh George it has been such long time, I'm sure John can spare me for while if you would like to come into the back room?"

"Not tonight Joan, I have business to do. I'll be returning in few days time, maybe then." He said, dismissing her advances, but not before he had pressed a florin into her hand and separated himself from her embrace.

"John, my friends and I don't want to be disturbed tonight. I suggest that you close up while we're here."

If George wants the Inn to himself he gets it. The last Innkeeper to deny such a request ended up watching his Inn burn to the ground. John went around the bar, locked the door and closed all the shutters, so that visitors couldn't see what was going on inside.

"Joan, bring me a tankard of ale." George demanded.

George took off his hat and coat, revealing a pair of pistols clipped onto his waistband, one partly covered by his waistcoat, the other in full view. A cutlass was hanging from the left side of his belt. He flung his outer clothing onto the chair, previously occupied by Joan and went towards the fire.

"It's a bit cold." George said. "You've a good fire going tonight John".

"Aye it's cold so I though a fire may bring in a few travellers." John replied, not that George was listening.

George went over to the table to join Jethro and the Frenchman. Jethro introduced the Frenchman to George. For a few moments the three of them spoke in French, thinking that the other two people in the barroom would not understand what they were talking about.

As George was about to speak, Joan arrived with the tankards. "Sit beside me Joan." George beckoned, returning to English.

Not wanting to offend, or more likely frightened not to obey, Joan placed the tankards before the three men and then reached over to a chair from the next table and drew it over, next to George and sat down.

Joan could read the signs. She knew that George wanted her as a distraction for the other two men. So as she sat down she leaned forward towards Jethro and the Frenchman, knowing that the front of her blouse would fall open giving the men a good view of her cleavage. With a quick flick of her thumb she sprung open one of the retaining buttons and pulled down the front of the blouse just before her rear made contact with the chair. The effect was that her bosoms had the attention of all those around her and with subtle movements she would be able to distract the men and give George any advantage he was looking for.

By now the three men had returned to talking in French.

What Joan had to look out for was that any movements she made did not appear to coincide with what they were taking about or they would realise she understood every word they said.

"Tell me about these letters Philip." George asked.

"Well I'm not to sure exactly what they contain but my sponsor says they are very important for France and aren't to fall into the hands of the English authorities."

"For that kind of cargo I would expect you are receiving a good wage?" Jethro put in.

"I'm not being paid to deliver these letters." Philip said.

This raised concerns for George, if Philip is not being paid, what's in it for him? Unless he missed his guess these letters were not in the best interest of England and were likely to be communications with French Agents or sympathizers. To be caught with these meant the hangman's noose for sure.

"If you're not being paid, what's in it for you?" George asked.

"I'm told that on the days I carry these letters the French Navy and Customs will turn their eyes as my lugger goes passed." Philip replied.

"That will be good for us as well." Jethro said, trying to impress George.

"We'll be able to bring more goods, with one of our obstacles removed."

George became angry with Jethro.

"Don't you understand what these letters are? If we're caught with them we'll be put to the gallows."

"Just because the French let Philip through doesn't mean that our Navy will. I'm dam sure the Customs men won't." George said to Jethro but facing the Frenchman.

"I need something for my trouble, a big something Philip." George said, this time directed at the Frenchman.

"You'll have the larger cargo in one trip and the profit from that, surely that's enough?" Philip said, thinking that the only thing that George thought about was profit.

"You may be working for your country for nothing but I'll be betraying mine. For that I need to be well paid." George said. Then he directed the next question towards Jethro.

"And why aren't you taking this on? You seem to be full of the idea of a larger cargo and bigger profit. Does you neck mean less to you than mine does to me?"

"Philip didn't want to chance landing his cargo in such exposed places as across the marshes, Hastings or the Bulverhyth areas. They are very dangerous places, so he asked me for some help." Jethro replied.

"I'd love Jethro to take on such a large landing but this is your area George and only a fool would come into your area uninvited." Philip put in.

George understood this and appreciated the sign of respect that Philip was showing him.

"George, the Customs men have been closing in on us on the marshes. It is getting very dangerous for us all. Even Philip has suspected that a navy cutter has been lying off shore, waiting for him." Jethro said.

"There'll be people to collect the letters near the coast but they're not willing to chance being captured. They treasure their necks." Philip added.

He let that fact sink in before continuing. "The Downs offer good cover and the many tracks leading away from the sea, this means that they can get far inland with less chance of being seen."

"I'll need ten sovereigns for each letter." George said.

There was a silence, Joan reached forward and picked up the three empty tankards, they may have been talking but it didn't stop them drinking.

"Well!" George cut in.

"Yes, Yes," spluttered Philip hurriedly. His mind was on Joan's cleavage, not on the business at hand.

"Good, when do you want to start? When will the first delivery be made?" George asked.

Philip suddenly realised what he had just agreed to.

"No, I didn't mean to say ten sovereigns for each letter." Philip was flustered; this would cost him dear.

"I meant, I can offer two sovereigns for the letters on each trip. That's the most I can pay."

George pulled out one of his pistols and thrust it in Philips face and cocking back the flint, in a practiced movement.

Philip had sweat poured down his face as he realised his answer could decide his very life.

John was an experienced Innkeeper, he could sense when trouble was brewing. He quickly drew up three tankards of ale ready to intercede if it became necessary. In the mean time Joan had picked up the empty tankards, on the table and started for the bar.

"Joan, get back there quickly and do something, I don't need bloodshed here tonight." John instructed her.

Joan dropped the empty tankards onto the bar and took up the three full tankards and went back to the table. She still couldn't show that she had understood their conversation so she thought quickly, how could she defuse this situation without George becoming suspicious?

"George, he only smiled at me. He wasn't making a pass at me. There's no need for you to act so jealously and any way, you said you weren't here for me tonight." Joan said, as she placed the full tankards onto the table.

"Keep out of this." George snapped in French, not for an instance taking his eyes from Phillip or his pistol from its line of sight. Anyone else may have reacted, but Joan stood still.

"What was that George, I don't understand?"

George realised what he'd done and calmed down.

"This is man's business and has nothing to do with you Joan." George said, this time in English.

"Sit back down while I finish off this matter and then you can have your Frenchman."

"Well Philip, what is your answer?" George had returned to French again, placing the barrel of his pistol firmly between Philips eyes.

"I'm sorry George. Yes it'll be ten sovereigns." Philip splutters out.

"And when will I be paid?" George still had not lowered the pistol.

"You wouldn't accept payment into your bank, by one of our contacts?" Philip asked. Sweat now streaming down his face.

If Philip thought he was dealing with an idiot he was in for a rude awakening. George brought the butt of the pistol hard down onto Philips hand, not sufficient to break any bones but enough to cause pain.

"I'm no fool Frenchman. I'll not have anyone being able to trace such payments to me. I get cash before I move to the coast or you take the letters back with you."

"I'll arrange this for you. The person who'll be collecting the letters will bring the money." Philip said.

George seemed to settle down. He returned the flint back to its safe position and then clipped the pistol back onto his belt and sat back.

"Can you ask the Frenchman if he has any perfume with him?" Joan asked George.

"I have not seen any French perfume for a long time and Master Turner said there are some exciting new ones about now." Joan said with a smile.

"He's not a travelling salesman Joan. He's just a fisherman over here to have his lugger repaired in Newhaven, he's not on holiday." George said.

"Pardon me George." Philip said, in English,

"I do have some bottles in a bag on my horse. I'll get them my Cherrie." He said, smiling at Joan. With this he rose and headed for the barroom door.

Phillip needed to get some air, George was a frightening man and so he needed to recover his poise before entering into discussions about the cargoes and the price. If he is careful he'll be able to make up the cost of the letters from the sale of the cargo.

"John let the man out." George ordered.

George was not worried that Philip would do a runner. Henry was outside and could well look after the Frenchman. What concerned him was what he would return with. George thought quickly, how could he neutralize Jethro at the same time covering the door? George's eyes strayed towards Joan's ample bust and remembered the reaction of Jethro, when he had a chance to view them earlier.

Henry was surprised to find the barroom door opening and the Frenchman walking out. He reached for his pistol and pointed it at the man.

"I'm just collecting a bag from my horse." The man said.

Henry watched him very carefully. He moved the horses so that he could keep an eye on the Frenchman, until he returned to the Inn. The man was just getting a bag from over his saddle and taking it back into the Inn. Henry relaxed, when the barroom door closed again.

George lent over towards Joan and whispered "Start to giggle girl and do not stop until I sit back." He instructed.

Joan did as she was told and started to giggle like a little girl.

"Before that Frenchman comes back I want you to give Jethro a good view of your breasts and give him the same smile that you did for the Frenchman earlier." George whispered again.

"Do you understand me, make no mistake your life and mine may depend on it." George said.

"Yes, stop that you naughty man, you said you didn't want me tonight." Joan said, turning to look at George's face. George sat back and Joan stopped giggling.

Joan guests that the Frenchman wouldn't be long, so tried to judge her action so as to co-inside with his return.

George slid his left hand over the butt of his second pistol and started to ease it free. George had to be sure that Joan did her job now or he could find a shot in his back from Jethro.

Although John may not like George, he wasn't having strangers killing one of his customers. John had also read the situation, after seeing Jethro arm himself earlier. He armed himself with the two pistols he kept under the bar, one would be aimed at Jethro and the other would be used on either George or the person coming through the door, whichever one posed the greatest threat to John's own life.

The only person in the bar who wasn't prepared for action was Jethro and this was his saving grace because had he been ready to kill George, both he and Philip would have ended up dead.

A few moments later Joan heard the sound of someone coming down the steps to the door. She half rose from her seat and leaned across the table towards Jethro. Ensuring that her blouse fell open sufficiently for her ample breasts to be in good view to any red blooded man.

As the door opened she reached over to pick up Jethro's Tankard. As she looked up her eyes followed Jethro's face from his chin, passed his drooling mouth, up his lumpy nose and looked into his eyes. Jethro was not looking at her face. Her job was done. The door opened and Philip walked in. He wasn't carrying pistols or any other weapon, just a bulging bag. He may not be a travelling salesman but he was always prepared to show samples of what he could supply.

Everyone relaxed as Philip approached the table. Joan took a deep intake of breath, which kept Jethro's attention and oblivious to what had been going on around him. Joan picked up the other two tankards and headed over to the bar, for refills.

"Here you are my Cherrie. Look through these and see if you can find one that will match your charms." Philip said, as he placed his bag down on the table in front of Joan's chair.

Joan was soon back at the table, with three tankards of ale, placed one in front of each of the men.

"Thank you Sir." She said, and began to rummage through the bag, taking out bottles that took her eye.

George now wanted to get down to the specifics of the business of the day, the Brandy, Geneva, Lace and tea. These were all goods that he had ready customers for and couldn't currently supply in sufficient quantities. George was expecting a delivery in two days time so didn't need another one for a few days after that.

It was George's experience that once he had paid off his men, most of them would visit local inns and public houses with their new found wealth, others took brandy or Geneva as payment and soon drank it dry.

George was of the opinion that Philip would be keen to start deliveries very soon but He needed to put him off for a week. After all the increased trade and the extra for the letters would make him rich and he would be able to retire from this very dangerous activity.

"Now Philip," George had returned to French again.
"We need to talk about what I need and can you supply it in the quantities and quality that my customers demand."
Also returning to his native French, Philip replied.
"Jethro will confirm that I can supply all the usual goods at the top quality, in any quantity you require and at the lowest prices."
He was into his selling mode now but it would take more than a smile to charm George. What Philip had already learned was that he was dealing with a very dangerous man. He would have to tread very carefully, especially if he was to walk away with a healthy profit.
"I do sometimes have trouble in getting Chantilly Lace but all of us have that problem from time to time as you will already know." Philip said, trying to flatter George with knowledge that he may or may not possess.
"I have a demand for Geneva at the moment. Have you any problems with that?" George was prodding now. He knew there was a new distillery in Dunkirk especially to supply the needs of the illicit trade with England.
The French authorities didn't mind this trade as they saw it as a way to get the English gold coins to melt down for their treasury coffers.
"That's alright. I have a boat that sails along the coast to Dunkirk. It one can get as much Geneva as I require."
Philip looked into George's eyes when he said this. He knew that George was testing him and he didn't want to come up wanting.
"What about the tea? I only want the best you know." George was on a roll, he felt that Philip would say or do anything to get his order. Even if it was only so he could please his French masters.
"I've some friends who sometimes come across ships returning from India, where the captains realise that they can get more for their cargo selling it to us than landing it at the customs sheds in London." Philip was hopping that this was impressing George.
"My friends have a warehouse. I can get whatever tea you desire."
George was impressed. Either this Frenchman was as good as he said or he had been very well briefed, by a first class smuggler. George chose to believe him. After all he had left him in no doubt as to what would happen to anyone who crossed him.
George put his hand into his left inside pocket and drew out a piece of paper and handed this to Philip.
"If you can deliver this on the night of the twenty fifth, at Exceat, we will be able to do business." George said.
Philip took the list and read it, there were one or two items that he had not expected to see but he knew that his reputation was on the line so he would have to pull out all the stops to fill this list.
"By the twenty fifth, I'll be able to land all these goods at Exceat; I'll be in touch with you, about the times as they will depend on the tides."
George was not happy with this arrangement and quickly thought of another way. If there was to be a French agent collecting the letters then Philip or his masters would need to contact them so that they knew when to come and collect the letters. George thought that he could utilize the agent to pass the message.

Turning to Joan and returning to English George said, "Joan would you like to show Jethro the treasures you keep in the back room."

Jethro did not understand why he was being dismissed but could he be about to see more of the treasures he had already been looking at.

Joan was not too happy at being dismissed

"I don't think I've much in my room that will interest Jethro, George, and what is there would be too expensive."

Joan was staring directly into George's eyes, she was trying to tell George that she only took people to her room if she liked them and Jethro didn't fall into that category, by a long way.

"I'll make it up to you." George said, as he slipped two sovereigns from a hideaway pocked, in his jacket, into Joan's hand.

Once Joan and Jethro had left the barroom, George told Philip how he wanted to be informed of the times and tides he would be delivering the goods. At first Philip was not sure he could achieve this but once George explained that he didn't want any contact with Jethro, again, Philip agreed.

"Can you give my friend a room for the night John?" George asked.

"Yes there'll be no problem with that George."

"I'm sure that we can find you a suitable room Sir." John said, addressing the Frenchman.

George smiled. "Have a good journey home Philip. I hope to hear from you soon."

With that George left the inn, not waiting to bid fair well to Jethro.

Henry was not sure if he had enjoyed just sitting there, waiting for George's return or was it the fact that he saw no one about. In Aldfriston there was always someone about, even at this time of night.

When George came out, Henry wasn't sure if he was happy or not. Firstly George smiled when he saw Henry but then his face changed into anger. It defiantly was not the time to ask how the meeting went.

George remounted his horse but instead of heading back the way they had come, he turned it around and they headed out of the village towards Walnut Street. For the first ten minutes, George said nothing but then he turned to Henry.

"I don't trust that Jethro. If things go wrong we could swing."

"What the hell has he got us into?" Henry asked.

"That is none of your concern but hell will arrive if he crosses us."

They rode on for about half a mile before George spoke again.

"I'm going to finish him. He's too stupid not to tell on us."

"We can't do that." Henry protested.

"Yes we can and we will." George stated.

Shortly after they had passed the driveway into Filtching Manor, they came across a small chalk pit, cut into the right hand side of the road. Opposite this was a long drop down into a deep ravine and at the bottom a stream broke to the surface and ran towards Walnut Street.

"We'll wait here. He has to come this way to get home." George said.

The two of them backed their horses into the chalk pit and sat there listening for the sound of a horse coming from Jevington. They didn't have long to wait. It sounded as if there was only one horse.

The moon was bright tonight so Henry and George would be able to identify their quarry quite easily. It was George who saw the horse, first. He moves his horse forward into the road, followed closely by Henry.

George had already drawn his pistol; it would do the talking for him. As Jethro drew up, on the opposite side of the road, George fired his flintlock directly at Jethro's head. Although not the most accurate of weapons, at this close range he couldn't miss.

Jethro had been in another world, the French Captain had given him two sovereigns for arranging the meeting. He was thinking of just how he was going to spend it. Before he could react to the appearance of George and the distraction of a second horseman, he faced a flintlock pistol being fired in his direction. He had no time to move or urge his horse away from this trap. It was too late now as the shot was on its way. It came in to his face just below his eye socket and went up, behind the eye, into his brain and everything stopped.

His horse was scared by the sound of the flintlock firing and reared up sending, the now limp Jethro, off his back and over into the deep ravine. When the front hooves touched down it galloped off towards Walnut Street and home.

With the departure of the horse, George looked down on the road but there was no sign of Jethro. What he could hear was like a large item falling through the trees and bushes, down into the ravine and the stream below. He had no doubt that he had hit his target and was just as sure that Jethro was now, or would soon be, dead.

It had been George's intention to return back up the road for half a mile and then branch off the road and head back into the hills and the quickest way back to Aldfriston but just as they were about to turn their horses in that direction a sound drifted towards them, from the direction of Filtching Manor. They heard the sound of coach doors being slammed.

"If we can hear them, they most likely heard your shot, George." Henry said.

"Aye, we had better follow that horse and then find another way back home." George answered.

With that the two of them headed towards Walnut Street. As soon as they could, they would turn off this road and head out across the fields and find a track that would take them back up on to the Downs and across to the Cuckmere Valley and home.

"I know some of this area." Henry said. "I'll lead the way."

At the end this small valley the road had fallen down to be level with the stream. Henry turned to his left and urged his horse to jump over the stream. George followed behind but his horse was reluctant to jump the stream as it saw the reflection of the moon shining up from the rippling water. It stopped suddenly and nearly threw George off headfirst into the water.

George wasn't at all happy with this. He backed the horse up and them urged it forward and shouted at it to jump the bloody water. It realised that its master was very angry and knew that if he didn't jump this time, he would receive a beating.

This time, as it neared the water, instead of looking down he just closed his eyes and jumped. When he realised that he was safely over the water, he opened his eyes and looked around. About three hundred yards, to his left, he could see the other horse and rider galloping off and so he headed after them, as fast as he could go.

In a short time the pair of them reached a cross track. To their right, this led to Folkington. In front of them the track led to some fields and across them they could reach Windover Hill, which crossed above Wilmington and would lead them down to Aldfriston. Henry said that this way would get them home both safely and quickly.

Before they set of George needed to reload his discharged pistol. George moved his horse into the moonlight while Henry kept in the shadows. George was not the type of person to allow himself to risk running into a fight with only one loaded pistol. From his small bag, he took out the powder bottle, a piece of wadding and a shot ball.

There was sufficient light for him to measure powder into the barrel and ram it home with his rod and then roll in the shot, this was then followed by the wadding. George used less wadding than most men and more powder. He found this gave him greater range, thus allowing him to take on his foes at a further distance than they were able to do. The only problem was that if he got it wrong, the wadding would not hold and the shot would fall out, followed by the powder.

"OK Henry, let's get home." George said, as he stuffed his loading equipment back into the bag.

Once they had crossed Windover Hill, they took a track ahead of them, which ran parallel to the Lullington village road and behind the village, but away from it. George thought that there was less risk by going over Lullington Heath, so they turned up the track and then took the left fork over the Heath.

The clouds had virtually dispersed and so the full moon was in full view, giving out such a bright light that the journey was nearly like being in daylight. This of course had very great dangers for George and Henry. They were on unfamiliar ground and didn't know places to hide up, if the occasion demanded it.

They could see for miles but so could the Dragoons and Riding Officers. George was hoping that the Riding Officers would be scouring the coastline, looking for the landing places and not yet come inland, to search for the carts and pack horses moving the goods away from the coast.

They rode on, searching the countryside as they went. Even though they didn't know this area well they were well aware of the types of places where people could hide up.

As they started to descend into the Cuckmere valley they came across various tracks that crisscrossed this side of the Downs. Both of them relaxed now, this was their area and they knew each and every tree and bush this side of the hill.

They went passed Fore Down and started to descend into Lullington. Before they reached the place where the track split off towards Littlington village Henry said "I'll leave you're here, George. see you on Tomorrow."

With that said Henry turned his horse and headed down into the valley. George could see a light in the window of Henry's cottage, which nestled at the end of this small valley.

George urged his horse on. He still had several miles to travel before he was safe in his village. He reached Littleington without encountering anyone, he decided to would slow down so as not to attract any attention.

As he turned off the road leading to Lullington and headed towards the bridge over the river Cuckmere and into Aldfriston, he came face to face with a Dragoon patrol.

They were but twenty yards in front of him and heading his way. He had no time to turn and flee. It would be of no use anyway. His horse was quite tired after the journey over to Jevington and back.

His only hope was that in the darkness of this road, although the moon light provided some light, there were trees on either side of the road here and so much of the available light was obscured and put him in near darkness. He pulled his hat down further over his eyes and tried to lower his shoulders so as to look smaller in the saddle.

As he rode forward the Dragoons parted to let him pass between their ranks. Halfway through the Dragoons, he saw that a large black horse and its rider had blocked his path.

"Good evening George." Sergeant O'Riley said.

George looked up and in the near darkness he could see that the Sergeant was holding a pistol in his hand and it was pointing in George's direction. He quickly looked around and found that each of the Dragoons was also pointing their pistols in his direction.

"Now put your hands up, like a good man." Corporal Jones said, from just behind his left shoulder.

To re-enforce his request he thrust the barrel of the pistol into George's shoulder.

George thought there seemed no point in trying to escape at this time. These men would shoot him dead, without a second thought. Putting his hands up, as ordered, he asked why they were stopping him, he hadn't done anything wrong.

"You're under arrest for the murder of Jack Clarke at the Newhaven Customs House. That is what you've done George."

"That wasn't me, I wasn't there and I can prove it."

"I expect you can find twenty of your friends to say you were in the Star Inn, all the time, aye George."

"That's right, I can." George said.

"The only trouble is that we have two Customs Officers and a Constable that will swear that you were in Newhaven.

George thought for a moment, would they take him to Lewes. If so he would be all right, there were three Magistrate's in Lewes who were in his debt. If they took him elsewhere he may need to call in a few favours to get the Magistrates, in whatever town he was taken, to release him.

One of the Dragoons, to his right lent over and relieved him of his two pistols and the cutlass. He wouldn't be able to fight his way clear now.

"Now put your hands behind your back, please." Corporal Jones said.

Taking a rope from his pocket and tucking his pistol into his belt with the other hand, he reached over and tied up George's hands.

"Not so tight, I can't feel my fingers." George called out.

"You won't need your fingers were your going." Sergeant O'Riley said.

John reached down and picked up the reins of George's horse and led it behind his own. The troop was now moving of, away from Aldfriston and out of George's area of influence. As they reached the road they turned towards Lullington.

"Where are you taking me?" George asked.

"To our barracks in South Bourn, you'll be safe there until we can transport you to London." The Sergeant said.

London, they can't do that, thought George. If you're arrested in an area you are supposed to be tried in a local court.

Sergeant O'Riley sensed George wouldn't be happy with what he had just been told and no doubt bewildered by it as well.

"You killed one of His Majesty's Customs Officers George. That means you have to appear in one of His Majesty's courts in London."

CHAPTER 33
I remand you to the Old Bailey

George had spent an uncomfortable night in the goal house at South Bourn barracks. The room had no window and the door was made of solid oak, with both the hinges and lock on the outside.

He had felt around the room, in the total darkness of the night and found nothing that would help him escape from the predicament he had, by chance, found himself in.

Before he had fallen asleep on the straw which was lying in the corner of the room, he had tried to work out how he got here and, to him more importantly, how he was to get out of this situation. If he escaped he wouldn't be able to return to his home and the safety of his gang. The authorities would be after him. He would have to leave the area.

Being dark George had no idea of the time. He had woken several times in the night and on realising his situation he would close his eyes and fall back to sleep. He saw no benefit in using up energy that he may need later.

The first sound he heard in the morning was that of the door being flung open and daylight pouring into his small room. He shielded his eyes, with his hands so that they could adjust to the change in light. As he lowered his hands he could see the shape of a Dragoon standing in the doorway, looking down on him.

"Good morning Mr. Styles." Sergeant O'Riley greeted. "I hope you had a good nights sleep and are rested."

"Go to hell." George replied.

"That treat has been reserved for you George."

"There's a bucket of water in the next room and a meal for you on the table."

Sergeant O'Riley was not in the mood for George's threats so decided to take the upper hand.

"You have ten minutes to wash and eat. Then you'll be taken to the Magistrate to remand you to our custody and transportation to London."

This hit home. George realised what he had thought of as a nightmare was reality. He had been arrested and was in danger of loosing his life.

He rose and followed the Sergeant out of the cell and into the room outside. As the Sergeant had foretold, there was the bucket for him to use to wash and on the table was a tankard of ale and some bread.

"I'll be back in ten minutes George, make yourself presentable. Mr. Smithers doesn't take kindly to people entering his court unwashed."

With that the Sergeant and a Dragoon left the outer room and George could hear a lock being turned on the outside door.

He went to the only window in the room and saw that outside the goal house were stationed three Dragoons, all with carbines and cutlasses. The Sergeant was taking no chances; thought George. He decided that now was not the time to make an attempt to escape. There would be plenty of time for such thoughts once outside the barracks.

As the ten minutes was up, the Sergeant and his men entered the room.

"You'll come with us now Mr. Style." Sergeant O'Riley ordered.

George walked towards the door but was stopped before he reached the entrance, by one of the Dragoons

"Hands behind your back please Mr. Styles."

George turned his head around and saw that the other Dragoon held some rope in his hands, ready to bind his hands.

"Sergeant there's no need for this. I'll cause you no trouble."

But this was falling on deaf ears. His hands were grabbed and brought around to his back and rope was bound around his wrists then firmly tied off.

"There's no need for the rope to be so tight, I'm not going to escape, not with you Dragoons guarding me." George protested.

No one was listening to him; he was thrust in the back and propelled out of the door. The Dragoon who was blocking his way was now standing outside, waiting to receive him in the open air.

Sergeant O'Riley had been lucky to come across George on his patrol the previous night. He had no intention of losing him before he handed him over to the jailers in London. If word got out that George Styles had been arrested, his gang would search him out and organize an attempt to release him. They had proved their worth when they had attacked the Customs House in Newhaven, so he was taking no chances.

George looked up and in front of him was a closed carriage, drawn by two black horses. The driver was a Dragoon, in full uniform and fully armed with cutlass and pistol. Sticking out from under his feet was the butt of a gun, which George took for a blunderbuss.

Behind the carriage were four mounted Dragoons and a spare horse, which was for the Sergeant. Escape was going to be harder than he thought.

"Get in the carriage Mr. Styles, if you please." The Dragoon said.

George didn't move quite as quickly as the Dragoon thought was right so he pushed his pistol into his back, with some force.

"Now Mr. Styles." He insisted.

George realised he would have to go along with them, play their game for as long as necessary. Then escape!

After he and the two Dragoons had entered the carriage it moved off. George had his back to the horses and his guards sat opposite him, each with a pistol in their hands. One of these pistols may misfire, as they did quite often, but the chances of both of them not getting off a shot was unlikely.

The journey to the Magistrates house took ten minutes but with the state of the roads around the town, George would have preferred to have ridden a hundred miles on his horse, than taken this journey.

When the carriage stopped outside the Magistrates house, the Dragoons in the carriage made no attempt to leave or prepare George to leave the carriage. They just sat there looking at him, apparently waiting for him to try to escape so that they could shoot him dead. If there was a reward for his arrest he was sure that they would collect it whether he was alive or dead.

George could hear someone walking up to the Magistrates door and knocking. After a short time the door was answered and he could hear the Sergeant asking to see the Magistrate. The Sergeant was admitted to the house, so George sat and waited for developments. He knew this Magistrate and had heard, that among all those around, this one was not easily bribed.

He didn't drink or smoke and his wife was not the fashionable type, so the latest laces from France couldn't be use as bribes. With the exception of some of tea, there was nothing that would entice this man not to do his duty and this was the wrong time of year for new season tea.

"It must be very difficult for you boys to leave the Dragoons, having little money to take away with you to start a new life." George said to the man sat opposite him.

He saw no reaction from him so he looked at the other Dragoon.

"You also." He said pointedly.

Neither man gave him any indication that they were listening to him.

"A man could set himself up well with a hundred sovereigns."

Still there was no reaction from either of them.

"And for two hundred he could get himself a beautiful wife as well."

This did bring a reaction from the youngest of the Dragoons.

"Aye I could go home and buy a few horses and start trading them on the farm next to my father's." He said, turning to his friend.

"Yes and the Sergeant would come over and find you, take back the money and if you were lucky, bring you back alive to stand trial."

He let that sink in for a moment then continued.

"If you were not lucky he would kill you where you stood for betraying the Regiment." This did sink home.

"And you Sir would die because you would have caused our Sergeant to punish one of his men, an expensive few sovereigns I think."

George saw that he wouldn't be able to bribe these men, especially if the older Dragoon was guarding him.

Before he could come to grip with these thoughts the door of the carriage was thrown open, standing outside were the Sergeant and the Magistrate.

"Is this the man you have arrested Sergeant O'Riley?"

"Yes it is Sir, George Styles from Aldfriston, the leader of the Aldfriston Raiders, you have heard of them I presume?"

"Yes Sergeant I have heard of Mr. Styles and his gang."

George expected to be brought down out of the carriage and into a courtroom but that didn't appear to be what either man had planned for him.

"What are the charges, Sergeant?" The Magistrate asked.

"He is charged with murdering a Customs Officer at Newhaven and of stealing contraband secured in the Customs House at Newhaven." The Sergeant reported.

"What have you to say for yourself Mr. Styles?" The Magistrate asked.

Without waiting for him to reply,

"As I thought, you can't answer the charges. Take him away Sergeant. I remand him in your charge, for delivery to a Goal of your choice, in London, where he can be tried for these devilish offences."

The Magistrate turned around and returned to his house, not looking back or listening to the abuse that was flowing from George's.

"Stop that at once." Sergeant O'Riley shouted.

"You're now my prisoner. You are going to London to meet the hangman at Newgate Prison."

With that he slammed the door closed and ordered the driver to move on.

255

Sergeant O'Riley turned to one of his troopers.

"Stan, go with the Magistrate and get him to write out the charges and say that he has given George over to us for delivery to goal, in London. Ensure that he signs and dates it."

"Which way are you heading?" Stan asked.

"Through East Bourn, Ratton, Willingdon and on to Swings Hill, you should be with us by then."

Was this to be George's last journey? Had he just started to amass his wealth only to hang without enjoying the fruits of his crimes? Not if he could help it.

This journey was going to take all day and if luck was in, they would have to stop at some inn along the way. Even guards such as these wouldn't travel once it got dark and although this was early morning, by the time they reached the outskirts of London, night time would be drawing in.

George had realised that the younger of the two liked the idea of the two hundred sovereigns and was thinking it may well be worth the risks involved.

"Can't you loosen these ropes around my wrists?" George asked, directing his comments at the older of the two Dragoons.

"They're cutting into my hands."

"It's the rope around your neck you should worry about. You won't need your hands after that." The Dragoon said, with a chuckle.

The younger one joined in the laughter.

"So you think this is funny do you?" George asked.

"When my men catch up with us, in Forrest Row, it'll be me who is laughing and you two will be dead."

"Your men don't even know you've been arrested, let alone on your way to London. This is the normal Regimental carriage trip up to London. You should know about this, you normally plan your busiest nights when our officers are away from barracks." The older Dragoon said.

"Your men won't know of your arrest until news of your hanging finds its way back to the Cuckmere Valley."

A small plan started to fester in George's mind, if he could let his man see him, as the carriage went past, they would alert the rest of the gang and before long a rescue party would set off to release him from his mobile goal.

In the next hour George would need to attract as much attention to the carriage as possible. He couldn't leave it to a chance that his man would see him. If they sent old John Turner over it would be lucky if he even saw the carriage let alone the travellers inside.

As the carriage started up the small hill into Willingdon, George saw his first chance to get a message out. At the top the villagers would meet.

With the curtains still covering the windows of the carriage, there was little chance of anyone seeing in. He would have to draw one aside.

The carriage was slowing now and George saw this as an opportunity to look out. He moved forwards towards the curtain ready to peer out.

"Sit back Mr. Styles or you die where you sit." Ordered the Dragoon.

"And not a word or you'll not hear its end."

George found a pistol pointed directly at him. He turned to protest to the younger Dragoon and found that his pistol was also pointing in his direction.

"I just needed a bit of air lads, that's all." He protested.

"You can have all the air you want once we reach Newgate Prison."

They passed through Willingdon without stopping. Although there were a few people around, they took no notice of the Dragoon's coach, as it passed through each week.

Before they reached Swings Hill Stan had rejoined them and handed the letter from the Magistrate, to his Sergeant.

Had George been able to look out of the carriage, as it passed the Hailsham woods, he wouldn't have been identified, for it was John Turner that was on lookout today. The only reason he knew it was the Dragoons carriage was the fact that there were five outriders accompanying it.

The journey became very tiring for the next three hours, each time George tried to draw the curtain a pistol would be levelled at him.

By this time George had no idea where he was, had he passed Uckfield or not, he didn't know. He was hoping that they would have stopped at an inn before they reached the Ashdown Forest. If so he would have been able to get some sort of message to the local gangs of ruffians, to release him from his captors. Once they were passed the Ashdown Forest his chances of escape would be greatly lessened.

Sergeant O'Riley was well aware of the risks of losing his prisoner, whilst travelling through the Ashdown Forest. He had made detours around the various villages in the forest, so as not to raise questions as to whom he was carrying or for that matter what cargo he may be carrying.

It was noon by the time they came out of Ashdown Forest. Well past the time he would have normally have stopped to rest his horses and feed his men. The first village he came to was much too close to the forest for his good so he continued for a further three miles until he came to East Grinstead. Here he called a halt at the inn.

"Good a chance to stretch my legs at last. I thought we were never going to stop." George said.

"We wait for the Sergeant to give the orders Mr. Styles." The older Dragoon said, raising his pistol again.

The door of the carriage opened and the Sergeant came into view.

"You two can get out now and stretch your legs and get a meal in the Inn." He said to his men.

"What about our prisoner, who is going to look after him?" The younger Dragoon asked.

"Mr. Styles will be staying where he is and if he attempts to escape he will be shot dead, if he even looks out of the carriage he will be shot." Looking at George. "Do I make myself clear George, you stay here and I'll send you some food out, if you try to leave the carriage I'll have you shot."

"You're not a very nice man Sergeant O'Riley. Your men are right about you. You have no heart."

"May be, but my men and I have never lost a prisoner and I've not lost a man who was doing what he was told."

With that he turned and walked away from the carriage. The two Dragoons left the carriage and, after ensuring that the carriage doors were closed and the windows covered, they to went into the inn.

George was a careful man; he hadn't survived this long by being careless. What had brought him to this place was just bad luck, now he had to get himself out of it. He could see that there was a gap in the cloth, covering the door beside him, so he manoeuvred himself so that he could peer through and see if what the Sergeant had said was true.

To his dismay there were two Dragoons looking directly at the door and as he started to move the cloth to one side, to get a better look around, he saw one of the Dragoons pick up his carbine and raise it to his shoulder and aim towards the carriage.

George needed no second invitation to release the cloth and cover the window again. He waited for a shot to come whistling into the carriage, but none came.

As promised the meal arrived, together with a tankard of ale, all compliments of the Sergeant. The Dragoon untied his hands, guarded him while he ate and drunk his ale. Then he retied George's hands again.

Once the meal was consumed and the chattels returned to the Inn, Sergeant O'Riley organized his men ready for the remainder of the journey. He looked around, just before he gave the order to move off and saw two men standing at the corner of the inn.

To a trained eye, like the Sergeant's, these men were not there to wave them off. Mounting his horse he rode over to where the men stood.

"If you are thinking of following me and my men I'll warn you now that you won't live to tell what you see."

"We are doing nothing wrong." The first man said.

"No, and your not going to. For I'll see you dead before I allow any harm to come to my troops."

With that he drew his cutlass and lifted off the hat of the first man, with the point of the cutlass. Pointing it now directly into the eyes of the man.

"Do I make my self very clear?"

The man definitely took the point and after he had picked up his hat he and his friend left the Inn, deciding that these were not easy pickings for the gang of cutthroats they belonged to.

Several gangs worked in the woods, north of the village, robbing travellers that past through their area. Coaches were more difficult to rob, as the gangs worked on foot and the coachmen would use the speed and weight of the coach and horses to evade them.

They mostly picked on small groups or loan travellers who travelled mostly on foot or leading horses and carts. Highwaymen would attack the coaches as they could match the speed of the coach. Being off the ground they were on a level with the coachmen and thus their pistols made a big impression on these men.

Sergeant O'Riley had no intention of being the pickings of such gangs. Highwaymen wouldn't attack a troop of Dragoons.

The rest of the journey was uneventful. No one would risk attacking a carriage and a troop of Dragoons, away from the cover of the forests. There were a few villages to go through before they reached the River Thames and the bridges that crossed it.

Once they were over the river they headed for Newgate Prison.

At first the guards didn't want to take him in, as they had received no notice of his arrival but Sergeant O'Riley handed him the letter from the Magistrate in South Bourn. He then agreed to put George in a cell to await his trial.

Having deposited their prisoner they knew that they wouldn't get back to barracks before nightfall. The Sergeant decided to go to the nearest barracks, in London, to ask that his troop and their horses to be allowed to rest there for the night.

They all had a good night, The Sergeant was taken to the Mess and given a meal and, over drinks he recounted the capture of the smuggled goods and the capture of George Styles.

Although his men were not looked after in such style, after they had taken care of their horses, they were give a meal and then they sat around and told their version of events over the last few days.

The next morning they gathered together the horses and the carriage and headed back towards South Bourn.

Chapter 34
The search is over

Graham got up early today. He wanted to get out and about before others were around. Although he felt good about being able to clear Mark's name, not finding him was a worry.

Mrs Jefferies heard Graham coming down the stairs. He appeared to be trying to creep about her house and she didn't like that.

"Mr Johnson, is that you?" She called.

"Sorry Mrs Jefferies I was trying to get out without disturbing you."

"You're not going out without a meal inside you. Give me a minute and I'll be there."

"You don't need to trouble yourself."

"It's no trouble."

Graham realised he had better do as he was told. He was likely to be out for most of the day, so a good meal inside him would sustain him until he was either back here or found an Inn where he could get a meal.

While he was waiting for Mrs Jefferies to arrive he checked his pistols to ensure that they were loaded and that the power was dry. Having completed this he placed them on the shelf, by the outside door and checked his riding boots were there.

"Where are you going today?" Mrs Jefferies asked, as she entered her kitchen.

"I'm not sure. Now that Mark could have changed the half-ankers of Brandy and Genever into money, he could have gone anywhere."

"Mark only knows here abouts and Chichester. He wouldn't stay around here, not while he thinks you are all after him. He wouldn't go home either." Mrs Jefferies said.

"Yes, that's my problem. If he's still around, how to I get a message to him that he's not wanted. If he's left the area, well that's it." Graham said.

By now Mrs Jefferies had made breakfast for the pair of them and placed two plates on the table. Each one had cold meats, cake and bread. She collected the two tankards of ale and placed them beside the plates.

"Have you told Barbara Mark is clear and should come and see you?"

"Yes, she was the first person I told. The only problem is that I don't expect Mark to head back that way. I wouldn't if I was him, far too dangerous." Graham said.

"Can I help?"

"You could spread the word around Seaford. Has anyone seen Mark? Have they heard of his whereabouts? Could they pass word for him to come and see either of us?" He suggested.

"I can do that. I'll start with Fred and Simon. They get customers from all around, they may hear something."

"Don't forget Mrs Midhurst, she gets people in from all around." Graham suggested.

"I can't go into the Duke's Head."

"Then go around to her kitchen. She'll see you there and others won't think badly of you."

261

"I'll do that. What time do you expect to get back?" She asked.

"Before dark, I hope. I'll try to get out and see Bob Climpson, if I can. He may have heard something by now."

"You had better be on your way then."

Graham picked up the last mouthful of meat, washed it down with the dregs of his ale and got up from the table. He took his pistols down from the shelf and put them into his belt, put on his riding boots, coat and hat. He was now ready for the days work.

"Bye, see you later and good luck." He said, as he left the cottage.

His horse was in its small stable, at the cottage. He looked up as Graham approached and whinnied to acknowledge his arrival. It took Graham only a few minutes to get him ready for their days work. The reins were easy to fit and once he had led him out of the stable, he was able to get the saddle thrown over his back and fastened securely.

There was no way that he was going to enter Aldfriston so soon after all the troubles. They were still hurting from the death of their three young men. After their attack, on the Customs House, he would need Dragoons, with him, if he was brave enough to go there now. It would be a few weeks before he could even consider doing that.

Which way would Mark go once he had the Brandy? Graham couldn't think of him heading into Seaford. That would be silly and Mark wasn't a silly boy. He would want to make as much distance as he could from Graham and Newhaven.

That would mean going east, towards Friston and South Bourn. Then it struck him that he wouldn't do that. The Dragoons are barracked in South Bourn and they come through Friston, on their patrols. No, that wasn't a safe place for Mark. Where would he go?

It suddenly struck him. One day he had told Mark about the smugglers who worked in the next valley. Jevington was the only place he could go. They had an Inn and their Innkeeper was said to help out the authorities, with information. Maybe he would have heard about young Mark.

He urged his horse forward, headed over Seaford Head, down into the Cuckmere valley and along to Excet Bridge. Although he didn't know the countryside around Jevington, he had been told of the tracks leading through West Dean, into the hills and ending up in the Jevington valley. He would take that route but be very careful. Being very much a foreigner and, if he was recognised, a dangerous one at that.

Riding Officers were not welcome around smugglers areas and it was known that the best Genever, smuggled into this country, came through this valley in great quantities. 'Crowlink Gin' was not only well sort after but its fame spread across the country. Ending up in far away places such as London, Birmingham and other large cities.

No it was worth the risks. If he could find some trace of Mark or that he had passed this way, he would be making some progress in his quest.

As he rode into West Dean he noticed that there were few people around and those that were there were not interested in giving any information to Graham. He headed out of the village on the track that led into the hills and the next valley.

On his way he noticed a large house, set back from the track. It was an imposing building, not the type of place that would entertain a fugitive. He rode on passed and headed down the valley to Jevington. Before entering the village, Graham took out his pistol and held it across his lap, in his right hand. This way he was ready to defend himself but with his left hand holding the horse's reins but covering the pistol, this fact would not be obvious to the villagers.

His best call would be to go to the Inn and speak to the Innkeeper. If anyone knew what was going on, it would be him. The road that went through the village only had a few lanes that led off it. The majority of the cottages and houses were along this road so he assumed that the Inn was along here, somewhere.

After climbing a short hill, he could see the Inn, some hundred yards ahead of him. He replaced his pistol into his belt and, as he arrived at the inn, he found somewhere to tether his horse. Now he would have to be careful. If he was suspected of being from the authorities, he'd get nought.

"Good day a tankard of your best ale." Graham asked, spotting the man behind the bar.

"I'm not open yet." John Pettit replied.

"I've travelled a long way and have a long way to go, just a tankard." Graham said.

"What's your business?"

"I'm looking for the son of my employer. He ran away and his Lordship is worried." Graham lied.

"Well he's not here."

"His Lordship has told me that I can pay a reward to anyone who helps me find his son." Graham teased.

"How much is the reward?"

"That depends if I catch up with him today or not."

"If I've seen him, what's in it for me?"

"I'll give you a florin now. If I find him, then it'll be a sovereign." Graham said.

John thought about this. A florin was not very much but a sovereign was a good amount, even for him. There was something about this man that didn't ring true. This man looked very much like a fighter, someone who could look after himself. John knew of no aristocrats who would employ such as him. Was this a trap? But then he had not asked about anything that he would expect one of the Excise men to ask. This wasn't a man to be trusted.

"I saw a young man ride passed here yesterday." John said.

"Did he have anything to sell?" Graham asked.

"No, he just rode on passed and headed down towards Walnut Street."

"How was he dressed?"

"Just a riding coat, three cornered hat, that's all I can remember."

That was about as vague a description as Graham had ever heard. This man had either seen Mark or he was trying to get the florin for nothing.

"What about his horse?"

Now this would tell him if this man was lying. Anyone living in the country side couldn't help but notice the quality of Mark's mare.

"He rode a brown horse, but it was nothing special." John replied.

"Well that's not the person I'm looking for. He rides a good mare, dresses well and you would've noticed his fine cutlass." Graham said, with a smile.

He now knew that the Innkeeper had seen Mark and also, Graham was sure, he would've purchased the Brandy and Genever from him. The direction he said Mark had gone was also suspect but it was a start.

With that he returned his purse into his coat pocket and turned to leave.

"Just a minute, you said you wanted a tankard of ale." John said, as he came around the end of the bar.

"You said you were closed. Anyway as you haven't seen the boy, I must be on my way." Graham said.

Graham had been careful not to let the Innkeeper see the extent of the money he was carrying. Had he done so, it was possible that John may have considered robbing Graham.

He would follow the Innkeepers direction as to where the young rider had gone. At least it would get him out of this village quickly. There were just two farms to pass then he would be on his way and out of any danger that this man may cause him.

Once he had remounted his horse and rejoined the road, not knowing this area, Graham took out one of his pistols and held it in his right hand. He could well control his horse's reins with his left hand. The trees and bushes, along this road soon closed in, so there was less light and he couldn't see very far ahead. He worried that he was riding into trouble, so kept his whit's about him.

It wasn't long before he came to a hamlet, just a farm house on the top of a hill and a few cottages spread along the road. At the end of these he found an old manor house, to his right, set back from the road.

Would Mark have called in here? By the time he got here, he would have been both tiered and hungry. His boyhood charms could easily have got a cook to give him a meal. He would ride in to if Mark had called.

Graham rode up the short driveway to the main entrance, dismounted and left the reins hanging on the ground so his horse would stay where he was until his master returned. He strode over to the imposing door and knocked. In a short while the door was opened and before him stood an imposing man, holding a flintlock pistol.

"What is your business here?" The man asked.

"I'm looking for a young man who might have come this way, in the last day or two. I was wondering if he may have called here in search of some food and drink." Graham asked.

"No and he wouldn't have been welcome, if he had." The man said.

With that he closed the door, dismissing Graham without further ado.

Well he had to try. Now he would be on his way into Walnut Street and try there. If he had no success there, he would start to head towards Lewes and ask about Mark, along the way.

As he rode into this village, a man walked up towards him and held his hand up as if asking him to stop. Graham did as he was bid.

"Good day to you Sir." Graham said.

"Good day to you." James Watson said.

"I'm the Petty Constable hereabouts. What is your business?" He asked.

"I'm looking for a young man who may have come this way, you may have seen him. He was riding a magnificent mare and carries a brace of excellent pistols."

"I've not seen anyone like that around here. When was he this way?" James asked.

"A day or two, I believe." Graham said.

"In that case, defiantly not."

"If you do see such a young man, would you tell the next Dragoon patrol that comes this way and where he was headed?" Graham asked.

"What's in it for me?"

"There's a sovereign if word gets back to me, and I am able to catch up with the young scoundrel." Graham said.

"And who are you Sir?" James asked

"I'm the Riding Officer from Seaford, Graham Johnson." He replied.

With that the two men went their separate ways. James back to his house and Graham of towards Folkington, via Swinses Hill. There were no cottages at the hill, just a road junction. Graham knew that he needed to turn left and follow the contours of the Downs, keeping them to his left. If he did that, he'd find himself in Lewes by midday, provided he didn't get waylaid.

It was a quite morning, he saw no one on the road until after he had crossed Chilver Bridge, then he saw a man leading a horse and cart, coming towards him.

"Sir, have you seen a stranger here abouts, in the last day or two?" Graham asked.

"Only you, Master." The man replied.

Graham rode on and crossed Berwick Common, there he took the track that led into the village of Alciston. The actual road he had been on bypassed the village but Graham wanted to ask here, in case Mark had doubled back, once he had money.

He asked three people, in the village if they had seen the young man he was looking for but no one was going to tell Graham anything. He was back in his home area, not only did he know the people around here but they knew him.

Once he left the village and rode on towards Firle. Here he would stop for a drink and some food at the Ram Inn. Hopefully Jim would have heard something.

He had no more success here than he had had in the other villages. It appeared that Mark had just disappeared. It was time to seek out Bob Climpson and see if he had any more luck in finding Mark.

Graham saw no point in going into either Beddingham or Glynd. They were unlikely to tell him anything, even if they had seen Mark pass their way. As such he rode along the track that passed Ranfcomb and would bring him into Cliff, on the outskirts of Lewes, where Bob lived.

As he rode up towards Bob's cottage he saw him coming out of his front door. Once Bob recognised Graham he stopped what he was doing and waited for him to arrive. It was obvious that Graham had come to see him but he knew that he had nothing to report to him about Mark.

"I see you haven't found Mark yet, Graham." Bob greeted him.

"No, not a sign. I've a feeling he did pass through Jevington."

"Come in the cottage. I'm sure Angela can rustle you up a bite to eat."

"I'll come in but don't bother Angela. I've already eaten in Firle."

He dismounted and tied the reins onto a post, outside Bob's cottage then both men went inside, sat down and talked all about the last couple of days. Graham told him about the half-ankers of brandy and genever that Mark had retrieved and where he thought he had sold them. With the money he would have received for them, he would be able to go wherever he wanted.

It was agreed that they would stop searching for Mark. If word came about that he was in the area, they would try to contact him but there seemed little point now.

Chapter 35
He'll be back

When Mr Williams awoke, that morning, he was not at all happy. A few days ago he was seen as a great Comptroller. He was the man responsible for capturing the largest consignment of contraband, this year. Now he had to find a way of reporting that it had all gone. Taken back by the very smugglers his men had captured it from.

When he walked into the dining room, his wife was already sat at the table and was eating her breakfast.

"Is there any news of Mister Mark?" She asked.

"Who cares about that young man? He let me down and if it hadn't been for him George Styles wouldn't have been able to take his goods from the Customs House." He snapped.

"It wasn't his fault, it was ...." She began.

"Then whose fault was it? It wasn't mine. I was in London." He said.

This was a sign for her to stop talking. She also realised what she was about to say, when he interrupted her.

Ann knew that her husband was a vindictive man. He was already looking for someone to blame for what had happened and Mark seemed to be the one at the top of his list. If he knew what he was really doing that night, if he caught up with him, he would see that Mark went to the gallows.

After breakfast, Mr Williams left the house and headed to the Customs House and his office. He had a report to write and needed a place of peace and quite to compose this work of fiction. What he couldn't see was that none of his men had done anything wrong.

Had Mark been at the Customs House, when George Styles and his men attacked, he would have had two bodies, instead of just the one. As Mark was one of only two people who had been able to put George in Newhaven and at the Customs House, he should be pleased.

It then struck him that Mr Downer, Marks father, was in charge of the investigation. If anything went wrong, it would be him who would carry the can. This made him feel better about it all now. He could write the report without mentioning his involvement at all.

Ann Williams had gone down to the kitchen to talk to Mrs Damson about the household duties and the menu for the week. As she was approaching the kitchen door she could hear a girl crying. Mrs Damson never brought her daughter to work so who was this? As she walked through the door she saw Barbara sitting, slumped on one of the kitchen chairs, sobbing uncontrollably.

"What's up with Barbara Mrs Damson?" Ann asked.

"It's young Mister Mark, madam. He promised Barbara that he'd return to see her last night, but he didn't turn up."

Ann walked up to Barbara and pulled up a chair beside her and sat down. She put her arm around her and pulled her towards her.

"He'll be back my dear. If he said he would come and see you, he will."

"But he was so angry with me, when he left." Barbara said, trying to wipe the tiers from her eyes.

"Why was that?" Ann asked.

"Because I told Mr Williams that I hadn't seen Mark the other night, the night of the attack."

"I know my dear. He was afraid. He was in trouble and had lied about seeing you that evening. When he found out that they had already spoken to you, his lie was seen through and he was in big trouble." Ann said.

"But he could have told the truth." Barbara said.

"No he couldn't, believe me. Had he told the truth he'd have been in even bigger trouble that he is now." Ann said, looking at Mrs Damson.

Both women knew what she was saying and neither of them wanted Barbara to know of their individual involvement in what went on that evening.

Mrs Damson came over.

"Barbara, Mark will be back, I know he will but it may take a while. In the meantime you need to prepare for when he does. Stop your playing about with the other boys and that man of yours. Be ready to give all of yourself to Mark." Mrs Damson said, as much to Mrs Williams as to Barbara.

Ann knew that Margaret was right, what she had done the other night was wrong in so many ways. She was going to have to put Mark completely out of her mind. She knew it was going to be difficult. He had given her such pleasure and she knew that, given time, she could have taught him so much more on how to please a woman.

Now she would have to go back to joining Mr Williams, in his bed on Friday nights. There would be no excitement and little pleasure to be had, for her. All she would be doing is comparing her husband with how she felt with Mark and he would come up wanting.

"Mrs Damson, I'll have a bath in my room, this morning. Will you see that I get plenty of hot water?" Ann said.

The next day was a quite day for them all. Graham went about his duties, patrolling the whole of his area, as far inland as Little Horstead, keeping to the right of the River Ouse. He made his way, via Terribbe Down, to East Hoathly. From here he started back towards the coast, riding through the villages and hamlets of Ripe, Chalvington and Selmeston. For the last few miles home he took the long way around the Downs to bring him back to Seaford via Beddingham and Denton rather than the shorter way through the Cuckmere Valley.

Although he was known, throughout the area, few people would talk to him and even fewer would give him any information. From those he did talk to, none of them said that they had seen Mark or his horse. He was beginning to think that it was possible that Mark was still near the coast. After all he had grown up along the coast in Chichester, and it was that countryside that he was most familiar with.

Barbara found that she was able to put all her other boys and man friends out of her mind. The married man was persistent but Barbara was having none of it. She told him that unless he walked out on his wife, that instant he wasn't going to have her again.

As far as the local boys were concerned, Barbara was just a play thing. They were all developing relationships with other girls and as such she was of lesser importance to them.

Her father was careful to ensure that she was not left alone at night, just in case George Styles or some of him men came calling. He was still afraid Barbara was in danger for what she did that night. He was unaware that George had been arrested and that the members of his gang had other things on their mind than to bother with Barbara.

Mrs Williams spent the day with her needlework, designing a cover for a chair, in her bedroom. The picture was of the local country side with a fine black horse being ridden by a young man. To her, this was Mark but to others it could have been anyone.

Mr Williams spent the day rewriting his report as he realised that he had tried to put the whole blame, for this tragedy, on both Bob Climpson and Mr Downer. To show he was in charge of his own area, he would need to show he had taken charge of the investigation with just a limited help from Mr Downer. He wrote that he had sent for Mr Downer, where in fact it was Bob who had done that, even before Mr Williams arrived back in Newhaven.

Happy that his report was ready, he would wait a day of two before he took the coach to London and The Customs House.

Chapter 36
So this is where you are

It had now been three nights that Mark had slept in this bed. Over the last two days he had been helping out around the house, doing odd jobs for Miss Badger and entertaining her daughter with tales of smugglers.

He lay there watching his room brighten, as the sun rose. Being that the house was set deep into the hills around it, the light was late arriving. Miss Badger had told him he would have to be gone before lunch time.

Closing his eyes he could hear the skylarks singing high above, the black birds, pigeons and the occasional pheasant calling. It had the start of a very lovely day and he felt lucky to be alive and free.

Another sound came to his ears. It was of someone approaching his room. It wasn't the heavy sound of boots on the stairs, which he would expect if the Dragoons or Customs officers were coming for him. This was a softer footfall, more the sound of a ladies shoe. Because of this he relaxed and kept his hand away from his pistol.

The door opened slowly and the face of Miss Badger appeared.

"Oh you're awake then Mister Mark?" She greeted him with her usual smile.

"Good morning Miss Badger, I was listening to the birds singing and contemplating the day ahead."

"There's no hurry for you to leave. Well as long as you're gone by midday that is." She said, as she moved into the room and stood by his bed, looking down at him.

"I brought you a mug of tea, I hope you enjoy it. You can have your breakfast when you're dressed." She said, as she put the tea down on the small table beside the head of his bed.

"Thank you. I'll be up soon and will leave once I've eaten. I don't want to put you in danger of being found with a stranger in the house."

Instead of leaving Miss Badger sat down on the bed and rested her hand on the blanket. Mark didn't know what to think. The last time he had been in a ladies bedroom, he'd got himself into all sorts of trouble. That ended with him being on the run and hiding out in this very house.

"I wanted to thank you for all the help you've given me around the house and for entertaining Carol the way you have." She said, as her hand moved up his thigh and onto his stomach.

"There's no reason to thank me Miss Badger. It's me who should be thanking you for letting me stay."

He suddenly realised what he had just said. Here was a woman sitting on his bed, running her hand over his. Miss Badger didn't seem to need an invitation. She smiled, took her hand up to the top of the blanket, pulled it away from his body.

Mark rarely wore clothes, when in bed and tonight had been no exception. He was now laying there completely naked. She watched as he became more aware of her presence.

"I see you really do want to thank me then Mister Mark." Miss Badger said with delight.

Before Mark could say or do anything she put her hand between his thighs.

"Miss Badger, I was thinking more of paying you with a sovereign so that you could buy something for yourself and Carol." Mark said.

Sex had brought him nothing but trouble ever since Barbara had seduced him in the barn.

"I don't need money, I need a man and I've one here." She said, with a voice of authority.

"I haven't had a man for a few years now and I'm not going to be deprived of one now." She said.

She released her grip of him and stood up. It was not a signal she was leaving but to give her the opportunity to undress.

Mark lay there and watched as she raised her dress up over the head. First into view came a pair of very shapely legs, far slimmer than he had imagined, from the way her dress hung over them.

Next were her pants, more like a pair of shorts than anything else but showing the colours and pattern of having been cut down from a dress.

As her dress went over her head and fell down her back, Mark looked up and watched her breasts as they came into view. From never having seen breasts before, in the last week he had viewed three completely differing pairs of breast, each one having a delight the others didn't.

In Miss Badger's case they were large but appeared to be very muscular, standing out with no more support than the muscles around them. Before he could take in more she lent forward to take off her pants, but Marks eyes were still affixed to her breasts and how they swung as her body moved.

"Do my breasts offend you Mister Mark?" she asked, having noticed how much interest he was paying to them.

"No, not at all, I was just admiring them. They're magnificent, absolutely magnificent." He said, in the spirit of a boy with a new toy.

She moved back to the bed, now completely naked.

"Then you shall have them all to yourself." She teased.

Before he could answer she was climbing onto the bed and sat astride him, just above his knees, looking into his eyes.

"I see you still want to thank me. It's now time for you to pay your bill." She said, as she started to run her hands up his legs and brushed her fingers over him. She moved her hands up towards his chest and levered her body forward.

"You can take hold of my breasts now Mister Mark." she said, more of an order than anything else.

He didn't need asking twice, his hands moved directly to cup her breasts. They really were as solid as he had imagined. The muscles were very strong and instead of allowing his fingers to sink deep into the fleshy part of her breasts, they resisted.

Whilst he was taking in all of this, Miss Badger was lowering herself onto him and taking him inside her. She now realised how much she had missed this. After lowering herself on to him she felt the warmth of him. She closed her eyes and felt as if he belonged to her.

Miss Badger was not feeling Mark's hands on her breasts, there were no feelings coming from that area of her body. Her mind was just concentrating all its efforts on the feelings it could gather from lower down.

She kept up her movement for what seemed to be a long time. All the time her eyes stayed shut and her mouth was open, allowing her to take in the air that would replenish the energy she was expending.

Mark held her breasts for a while but then removed his right hand and placed it on her ribs. He did the same with his other hand. Once both hands were in place he started to move them down, leaving her ribs and taking his hands down the centre of her stomach. These muscles were not as firm as those of her breasts. In fact there didn't appear to be any muscles there at all. Although she wasn't fat, there was little resistance to his fingers pushing against her.

He moved his hands out to hold her hips. He pulled her towards him, in time with the movement of her body. Miss Badger opened her eyes and looked down into his eyes and smiled. She was so much enjoying this that she failed to realised just how much noise was being made by the bed, as it creaked and banged on the floor.

As she felt ripples coming through her body she was interrupted by the sound of Carol calling.

"Mother, Mother, where are you?"

She wanted to call out and tell Carol not to come up here but to do so would break the moment, so she ignored her daughter's call and pushed harder towards Mark.

Mark realised what was going on. He didn't want Carol to walk in on the two of them. He wanted to help Miss Badger by using his legs to lever himself towards her. She was not going to leave him until she had reached her peak.

They could both hear Carol coming towards Mark's room. There was nothing they could do about the noise the bed was making and Miss Badger was not going to stop, not just yet.

Carol came closer and closer, Mark could see Miss Badger was not listening to Carol's footsteps. She was looking up at the wall behind Mark's bed and holding back the murmurs she had been making. If she finished with Carol outside the door, there was no knowing how much noise she would make and whether Carol would then walk in on them both.

"Carol." Mark called   "Your mother's gone to the barn to feed my horse." He lied.

He hoped that this would send her on her way, to find her mother. By the time she found out it wasn't true, her mother would have finished with Mark and disappeared back into the house.

"What's that noise I can hear?" Carol asked.

There was no way Mark was going to tell her that and with her mother's face showing the strains of holding back her ecstasy Mark had to dismiss Carol quickly.

"Go find your mother, Carol. I'm packing now and need to leave very soon. Ask your mother if she can do me something to eat. Go quickly now." He called.

All the time this was going on Miss Badger was moving quicker and quicker. She could never remember feeling like this, never so satisfying, never with such excitement. The possibility of being discovered heightened the whole experience.

The moment she heard Carol running back down the stairs she let her self go and flood her body with the emotions of a great lasting longing. With that completed she let herself flop down onto Mark's chest and his lips reached up to kiss her.

Because of the energy used, both of them were exhausted and failed to take any notice of time. Miss Badger was now enjoying the lingering kisses that Mark was heaping on her. She moved off his body and lay beside him, allowing him to run his hands over her body.

Mark was in no hurry to bring about an end to this encounter with his latest lover. He was prepared to take his time and as well as satisfying her, he wanted to explore the contours of her breasts, again.

Carol couldn't find her mother anywhere, this frightened her. Her mother had never left her without first telling her where she was going and when she would return. Had something happened to her, had someone come into the house and taken her?

As Mark was in the house and, from what he had said, he was packing to leave. She would go back and see him. He would know what to do; he would have some idea of how to find her mother.

Carol started up the stairs, this time she couldn't hear any of the sounds she heard earlier. As she made her way along the short corridor to his room, she could hear different sounds coming from his room. These were more like a woman not a man.

She stopped outside his door to listen. She didn't want to walk in on Mark, if he had a visitor but she was very worried about where her mother was. It was because of these concerns that she decided to ignore her mother's instructions of never walking in to any of the rooms in the house, if a guest was there. She couldn't hear any sounds coming from Mark's room, so she lifted the catch to his door and walked in.

What she saw in front of her was a complete surprise. On Mark's bed was not only Mark but also her mother and they were both undressed. Mark was kissing her mother's breast. She was lying there with her eyes closed, with a gurgling sound emitting from between her lips.

Even though Carol was only twelve, she was developing the body of a woman. Her breasts were enlarging and she was capable of becoming pregnant. Her mother had told her some very basic details about sex but this was the first time she had seen a naked man.

Neither Mark nor Miss Badger had noticed Carol enter the room. They were now nearing the point where each of them would either end what they were doing or start again. Miss Badger whispered that she wanted him.

Mark didn't need any encouragement. He removed his hand from her body and rolled over, to be above her, placing his legs between hers. This time it was his turn to do the work. Because of the way they were both feeling and the fact that may be their last chance to enjoy each other, it took only a few moments before they were both satisfied.

Carol stood there, watching and saying nothing. What she had to say could wait until they realised she was there. Then she would have her say.

Mark looked down at Miss Badger, funny he thought, he didn't even know her name. Here they were naked and in each other's arms. Still as he was leaving today, it may be better that way. Mark lent forward and kissed the tip of her nose, then up the ridge of her nose to kiss her eyelids.

Miss Badger was feeling so good just now. This was the first time for many years that she had made love to anyone and in her mind it had been the best. Not even her partner had brought her to such heights, she felt really good right now.

Mark rolled off her and she opened her eyes and looked up towards the ceiling, Mark was doing the same. Neither of them had seen Carol standing at the foot of the bed.

"So this is where you are." Carol said, indignantly.

Both Miss Badger and Mark sat up and looked towards where the sound had come from. Mark tried to cover himself and Miss Badger tried to cover up her breasts and put a hand between her legs.

"What are you doing entering Mister Mark's room without knocking?"

"Looking for you"

"Mark said you were outside. After I couldn't find you there, I was worried and came to see Mister Mark. To see if he could help me find you." She said, with tears starting to run down her cheeks.

Miss Badger forgot about her modesty and got up from the bed, walked over to her daughter and took her in her arms.

"I'm alright my love, you don't have to cry. I wouldn't leave you."

Mark looked at mother and daughter, holding each other. During his stay he had noticed that they relied on each other. What had happened today would put a strain on that relationship for a while. Yes it was definitely time for him to leave.

He got up and dressed into his travelling clothes. Mark picked up his bag and quietly walked towards the door.

"Mark, please don't leave." Miss Badger said.

"Carol would like you to stay." She pleaded.

"No it wouldn't be right to come between the two of you. I have defiantly overstayed my welcome."

Mark left the room, with Miss Badger still naked and Carol standing with her. He went down to the kitchen, placed his bag beside the door and put on his riding boots. He needed some food before he left and was confident that Miss Badger would feed him, when she was dressed.

Mark left the kitchen and headed for the barn, he wanted to see to his horse. Feed her and put the saddle on, ready to leave after his meal. Mark was just finished when he felt someone close to him. He spun around and found Carol advancing towards him.

"Is the food ready?" Mark asked.

"Yes, mother sent me to ask you to come and eat."

Mark turned back to his horse and finished tightening the girth.

"You really don't have to leave Mister Mark." Carol said.

"Yes I do, your mother won't want me around, after midday."

Carol realised Mark had to go but she hadn't seen her mother as happy as she was right now. Her mother worked very hard for very little pay, she hardly had sufficient money to keep them both in clothes. If it weren't for her skills with the needle and was able to re-use the clothes discarded by those of the house, they would be in a very bad state.

Mark had now completed his tasks so, with Carol, he left the barn and returned to the kitchen. Miss Badger was standing by the stove, making a pot of tea. On the table were cuts of meat, bread and biscuits.

With the tea made, Miss Badger came over to the table, sat to the side of Mark and poured out a mug of tea for him, Carol and herself. Plates were also laid for Carol and herself. Miss Badger indicated to Carol that she could begin her meal.

The breakfast meal, for the first time since he had arrived, was eaten in silence. All of them full of their own thoughts. Both of the females wanted to ask Mark to stay but neither would do so. Carol had been told by her mother not to ask him to stay and she wasn't going to ask a man, especially one as young as Mark, to stay around for her needs, however much her body was screaming out for her to do so.

After the meal was finished Mark stood up, looked at the two others at the table and, without saying anything went towards the door, lifted his hat from the peg by the door. It was then that he remembered that he needed to give Miss Badger something for hosting him for the last three days. Taking out his purse he removed a sovereign, walked back to the table and placed it in front of Miss Badger. He then turned and returned to the door.

He didn't want to look back in case it weakened his resolve to leave but he couldn't walk out on them without saying goodbye. So, without looking back he said "Goodbye," opened the door, stepped out.

Miss Badger and Carol wanted to follow him and ask him to return. They just sat there and finished their meal, listening for the sound of Mark returning, dreading the sound of him riding out of the barn.

Mark, on the other hand, needed to get away as quickly as he could. His sexual exploits had brought him nothing but trouble and he didn't want this latest experience to turn sour on him. His horse was ready so he led her out of the barn and jumped up into the saddle. Soon he was out on the track and on his way.

He had no choice on the direction he took. Turning left would take him back towards West Dean and the Cuckmere valley. He couldn't go there, as he was wanted by the Customs authorities.

The only choice he had was to head for the London road, at the end of this valley. This would allow him to get out of the area and away from any pursuing authorities.

Going through Jevington would be a risk so he took the tracks that he used when he came back from Jevington, the other day. He wouldn't need to go out over the downs first. He was sure that the Dragoons wouldn't be up and about this early in the day.

After leaving the first part of the track he headed up on to the hill, he could join a track to Folkington, bypassing Jevington.

This journey was a pleasure, he could look out over the country side and admire the wonderful view that it afforded.

There were no workers about so he didn't need to hide his face. He could be himself for a while.

As he started to enter the village of Folkington he noticed that a rider was heading in his direction but he was being stopped and spoken to by a man on foot, holding what looked like a blunderbuss. Mark didn't need to be seen but he was interested to hear what these men were talking about. He had noticed a hedge to his right went along beside the track he was on. If he rode on the other side of this hedge, he could come alongside these two men and listen to what they were talking about. He judged that the hedge was high enough to hide both himself and his horse, provided he dismounted halfway along.

Mark was quick to act and took his horse behind the hedge and after fifty yards he dismounted and walked beside the horse until he came level with the two men. Mark listened and took in all that they were saying.

This changed everything. If he was quick he could take advantage of this information.

Chapter 37
Sampson. You're back so soon

The last time Mr Williams had been to this Inn he hadn't realised what he had left behind. Everything seemed to be going along so well. He commanded a good group of Riding Officers and controlled the local Customs cutter. He had just captured one of the largest consignments of contraband that year.

Tomorrow he was going to report that the consignment had been recaptured by the smugglers and one of his officers had been killed, trying to protect the Customs House and the contraband.

There would be no celebrity drinks tonight. In fact he just wanted to go to his room and hope that he could get a good nights rest, in preparation for tomorrow's inquest.

The morning came much quicker than he realised. There was a knock on his door and a large woman walked in, carrying a jug of water, which she placed on the small table, next to a bowl. She then turned, walked out and closed the door.

The sun was starting to lighten the sky and it appeared through the dirty windows in his room. The quicker he got up and left this place, the quicker he could get this all over and return home.

As he left the Inn, he paid the shilling for his room but said that he wouldn't need it again tonight. The Inn wasn't too far from the Customs House. The streets were like cesspools. He had to watch everywhere he placed his boots in case they stepped into something very nasty. All this made his journey much longer than he had anticipated.

He knocked on the big door, at the entrance to the Customs House and was greeted by a man in uniform and carrying a large stick. As Mr Williams had been there only a few days earlier, the man recognised him and let him into the building.

The reception desk was across the large entrance hall. Mr Williams walked over and rang the bell which was on the corner of the desk. There was no answer, so he rang it again, this time louder and for longer.

"A bit early for all that." Came a voice behind him.

He turned around a saw that the only other person in the hall was the man who had let him in.

"What time will anyone be here?" He asked.

"About half an hour, I would say but if you need to see anyone, that'll be about an hour."

Without thanking him for the information, he walked over to a set of chairs across from the reception desk. He would wait there.

While he waited he had to think things over. He couldn't be blamed for the loss of the contraband or the death of his officer as he was here, in London. He had already written his report about this and had firmly put the blame on Bob Climpson, as he was in charge while he was away.

It was how he was going to tell them about the enquiry and Mr Downer's insistence of taking control of the whole thing. This would show that he could not control his area.

It suddenly crossed his mind that if they didn't like what he had found out then he could put the blame firmly on Mr Downer. Pointing out that it was his son that had caused a lot of the trouble and it was possible that Mr Downer was trying to cover for his son.

"Yes, Sampson, you've got it. You're in the clear." He said out loud, with a big smile crossing his face.

"Pardon Sir." The guard said.

"Nothing my man"

He felt good now. He could face the men, knowing that he could pass the blame off on others.

The half an hour seemed to last forever but eventually an old man came into the hall, from a door behind the reception desk, and sat down.

Sampson got up and walked over to the desk.

"My name is Mr Williams, Comptroller from Newhaven. I have an important report to give to Mr Jacobs."

"Would you hand it to me Sir? I will see that he gets it."

"I need to hand it to him myself. It is very important. One of my men was killed the other day."

"I'm sorry Sir but all reports have to be sent up to Mr Jacob. If he needs to see you, he will call for you. Would you go and sit back, over there. I'll call you if needed."

"My man I'm the Comptroller from Newhaven. I'll not just waiting to be called."

"In that case, if you would call back, after lunch, I expect I'll be able to tell you if Mr Jacob will see you."

Sampson was starting to get very angry. Did this man not realise what an important man he was. He was no used to being treated like this. Just as he was about to let out an outbursts of abuse to this underling, he heard the sound of footsteps coming up behind him.

"A problem Mr Smith?" The guard asked.

"No thank you John. Mr Williams was just leaving."

"This way Sir" John said, as he took Sampson by his arm and guided him towards the main entrance.

Before he realised it, he was standing on the top step of the Custom House and the door behind him had closed. What had just happened? His world was falling apart.

He walked along the path, beside the Thames and before long he had arrived at an Inn. He needed a drink and something to eat. It seemed that he had the whole morning to fill before he returned to the Customs House.

Not realising where he was, he walked in and everything looked very familiar. Last time he had been in London he had been taken to an Inn, just like this one, and had a very enjoyable night.

"Sampson. You're back so soon."

He looked over to where the sound was coming from and, advancing towards him was a large woman, older than himself and showing far more of her womanly body than was proper.

"Have you come back for second helpings?" She asked.

"Sorry. I don't know what you're talking about." He said.

"On Tuesday you and I spent the night in my room." She replied.

God, was this the woman? I thought she was much younger and slimmer than this woman.

"I think you are mistaken, madam. The lady I spent the night with was not you." He said and turned away.

Two other women blocked his route to the door. They were also just as large and had similar wares on show. He was going nowhere.

"You don't insult Susan." Emma said.

"Not unless you pay her, that is." Sally said.

Mr Williams now remembered these three women. All three of them had spent the night with him and one of his companions. It had been a night to remember but now, being sober, he realised what a mistake he had made.

"How much?" He asked.

"A florin each." Emma said.

"But I thought you said I had to pay Susan?"

"We come in threes, like last time Sampson." Sally said, smiled and placed her hand between his legs and squeezed.

"I don't think I have...." He couldn't finish what he was saying as Sally squeezed even harder and the pain shot up to his head.

"If you agree, Sally will let go." Susan said, into his left ear, as she reached around and turned his face around to face hers.

"Yes, Yes, I'll pay." He stammered.

With that Sally released her grip but didn't remove her hand. Instead she gently massaged his aching body.

Susan smiled at Sampson, lent forward and kissed him on his lips. Then she released him and stepped back. Sally let go of Sampson and stepped back, allowing Emma to come forward and face him. To his surprise she opened up her blouse and revealed her breasts.

"You couldn't get enough of these the other night. Help yourself." Emma said, reached around his head and pulled him into her cleavage.

Oh yes, he remembered these. He had spent a long time with his face buried in-between them. His whole senses were saying that he should step back, pay the women what they wanted and leave. The only trouble was that the part of him that Sally had been rubbing was calling out for him to stay and enjoy the experience.

Before he stopped breathing, he managed to pull himself away from Emma then turned around and faced Susan.

"I only have a couple of hours. How much?" He asked.

"For you Sampson, a florin each will be right." She said, with a smile.

Before he realised what was happening he was being led up some stairs and into a room with a single bed against the wall. Sally closed the door and slid a bolt across, to stop Sampson leaving before he had paid.

Susan was the first to get undressed and lay on the bed. Emma and Sally undressed Sampson and led him over to the bed and told him to enjoy himself.

They stepped back and sat on the two stalls that were against the other wall and watched as he went to work.

He didn't know how long he had been with Susan but once she had decided that it was enough, she pushed him off, got off the bed and Emma took her place.

The same thing happened with Sally. She just rolled him over, towards the wall and climbed off the bed. She was replaced by Susan.

Susan could see that Sampson was not living up to his name so rolled him on his back and climbed on top of him and went to work. He thought all his energy was spent but no, he still had something left for Emma.

Emma climbed off, Sally returned and dangled her breasts in his face.

"For a florin, they're all yours." Sally said.

"I'm sorry but I don't have the energy for them." Sampson said.

All the women got dressed and waited for Sampson to do the same.

"Our money please" Susan said, holding out her hand.

Sampson brought out his purse and found the three florins that he had agreed to pay and placed one in each of their outstretched hands.

With that transaction completed, Susan slid the bolt back and opened up the door. The women stood aside and let Sampson leave.

To the women this had been an unexpected bonus. Normally their trade was carried out in the evenings. Doing it in the morning was a delight. They were rested and the man was not reeking of ale.

Mr Williams had not realised just how long he had been upstairs. He reached into his pocket and found his watch. It was half passed twelve. Time he got back to the Customs House.

When he arrived at the Customs House, the main doors were open and the Guard was stood inside. Mr Williams ignored the man. He was not being pleasant to a man who had basically thrown him out of the building, just a few hours earlier.

As he approached the reception desk, Mr Smith looked up and beckoned over a messenger boy.

"Take Mr Williams up to Mr Jacobs, boy." He said.

He completely ignored Mr Williams and Mr Williams did the same to him. It would be safe to say that he hadn't made a friend of either the guard or Mr Smith.

Mr Williams followed the boy up the grand stairway, until they had reached the first floor. The boy turned right and headed down a wide corridor, with big doors on either side. Mr Williams had not been to this part of the building before. At the last visit he had been taken down the left hand corridor, where there were smaller doors than these.

"I think you are taking me the wrong way boy." He said.

"You're to see Mr Jacob. He's waiting for you in one of these offices." The boy replied.

As they reached the second door, from the end of the corridor, the boy stopped and knocked. There was no instant reply so he knocked again.

The door opened and there stood Mr Jacob. He was a large man with greying hair and a full beard, which covered most of his features. He dismissed the boy and turned to Sampson.

"You're just in time."

"Come in. We have much to discuss."

This was a large office with a grand desk on the far side. Behind this desk sat a robust man, smoking a pipe. He appeared to be reading some papers and as such didn't look up at the latest visitor to his room.

Stood to the right of the desk were two men who were both wearing glasses and holding bundles of papers. They looked at Mr Williams, as he came in but switched their gazed back to the man behind the desk.

Mr Harrington eventually looked up from his papers.

"So, Williams, you went to all the trouble to capture the contraband and then lost it. What have you to say for yourself?"

"Sir, it wasn't my fault. I was up here, handing in my report to Mr Jacobs. It was Mr Climpson's job to secure the contraband." He said.

"If you think like that, I'm surprised that you captured the contraband in the first place."

"Mr Harrington, Mr Williams has limited resources and the smuggling gangs, in his area, are very violent." Mr Jacob put in, on his behalf.

"It's how you use your resources. That's the important thing. Have you commanded men in the field, Mr Williams?" Mr Harrington asked.

"I don't understand. I'm not a farmer." Mr Williams replied.

"I mean in the Army, on the battle field."

"No."

"I said that we should only appoint Navy or Army Officers. They know how to get the best out of their men."

"Right, let's see what we can do to get us out of this hole." Mr Harrington said, addressing the two men, stood to his left.

"By chance, one of the South Bourn Dragoon patrols came across a Mr Styles. Who was the leader of the Aldfriston smuggling gang. The one's who attacked the Customs House in Newhaven." Mr Laker said.

"How does that help us?"

"Well they transported him up to Newgate Prison, on a charge of killing Mr Jack Clarke, the night guard at the Customs House." Mr Quinton reported.

"And that helps us how?" Mr Harrington demanded.

"If we get a conviction, we can send a message to the area that he was arrested as a result of a tip off. That will cause havoc among the locals and may end the smuggling in that area." Mr Laker said.

"What evidence do we have that he did it?"

"The report Mr Williams handed in is very good. It contains evidence which he took from local people and his Riding Officers. With him being here, to give evidence in court, they will take what he says as evidence and we'll get the conviction we need."

"What do you think, Mr Jacobs?" Mr Harrington asked.

"How long before we can get this man in court?" He asked.

"Tomorrow" Mr Quinton said.

"Then so be it. Mr Jacobs, take Williams away and make sure that he's in court tomorrow morning."

"Mr Jacobs, can we have a word with Mr Williams, in your office, before we go?" Mr Laker asked.

"Yes, by all means."

"I'll get this all sorted out for you Sir and report back tomorrow, after the court hearing." Mr Jacobs said, addressing Mr Harrington.

The four men left the office and walked back down the corridor. This time they were going to Mr Jacob's Office. Somewhere Mr Williams was more familiar with and would feel more at home.

Once they were all seated in the office and the door was closed. Mr Laker looked at Mr Williams.

"How reliable is the evidence about the raid on your Customs House?"

"Well the evidence that Mr Styles was in Newhaven, to attacked the Customs House I got from the Ferryman's daughter. She was made to row him and a group of his men over the river, so that he could meet up with others of his gang." Mr Williams reported.

"Um, it appears that she jumped off the boat and left them to fend for themselves?" Mr Quinton said.

"Yes she did. She then swum back to the quay, ran back to her home and changed out of her wet clothes. She took one of my Riding Officers horses and rode into Lewes to fetch Mr Climpson."

"Did she see Mr Styles get off the ferry?" Mr Laker asked.

"Yes, just as she left the barn, with the horse. She looked back and saw him climbing onto the quayside, on the far side of the river."

"Good. That puts him in the area." Mr Quinton said.

"She also said that the reason that she jumped was that they said that they were going to attack the Customs House and she was afraid for the safety of one of the Guards, Mark Downer." Mr Williams said.

"Even better. That bit is not in the report." Mr Laker stated.

"Well no, it didn't seem that important at the time." Mr Williams said.

"Now, in the report, you said that this Mark Downer overheard Mr Styles not only admit to killing Jack Clarke but threaten others. You appear not to think that this evidence is any good, why?" Mr Laker asked.

"Well it was because young Mark would not tell us why he was late to his duty. At first he told us he had fallen asleep and was only awoken by the shot that killed Jack. Then he said that he had been in the Ferryman's barn, with his daughter but we already had her statement and that was not possible." Mr Williams said.

"So where was he?" Mr Laker asked.

"One of my Riding Officers discovered that he had been in bed with a lady. He wouldn't tell me with whom, to protect the ladies reputation." Mr Williams said.

"If we could get that young man up here, to give evidence, I'm sure that we could get the trial put back a day." Mr Quinton said to Mr Laker.

"You can't do that. Mark ran away and is on the run." Mr Williams said.

"Why?"

"Because I said that if he didn't tell me where he really was, I would lock him up in the local gaol. He pulled his pistols, disarmed all the men in the room, locked the Customs House main door, leaving us all locked inside and escaped over the river and away. I still have men out looking for him."

"You bloody fool, Williams. I know Mark Downer and his father. That young man is a gentleman. He would have been protecting the lady. If he said that Styles said what he said, then that is what happened." Mr Jacobs said.

"Right, this is what we will do..."

Mr Quinton then went through the evidence that Mr Williams was to give to the court the next morning. He emphasized how important that it was for him to say just what they told him to say. If not Mr Styles could be released or the trial could be put back until he had found Mark Dawson.

Once both Mr Laker and Mr Quinton were happy that Mr Williams would say and do just what they had told him, they said their goodbyes to Mr Jacobs and left the office.

"You'd better get it right or your career in the Service will be over." Mr Jacobs said.

With that said. Mr Williams was dismissed from his office and told to find himself an Inn but ensure that he was in the court, at the Old Baily, by nine o'clock sharp, tomorrow morning.

After leaving the Customs House Sampson had a decision to make. Did he return to the Inn that he had slept in last night or did he go along the Thames, back to the Inn he was in earlier and reacquaint himself with Susan? No, he would go back to the first Inn. He couldn't risk being late into court and if he drank too much again tonight he was very likely to mess up his evidence.

The walk back to the Inn was no easier than it had been this-morning, in fact it was harder, as even more rubbish and effluents had been deposited in the streets. He picked his way gingerly around the worst of this and eventually arrived back at the Inn.

"Good afternoon. I know that I said that I didn't need my room again tonight but things have changed. I now need to attend at the Customs House again tomorrow." Mr Williams said as he greeted the Innkeeper.

"Sorry Sir but that room has been let out. I do have another one you could have."

"I'll take that then."

The Innkeeper came around the bar and led the way up the narrow stairs. They kept climbing up and up the flights of stairs until eventually they reached the last step. The Innkeeper stood to one side and opened up the only door ahead of them.

"This is your room Sir." He said, with a smile.

Mr Williams squeezed passed him and entered the room. To call it a room would be an exaggeration, it was very small. The roof sloped down on two sides, leaving hardly enough room for him to stand up, in the middle of the available space. The only furniture, so to speak, was a horsehair mattress on the floor, together with a couple of blankets.

"I can't stay here."

"It's the only room I have available tonight. Had you told me this morning, you could've had your old room but that ones gone."

Sampson realised that it was getting too dark to go traipsing around looking for another room. He would have to make the best of this room.

"Can you send me up a chair and a candle?" He asked the Innkeeper.

"Yes Sir. Don't keep the young lady too long. She's a lot of regular customers coming in tonight."

With that, the Innkeeper went down the stairs and Sampson went over to the mattress and gave it a shake. There was a scurrying noise and he saw three mince running for the door. He picked up the blankets to throw after these departing rodents when he saw five more mice drop from the blankets and head after the others.

He was just about to leave the room and head back down to the bar room when a chair was being carried into his room. There was a lit candle, in a candle stick, sat on the chair. The little light it gave out was sufficient to mask the person carrying the chair.

Once the chair was in the room, he looked up and found himself looking into the eyes of a beautiful young girl. She reminded him of Barbara, the ferryman's daughter. She gave him a nice smile and placed the chair down in the middle of the room. She put the candle stick on the windowsill.

"Is there anything else I can do for you, Sir?" She asked.

"Is there no room better than this?" He asked.

"Only mine, but I'll be using that for a while." She smiled.

"How much would it cost me to spend the whole night there?"

"A sovereign."

"I'll give you half a sovereign now and the other half in the morning." He said, offering a half sovereign.

She held out her hand, took the money, turned around and walked out of the room.

"Are you coming?" She asked.

Sampson was quick to follow her. The sooner he got out of this room the better he would feel. They went down two flights and along a corridor, leading to the rear of the building.

"This is my room. Settle yourself in there. Don't come out or I'll be in a lot of trouble."

Sampson walked into the room. It was very nice. It was much like his wife's room, the same smells and all the trappings of a lady. The room was smaller than his wife's but that is all that could be expected in a building such as this.

He took off his coat and shoes and lay on the bed. Before he knew it he was fast asleep.

When Sampson awoke, in the morning, he found the young lady laying between him and the wall. She was not completely clothed, being naked down to her waist. He couldn't remember the last time he woke up to find a naked woman next to him.

He looked up to her face and saw that her eyes were closed and her lips were slightly open. He so much wanted to reach over and caress her breasts but felt wrong doing that to a sleeping girl. He sat up and placed his feet on the floor boards.

"You don't have to leave just yet." The girl said.

"I must, I have places I must be, this morning." Sampson replied.

He stood up and walked over to where he had left his shoes and put them on. He was about to finish dressing when he turned around and looked over to the bed. The girl had now moved so that she was laying down the centre of her bed and had removed her pants so that he could now see her in her full glory.

"You haven't had your sovereign's worth Sir." She said with a smile.

"Having a comfortable bed was worth the sovereign, my dear." Sampson replied.

"But you paid for all of this."

"The pleasure of seeing you naked was worth the sovereign."

He so much wanted to undress and ravish this beautiful girl but felt dirty, just thinking about it. She could only be about fourteen years old. No he couldn't do that.

He reached into his pocket and found the other half sovereign and placed it on her tummy. He watched as the coldness of the coin brought about an involuntary reaction as her tummy muscles retracted, seemingly drawing the coin into her belly button.

If he stood here any longer he would forget what he was in London for. He had to leave and get to the court. He reached into another pocket, in his coat and found his pocket watch. It showed seven o'clock. He had two hours to find his way to the court and get breakfast.

Sampson turned around and headed for the door.

"Turn right and leave by the second door. If dad catches you, you'll be a dead man."

'Oh my god, what have I got myself into?' He asked himself.

He had been silly in not bringing his flintlock pistol with him on this trip. How was he to defend himself against the Innkeeper? He was a very large and strong looking man.

He followed the girl's directions. Out side the second door was a staircase, leading into the Inn's yard. There was no one about so he carefully walked down the stairs, trying hard not to make a noise that would disturb the Innkeeper. Once he reached the yard he could see a passage leading away from the Inn. He followed this and it brought him out into a much wider street.

Here he was soon able to hail a coach to take him to The Old Bailey.

Chapter 38
Guilty

Mr Williams arrived at The Old Bailey courts just before eight o'clock. He was informed that the courts wouldn't be sitting until nine o'clock, at the earliest and that he should come back nearer the time. He asked if there was a place, near by, where he could get a meal? He was directed to an inn just around the corner.

As he walked into the inn a Soldier stood up and headed towards him. He wasn't sure who he was or why he was coming in his direction.

"Good morning Mr Williams, here for the trial?" He greeted.

"What trial?"

"Well George's, that's whose." He grinned.

"I'm sorry I don't know you." Mr Williams eventually said.

"Sergeant O'Riley, Sir. I was part of the party of Dragoons that captured the contraband, from poor old George."

"Oh, Sergeant, I'm sorry. I'm pleased to meet you."

"Would you like to join me? I was just ordering breakfast."

"That's kind of you."

Once they had sat down and the breakfast and ale arrived they ate a hearty meal, setting them selves up for, what could be a long day.

"I should be back in my barracks in South Bourn, now. A message was sent for me to remain in London and come here today. Do you know what they want me for?"

"No. I'm to give evidence, to the killing of Jack Clarke."

"But you weren't there!"

"I told them that but they want this case over quickly so I'm to tell them about the evidence I obtained, at the inquiry I held the next day. I just hope they'll take it. If not the case will be put off until we can find young Mark and get him and Barbara here for the trial."

Mr Williams looked at his watch and saw that it was time for the pair of them to make their way back to The Old Bailey.

As they walked in, Mr Quinton came over to them and asked if they had been to a Crown Court and given evidence before? They both said that they hadn't. He suggested that they went in to the court and listened to one or two of the cases, to see what went on and who would likely be asking them questions.

He led them into the court and found seats, towards the back of the public area, so that they could see what was going on but, once George Styles case was called, they could leave the court and await being called to give evidence.

For both of them it was an education. They had both attended Magistrates courts before but they had never been to a full court, with Judges, Lawyers, Recorders, a short-hand taker, to record what happened and for the first time they saw that a jury was present.

The accused would be brought up to the dock, from a stairway leading up from the cells, directly into the dock and they would be accompanied, the whole time, by guards.

They watched, with interest, the proceedings of three cases where the person was accused of 'feloniously stealing'. In each case the person had been found guilty. One was sentenced to Death, another to transportation to Australia and the last fined a shilling and confined to Newgate prison for a week.

The next case was called.

"Bring up George Styles." The Serjeant at Law called.

This was the signal for Sergeant O'Riley and Mr Williams to leave. As they got up, they saw Mr Laker walk in and move to the front of the court. He was wearing a cloak and a wig.

"Mr Laker is prosecuting." Mr Quinton whispered to Mr Williams.

"I will come and fetch you, when you are needed. Don't go too far from this door. This Judge doesn't like to be kept waiting." He said.

George was brought up to the dock and was accompanied by two burly men in dark uniforms. He looked around but could see no one he knew, with the exception of his lawyer, Mr Knowlys, who was sat just in front of the dock.

Once the Judge had taken his seat, overlooking the whole of the proceedings, the trial could start. The Serjeant at Law read out the two charges being brought against George.

"George Styles is charged with feloniously killing and slaying Jack Clarke, an officer of King George's Customs on 21st day of September 1786, at his Majesties Customs House in the port of Newhaven, in the county of Sussex. A second count of feloniously stealing, on 21st day of September 1786, 300 half-ankers of brandy, 200 half-ankers of genever, 10 bales of lace and 14 cases of tea from the Customs House at the port of Newhaven, in the county of Sussex, the property of King George."

The Judge asked George if he was guilty of these charges. George said no. The Judge asked Mr Laker to present the case for the prosecution.

The first thing he did was call for Sergeant O'Riley to give evidence. George was astonished that they had him here, in London. He lent forward to Mr Knowlys and whispered things in his ear about the Sergeant.

Sergeant O'Riley was sworn in and took the stand.

"Sergeant O'Riley can you please descript to the court how you came across George Styles and why you arrested him?" Mr Laker asked.

"I was on patrol, with my platoon of Dragoons, in the Cuckmere valley. We noticed George coming towards us so we split apart and allowed George to ride between our ranks. When he was half way through I blocked his way and my troop closed in on him and his horse. I arrested him for the killing of Jack Clarke and he was escorted back to our barracks in South Bourn."

"Why did you only arrest him on that single charge?" Mr Laker asked.

"Before we went on patrol, that morning, Lieutenant Hall had told us that if we came across George Styles he was to be arrested for killing Jack Clarke, a Customs Officer at Newhaven Customs House, Sir."

"What day was this?"

"The 22nd day of September 1786, Sir."

"How do you know George Styles?" Mr Laker asked.

"I have come across him many times during my patrols of the area."

"Why do you patrol the Cuckmere Valley Sergeant?"

"The Regiment is stationed in South Bourn to give assistance to the Customs people and to protect the Sussex coast from French raids, Sir."

"Are you aware of Mr Style's profession?"

"Yes Sir. He calls himself a Free Trader"

"What is a Free Trader, Sergeant?" John Phipps, of the jury asked.

"Smugglers, Sir." Sergeant O'Riley replied.

"What position does he hold among the smugglers?" Mr Laker asked

"I understand that he is the leader of the Aldfriston Raiders, the largest gang of smugglers in the area, Sir."

"Once you had Mr Styles in your cell, at the barracks, what was decided to do with him?"

"I was told that, in the morning, I was to take him to a local Magistrate who was to be asked to commend him into my charge so that he could be transported to London, to stand trial for killing one of His Majesties Customs Officers."

"When was this?"

"On 23rd day of September 1786, Sir."

"Why was he not tried at a local court?" Mr Laker asked

"I don't know Sir."

"Was it because he would use influence to secure his release?"

"I can't say Sir."

"Sergeant, are you in the pay of George Styles?" Mr Knowlys asked.

"No Sir."

"Have you received payment not to be around when a run was on?"

"No Sir."

"Then can you explain what happened to the Brandy and Genever that was left for you at Excet Bridge?" He asked.

"I know nothing of this Sir." Sergeant O'Riley insisted.

"You do understand that lying to this court is an offence, Sergeant?"

"Yes Sir, but I have not lied."

"Sergeant, once the Magistrate had committed George Styles to your charge, what did you do then?" Mr Laker asked.

"With my troop, he was loaded into a carriage and we brought him to Newgate Prison, to await trial."

"Sergeant, do you have a copy of the warrant issued for the arrest of George Styles?" Mr Knowlys asked.

"No Sir but I understand that Mr Williams has a copy."

"Who is this Mr Williams?" The Judge asked.

"Mr Williams is the Customs Comptroller at the port of Newhaven. He is our next witness, your honour." Mr Laker replied.

"Sergeant, how long have you known George Styles?"

"About a year, Sir."

"How long have you known his profession?"

"About a year Sir."

"How do you know that he is the leader of the so called gang?" Mr Knowlys asked.

"He was the second in the gang until he had a fight with the leader, a Mr Cockburn. After the fight, it is common knowledge that George took over the leadership of the gang."

"Did he kill this man?" Mr Knowlys asked.

"No Sir but he did shoot him."

"How did he not die then?"

"A patrol came across Mr Cockburn and dispatched him to hospital.

"Didn't Mr Styles and Mr Cockburn become friends again, after this?" Mr Knowlys asked.

"You would have to ask Mr Cockburn, Sir."

"Sergeant, is it true that you were given money to arrest George Styles and bring him to London, on a trumped up charge?" Mr Knowlys asked.

"I received no money, Sir. I just obeyed orders from my Officers."

"Is it not true that a large sum of money was offered for his arrest?"

"I believe that a reward was offered." Sergeant O'Riley replied.

"Then you and your men received this, is that not true Sergeant?" Mr Knowles asked.

"Any reward would go to the Regiment Sir, not to me or my men."

"So you arrested Mr Styles for your Regiment then?"

"No Sir. I arrested him because His Majesties Customs Comptroller issued a Warrant for his arrest for killing one of His Majesties Customs Officers."

"Mr Knowlys, I don't see where this is going?" The Judge asked.

"The Sergeant has provided no evidence that my client killed anyone, Your Honour." Mr Knowles replied.

"Your honour, our next witness will provide all that evidence. The Sergeant was here to give evidence to Mr Style's arrest." Mr Laker stated.

"In that case, shall call your next witness, Mr Laker?" The judge said.

"Thank you your honour. Call Mr Williams." Mr Laker said.

Sergeant O'Riley left the stand and was escorted to a seat at the back of the court, so that he was available, if he needed to be questioned again. As he took his seat Mr Williams entered the court and was escorted to the stand. He was sworn in.

"Sir, would you give us your name and profession." Mr Laker asked.

"My name is Sampson Williams. I am the Customs Comptroller at the Port of Newhaven, in the county of Sussex."

"Do you have customs officers under your command?"

"Yes Sir. I have 5 Riding Officers, 1 Apprentice Riding Officer, A crew for the Customs Cutter and a Customs Officer who also guards the Customs House when there are any goods secured there."

"Was Jack Clarke a member of your Customs staff?"

"Yes Sir. He was responsible for guarding the Customs House."

"Was he on duty on the night George Styles and his men attacked the Customs House?"

"Yes he was."

"Was anyone else on duty with him?"

"There should have been the apprentice, Mark Downer but he was not there at the time." Mr Williams reported.

"Where was this young man?"

"I can not say."

"Was he at his station?" Mr Laker asked.

"No Sir he was not."

"On 21st day of September 1786, how much contraband was stored in the Customs House?"

"300 hundred half-anker's of brandy, 200 hundred half-anker's of Genever, 10 bales of lace and 14 cases of tea, Sir." Mr Williams reported.

"Had you inspected this contraband, in the Customs House?"

"Yes I had."

"Do you see George Styles in the court today?" Mr Knowlys asked.

"That's him." Mr Williams said, pointing at the man stood in the dock.

"Are you sure?"

"Well it must be. He's the man charged." Mr Williams said.

"But have you ever met Mr Styles before?"

"No I haven't." Mr Williams admitted.

"Then this might not be the right man?"

"I can not say."

"Are we trying the right man?" Adam Kilsby asked, from the jury.

"This man admitted it was he, when the charges were put to him and Sergeant O'Riley identified him when he gave his evidence of arrest." The Judge stated.

"Did you see George Styles shoot Jack Clarke?" Mr Knowlys asked.

"No Sir I did not."

"Mr Williams, when you returned to Newhaven, from reporting to the Customs House, here in London, and found that all the contraband in the Customs House, had been stolen, what did you do?" Mr Laker asked.

"Mr Climpson reported to me and told me the investigations he had carried out and handed me a statement by Mark Downer as to what he had seen." Mr Williams stated.

"Your Honour, I have copies of this statement for the court and Mr Knowlys." Mr Laker handed a copy to the Judge and Mr Knowlys.

"In this statement, Mark Downer states that he saw George Styles standing over the body of Jack Clarke, is that so?"

"Yes Sir he did."

"He also said that he heard one of the men ask him why he had shot him. George Styles said that had Norman done his job properly, Jack wouldn't have got through their cordon and George wouldn't have needed to kill him."

"Are you sure that this is what was said? Could it not have been that this man 'Norman' had carried out the shooting?" Mr Knowlys asked.

"No Sir. This statement was taken within the hour of the killing. This young man has a good memory for facts."

"Could not Mr Climpson have put words into his mouth?" Mr Knowlys argued.

"No Sir he wouldn't do such a thing."

"Not even to put away such a man as George Styles?"

"No Sir, not even for him."

"Mr Williams, how can you be sure that George Styles was part of the gang who attacked the Customs House?" Mr Laker asked.

"Together with what Mr Climpson had reported and an interviewed we carried out with the ferryman's daughter, she confirmed that it was George Styles who was leading the attackers."

"How did she know this?" Mr Laker asked.

"She said that he made her row him and ten of his men over the River Ouse, in her father's ferry boat."

"Half way over the bitch jumped overboard, leaving me and my men to drown." George called, from the dock.

"As Mr Styles has just admitted he was there, there's no need for you to continue with this area of questioning Mr Laker." The Judge directed.

"After she jumped overboard, what did she do?" Mr Laker asked.

"Once she had got out of the water, she ran home and changed into some dry clothes. She then went to her father's barn and saddled Mark Downer's horse and rode off to Mr Climpson's cottage, in Lewes, to report what had happened."

"Mr Laker, are you calling any more witnesses to give evidence?" The Judge asked.

"No, Your Honour. George Styles has already admitted, from the dock, that he was there and was leading the gang who attacked the Customs House. You have heard the evidence of what was overheard between George Styles and one of his gang members. I believe that this puts him there and from his own mouth, admitted that he shot Jack Clarke."

"Right, Mr Knowlys. Do you wish to call any witnesses?" The Judge asked.

"No Your Honour."

"What about me? It's my life you're playing with. I want to give evidence." George shouted at Mr Knowlys.

"Mr Styles, do you think that is wise?" The Judge asked.

"Bloody right it is."

"Alright Mr Knowlys you can call George Styles to the stand, only he will give his evidence from the dock."

"Thank you your Honour."

George was sworn in and Mr Knowlys then had to ask him his first question, but he was not sure what to ask, without his client saying the wrong thing.

"Mr Styles, why were you in Newhaven, that night?"

"I was going to the New Inn for a drink." George replied.

"It's a long way from Aldfriston."

"Yes but Tom brews the best ale." George said, with a smile.

"What were you doing near the Customs House?"

"I heard a shot and went to see what had happened."

"We heard evidence that you admitted killing Jack Clarke." Mr Knowlys said.

"He couldn't have heard me, there was no one there." George snarled.

"Did your gang take the contraband from the Customs House?"

"They were my goods. The Riding Officer and Dragoons stole it from me. We were just getting it back."

Mr Knowlys realised that he couldn't ask any more questions that would help to prove his innocence of the charges against him. He sat down so Mr Laker could cross examine him.

"Mr Styles. You said that Mark Downer could not have overheard you. Why was that?" Mr Laker asked.

"Because he couldn't get passed my men, that's why." George replied.

"Then how did Jack Clarke get from the New Inn to be in front of the Customs House? Surly he had to get through your men?"

"That's different."

"Why is that then?"

"Because he's been around for years, that's why. Mark Downer only arrived a few months ago."

"You're saying that Mark Downer or anyone else couldn't have seen you kill Jack Clarke, is that right?"

"Yes, only Brian saw me shoot him." George replied.

"Mr Styles. You have just admitted that you shot Jack Clarke and that your gang took the contraband from the Customs House in Newhaven, is that correct?" The Judge asked.

"They were my goods. They didn't belong to the Customs." George stated.

"If you have no more witnesses, Mr Knowlys, I'll let the Jury come to their findings."

"I have no more witnesses your Honour." Mr Knowlys said.

"Gentleman of the Jury. You have heard the evidence and the words of George Styles. I need you to consider the two charges separately. Firstly did George Styles kill the Customs Officer, Jack Clarke? Secondly was George Styles responsible for taking away the contraband, stored in the Customs House, in the Port of Newhaven?"

The foreman of the jury turned and faced the other members of the jury, each one of them nodded towards him. He was sure that they had all reached the same findings as he.

"Your Honour. We have reached agreement on both the charges."

"And how do you find him on the charge of feloniously killing and slaying Jack Clarke, an officer of King George's Customs on 21st day of September 1786, at his Majesties Customs House in the port of Newhaven, in the county of Sussex?" The Judge asked.

"We find him guilty."

"And on the second charge of feloniously stealing, on 21st day of September 1786, 300 half-ankers of brandy, 200 half-ankers of genever, 10 bales of lace and 14 cases of tea from the Customs House at the port of Newhaven, in the county of Sussex, the property of King George?"

"We find him guilty."

THE END

Made in the USA
Charleston, SC
21 May 2014